# I Want 2 KNOW HOW

To Nick
Peace & Joy
Dawn Bolton

# DAWN BOLTON

**Outskirts Press, Inc.**
**Denver, Colorado**

This is a work of fiction. The events and characters described herein are imaginary and are not intended to refer to specific places or living persons. The opinions expressed in this manuscript are solely the opinions of the author and do not represent the opinions or thoughts of the publisher. The author has represented and warranted full ownership and/or legal right to publish all the materials in this book.

I Want 2 Know How
All Rights Reserved.
Copyright © 2011 Dawn Bolton
v2.0

Cover Photo © 2011 JupiterImages Corporation. All rights reserved - used with permission.

This book may not be reproduced, transmitted, or stored in whole or in part by any means, including graphic, electronic, or mechanical without the express written consent of the publisher except in the case of brief quotations embodied in critical articles and reviews.

Outskirts Press, Inc.
http://www.outskirtspress.com

ISBN: 978-1-4327-7476-9

Outskirts Press and the "OP" logo are trademarks belonging to Outskirts Press, Inc.

PRINTED IN THE UNITED STATES OF AMERICA

# 1

I don't believe I even felt the rain as I walked from my rental car the half block to the apartment building. But as a man with a neatly trimmed salt and pepper moustache and goatee held the door, I walked inside and went straight to apartment 4C. It must have been thirty minutes or maybe more that I had been leaning against the wall across from the Special Walnut stained door, but it seemed like thirty seconds. I supposed I had slipped into a coma of dark thoughts. When I awakened, I realized that I was soaked, chilled, and in a tight.

I raised my fist to knock, but stopped when I heard voices drifting through the door.

"That's definitely not the television." I mumbled to myself.

I could hear an unfamiliar female voice as well as the mellow vibrations of a very familiar man.

"My timing has to be the worst in the world. What am I suppose to do now?"

My answer appeared in the form of a piercing pain in my bladder. So, I knocked.

"What in the hell?", was the first thing that came out of Paully's mouth when he opened the door. "I thought my eyes were playing tricks on me. Where did you come from?" he bellowed.

"I don't know, but I do know where I'm going. To the bathroom, so point the way." I responded.

Following his directions, I hit the bathroom doing forty going north. With that bit of tension lifted, I walked back into the front room and finally saw the owner of the other voice I heard from the hallway.

"Rhap, this is Tanya. Tanya, this is the infamous Rhap, my best girl."

"Hi." I said with a smile that was forced, but I hoped looked real.

She responded with, "Hi, I've heard so many stories about you."

Tanya was a small framed, brown sugar toned girl, who looked 24 or 25 years old. She had a real pleasant face and wore about a 34D. Just Paully's type. I couldn't help but look at him and smile. Paully came over and put an arm around my shoulder.

"Oh yeah, we have 20 some odd years of stories together." He said. I ducked from under his arm and said." Don't try to make me look old by detailing the length of our friendship." We all laughed and then Paully sat down on the green pleather sofa next to Tanya. I eased down into the matching chair.

"Paully told me that you're the best child psychologist in the South."

"Well I don't know about all of that, but I can say that my heart is in my work."

"That has to be a difficult job trying to understand the workings of juvenile minds. How did you ever get into that profession?"

"Well, I guess you can say that it's one of those high school dreams that actually came true with a lot of hardwork and even more student loans. I've always wanted to help people and children are so special."

I suppose Paully thought I was going to start running off at the mouth because he interrupted me.

"Whatever! All I know is that you sure took the long road to Kiddie Land." Paully's amateur comedian skills were still quite amateur.

Tanya looked at him with a confused expression and said, "What are you talking about?"

I shook my head and responded.

"Your boyfriend, here, is being a smart-aleck, because it took me ten years to get my undergrad degree. But I make no excuses. I was doing it alone, which sometimes meant that I worked more than I went to school. Graduate school went much smoother."

"Oh I see. But Paully, that's not funny. I think that's courageous."

I looked at Paully and he looked at Tanya. They just stared at each other and after a few moments of silence Paully looked at me.

"I can't believe that you didn't call to tell me you were coming into town, Bozo Head."

"Well, I didn't really tell anyone. Uh, it was kind of spur of the moment."

"Oh, it must be great to be able to take time off whenever you like." said Tanya.

"Yeah." I responded dryly.

Paully caught my eye and I smiled a real weak one.

"Tanya come here a second." He said as he stood and walked down the hall. About five or six minutes later they strolled back into the room walking hip to hip, his armed draped across her shoulder. I thought to myself, "Isn't that sweet, they actually look cute together."

Tanya spoke first. "Well. It was nice meeting you, Rhap. I'm going to get on out of here, but maybe we can all go out while you're in town. How long are you staying?"

I didn't know what to say because I didn't know what I was doing in Chicago in the first place. And I must have looked as confused as I felt, for when I looked up at the two of them they looked confused too. So I said, "You know, I'm really not sure."

"Okay, well you two figure it out and let me know."

Tanya gave Paully the love eyes and said, "Okay, I'm out and Paully call me later."

With Tanya gone, Paully stared me down like old times and started in like Running Bull.

"Rhap, what's going on? What's the matter? And don't even think about doing your "Eisenhower Rush Hour Shutdown" either. Just spill it."

"Paully, I really don't know." I said as tears welled up and wouldn't stay back.

"Oh Shit, Rhap come here."

He pulled me into his arms. Then, I started boo-hooing like some kindergartener who'd wet her pants. Paully said nothing. He just held on and caught tears and snot on his DePaul sweatshirt. I felt awful inside but being comforted by my best friend made the pain start to numb. We sat down on the sofa when the tears subsided a little and Paully asked again what the matter was. I huffed out the last of my crying spell and started in on the Nightmare at Beacon's Court.

"About four months ago, I was in Wal-Mart getting my regular household supplies and minding my own business."

"Hold up, Rhap! Girl, you are sopping wet and shivering! Let me get you something to put on before you mess up my fine Italian leather sofa."

I laughed and said, "Yeah right, leather!"

Paully left and came back with a pair of grey Russell sweat pants and shirt.

"Here, put these on and I'll take your wet stuff. Is your coat that wet too? Did you have a coat on?"

"No, I forgot it at home." I responded quickly.

I walked to the bathroom to change. The first look in the mirror almost made me start crying again. I looked a mess. My face and eyes were puffy. My clothes were plastered to my body. But at least my hair didn't look too bad, since it had been pulled back into a ponytail. I couldn't help but feel embarrassed just thinking about what I must have looked like to Tanya. Well, so much for first impressions.

When I came back into the front room Paully handed me a mug of hot tea with lemon. The first sip told me that he remembered to drop in a piece of peppermint candy. "That's what friends are for." I thought.

"Now let's get back to the story, he said."

"Okay, like I said, I was shopping and minding my own business. I'd parked my cart at the front of the cleaning supply aisle and walked down to pick up what I needed, right? Then, I went up the next aisle. When I got what I needed I went back to my cart and headed for the register. I felt someone tap me on my shoulder and say excuse me. I turned to find this 6'2" smooth and fine chocolate chip. I mean, Paully, he made my heart skip a beat. Then he says in voice as rich and smooth as his skin, "I'm sorry, I think you have my buggy."

I turned back and looked into the cart. There was magic shave and some other stuff that I knew wasn't mine. Slightly embarrassed, I apologized, grabbed my cleansers and air freshener, and left to find my cart. I really didn't think it was a big deal. In the parking lot, he approached me again. This time he offered his card with a request for me to give him a call sometime.

At that point, my throat got a little tight, but I managed to thank him, take the card, and turn away. I didn't look at the card until I was almost home. It read, Karl Jeffreys-ReMax Real Estate Representative. On the back he'd written his home number with a note to please call.

Paully, I thought then that he might be for real, but I didn't call that night. And after that, I just forgot about it. Then, I ran across the card in my wallet about a week later and called. It was about 10:30 p.m.

I dialed the number and he answered, I asked for him, and he identified himself. I said, "Hi, are you busy?" and he said, "Not for the lovely buggy snatcher." I couldn't believe that he knew who I was, right off the bat, but he did. I mean, I never even told him my name when we met. It was as if he was actually waiting for me to call. Anyway, his little pun gave us a tension releasing laugh and then we starting chit-chatting.

I started out all polite, but you know me. I gave him the dare to tell the truth drill.

"I know you did!" Broke in Paully. "Do you know any other way?"

"Hell no!" I said.

I was feeling even better now and Paully could tell, because he pulled off his socks and started the old, old habit of rubbing and popping his toe joints. I couldn't help but smile with the warm at home feeling that watching this tedious act gave me.

"Anyway." I started again. We talked about 3 hours that night about any and everything. He told me that he had been engaged for a year while he was in the Air Force stationed in Saudi. But when he came home she broke it off. Apparently, she couldn't take Karl's constant depression. Therapy helped him get through the depression but by then he didn't want her back.

Paully, he was the perfect age, intelligent, sensitive, and fine. That night it felt like I was talking to an old friend. We seemed to just click like legos.

"Rhap, how old is he?"

"Thirty-five."

"Okay, go on."

"Alright. It was real close to 2:00 a.m. when I tried to pull the conversation to an end. He asked me to meet him for lunch after church the next day. I told him that I would. You know I figured I'd end up playing chicken and cancelling an hour before. But Paully, I didn't. We met and had a great time. I even let him kiss me when we left the restaurant. I mean, that's how right it felt."

"Dog Rhap, don't start that crying shit again." whispered Paully.

I dabbed at my eyes with the sleeve of the sweats and drifted into a moment of silence before I began again.

"We loved all the same things like movies, the zoo, concerts, museums, and literature. We even roasted marshmallows in the fireplace during the summer. Everything was great! We spent quality time together and didn't let our hectic work schedules interfere. He made me feel good all over, through and through, over and over again. So before I knew it, I was falling in love. Can you believe it? Seven weeks into this and I'm in love!

Paully interrupted, "Sounds like the double-d-w to me."

I popped his head with a synchronized,"Boy, shut up!"

We laughed and I continued.

"But seriously Paully, it wasn't that at all. Although, he was on it! I smiled. I mean the way he listened and talked to me made me feel a way that I've never felt before. It was like we were living one life. I've been in love before but never this intensely"

"Well then, what happened?" Paully had a truly bewildered look on his face. I fell silent again and in my mind all I could see was Karl's Hunter Green Cherokee glistening in the glowing rays of a quiet moonlit night.

"Yellooooow?" called Paully. Snap out of it and tell me what happened."

"Okay, I said, I guess it was about a month ago when Karl told me that his old roommate was moving to Atlanta from New Orleans. I thought that was fabulous because he had taken a few weekend trips down to hang with him and I figured that now those weekends were mine. But when he finally moved, it seemed that I saw Karl less. At first, I didn't say much about it, but I started missing him and I told him so. We talked about it. Then, the very next day he came by with two tickets to Miami. Paully, I was floored! I had never had anyone take me on a trip or even want to for that matter."

"Now that was smooth." Paully said.

"Yeah, I know. So anyway, things went along smoothly and in hind sight I guess I preoccupied myself with getting prepared to take off from work. So I didn't notice that I still wasn't seeing a lot of him.

So last week, I guess it was Sunday night, we were at my place watching Cornbeard, Earl and Me. He told me that he had to go Savannah for his job. He was to be there from Thursday to Saturday. We were to leave for our romantic getaway on Sunday, so he wanted to have his ticket changed and leave from Savannah. We would meet at the airport in Florida. So I gave him his ticket and he made the changes. At least, I assumed he did."

I paused to take a sip of my now cold tea. Paully was totally entranced in the story so I continued.

"Okay. Karl and I had lunch on Thursday before he left that evening. And we talked briefly that night and Friday night. On Saturday, Corie called me about 8:00p.m. and invited me to this party that one of her friends was having that night."

"Is Corie the chick that went to GSU with you?"

"Yeah."

"I met her at Fat Tuesday's, right?"

"Yeah, yeah. Now listen. I told her that I had to pack but that I would drop her.

When I picked her up, she directed me to the Beacon's Court Apartment Homes, right?

The name sounded familiar to me and I told her that I thought that Karl's friend from New Orleans stayed in that complex. It was just a pure innocent recollection. No big deal. Well, Corie got out and I watched her go into the party. Then, I started to get out and go tell her to call me if she needed a ride home. All the while I'm thinking about getting home so I didn't miss Karl's 11:30 call.

So, I'm getting out of the car and I notice a guy in jeans, no shirt, and no shoes coming down the stairs opposite the ones that Corie had just ascended. I just glanced at him as I was locking the car door. Then, I hear a lady calling out from an apartment to him. She only had the door opened enough to stick her head out, but I could see that she was wearing what appeared to be just a bra and panties.

Now get this! She yells, "Karl! Baby, look behind the driver's seat.

Bam! I look at the guy again and he's turned so that I can see his profile. Paully, it was Karl alright, my Karl.

I burst into tears once again and Paully, without uttering a sound, put his arm around me in comfort.

"Why does this hurt so bad?" I sputtered.

Paully responded, "Deceit hurts the most when it's someone you love."

After I settled down from what was to be the last cry of the night, Paully suggested that we go to get something to eat.

"Let's get some pizza since you claim not to be able to find real pizza in Georgia." Paully said.

"Oh yeah, now that's the ticket." I crooned.

We walked out into the brisk night air which is typical for Chicago in October and headed for my rental car. I handed Paully the car keys as we neared the car.

"I must have chauffer written on the back of my jacket." Paully commented only to receive a sly smile and a wink from me. As soon as he cranked the car, Paully jumped at the blast of Nancy Wilson singing The Other Side of the Storm.

"Shazam! Girl, I'm surprised that you could even hear yourself think with this junk so loud!" Paully shouted as he searched for the volume control.

"That was the idea, dummy, not to be able to think." I countered and readjusted the volume.

After Nancy, I pulled Exodus out of my purse and we went jamming down the Dan Ryan with our heads bobbing to the Reggae beat. As we pulled into Giodanni's, Paully proclaimed, "Bob Marley will always be the king of reggae!"

My stomach winced with the first whiff of garlic and oregano as Paully opened the door to the restaurant. I was instantly reminded that I hadn't eaten anything since lunch the day before. As soon as we were seated, I asked for an order of garlic bread and a pop. We ordered a large Supreme minus the onion and I gobbled down four slices as oppose to my usual two. Paully assisted the pizza in keeping my attention away from thoughts of Karl by reminiscing on old times and telling funny tales from his job.

Overall, dinner was good but the drive back to Paully's was even better because I slept the full thirty minute ride.

"Alright Rhap, wake up because I'm not carrying your overgrown butt anywhere." Paully barked as he parked. "You can have my bed tonight and you're in luck because I just changed the sheets."

"You mean that it's the first of the month again?" I teased.

"Keep it up if you want to and you'll be sleeping in this borrowed car." He threatened.

Once I laid on Paully's motionless waterbed, I was instantly bright eyed and couldn't seem to even borrow a wink of sleep. I kept thinking about what Paully'd said earlier. "Deceit hurts the most when it's someone you love." The words were true and quite insightful but, they still couldn't relieve the dull warm pain that I felt somewhere between my stomach and heart each time I thought about Karl and what I thought we had. It seemed as if all of the events that transpired in the last four months were a constant reminder that happiness in my life was only a temporary condition. Lying there with my eyes closed, I succumbed to the fact that I was not going to get any sleep that night. On the other hand, Paully slept like a log and sang a bullfrog melody all night long.

# 2

I must have dozed off sometime during the wee hours. I awakened to the sound of the shower running and Paully singing, "I Want to Go Outside in the Rain".

I rolled out of bed and went into the kitchen for a glass of juice. Unfortunately, the only beverages in the refrigerator were Kool-aid, Red Stripe, and milk. So I settled for a glass of water. As I filled my glass, I noticed that Paully still had his bedding sprawled over the sofa.

"I shouldn't have taken my poor buddy's bed. Tonight I'll sleep on the sofa" I thought while I folded the sheets and comforter.

Paully came out of the bathroom bright eyed and energized.

"Good Morning lil' sexy! You know your morning look ain't bad."

"Good morning, Paully. And I can tell that it's a good morning for you."

"Baby, I slept good last night."

"I know that you snored all last night."

"Oh, now don't start because you were doing some snoring of your own this morning."

"Whatever, man."

"Well, how are you feeling?"

"I'm okay. You know I have to realize that it's happened and I have to deal with it."

"Sho ya right. So what's on your agenda, today?"

"I don't know. I really hadn't thought about it at all. What time do you get off work?"

"Not going today – eh, eh – I'm not feeling well. Think I may be coming down with the flu or something."

"You are so crazy, boy. Don't tell me you called in sick."

"I sure did."

"You shouldn't have done that Paully. Dag, I don't want to be an inconvenience. You know I can get around this town alone."

"Yeah, I know." Paully said as his face transformed into the face of a pouting little boy. But I figured you really shouldn't be, uh, alone."

"Okay here goes Mr. Sensitivity again. Look, I'll be fine."

"Sure. It's done so get over it and tell me what's up for today."

"I don't know. Let me think about it in the shower." I said.

"Bet!" Paully shouted as he plopped down on the sofa.

I turned and headed for the bathroom and then remembered that we'd left my bags in the trunk of my rental. So I turned and flashed Paully a smile.

"Paully, would you run down and get my bags out of the car?"

"Dag girl, I was just getting comfortable." He pouted as he slid off the sofa and glanced over the room to locate the keys.

"Well, if you want, I'll just keep on this t-shirt of yours and my same dirty drawers and we can just hang out all day. Funk and all." I smiled.

"Forget that! I'll be back in a be- bop minute and with that he headed out of the door in an exaggerated run.

A few minutes later Paully sauntered through the door carrying my garment bag over one shoulder and my overnight bag over the other.

"What are you doing? Get off my couch! Why aren't you in the shower?"

I gave him a quizzical look, then questioned. "And what was I to put on when I got out of the shower?"

"Oops."

"Just give me my bags!" I snapped and marched off into the bathroom. The hot water from the shower was both soothing and meditative. Thoughts of Karl were soothed over by the relaxing feeling of being with someone who knew me and cared for me and my well being. Somehow I knew then that this too would pass.

After my shower I slipped on a pair of khaki chinos, which were the only pants I had other than the wet jeans from the night before. I was even less fortunate when it came to tops, so I chose a short sleeve chocolate rayon top. It was the warmest thing I had. I realized that I really should have repacked before leaving for Chicago. But at the time, all I could think of was getting away from Karl and that situation. While blowing out and bumping my hair, my mind drifted back onto the recollection of returning to my condo in a daze, looking at the blinking answering machine light, and debating over ripping up the airline ticket, driving back and confronting Karl and that half naked witch, or calling Karl and begging him not to leave me. Then, contrary to any of those options, I paid fifty-five dollars to have my ticket changed from destination Miami to destination Chicago. And there I was. What a wild and blurry 36 hours it had been.

All refreshed and dressed I met Paully in the living room.

"All set, Home Slice?"

"Yup. Let's hit the street." I said.

Then Paully responded, "Looks like you're ready to freeze in the streets, girl. Where are your sleeves?"

"I don't have any. Remember I'm suppose to be on the beach, charcoaling." I answered, surprised that I was able to say it with a smile.

"Oh yeah, I forgot. Well, let's find you something to keep you warm."

I followed Paully back to his bedroom. He shifted around in his closet and came out with a brown Polo sweater. After a little more searching, he gave me a black leather bomber. I slipped on the sweater, which surprisingly did not swallow me up and threw the jacket over my arm.

"Okay, let's hit the road. The first stop is Little Jack Horner for a western omelet and raisin toast." I said.

"You got it. But let me make a pit stop before we leave, because you know I can't stand those crusty public bathrooms."

As Paully headed for the bathroom, the phone rang for the first time since I arrived. I almost touched the ceiling because it scared me.

"Rhap, catch that for me." Paully called over his shoulder.

"Hello?"

"Hi, is Paul there?"

"Just a minute. May I tell him whose calling?

The voice sounded slightly familiar and very irritated.

"Tanya." The voice said.

"Tanya, hi, this is Rhap. Girl, Paully's in the bathroom. He'll be right out. So what's going on?"

"Not much, girl, I was just checking in with him, since he hadn't called." She responded with a slight hint of tension still evident in her voice.

I quickly searched for the correct tone to use with my next words in order to defuse the situation rising.

"He forgot to call you? Well, I have to take the blame, because I kept him out late last night trying to feed my face. I'm sorry."

"Oh, that's okay. I know he probably pigged out and then passed out himself." Tanya said.

"You know it!

We both laughed. Mission accomplished, Tanya was comforted. Then, Paully came strutting back into the room.

"Here he is, Tanya. Hang on."

I covered the mouth piece with my thigh and whispered to Paully, "You forgot to call."

Paully's face showed mock fear as he took the phone.

I took his car keys from his hand and jiggled them as I walked to the door and whispered, "I'll meet you at the car."

I walked down the stairs and realized that I didn't even know what kind of car Paully drove. So I looked at his keys to check a manufacturer's name. But to my surprise, there were three car keys on his chain, two Ford keys and a Honda key amongst the jamboree. I decided not to take the chance of being picked off as a car thief and just waited inside the foyer for Paully to come down.

I only had to wait about 10 minutes before he came galloping down the stairs looking very much like a teenager heading out to the basketball courts.

"I thought you were going to the car?" He said as he hit the landing.

"I would have if I knew which car to go to." I responded.

Paully smiled and said, "That's what you get for not keeping in touch with a brother."

I had no defense because I hadn't called or written Paully in about six months, and that was unusual. Life just seems to have a way of putting the soup on the back burner in order to cook today's meal. Even so, Paully was never far from my heart.

Paully and I met when I was five years old on the playground outside of T. Stone Elementary. It was my very first day of Kindergarten. I was so excited and my mother was holding my hand very tightly. I'm sure she was the nervous bundle that I should have been. She walked over to another woman who was very tall, tan, and thin. The woman was wearing a house dress the prettiest shade of pink with a pale green trim around the neck, arms, and skirt. I remember that it reminded me of rainbow sherbet on a plain cone. The lady was with a scrawny boy with his hair cut so short that he looked bald. Mother started talking to the woman about who the kindergarten teachers were and how she hoped that I wouldn't cry all day. While they were talking a short dumpy lady with black rimmed cat glasses, walked up to us and asked both mothers our names. She checked a list in her hand as both of them responded. Then, I noticed that the little boy was now standing in front of me so that I couldn't see all of the other kids standing, walking, and some even running around. So of course I pushed him and said, "Move doe doe."

My mother snatched me and pinched my shoulder, which was her notorious signal to cool it. I was so mad that I turned my back to all three of them. Then Momma said, "Rhapsody, this is DePaul and guess what? He's going to be in your class. You two can be friends."

Yeah, like I wanted to be friends with a doe-doe. A moment later a man started telling the parents to put the children in line with their teachers. As my mom started walking me toward the stubby lady, I snatched my hand out of hers. I wanted to walk to my line like a real Kindergartener.

With my head up, I look over at DePaul and he followed suit and crossed in front of his mother to walk next me and lined up right behind me. Our line walked into a large room with yellow walls. The teacher started calling names and showing us where to sit. I was the third student called because my last name is Austin. Paully was soon after with the last name of Dupree. When we were seated I focused on the teacher, watching her mouth as she spoke, her hands as she pointed, her body movements as she greeted and seated all of her brand new students, and I even watched her eyes as she focused and refocused on the names she read from her roster. Then from behind me I heard a strange sound.

"I know how to write my name and my phone number."

It sounded like someone talking to me through a cardboard roll from used up paper towels. I turned around in my seat to see where it came from.

"I can count to twenty, too."

It was doe-doe's voice! I was awed and fascinated. I wanted him to talk more just to hear his voice.

Well, that was the beginning of a strong friendship. We came through kindergarten with many bumps and scraps and pasted paper. Next, on we went through the hormone infested grammar school years. Then, we pimped through the high school years filled with sports, study halls, and even some summer school for me but not for Paully.

We stopped at a black Ford Explorer

"I should have known that this was yours, rugged man." I teased Paully, but the truck had Paully written all over it.

"Well, with the snow, ice, and rain Chicago gets, this is the only way to go." Paully responded. "I also have a convertible 5.0, but I mostly drive it during the summer. It's my chick magnet."

"Where is it?"

"I keep it in Mom's garage."

"How is Mom Dupree?"

"She's fine and still thinks she's my sister." Paully chuckled. "You better get over to see her or she'll kill you!"

I thought on that a moment. Mom Dupree has always been my second Mom and the more perceptive of the two when it came to me. She could read me by looking at my face. There was no way she wouldn't be able to tell that I was troubled about something. And there was no way I was going to be able to go into this fiasco with her. Not now. I just wouldn't be able to take it. Right then, I decided I would not be visiting Mom Dupree this time around. So I simply did not respond to Paully's statement. Instead, I changed the subject.

"Paully, what did Tanya have to say? Is she mad?"

"She'll be alright. I just turned on the charm and she melted back into my mold."

"Yeah, right!" I laughed. You better be careful or you'll find that mold busted. She seems pretty cool. Why don't we pick her up to have breakfast with us?"

Paully hesitated as he stopped at the stop sign on the corner. Then said, "Naw, I told her that we'd go out for drinks tonight."

"Bet."

At Little Jack Horner, the tiny parking lot was full as usual, with a constant flow of traffic. I got out of the car to go stand in line for a table while Paully waited for a parking space. After a few minutes Paully joined me and we chit-chatted while we waited.

"So Paully when will you be coming to the ATL? It's been at least two years since you've been."

"I know. But maybe I'll be able to get there this summer. I wish they still had Freaknik down there."

"I can't believe you are talking about Freaknik." I responded. "Oh, wait a minute. I know what it is. You want to go find you some SYT. Paully wants a Sweet Young Thang." I mocked.

"Woman, just shut up!"

When seated, we didn't even have to look at the menu. Paully ordered Horner Eggs over easy and raisin toast. I ordered a Western Omelet, hash browns, and raisin toast. I can't remember either of us ever ordering anything different. We talked a little more as we waited for our food. Then, most words were replaced by smacking and moans as we ate and sipped brut cups of java. The omelet was even better than I remembered and it didn't last long on my plate.

While finishing our last cup of coffee, I started reminiscing.

"Paully, do you remember when me, you, and Cocoa use to go to the park on 81$^{st}$ and Damen to swing on the swings and get tipsy on Bartles and James?"

"Yeah Buddy! Whenever anyone lost a job or you or Cocoa lost a man."

"Hold on! What about when you thought Alisa was pregnant?"

"Alright, Alright! Let's just say that whenever any of us were having hard times, we could be found there. Three fools on one see-saw."

We paused for a moment in recollection, smiled, and then laughed. I laughed until I thought my omelet was going to come back. Paully broke the laughter with a brilliant idea.

"Rhap, check this out. This is the perfect occasion for one of our playground parties. Let's go by Cocoa's."

"Let's hit it then." I joyously responded.

After we paid the bill we jumped in the Explorer and headed East on 79$^{th}$ street. Cocoa has lived on 85th and Champlain all of her life and still lives there with her mom, dad, and baby brother. Her sister, who is only 9 months older than Cocoa, moved out last year. Cocoa and I never missed a chance to tease her about shacking. Although at our age, we're probably more jealous than anything else.

Traveling along 79$^{th}$, I stared out the window taking in all of the common and not so common things. The sidewalks were buzzing with people. There were guys hanging out on the corner and in front of apartment buildings, and older people just making a trip to the corner store. I had to smile to myself at the familiar way that the car traveled along the street hitting potholes every two to three seconds. They'd had an early snow and the sight of black snow and ice pushed up against the curbs sent a strange warming sensation through my gut. To many people this would be an awfully ugly picture, but I just loved it.

As we turned on to Cocoa's street, I could see the wrought iron gate around her house had been painted white to match the trim of the tan brick bungalow. We parked and walked up the porch. The evergreen bushes were evenly trimmed and a bit taller than I remembered. Paully pushed the doorbell and we waited for someone to answer the door. We could hear the locks tumbling and then Canyun, Cocoa's brother, peeked out of the door. Instantly, a giant smile broke into his stone chiseled face and he pushed the storm door open.

"This can't be old Nappy Rappy. Girl, what's up? He yelled as he stepped outside and gave me a giant bear hug. He had grown quite a bit since the last I saw him. Canyun was about 6'3" and looking very much like a man.

"Hey Brat!" I smiled. "Look at you standing here looking grown. And what's with the hair under your nose?"

Canyun ran a finger over his mustache and said, "What can I say? Gotta keep my lip warm."

I laughed and let go of his other hand.

"What's up man?" Canyun nodded to Paully as they exchanged a hand grip.

"You got the best hand." Paully replied.

"Come on in. Cocoa's up in her room. I'll go get her."

The living room and dining room were exactly as it always had been with tan sofa and love seat, and two Queen Anne chairs all covered with plastic. The mantel was filled with graduation, prom, and family portraits. There was a wall to wall mirror behind the mantel with faint etchings of sailboats on water. The same old antique white, fat bellied, French provincial lamps were sitting on end tables on either side of the sofa. The dining room table was draped with a white lace trimmed table cloth and fully set for a party of six. The only thing noticeably altered was the carpet. The room now rested upon a soft cloud of cream Berber as oppose to the old brown sculptured carpet.

When Cocoa came bounding down the stairs, Paully and I just smiled and shook our heads. Cocoa looked the same except for her cute Halle Berry bob cut. She hugged me, as I stood, with her tall, thin frame and that crazy crooked smile. Although she hasn't been a flight attendant for two years, she has kept her 5/7 figure. I noticed that she was currently wearing green contact lenses and a lower set of braces.

"Girl, I don't believe this. What are you doing here? When did you get here? You are a trip! And look at you, all cute. Must be a new man. What's his name?"

Then she looked at Pauly as if it were an after thought.

"All junk. And where did she find you, boy?" she said as she hugged him.

"I don't believe this! I thought Canyun was joking."

I laughed and shook my head as I sat down. Coming home was feeling more and more like just what the doctor ordered. I had two good friends, a warm welcoming, and a familiar non-threatening environment. The memories flooding my head were all good.

Pauly sat in one of the chairs and Cocoa sat next to me. Then we chatted and filled Cocoa in on our plan for an outing. Of course she was gung-ho and dashed upstairs for her shoes. When she returned she asked us if we had spoken to her moms and pops, which we hadn't. So we followed her down stairs to the recreation room which was divided into two areas. Mr. and Mrs. Rays were sitting in the first part watching television. Mrs. Rays screamed when she saw us and jumped up to give Pauly and I squeeze. I hugged Mr. Rays and then answered the usual what's going on questions. I noticed that Cocoa and Pauly had moved into the back area so I dismissed myself and went to find them. I suppose I was subconsciously saving myself from the possibility of having to talk about my marital status. Our parents always got around to that form of questioning.

I walked into the back room and found Cocoa, Pauly, Canyun, and another guy about Canyun's age. The two young men were shooting pool and talking junk. It was nothing unusual. Canyun introduced me to his friend and we shook hands. As Trayu took my hand I noticed that he had the cutest little dimple in his right cheek. Yeah, he was a little cutie.

Canyun cleared the eight ball into a side pocket and instantly started an exaggerated funky dance around the table mocking Trayu.

"Alright Pauly, it's time for you to take a whipping." Canyun invited.

Pauly held up his hands in protest, "Naw man, I can't help you right now. I've got other plans. You see me and my girls got to make an important run."

"Man please, you are just copin' out."

"Naw, I'll tell you what. You just give me a couple of hours and I'll be back. So be ready to take your whippin' like a man, because I'm just the man to give it to you." Paully huffed.

Cocoa, Trayu, and I bent over in laughter. Even Canyun couldn't keep from chuckling a little himself.

"Man, please, I see I'm going to have to show your narrow behind. You see, I am the man when it comes to this table. I'll tell you what. Me and my man here will go with you just to make sure you don't chicken out."

"Hold on Lil' Bro'. No way, I don't need you two young backs in the picture. I can handle these two all by myself. Maybe I'll teach you how to do that when you get a few more years on you."

We all laughed again as Canyun instructed Paully to get out of his face, but not to forget to come back for his whipping. Needless to say, the three of us headed upstairs, still snickering about the testosterone battle. It felt good to be with Cocoa and Paully and I could only hope that they were feeling the same type of comfort.

We took Paully's car because Cocoa's little Miata was surely not going to seat us comfortably. Then we headed over to the Five Dot Liquor store and picked up a four pack of Fuzzy Navel Bartles and James, a four pack of Jack Daniels Lynburg Lemonade, a bag of starlight mints, and a bag of Jays Salt and Sour potato chips.

The park was pretty much as I remembered it. The swings were hovering over wider and deeper ditchings made by the constant foot starts and dragging stops from children with hearts still full of play. The three see-saws looked to have a fresh paint job of afro centric colors and the slides still beckoned all who dared to come feel their thrill. The two tennis courts were still covered with a thin sheet of snow and ice. The basketball courts were modestly put into use by young men, some of who should have probably been in school, and older men feeling their oats.

We took our regular spots on the swings as we chattered about Da Bulls and Da Bears. Paully busted out the coolers and fulfilled our requests, while I grabbed the chips and started a slow, low swing. Soon all three of us were crunching, sipping, swinging, and taking in the atmosphere in near silence. What a wonder it is to feel at home in a place that has been visited too infrequently. But as fate would have it, Cocoa would soon get around to asking about the reason behind my unexpected visit.

"Look girl, now don't get me wrong, I'm straight up ecstatic about seeing ya. I mean you gonna always be my sconnie, cause that's the way it is. But I know that this pop in thing just ain't you and this park date makes it even more suspicious. So fess up and let's talk about what's going on."

I took another swig from my drink and swallowed it real slow while sneaking a glance at Paully's somber expression. Cocoa couldn't take it.

"Girl, come on and spit it out!"

"Okay, okay! Just let me start by saying that I'm cool with it right now. Cause girl, you know I'm strong and been through worse."

"Rhap, spill it!" Cocoa interrupted.

Well, that was enough to get me started rolling through my unfortunate tale of deceit. It didn't seem to cause as severe of chest tightening as it had before, which was a good thing. I suppose it was due to the sense of confidence that comes with having your very best friends by your side. With backup like that, you can take on the Jolly Green Giant.

As I talked and sipped, I noticed Cocoa's facial expression hardening and her breathing deepening. She did not like what she was hearing. She was looking like a pinless grenade. The moment I finished, Cocoa opened her mouth slowly and released the blast. And boy it was rippling!

"I'm sick and tired of all these stuck up, I got it going on Negroes, running over us. How do they expect us to bring our people up and out when they keep digging new holes to add to the many we are already climbing out of? You know, to me these fools who continue to shatter our faith in relationships are just as bad as the crack dealing jokers on the corner. They're both doing the same thing, lessening our chances or possibilities of building a stronger, peaceful, and intelligent race. You see, dope dealers can turn judges, doctors, and lawyers into thieving scrubs. And these stank pretend Casanovas can turn loving, gentle, nurturing women into crass, untrusting maniacs. Plus, they both leave innocent children, who are supposed to be our bright future, deprived and confused.

Does this fool have any children? Forget that, does he have any children that he's taking care of? If he does, he's probably sending them the bare minimum of child support and spending next to no time nurturing their minds and preparing them to live a righteous life. I'm telling you I want to know not when a change is going to come but when are we going to make a change.

Look Paully, don't think that I'm just coming down on the brothers, cause we have quite a few sisters out here aiding the destruction of human minds and bodies. Shoot, we have to start using our heads instead of our snatch in order to build meaningful relationships. That's the only way a change is going to come."

Paully replied almost immediately.

"Let's be real. It is what it is and it crosses all barriers. Men are just gonna be men, players gonna be players, and hoochies are gonna be hoochies. It don't matter the size, the shape, or color. That's just the way it is."

Then he added.

"Besides, it's true what they say. When your eyes are closed, all slap is the same."

Pleased with himself, he burst into a round of laughter.

Cocoa and I looked at each other and shook our heads. Then we snickered just a bit and sipped our juice. I had no idea that my story would send Cocoa spinning like that. My girl just went off. But I had to admit that she made valid points. After Paully relieved his funny bone, even he had to admit that Cocoa spoke of much truth.

We chatted about the ordeal a little longer until the park started to fill. This meant that school was out and soon we would only be able to hear basketballs and smack from the wanna be Jordan's. It's amazing how no matter what the weather, a basketball court is never lonely.

We decided to head back to Cocoa's and chill a bit.

The ride was carefree and full of jokes. Cocoa shared some of the crudest and corniest jokes around that she'd picked up during her travels. And Paully tries so hard to be funny that we usually end up laughing more at his effort than any of his jokes. We were all still full of laughter as we walked into Cocoa's.

Canyun was true to his word, for he and his sidekick were in the basement awaiting our return, munching on a couple of Italian beefs and Tahitian Punch. The room was in a slow groove with Stanley Jordan setting the mood. Canyun let out a confident whoop when he saw Paully.

"Oh yeah, it's on now. Rack 'em up, chalk it, and let the sticks slide. Now, tell me how you'd like to take your whippin' — hard and fast or with a slow groove?"

Paully could only laugh and shake his head.

"Look young blood, you can talk all the junk you want before your whipping and after it too if it makes you feel better. But all I ask is that you don't cry in front of the ladies. You see, no woman wants to witness tears of defeat from a man. But you wouldn't know anything about that, son."

At that, we all hooped and hollered. Cocoa and I knew that we were in for a real treat. "Tell me what woman doesn't enjoy watching men strutting their chest feathers. What the men don't understand is that we enjoy it because they look so ridiculous." Cocoa laughed.

It was decided that Canyun and Trayu would play first and Paully would take on the winner. Canyun walked away the winner leaving Trayu with four balls on the table. And of course, being the gentleman that he is Canyun asked Paully if he wanted to withdraw from the pending challenge. But it came out more like…

"Look Gramps, I'll understand it you want to back out now that you see what I'm made of."

Paully just flicked his chin and began to chalk his tip.

"Man, you need to rack the balls. You see, I'm the reigning champ on this table." Canyun interrupted.

"No way man, you see my arthritis prevents me from doing that."

Once again, Cocoa and I bent over in laughter.

Canyun and Paully dueled it out on the table so hard that I do believe they both were sweating. In the end, Canyun kept his title. Along with the title, he kept his tongue lashing going strong. Paully made some comment about the liquor messing with his reflexes and then dismissed himself to go call Tanya.

Paully returned with an announcement that it was time for us to depart. He'd made a date for Tanya, he and me to go out for dinner and drinks. For various reasons, I did not want to join the couple so I suggested that Paully and Tanya take this time to be alone. Besides, Paully needed to be trying to make up for his behavior the night before. Of course, Paully didn't think so. Remember, he is the man and he had Tanya under control. Yeah, right. I've heard that declaration more often than I'd care to admit. But after checking with Cocoa for a ride back to Paully's and retrieving a spare key from him, I sent Paully on his way. He still seemed kind of reluctant about leaving me, but I refused to take no for an answer.

With Paully gone, the four of us paired off and played some team billiards. The first couple of games were ladies against the guys. Although Cocoa and I put up a good fight, we lost both games. Even with Cocoa's expert bank shots we still pulled up short. After the second game, we sent the guys to White Castle for our dinner. Then Trayu suggested that we play some mixed doubles. I paired up with him and Cocoa with her brother. We were into our third game before I knew it. On the table, there was one solid for us, one stripe for them, and the black beauty. Trayu put a little English on the 2 ball and sank it. The 8 ball was set up perfectly for the left corner pocket at the top of the table. I glanced at Canyun and Cocoa because the room fell silent. Canyun had that serious, *I know he better miss this*, look on his face. But Cocoa was nodding pretty heavily leaning against the wall.

Trayu sank the ball with ease and I hopped up and down yelling, "Yes, yes, yes, baby, yes!"

He gave me a high five and then grabbed me and swung me around off my feet. I guess those well defined arms did have some strength in them. It was a strange and comforting feeling. Maybe it was the alcohol or maybe the result of the insult I'd endured recently, whatever it was it was a good feeling that I wished would have lasted longer than the few seconds it had.

After the excitement died down, I figured it was time to head back to Paully's. Cocoa was dozing over in the lounger.

"Girl, you better wake up, so you can take me home." I called hopefully, trying to snap her out of it. But she just groggily attempted to sit upright. I figured I might end up spending the night there. Although the notion wasn't appalling, I would have preferred being at Paully's. Being there would probably leave me a little solitude to do some more reflecting. I really needed to put some thought into what I was going to do when I got home. Eventually, I would have to go back and deal with Karl. This thing wasn't just going to dissipate.

"Hey, I can give you a ride." Trayu offered.

"No, that's okay, but thanks for offering." I declined as I pushed Cocoa in another attempt to get her going.

"Aw, come on, it's not a problem at all. I'm not the biting kind and I won't even bother you with small talk. I'm a complete gentleman. Tell her, Canyun, man."

"Yeah, he's cool. You know I don't hang with no fools. Besides, I know you'd rather ride with someone that's awake. Tell me I'm wrong?"

I felt stuck. Trayu had this adorable look on his face. His little smile made me want to just hug him like my favorite teddy bear. Cocoa was awake enough to agree that Trayu's idea was a suitable one. She was partially agreeable because it would allow her to hit the sack.

Finally, I accepted Trayu's offer, still feeling a bit uneasy. I kept repeating to myself that everything would be fine and I'd make it back to Paully's safely.

After Canyun went to check to see if his parents were still awake, I said my goodbyes and promised to call when I got to the apartment. Trayu and I walked to his car. It was a typical young man's vehicle. Pleasingly, it wasn't ghetto. He drove a blue Chevrolet, no older than

1990, silver spiked rims, major stereo system, and neat as a pin on the inside.

Once inside he quickly changed the station to 107.5. I suppose he was trying to be respectful to his elders by not forcing me to listen to any rap. We sat there for a few minutes to let the motor warm. Very little was said other than a few comments about our win and the weather. But as I sat there I caught myself sensualizing the smell of his car and the vibration of his voice as he softly sang/hummed the tunes on the radio.

I was brought back by his voice strengthening to ask something.

"I'm sorry, what did you say?" I stammered.

"Do you have any brothers or sisters?" he asked.

"Yes, I have a younger brother. He's twelve and already one of the greatest people you could ever know. I think it's because he came along when both my mom and stepfather had experienced the best and worst of life and therefore had more knowledge of what children really need to know. Aslen is intelligent, funny, and kind. He loves sports, too. He's a great soccer and Lacrosse player."

"Le who?"

"Lacrosse. It's a field sport played with a ball and a net on a pole that's used to pass and catch the ball."

"What about good old b-ball? You should let me introduce the kid to the rock."

"Oh he likes basketball, too. As a matter of fact, he's like his big sister and enjoys all sports, but soccer and lacrosse are his favorites. He's extremely agile and has super endurance. Actually, I admire the way he goes after the things that interest him, regardless of what his friends are doing. He's always been that way and I believe that's a trait that will take him far in life."

"But lacrosse. I still don't get it. Maybe I'll check it out on ESPN or something."

"You should and I'll see if I can get my lil' bro' to run you around the field."

With the ice broken, we let our conversion follow a carefree and easy course. We talked about his recreation center and high school basketball adventures as well as his post high school life. He was currently attending the International Academy of Design & Technology. His school of choice was Howard University, but his parents refused to send him away to school. His mother just wanted to keep her baby close to home. On the other hand, his father's motivation was to keep an eye on him. The chance of losing his son to a life of partying, drugs, and melted ambition was a risk he was not willing to take. Trayu said that initially his dad's attitude angered him and put a strain on their usually close relationship. Fortunately, they had both come through the drama unscathed and were cool again. Trayu still met new friends, such as Canyun, and enjoyed learning more about what the city had to offer. As for myself, my appreciation for Chicago didn't materialize until after I moved away.

Trayu asked if I'd left a boyfriend behind when I moved to Atlanta.

Technically I didn't, because Randall and I had been broken up for almost two months before I left. We were still kicking it every once in a while, but he wasn't my man.

"So you left and broke the brother's heart." Trayu said.

"No, I don't think so. Hold up! Don't try to make me into a villain." I laughed. "He may not have wanted me to move, but I don't think I broke his heart."

Just as we turned on to Paully's street, Trayu asked, "Have you ever broken anyone's heart?"

It was the wrong question to ask but perfect timing, because we were only a good 60 seconds away from the apartment. Although the thought of answering that question aroused the emotions linked to my present heartbreak, I figured that I could hem-haw my way out of it until he dropped me off.

"Well, I'd have to say no or at least not that I'm aware of." I said as I reached for the door handle. Trayu jumped out of the car with me and proceeded to walk me to the building. The night's air was not too bad for this time of year and the sky was just the way I like it, deep and mysterious with an abundance of inviting sparkles. I turned to face him as we reached the foyer entrance.

"Well, Mr. Trayu, thank you for being so kind as to see me home safely. I really enjoyed your company. Let me give you some gas money."

His dazzling smile tickled me as he suggested that I let him escort me to the apartment door. I assured him that that wouldn't be necessary and on the verge of being inappropriate, since I'd just met him. He let it go rather easily, declined any money, and asked for a hug instead. I relented and stretched out my arms. He gathered me up and I was sure that I could've stayed in the warmth of his arms for hours. Hugs are one of my most favorite things; they can ease just about any pain. You can tell a lot about a person from their hug and through the years, I've experienced quite a few of them. Trayu's hug was neither restraining nor aggressive. It had a firmness that was teetering between comforting and sensual. I'm not exactly sure how long we held each other, but as soon as I felt the stinging in my eyes, I broke the embrace. I had to get inside before any tears had the chance to break through. I thanked him again and headed up the stairs. I thought I was home free until I heard his voice echo up to me.

"Rhap, hold up."

I stopped and watched him trot nearer.

"Take my number. I would really like to talk to you some more."

Now you know that I took the number. How could I not. I could feel his nervousness and see the hopefulness in his eyes. After I took the number, he trotted down the stairs like a child headed out to play. His apparent happiness brought a little grin to my face as I headed toward the apartment.

As I tried the door key, I listened to see if I heard any voices coming from inside. I heard nothing and as I entered the dark apartment I was sure that I was home alone. Mixed feelings overcame me. It would have been nice to spend a little time chatting with Paully. Then on the other hand, I was glad to have a little quiet time with my thoughts. Of course, I knew that I was going to rehash my recent trauma, but it's what had to be done in order for me to get real with it, deal with it, and move past the pain of it. That's how I'd learned to cope with all of life's problems. It's worked up to this point, so I saw no need to change the program.

I decided to shower, hop into some comfees and make my sofa bed for the night. Then, I would say my nightly prayers and lull myself to sleep with thoughts of what to do about that low-down cheating and lying Karl. It was a pretty solid plan.

The shower was nice and hot with great water pressure. So much so that I felt sure that sleep was going to overcome me before I could properly prepare my narrow slumber unit for the night. It had been a long fun-filled day and I had to remember that I hadn't had a good nights sleep in three days. My not so young body was well over due for some rest.

Unfortunately, my present state of fatigue could not save me from my overactive mind. I thought that I was drifting peacefully into sleep when all of a sudden, a vision of Karl and I spooning burst to my mind. From there I rambled through various happy times we'd spent together. I thought about the wonderful, sun-filled vacation we'd planned. What if we'd actually had the chance to take it? How long would it have taken me to find out the truth about his commitment to our relationship? Hell, I'm sure that if he had his way, it would have gone on forever. I was up for a forever with him. Karl was my "it". He was the "it" that everyone waits for; the "it" that I never understood until him. Now, it looked like Karl was giving "it" to someone else.

I wondered if she knew about me? I suppose she could know and not care. She could be thinking that a part-time lover is better than nothing. I'd rather have nothing!

"Damn, I just want to sleep!" I yelled at myself.

But the voice in my head kept going.

Would I curse him? Maybe I should just totally avoid him and act like he never happened.

I guess I could try to turn my back on what happened and move on. But that's easier said than done. I couldn't turn my heart off, that would make me inhuman. I'd have to say something, I guess. Maybe cursing him out wouldn't be the best thing to do. I didn't want to take the chance of coming off like some hysterical crazed maniac, rolling my neck, batting my eyes, and swinging my arms.

I had to laugh at the thought of myself playing Miss Ghetto Fabulous. Behaving that way would surely let him off the hook.

He'd be thinking, "Look at this fool. See how women act. That's why we do what we do."

"Oh no, he won't get that from me. I'd be cool and composed and even eloquent in my speech. I want him to know how much he hurt me. I want to make him feel ashamed of having it in him to do another human being, a good strong loving woman, wrong. But, I won't dare let him think that he ruined me. I won't let myself be ruined by him. I'm too strong for that. At least I hope so. Yeah, I know so. Okay that settles it! I will definitely talk to him. What I'll say, I don't know, but I'm sure it will come to me. Maybe I'll write it down. Make some note cards. Practice in the mirror.

I could feel the aching in my eyelids and I knew it was way late.

"I've got to get some sleep. Shoot, I'll give it more thought tomorrow." I resolved.

# 3

Paully came in the next morning while I was frying up some Parker House hotlinks and eggs for breakfast. I had been up long enough to shower and go out for a Sunday Sun Times, papaya juice, and Dunkin Doughnuts coffee. It was the last day of my impromptu visit.

Paully was all smiles as he greeted me with a hug that lifted me off my feet.

"Hey girl, what ya cookin'?

"I'm making myself a Chi-town breakfast sandwich. You want one?" I said.

"Well, I guess so, but I thought we would go out for breakfast."

"Paully, I didn't know. It's not like I heard from you last night. I guess you were tied up, huh?" I winked.

"Rhap, you're stupid. Naw, I was going to call you, but lost track of time. I thought you'd still be sleeping when I got here."

"No baby, I've been up and out already. I have a flight out this evening. I guess I'm a little anxious."

"When were you going to tell me you were leaving today?" he asked with a furrowed brow.

"Calm down! I just made the plans this morning. Geez, I'm sorry."

"It's cool."

Paully's little mind was working away at something. I could tell because he got real quiet and was biting his upper lip. I have known that look since eighth grade. The first time I remember seeing it was when we were taking a practice test to prepare for our high school entry test. Mrs. Rome had been priming us for our next educational stepping stone for most of that school year. We'd had various class discussions about what high schools we wanted to attend, our college ambition, and our career interests and options. That year we learned what academic reputations were and how they could better our college chances and choices.

By the second semester, most of the students spent lunch hour talking about colleges and careers. A few of our classmates even started wearing collegiate sweatshirts on occasion. The focus of that semester was to prepare ourselves to test well enough to get into the high school of our desire. In order to do so, we took weekly exams covering the basic academic areas. Every Friday morning, Mrs. Rome transformed our classroom into a testing center. We were to come with no books in hand and two or more number two pencils. We still recited the Pledge of Allegiance and sang Our Country Tis of Thee, but after that we were to be seated and prepared to test. Mrs. Rome would always have her desk cleared of everything except for her coffee mug, a kitchen timer, extra pencils, a magazine or novel for her entertainment.

The first week of testing, Paully was seated two rows to the right of me. I remember thinking that he was mad at me about something, because he had been unusually quiet during our walk to school. I couldn't figure out what was wrong and I kept looking over at him as if I would magically be able to read his thoughts. He would feel my stare and look at me, but I couldn't read his face.

Then Mrs. Rome began giving instructions and the class fell silent. We were allowed to ask a few questions and then testing began. I finished the first part on Spelling before the timer went off, so I was looking around at the other students. They all looked very serious, except for Richard Bean; he was playing with his pencils and doodling on the edges of his paper. He was never serious about any school work. I look at Paully just as he laid his pencil down. He had this weird look plastered on his face as our eyes met. It kind of looked like he was constipated or had his finger stuck in a tight hole. I smiled and winked at him, but his expression did not change.

We tested for three hours, including two fifteen minute breaks for the restroom and a snack. When we finished testing, we put our desks back into order and were allowed to talk and play games for the twenty to thirty minutes left until lunch. After lunch, we would either play kickball or piggy for the rest of the afternoon. Paully and

I played a homemade version of handball against the building and I finally got him to talk about what was bothering him.

He told me that he hated taking tests. It made his stomach ache. I reminded him that he always did well on his tests, almost as well as me. But I guess these tests felt different to him. At least that's what he said. They were more important and he didn't know if he could do well on them. He even said that he felt like he would not get into any high school. That was my first experience with test anxiety, although I didn't know what it was called back then. Paully eventually learned to get a hold of his anxiety issues in school, but whenever he was nervous about anything, that same look could be found on his face. He had that look now.

"What's up, Paully." I inquired.

"Hey, I was just wondering...I know we haven't really talked about it...But I was wondering what you planned on doing....You know... when you get home. I mean...like what are you going to do... you know... how do you plan on handling this thing...with old dude...uh Karl? Are you going to try and talk to him or see him? Because you might want to talk about it before you do anything. You know...like plan it out."

He was definitely fumbling with his words, but I understood what he was trying to say.

"Hey." I interrupted. "I'm not going to act crazy. And I promise that I won't cut him or key his car or anything like that. I have thought about it, shoot, I thought about it for quite sometime last night. Which is, partly, the reason I've decided to head back."

I paused in order to recall and organize my thoughts from the night before.

"I believe that what I'll do is talk to him and let him know exactly what I know and how I feel. You see, I'm clear on what I know but I'm sure that there's got to be more. I know I can't just ignore his deceitful antics, and if I don't get these feelings off of my chest, I won't be able to move past this. It will eat away at me and then I'll end up building a wall blocking out any future chances of love. So, I know I have to talk to him. I don't have a specific dialog yet, but I've got a pretty solid outline. Look, why don't you grab the juice out of the fridge and let's eat."

I had to change the subject if for no other reason than that I was tired of it. We gathered our breakfast and sat down at the smoke tinted glass butcher table and began chowing down. But Paully couldn't let it rest for long.

"Rhap, what are you going to do, confront him at his j.o.b.? You know you don't need to go embarrassing the man on his job."

"Oh please, now you know that's not my style." I said. "No, I'll probably call him at home and set up a date to talk face to face."

"Hold up! I just thought about something. Where is homeboy, anyway? Weren't you supposed to meet him in Florida? What you think he did when you didn't show? Rhap, he might be thinkin' you dead or something. Did you call him?"

"Hell no, I didn't call him! For what? He didn't deserve to be fore warned. He didn't fore warn me. Look, I don't know what he thought or what he did. But I figured he would eventually try to call me and I planned for that. My cell phone has been off since I got on the airplane, so he'll probably call the home phone. I always forward my home phone to Corie's place when I'm out of town. So I called her and gave her a quick run down of what happened from the airport. I told her that he'd probably call. My instructions were to tell him that I had a family emergency and had to fly to St. Louis. Other than that, all she should tell him that she knows is that I'll be back in a few days."

"She won't have a problem playing dumb to him?"

"Paully, that girl was so upset when I told her, I thought she was going to do a drive by on his butt. She probably enjoyed lying to him." I laughed.

Paully laughed, too and almost choked.

"You women know y'all can get real foolish."

He took a swallow of his juice and continued. "So you mean brotherman doesn't have a clue as to what's up? He doesn't even know that he's been busted?

"Not if Corie did what she was suppose to. Therefore, I shouldn't have a problem hooking up with him to talk. He'll probably be itching to see me and tell me off about standing him up. Naw, he'll probably continue to play the role and act all concerned and sympathetic about my so-called emergency, which made me miss our very special getaway. But he will be in for a real shocker when all the bricks fall."

We spent some time finishing up breakfast. Dang, that sandwich was shole good. Then we talked about what to get into on my last day. Paully suggested going down to Navy Pier and hanging out or maybe going to the Water Towers and doing some shopping. But suddenly, the thought of going out at all was unappealing. I kinda just wanted to chill out there and maybe watch some old movies. I shared my thoughts with Paully and it was cool with him. He went off to shower and change and I started washing up the dishes. I thought about calling Corie. I should check to find out what had transpired over the last couple of days. She was expecting a call from me anyway and I didn't leave her any numbers. Hell, I didn't even know where I'd end up other than the city of Chicago. I decided to call her sometime before I left for the airport.

A refreshed Paully sauntered in and suggested that we go and rent some movies. It sounded like a good idea, so off we ventured. We picked up Mo Better Blues and Cleopatra Jones, stopped at Jewels for movie refreshments, gassed up the rental car, and headed back. With the exhaustion we felt as we plopped down on the sofa, you would have thought we had just run a 3200 meter relay. I felt like I could use a quick rejuvenating nap, so I suggested we watch Mo Better Blues first. That way if I happened to doze off I wouldn't miss out. I've watched that movie at least twenty times.

Paully and I chatted as the previews ran. I told him that Trayu had dropped me off the night before.

"What's wrong with you letting some strange dude drive you home in the middle of the night? I don't even know that dude and neither do you. And what if something had happened? I wasn't even here to help you."

Paully was trippin'

"Dag, don't bust a testicle!" I joked. Both Cocoa and Canyun said it was cool and they both know him. Besides, it was probably safer for him to drive me home than half sleep Cocoa. Paully, everything was cool. He was the perfect gentleman and he seems really sweet."

"Sweet? Don't tell me that you're diggin' that young buck." Paully teased, as he busted out in laughter.

"Shut up! I'm not diggin' anyone. But he did give me his number. Said that he liked talking to me."

Paully laughed even harder.

"Rhap, you're trying to pull jail bait. How do you plan on asking for him when his mommy answers the phone? Say you calling to speak to Mrs. Jones baby boy?"

He was laughing too hard now and I was getting perturbed. So I just put on a pout, tuned him out, and started watching the movie that had begun. He finally caught my drift and tried to make up for his rudeness.

"I'm sorry, look, I was just joking around." He said.

"No you weren't, so don't even try to pretend. It doesn't matter anyway. If I feel like calling youngblood, then I'll call him. It doesn't matter what you or anyone else has to say. I got to do what feels right for me and only I know what makes me feel good." I definitely stated.

Paully just sat there looking down at his coffee table before he could come up with a reply.

"Rhap, I truly didn't mean any harm. I've known and loved you for most of my life. I care about you and I even worry about you from time to time. When you hurt, I hurt. When you're happy, I'm sharing the joy. So of course, I would rather you be happy. You deserve the best, better than what you had with what's his name."

Paully put his arm around my shoulder and pulled me near.

"You have such a giving heart; you're insightful, intelligent, fun as hell, and a good listener. I know this for a fact and to tell the truth, you're probably the model I use in selecting my women. Come on now, every man wants a woman like you. Even if they don't, they should. But every man is not worthy of having a woman like you. Rhap, I just want you to be patient and don't settle. I want you to not give up. Just keep your eyes and heart open, so you can see when he comes. You never know, he might be sitting right under your nose, just waiting for you to take notice."

He paused.

"Rhap, I just want you to want the happiness that you deserve. And if I can help you get it, I promise to do my best."

Tears were slowly rolling down my cheeks and Paully hugged me tighter. He didn't speak another word. Instead he continued holding me close and rocked me ever so slightly. I loved having him comfort me, because I knew that it was coming straight from his heart. It wasn't pity, I was sure. It was comfort brewing from pure unconditional love. I was really going to miss this when I went home. With the drama I would be walking into, I was going to need some comforting arms. We stayed close in this same way for a long while, so long that we both drifted off to sleep.

I awakened first, jolted by disturbingly dreamy pictures of being cursed and shoved by several women as Karl stood smirking in the background atop a golden platform. Paully jumped a little but recovered quickly by pulling me closer, kissing my forehead and whispering, "It's okay."

That worked for me.

# 4

I was on Flight 724, destined for Atlanta Hartsfield-Jackson Airport. "What irony, 724 are the first three digits in Karl's phone number." I thought with only a slight surge of warmth in my chest. The visit home was good. Heck, it was more than good. It was exactly what my aching heart needed. I'm sure that I didn't know that that was the therapy I needed, but I suppose that my alter-ego knew and that's what lead me there.

Three days of rest, relaxation, retrospect and frolic. Paully was still my best buddy without question. I could only hope the recently acquired peaceful feeling would carry me through the next couple of days back home. I was heading back to the scene of the crime, where I would undoubtedly have to face the perpetrator. On one hand, I was fearful of even hearing Karl's voice, yet on the stronger hand I wanted to deal with the situation and put it behind me. The flight was soothing and quick. I slept through at least an hour of it. As the landing awakened me, I felt a quickening of my heartbeat which was accompanied by the yearning to lie in my own bed. I waited for all but two passengers to exit the aircraft before I grabbed my bags from the overhead compartment.

After retrieving my car from the economy parking lot, I headed to the home-front feeling pretty confident and calm. The foremost thoughts were to mentally organize my work schedule for the week. I'd put in a bit of overtime the previous couple of weeks in order to prepare for my Florida excursion. Therefore, I was not worried about being slammed upon my return.

Flipping through my mental agenda, it appeared that I would have a pretty easy going week. Only the regular conferences and check-in sessions were on the books along with my Thursday Teen Anger Management Group session. Sometimes the one-on-one sessions can get a little boring. The regular question and response format becomes predictable after a while. It seems that I keep giving the same advice and suggestions to the same problems coming from the same people. If they would just try using some of the suggestions, they might see clear to the success of critical thinking and problem solving. The kids keep doing the same things and always become agitated with the resulting consequences. So, I try to get inside of their minds and figure out the basis of the inappropriate behaviors. Then, we can brainstorm and develop some evasive steps to lead them toward a more trouble free path. It used to amaze me to see how the same behavior exhibited in various children can be a result of so many different underlying problems. It's just as surprising to find that the majority of the time the child's inappropriate behavior is directly correlated to the family or homelife. The direction, attention, and discipline the child receives from their parents and or guardian, most often set the foundation of the child's life launch pad. This holds true whether the parents are lawyers, doctors, crack heads, or homemakers.

The Anger Management group provides a bit more excitement on the other hand. I believe its' energy and effectiveness comes from the empowerment that it alludes to its' members. The constant generation of ideas or equivocal techniques coming from the mouths of babes, so to speak, sometimes is more acceptable to the group than my own suggestions. Often I find that my suggestions usually return to the discussion floor in the disguise of street slang. It doesn't matter as long as the point gets across and by chance helps someone. It constantly amazes me to see how these very troubled kids find ways to help each other, yet they rarely seem to question themselves as to why they have never taken their insightful thoughts and applied them to their own lives. Overall, I think the group has made a decent amount of progress. Suddenly I was hopeful as to the success of a good many of those kids. I was interested to hear the updates for this week.

Obviously, my mind was working overtime, because suddenly I was only minutes from my condo. My bladder was awakened as if on cue by vicinity. This made me jiggle a bit and accelerate. I began stripping as soon as I hit the foyer. I shut off the security system and bee lined for my porcelain throne. From there the Nubian Princess headed for the royal waterfall for a warm lengthy cleansing. After the shower I put water on for a cup of Chamomile tea and retrieved my mail from the mailbox. I left the tea steeping while I put fresh linen on the bed. The chamomile and baby fresh bed made reading the mail nearly impossible. Sleep snuck up on me and quietly lulled me away without a peep of resistance.

In the morning I felt quite rested. I had a bowl of frosted shredded wheat, a glass of grapefruit juice, and a cup of Earl Grey, while I finished reading my mail. As I went into my bedroom to grab the dirty linen for the wash, I noticed my work pager. My friends tease me about being the only person still using a pager, but it works for me and my clients. When I checked the pager, of course I spotted Karl's cell phone number several times and immediately deleted them. I wasn't ready to deal with that just yet. One of the other numbers that I recognized was from one of my clients. The message left was for me to call Tiana. The next time the number appeared, it didn't have a text message attached. It was kind of weird to have two pages from Tiana. We didn't have an appointment until Thursday. I figured that I should go ahead and give her a call. The phone was answered by someone I didn't know and there was quite a bit of noise in the background. So much noise that I had to ask for Tiana twice before I was heard. The person on the other end just slapped the phone down without saying a word. The only reason I knew that they didn't hang up was that I could still hear the noise in the background. "Sup." Tiana answered in a low gruff voice. Definitely not the voice you'd expect to hear from a thirteen year old young lady.

"Hi Tiana. This is Ms. Austin. I just got back in town and received your message. So, tell me what's up."

I usually try to keep my language as professional as possible in order to set an example for the kids, but every once in awhile I slip. She didn't say anything.

"Tiana, is something wrong?"

The silence was deafening and cold. But her response was even colder.

"Naw, look, you gonna be in your office?"

"Well, I'm at home now but I can be there in about an hour." I said.

I could tell by her intonations that she was in a position where she couldn't talk freely.

"Aw right. Bet. I'll catch ya."

Now that conversation made me a little nervous and had a few butterflies dancing the sugar plum fairy in my stomach. I couldn't really pin point what I'd heard in her voice. It wasn't anything I could recall having heard before.

Tiana and Kieron had been clients of mine for almost two years now. They were my first pro-bono case. Actually, they are my only pro-bono case. I ran into their grandmother in an elevator and somehow she ended up telling me about her grandson and granddaughter being on probation. The anguish in her voice almost drove me to tears. Then the next thing I knew, I was giving her my card and offering my counseling service to two very angry and confused young teens. But I have to admit that Tiana and Kieron are two especially bright kids and I've grown attached to them. They've opened my eyes to what our young black youth have to deal with on a daily basis.

I decided on a quick shower, so I could get to the office with time to prepare for Tiana's visit. What was that I heard in her voice? I just couldn't put my finger on it. Well, there was no need to dwell on it, for I would be finding out for sure in a short while.

I thought about calling Corie, but decided that I should wait until after I finished the session with Tiana. It wouldn't be fair to go in preoccupied with my own problems. Maybe I was avoiding the call, but no matter, it was definitely going to have to wait.

I put on a pair a Levis, short-sleeve mock turtle, and topped it off with a blue flannel shirt. I slipped on my Muzunos, grabbed my briefcase and headed out the door. Traffic was light and I made it to the office in no time.

My first task was to open my windows a crack and sit a cone of Star Sandalwood incense on the ledge. Next, I hit the box frig for a bottle of papaya juice to perk my senses and calm my nerves. I decided to put on George Winston's December CD to clear the air. At last, I felt that I had freed my space enough to sit at my desk which was actually a 6'x4' cherry wood table I'd picked up from a garage sale in Dallas, Georgia.

It was perfect for my needs and sense of focus. It was spacious and free of defined obstruction, yet possessed clear boundaries to function within. Of course, my life was not that simple to corral, but it worked for the office. A set of fine cherry stained, laminate covered file cabinets behind my desk kept organization of office materials and files manageable. I had created the perfect workspace to keep my incisive, deductive, and creative thoughts flowing.

I got comfortable in my leather computer chair and set it on low vibration, put my feet up on one of the file cabinets, and sipped on my beverage as I looked out over the Midtown view. Times like this almost bring me to a state of pure euphoria. My mind felt clear, my thoughts poured pure, and my heart fluttered lightly.

By the time Tiana knocked at the door, I felt prepared to listen and advise. All of my anxiousness had subsided. Which side it had ventured to I didn't know but it was good to have it out of my gut. Tiana cautiously walked through the door upon my beckoning and sleeked over to the chair in front of my desk with her head low and slightly cocked to the side. She was dressed in an oversized Old Navy down jacket with a skull cap pulled down over her standard ponytails that hung down just past her shoulders. She had on baggy painter jeans and a pair of timberlands.

"Hey Tiana. It's good to see you. Why don't we go over to the conversation nook?" I said as I came from around the desk and headed towards the west wall of the office. The conversation nook was just an area to the left of my desk that housed three comfortable conversation chairs forming a triangle.

"Would you like something to drink? I have some juice, coke, sprite, and bottled water."

"Naw, I'm cool."

Tiana's reply was so dry that it stopped me in my tracks. I looked at her and instantly I thought of the feeling "distraught". Yeah, that was it, she was distort or in deep despair for sure. About what was the question.

"Come on, have a seat."

Tiana unzipped her jacket and slowly sat. Her cute little cherub face was so somber that she almost looked angry. What could possibly be the matter?

"Okay girl, what do I owe the pleasure of your company to today? Is Kieron with you?"

Tiana's head sunk lower as she shook it. I thought that she might be crying, so I softened my voice a couple of notches. I reached over and touched her knee.

"Tiana, what's wrong?"

She drew her shoulders up a bit, but didn't speak, so I waited.

"Kieron's not coming." She finally whispered.

"He's not going to be coming neither, cuz he got killed on Saturday."

I snatched back my hand as if someone put a match to it. Then, I slid my chair closer. I knew that I didn't hear what she'd just said. I couldn't have.

"What? Tiana are you serious?"

"Hell yeah, I'm serious! Would I lie about something like that? Why would I joke about my only brother being dead? That shit ain't nothing to joke about. He's dead! He's gone! I ain't got no big brother no more! I ain't never gonna have a brother no more!"

"Tiana was glaring at me and yelling as tears ran down her face. Then she just stopped and pulled in all the air she could get and hung her head as she slowly exhaled.

I got up and retrieved the Kleenex from my desk, walked back over and gave a few to Tiana as I rubbed her shoulders in comfort.

"Tiana, I'm so sorry. I didn't mean to upset you. I'm just in shock. Baby, I'm so, so sorry."

She just kept her head buried in her jacket as she held the tissues to her face. I just let her sit and gathered herself. She would speak again when she felt ready. Meanwhile, I would try to comprehend what she'd already spoken. How could Kieron be dead? Killed? Who would want to kill him? Why would they kill? He's such a sweet kid. He's just a kid. He wasn't even old enough to drive. What happened? Was he struck by a car? Fall? Eat poison? What? What? What could have happened? The thoughts were coming as fast as my tears. I quickly wiped them away. I had to pull myself together for Tiana. Oh my God, Tiana had lost her brother, her best friend, her hero. What was she going to do?

"Tiana, we can talk about it if you want or you can just be here. It's fine. I just want you to do what your heart needs. Okay?"

She nodded her head without uncovering her face. I got out of my chair and sat on the arm of her chair and put my arm around her shoulders. My thoughts drifted back to Kieron. Kieron was a handsome boy. Actually, he and his sister could be mistaken for twins. They were two years apart in age, but their close relationship nearly cancelled out the chronological differences, except for the fact that Kieron definitely played the role of protector to Tiana. I suppose he was the closest she would ever get to having a father and he knew it. They were the best of friends and as tight as support hose. When we first met, they made it clear to me that if they were going to see me, they would see me together or not at all. Of course, that arrangement worked fine with my schedule and that's the way we started.

Kieron and Tiana always kept me in stitches with their antics and stories from the hood. Their grandmother, Mrs. Menden, was often the topic of their hilarious stories. They joked her out just to get a laugh about how out of touch she was with their world. But they listened to her lessons and held them dear although they didn't think that they really applied to their lives. It was obvious that they loved her but boy did they think she was funny.

The two of them worked well together in our sessions, but they also had rifts. Problems usually arose when Kieron would scold Tiana about what she was doing or instruct her as to what she should be doing. Kieron was quite intelligent and even more street-wise. He didn't take as much care with school matters as he did with making cheese. On the other hand, he was very serious when it came to Tiana and school. He hounded her constantly about her studies. He expected her to put school first, second, and last. Kieron tried to keep her away from his street doings and the people with whom he associated. But the more he tried to keep her away the harder she tried to hang with him. During one memorable session, Tiana was complaining that he wanted her to sit a home and study and read and junk while he got to hang out and have fun. She was extremely angry that day. Kieron sat back and let her vent until she was exhausted. Then he looked straight at me and said his peace.

"Ms. Austin, I understand how she feels, you know. And I know she thinks I'm trying to keep her from having fun. But I'm going to explain to you like I did her. It ain't no fun out there. Not where we are. I'm out there, yeah, but I'm working a plan. And the plan I got is going to get us to a place where she can have some fun. You know, the clean and safe fun that kids are suppose to have. Now, I know that you know what I'm saying. Tiana is real smart. She got brains, you know, I mean she trips me out sometimes with the stuff she knows. She makes good grades easy. So, I know that she can make great grades if she put everything into it. Then, she can get a scholarship or something to one of those colleges like Famu or Spelman, you know. Cause you know that MaDear ain't got no money for college. Tiana is smart and she can have that if she stays focused on the right things. See, that's why I stay on her about studying. I ain't trying to be mean. I just want her to have a chance at some real happiness and have some real fun. If she hang out on the streets, she ain't gonna find nothing but what's out there. Misery. Man, it's all misery."

I told him that I understood what he was saying. Then, I proceeded to tell him that not only did Tiana deserve happiness and sunshine in her life, but so did he. And there are safer ways to get it other than the streets. He was just as intelligent and industrious enough to go to college. They could even do it together.

"Yeah that may be so, but right now I got to look out for little sis. She can be mad if she wants, but that's what I'm gonna do. And she knows I'm right!"

Boy, that Kieron was something. He really loved his sister and grandmother. I realized that I was already talking about Kieron in the past tense. It saddened me. I shook my head a little and stood as I whispered, "I'll be right back."

"Don't call MaDear!" Tiana snapped.

"No, no, I'm not. I'm just going to get you something to drink."

I retrieved a bottle of water from the frig and poured some into a clean mug. Tiana accepted the water and quietly drank. After a few minutes, she spoke again without raising her head.

"Ms. Austin, I'm sorry about cussing. I wasn't mad at you, really. I just kinda lost it. I'm really sorry. I don't know, I just been trippin' about everything that's happened."

"Tiana, it's okay. I know you didn't mean any harm. You have the right to be upset. So don't apologize, at least not to me."

"Thanks, but I really am sorry. I just wanted to come and talk to you. I think I needed to talk. MaDear....Well, I can't really talk to her right now. She's more messed up than me. You know how she gets. And all those folks hanging over at the apartment.....I shole ain't gonna talk to them. They don't know me and they don't know Kieron. But you know, you always said we could talk to you and I ain't got nobody else right now."

"Well baby, I'm right here right now and that's where I want to be. You can talk about whatever you want."

"It's just so weird. We got up like every other Saturday. We ate frozen waffles and watched cartoons. Then we went to the mall with MaDear. He talked MaDear into buying this church dress at Sears. It's really pretty. We stopped at the bookstore and he told me that he would only buy me the new Vibe magazine if I got a book too. He picked it out of course. It was "For Colored Girls Who Have Considered Suicide/When the Rainbow is Enuf" by Ntozake Shange. He was always buying me some book. But I liked most of them books and I ain't never tell him that."

She paused.

"He got some sneakers from the Foot Locker, too. Then we went grocery shopping and Kieron and MaDear were acting all silly up in there."

Tiana kind of smiled.

"When we got home, me and Kieron put all the groceries up, made some bologna sandwiches, and watched some television. I think we watched X-men or the Highlander. Then, I was on the phone. I don't remember when he left the house. I been trying to remember, but I can't. I walked over to the arcade and figured he'd probably be there, but he wasn't.

She paused long, then continued.

"Next thing I know I'm watching them put him in an ambulance."

"What happened?" I asked.

"He got shot. I wasn't there. I was still at the arcade and Meek came and got me."

Tiana stopped and took some time to dry the fresh tears from her face. Then she proceeded to tell of the mishap as it was told to her.

Kieron was with his boys, Meek and Kevin. They were just chillin' outside of the laundry house, talking about maybe going to the skating rink that night. Kevin wanted to go to the teen club to meet up with some chicken head, but Kieron dogged him so bad that Kevin agreed to go skating instead. They figured they'd go home to change. Kieron said he knew that I was going to be begging to go with him. And after she started whining to their grandmother, he would have to take her. So he was just going to ask me to go and cut out all the drama. Meek told him that I was probably still at the arcade where he'd seen me on his way over to meet them.

They were headed to the arcade when two dudes, one about their age and the other a bit older, crossed the street. The younger one called out Kieron's name. Meek and Kevin didn't know either of the guys, but Kieron obvious knew the one that called his name, for he pulled up and waited for him. When he finally reached them he asked Kieron for some stuff. Kieron told him that he'd already told him that he didn't have anything. Kieron laughed and said that he knew that the dude still didn't have no money, so go bother someone else. The boy said he knew Kieron was holding because he was always holding. Kieron kept telling the boy he didn't have nothing, but the boy wouldn't believe him and started getting upset. Then, the older dude that was with the younger one, starting walking closer to them.

The next thing they knew, the other guy pulled out a piece. Kieron, Meek, and Kevin took off running. They heard Kieron yelp then fall. They thought he tripped or something and turned to look over their shoulder. Kieron was on the ground and the other boys were running down the street away from them. Kevin got to Kieron first and tried to help him up. When Meek got there he knew instantly that Kieron was hurt, but didn't know how. Kevin kept yelling that Kieron was shot, but Meek didn't even remember hearing a shot go off. All he knew was that Kieron was out and then he saw a little blood at the side of his mouth. Meek was talking to Kieron asking him if he was okay and telling him to hold on. Kieron's eyelashes fluttered and he took an eerie heavy breathe. Meek yelled at Kevin to go get help, but Kevin said he wasn't going to leave Kieron lying there.

So Meek took off. He ran into the laundry mat and reached for the phone behind the counter and quickly gave the operator the information and location. Then he headed for the arcade. When he found Tiana he grabbed her and told her to go get her grandma because Kieron got shot. She instead went running behind Meek back to Kieron and Kevin. The EMTs' were putting Kieron in the ambulance by the time they got there. There were two police cruisers on the scene as well and an officer was questioning Kevin. Tiana was hysterically trying to ask Kevin what happened when one of the officers asked her if she was related to the victim. When he found out she was his sister, he took her to the hospital in his squad car. Meek and Kevin were taken down to the station.

From the station, Meek called his aunt, whom he lived with, and told her to go get MaDear and take her to the hospital because Kieron was hurt. When Tiana arrived at the hospital the officer and one of the nurses were very helpful. They assured her that her brother was in good hands and asked if there was someone that they could call. Tiana told them no because she didn't want to call MaDear. She was scared. What would she say? How would she say it? No, she couldn't call MaDear. Tiana gave the nurse some of the general information she needed. Then they sent her to the waiting room with a promise to inform her as soon as they had any word on what was going on. The officer bought a soda for her and left to check things out. He returned with no new information and sat with Tiana until her grandmother arrived a short time later.

MaDear was hurriedly ushered in by Meek's aunt. She was a

bundle of nerves seeking answers to why Kieron was there. Tiana wondered how she'd heard about Kieron so quickly. MaDear hugged Tiana and instantly began questioning her. Tiana was dumbfounded and couldn't seem to get any words through her mouth. She just kept shaking her head through the tears. When the officer explained that Kieron had been shot, MaDear went shock still. Meek's aunt and the officer helped her to take a seat and Tiana moved to sit next to her. The officer explained that he did not have any details on the facts surrounding the incident and that the witnesses were down at the station. Meek's aunt said that Meek hadn't even told her that Kieron had been shot.

He just told her that he was at the police station and to go get MaDear and take her to the hospital and that Tiana was already there. That's all he'd said before he slammed the phone down. The officer said he'd go and see what he could find out. Meek's aunt went to go find a doctor to tell them where Kieron was. She returned and said that the nurse said that the doctor was still taking care of Kieron and that he would be in as soon as he could. Then she said she was going to run down to the station and check on Meek.

Tiana and MaDear sat anxiously in the waiting area with all kinds of thoughts running through their minds. Every once in a while Tiana would take MaDear's hand and tell her that Kieron was going to be okay.

Endless minutes seemed to past when finally the doctor came into the waiting area and approached MaDear. Tiana knew instantly that Kieron was no longer among the living by the solemn look on the doctor's face. She felt it so strongly that she never heard the doctor give her grandmother the grave news. She only saw his mouth moving and then her grandmother throw her hands into the air and open her mouth in a scream. Tiana walked up behind her grandmother and wrapped her arms around her. At that moment, Meek and his aunt walked into the room. The aunt rushed to MaDear to comfort her and the doctor moved away with a sorry upon his lips. Meek was frozen with a grimaced face. Tiana caught his eyes and knew well the pain and anger he was feeling. They helped MaDear back to a seat with

Tiana and the aunt on either side. An unknown hand provided some Kleenex during their struggle to comfort. They rocked, shushed, and rubbed until MaDear began to quiet her crying to a low moaning.

Meek stood off to the side against a wall frowning and clenching his fists. His aunt walked to him and embraced him slowly and quietly. Tiana knew he was hurting. He, Kevin, and Kieron had been the three musketeers for so long. Now there were only two and the missing one was her only brother. Tiana's thoughts were interrupted by the sudden movement of her grandmother. MaDear fell from her seat to her knees, her arms stretched to the heavens, with prayers to the Lord flowing from her heart past her lips. Tiana knelt beside her, embracing her. As she rested her head on MaDear's shoulder blade, she silently offered a prayer that Kieron was with God preparing to receive his angelic wings.

# 5

Tiana sat silently with her head in her hands after giving her account of the events that transpired just a couple of days before. She appeared so tiny and fragile. This image of her was so dissimilar to what I had experienced of her. Tiana was usually so quick witted and energetic. Now, I only saw a shadow of what one often expects to see in a child her age.

I let her sit for a few minutes before interrupting her solitude.

"Tiana, are you okay?" It seemed like such an inappropriate question, but I was at a lost for words. So, I just went with my first thought. Actually, there are not any real appropriate comments to make in the light of such a tragic situation. We just try to project the essence of compassion with every word we speak.

"I'm okay. My head is just pounding so bad." She responded.

"Do you want some Tylenol? I think I have some."

It is not my practice to give medicine to my clients, but if there was ever a time to make an exception this was one.

"Yeah, that might help. That's what MaDear usually gives us."

"Have you eaten? You shouldn't take it on an empty stomach."

"No, I ain't had no appetite."

"Well, let me see what I have."

I went to check the snack stash in my file cabinet and found the usual selection of peanut butter crackers, clif bars, and twizzlers. I figured she'd prefer the peanut butter crackers over the clif bar, so I grabbed a pack and retrieved another bottle of water from the frig.

"Here you go. Eat this and I'll go find the Tylenol."

She took the crackers and water. I waited until she began eating before I went for the medicine. I gave her two regular strength caplets and suggested that she lay down on the sofa for a little while and give the medicine time to kick in. She went directly over to the sofa, laid down, propped her head on one of the throw pillows, and pulled the

African print sofa throw over herself.

The CD had finished sometime during Tiana's re-accounts. I figured some music would help her rest. So, I put on an Enya CD and went over to my desk. Initially, I just sat staring out the window, not really thinking of anything in particular. I was just letting my mind rest and process the abundance of information that had been inputed.

I still had difficulty believing it all, but the depth of Tiana's sadness made it real. I could see in her eyes that she, too, was wishing that it was all a dream. Then she would be able to resume her carefree teenage life. Unfortunately, we both knew that that was not an option in this case. Tiana would never be able to forget this time in her life. That much was factual. Whether or not she would be able to go on and lead a positive and productive lifestyle was the challenge. Tiana had already lived a very heartache filled life and had only recently, living with her grandmother, found a place of peace. MaDear had provided a place where she could sleep with the lights off and dream sweet dreams. If I ran down the list of drama she'd experienced thus far, one could never believe that she had only lived thirteen years. Yet, Tiana rarely hesitated to offer her smile which simulated the brilliance of a rainbow. Such a sweet baby and life was once again throwing a fastball straight to the head. I definitely could not stop the ball from hitting her, but I would do my best to help her recover from the blow.

I caught myself nodding and jerked myself upright. When I glanced over at Tiana, she had already fallen asleep. The poor child was obviously exhausted. She probably had a difficult time resting at home with memories of Kieron surrounding her, not to mention the constant flow of people filing through their small apartment. I decided to let her take a very long nap. Almost an hour had passed since I sat down at my desk, therefore, she'd probably been sleeping for at least half that time and could use a bit more sleep. Besides, I knew that I needed to call Mrs. Menden. Tiana had been there for almost two hours and I was pretty sure that her grandmother did not know where she was. Tiana might be upset with me but I had to call and make sure that she knew Tiana was safe. Her grandmother would surely panic if Tiana was away from home for too long.

I prepared my mug for a bit of tea with a squeeze of lime juice and two starlight mints, filled the miniature coffee pot with loose Red Zinger leaves and water, then sat down to make the call. The phone was answered by an adult who identified herself as a family friend after informing me that Ms. Menden was taking a rest. I then asked her to relay the very important message of Tiana's whereabouts and her estimated return home. The lady assured me that she would relay the message as soon as Ms. Menden awakened and expressed relief that Tiana was resting as well.

I decided to let Tiana sleep another hour or so before I awakened her. Meanwhile, I would go over some files and redo the weeks' agenda for my group session. This would be the perfect time to touch on the subject of personal losses and grieving. In looking at my session notes, it appeared that we'd never discussed the grieving process. That is not to say that no one had experienced the loss of a loved one, for I'm sure one or more must have. Suddenly, I was bothered by the absence of this topic and wondered if it could be considered negligence on my part. Any who, no matter now, all I could do was pick up the ball and play.

I started by listing the stages of grieving; Denial, Anger, Bargaining, Depression, and Acceptance. Then I listed questions to present to the group leaving room for questions they were bound to surprise me with. From there I outlined possible responses and counter responses and/or explanations. Finally, I mapped out a worksheet for the group members to utilize. It's wise to provide different modes for the children to communicate through. Even the hardest of hardest kid has a sensitive area which negates verbal communication and deserves other means to convey their thoughts and feelings.

The agenda was showing the makings of an interesting session. A quick glance at my watch showed that over an hour had passed. I stopped to transfer my work to my desktop computer, then to a flashdrive and finally to my laptop. I make a habit of creating two back ups for fear of losing something important. Mistakes like that have a tendency to drive me crazy, because prevention only takes a few minutes. It took another thirty minutes to complete that task and it was time to get Tiana home. I hated to wake her. She looked so peaceful, but I needed to get her home.

One gentle shake of her shoulder was all that it took to wake her.

"Tiana, you feel better? It's time to go home. I called and left a message for your grandmother. I told her that I'd drop you back home."

"What? You called MaDear?"

"It's okay Tiana. I had to let her know where you were. I couldn't have her worried about your whereabouts, especially not now."

"What did she say?"

"Nothing that I know of. I didn't talk to her. She was sleeping. So I just left a message with whoever answered the phone."

"Who answered?"

"She said a family friend, Miss Kender, I believe."

"Oh you mean Miss Kendrell. That's Meek's aunt. She's been watching over MaDear real good. I'm glad she's there but all those other folks need to go home."

"Okay girl, let's head out. Are you ready? Is there anything you want to discuss before we go? Anything at all?"

"Naw, I just need to use the restroom."

Tiana left to freshen up and I wondered if she felt I was kicking her out. I truly wasn't. I just thought that her grandmother would feel better having her around. She treasured those two and worried about them constantly.

Once in the car, Tiana struck up conversation.

"You say that MaDear was sleeping?" she inquired.

"That's what the lady said. Well, she said she was resting so I guess we can assume that she was sleeping. How has she been holding up?"

"Well, she hasn't been sleeping much at all. I hear her all through the night. She's pacing around, cleaning the house, piddling in the kitchen, listening to the radio, or playing solitaire. If she's not fooling around the apartment, she's in her room reading her Bible. I know because her light is on and she never sleeps with the lights on. That's how I got over my fear of the dark. Cause when we first came to live with her, I was too afraid to sleep by myself so I slept with her. I always wanted to keep the lights on, but she would say that she couldn't rest her eyes with light shining on her lids. "Lights makes your eyes puffy and gives your skin wrinkles."

I would keep begging every night and finally she said.

"Baby girl, you come to me because you know I'm gonna take care of you and keep you safe with my love. And you're right about that. Chile, my love is gonna keep you safe and I love you in the light and the dark. So, you ain't got no need to be afraid of the dark or nothing else. Because my love is always with you just like God's love."

"I believed her and then I could sleep pretty good." Tiana finished up.

"Your grandma is a wise woman."

"Yeah, and she don't deserve all this stress. It's bad enough that she gonna be sad over Kieron, but then she got to deal with all this other stuff. Did I tell you that the funeral is suppose to be Friday?"

"No, you didn't. What time are the services?"

"I don't know. I don't think that anything is final yet. That's what I'm talking about. MaDear been trying to hold off until she finds my momma. We ain't heard from her in so long and the last address we had ain't no good no more. MaDear been making calls and relatives and junk been asking around, but can't nobody find her trifling butt. That don't make no sense. How she gonna call herself a mother? She don't come around or even call her own children. We can't even find her to tell her that her son's been killed. You know it's gonna be a shame if we have to have Kieron's funeral without his own mother there to say goodbye to him. Then again, it ain't like she really been a part of our lives anyway. What we need her for now?"

At this point I had to interrupt Tiana's emotional verbal attack.

"Look Tiana, that's not cool. She is your mother and she may have made mistakes but I'm sure she loves you and Kieron. All mothers love their children. Besides, how could anyone not love you guys. You're the best."

"Ms Austin, she don't love us. How could she? All the stuff she put us through, you don't do that to people you love."

"Tiana, you're mistaken. Haven't you ever heard that you hurt those you love the most? Look, your mom definitely has some serious issues. I may not know exactly what they all are but you must remember that the junk that she puts in her body probably does all the thinking for her. I realize that she has not done the motherly job that you, Kieron, your grandmother, or even what I would expect her to have done. But by no means does that connote that she does not love you."

Tiana snapped a response. She was obviously worked up.

"Motherly duties…motherly anything. Ms. Austin, I can't remember her ever being motherly. What I do remember is her leaving us alone in stank, cold, ugly, roach infested apartments. Sometimes locked in our room. I remember one time she didn't come home for two days and when she finally found her way home, she slept a whole 'nother day. We ain't never have no food in the house. We might have some saltines and if we were lucky there was some canned beans or potted meat. But if she had the munchies, then that was gone quick. Thank God for free breakfast and lunch at school. Shoot, me and Kieron would make it to school on time just so we could get something to eat. It ain't the school's responsibility to feed us…. that's a mother's job. But she acted like she couldn't even do that. She wasn't no mother then and you see she ain't no mother now."

"I hear you Tiana. And it may be hard to comprehend right now because you're young and your wounds are still fresh. But Tiana, you will have to eventually open your heart and see the underlying truth. When you are able to do that you will be able to see the errors of her ways for what they are. And you will stand a better chance of not making the same mistakes. Hopefully you will be able to forgive her one day and love her for being your mother if nothing else. I know that I am grateful for her giving birth to the two of you. You two are a part of my life that I treasure and I know your grandmother feels the same way. So try to focus on the good things and people in your life because that's what matters the most."

Tiana didn't respond this time. She just stared out the window motionlessly. Once again, I left her to her thoughts. I continued the route to her place. Rush hour traffic had begun and our progress was slow. I'm very rarely bothered by tight traffic. It gives me time to think and Tiana looked like she was using this time for that purpose as well.

I pulled onto Tiana's street and easily found parking in her apartment parking area. Kids were running around playing and laughing. Of the twelve porch fronts, at least eight had young men and women doning the stairs. Some were sipping from cups or brown paper bags but most were just shooting the breeze and listening to music. There were a few guys hanging out in and around a big burgundy Caprice that was supplying the air with thumping bass that was vaguely referable to the tribal uplifting of our ancestors' percussioning. I might have been able to find a better relation in the music had it not been for the distorted muffling caused by the huge particle board speaker boxes use to create the musical effect desired by so many young drivers.

Tiana's porch steps were occupied by a few youngsters probably 7 or 8 years old. They all called a greeting to Tiana as we approached and she greeted them all by name as she mussed each head. We walked into the building to ascend the stairs to Tiana's third floor apartment. As we started our ascent, two thirtyish women exited Tiana place with three toddlers in tow. Tiana spoke to them and they stopped to hug her as they reported there departure to go get dinner started for the kids. I walked pass them and waited for Tiana by the apartment door. When she reached the top of the stairs, she took a few minutes seemingly to prepare for her re-entrance to the mourning household.

As soon as I walked in behind Tiana, I saw Ms. Menden sitting on the living room sofa. She was somberly listening to another woman who appeared slightly older than she, dressed in a Sunday-go-to-meeting white skirt suit. Tiana walked over, sat next to her grandmother, and gave her a peck on the cheek. In return she reached over and stroked Tiana's head as their eyes met. They were silently checking to see how the other was holding up. This was the language reserved for loving members in a code developed in the heart. What the two of them found in response remained undetectable and unspoken to the others in the room.

Tiana directed her grandmothers' attention to my presence. I greeted Mrs. Menden with a combination hand hold and hug. She felt fragile and I wondered if she had been dieting or if it was the disintegrating effect of her grieving.

"Ms Austin, thanks for taking care of my baby here. When I heard she was with you I knew that she was okay. Cuz' you wouldn't do nothing less than take the best care of her. You've always taken good care of both my babies."

She paused ever so solemnly and then beckoned me to have a seat next to her. Tiana slid aside to offer a place between the two of them. I took a seat and Mrs. Menden introduced me to the woman who'd been conversing with her upon my entrance.

"Sister Bloom, this is Ms. Austin. She's the counselor that's been helping Tiana and Kieron. She's a godsend and they love her. Kieron used to talk about her all the time. I ain't never had no problem getting him to keep his appointments with her. Neither one of them. Yes Lord, she really has helped my babies. I don't know what we would have done without her. Ain't that right Tiana?"

Tiana smiled at me and said, "Yes Ma'am MaDear."

I couldn't think of a befitting response. I surely didn't think that I could accept the life saving title she was appropriating to me. But I didn't want to sink any negativity into the conversation. So I simply said, "Mrs. Menden, I don't know what they would have done without you."

She just patted my knee.

Sister Bloom announced that it was time for her to leave as she stood and gave Mrs. Menden a sisterly hug. Meanwhile, I surveyed the apartment. It was small but very well kept. The lighting was poor and there was not much natural lighting. The furniture was neatly arranged and had the glow of a fresh dusting. Pictures of MaDear and the kids were skillfully arranged on the wall. The mocha colored carpeting was worn but visibly free of lint and dirt. Overall the place looked the same as any other time I visited. That is except for the absence of Kieron's cheery voice and handsome face.

There were four other women present. Three women were sitting at the dinette finishing up plates of food and desserts, dressed much like Sister Bloom. Another woman was coming out of the kitchen drying her hands with a dish towel. She started clearing the dinette table as Sister Bloom summoned the other ladies. Tiana whispered that the woman cleaning was Meeks' aunt. Then she rose from the sofa and asked if I wanted something to drink. I requested a soda and off she went.

The group of church mothers gathered around MaDear to say their goodbyes. One suggested a prayer and MaDear stood pulling me up with her. We all joined hands forming a small circle. Meeks' Aunt joined us. As Sister Bloom began the prayer, MaDear broke the circle by unlocking her hands from the group.

"Wait! Where's my baby girl? Tiana?" she called. "Come in here for a minute, baby."

Tiana peeked out from the kitchen and realizing what was taking place, gingerly walked toward us. MaDear reached out and placed her between the two of us. With the circle now complete, Sister Bloom started the prayer session.

*"Let every head bow and every eye shut. First before all we want to thank you, Father God. We thank you for loving us all, Father God. We thank you for bringing us here together, Lord. We thank you for all the blessings you have filled our lives with through the years, Father God. Blessings like sweet Kieron. And Lord God we thank you for the trials in our lives. For, Father God, you know they make us stronger. You know, Lord God, that we are weak sometimes. Yes Lord, weak with our humanly hearts, weak with fear of this worldly world, Dear Lord. But Lord, we must remember as you told us as you placed it in our hearts, that the battle is not ours, it's yours, Lord. We know Lord, yes, we know Lord that there is nothing Lord that you will place on us that we can't bear. No Lord, not one thing. You carry the weight, Father God, for us. So we pray Lord, we pray to you for strength Father God, in this time of turbulence. We pray for our sister, your daughter Sister Menden. We know she is your child and a diligent servant. We pray to you to help this pure flower, Tiana, so young and yet growing closer to you everyday. We pray for them, Lord God, to remain trusting in you, Father God. For you know best, Lord God, your will shall always be done and it is always just, Dear Lord. Yes, they have to say goodbye to a precious loved one but you loved him best. We pray for your continued love*

*and guidance, Father God. We pray that you order our steps and keep our hearts full with your love. We pray this all in your Precious Sons' name, whom you sent to give his life for us, Jesus Christ. And all Gods' children say . . . . . "*

And in unison we all responded, *"Amen!"*, with a gentle squeeze to the hands held.

MaDear walked the Sisters to the door, I took my seat, and Tiana headed back to the kitchen. Ms. Menden returned to the sofa and lowered herself with a long heavy sigh. I put my arm around her and laid my head on her shoulder. A portion of the sorrow she was feeling seemed to eminate the air with each breath she exhaled. Although I wanted to offer her comfort, I knew that there was nothing I could do to ease her weariness. Nothing I could say to justify a rhyme or reason to this loss of life. So, we sat silently even as Tiana reentered the room with three beverages.

A couple of Tiana's friends came by the apartment and she grabbed her jacket and headed outdoors with them. Tiana made sure to ensure her grandmother that she would not go any further than the front stoop.

With Tiana gone, Mrs. Menden beckoned me to her bedroom for a private conversation. The notion that she didn't want Tiana to walk in on our conversation alerted me to the seriousness of the forth coming discussion. Mrs. Mendens' bedroom was a picturesque view of a princess quarters in the ghetto. It was amazing what she had created with such a small space and cheap furniture. Against the main full wall sat an antique solid oak bed with rolled front nightstands flanking either side. The headboard was partially hidden by two fluffy bed pillows and several laced throw pillows matching the white laced duvet. The nightstands each held miniature glass tear dropped lamps. The right nightstand also held a tattered white bible with gold-leafed lettering and page edging. The one window in the room draped shear white curtains with faint laced etchings. Ms. Menden had situated a cream colored wing back chair and a round glass table next to the one window. This was where she did her cross-stitching which was apparent from the white wicker basket full of supplies resting on the glass table. A large oak laminate chest of drawers stood against the wall next to the entrance. The last wall of the room was mostly taken up by a small walk-in closet that had bi-folding mirrored doors. She had accented the area by adding a decorative curtain rod above the framing and cinching a set of the window curtains. Ms. Menden's room was definitely a place devoted to peace and beauty.

She turned the chair to face the bed and directed me to be seated. Then she sat on the edge of the bed, kicked off slippers and gently propped herself up against the pillowed headboard. Ms. Menden closed her eyes for a moment and took a few deep breaths. She looked as drained as one who'd spent a ten hour day doing some serious manual labor.

"Whew, Lord have mercy." She whispered, then looked at me.

"Is there anything I can do to help out?" I asked.

"Baby, I don't rightly know right now. Things are so crazy. I mean it's hard to know which way is up most of the time.

She paused.

"Lord knows that my life has been well seasoned with trials and tribulations, but this one has been the hardest. And may God forgive me, but at the beginning of all this I questioned why the Lord had put this on me and how I was going to get through it. My precious baby's life has been snatched from me. But as God is my light, I ain't worried about making it through anymore, because I know He's gonna carry me right on through it all. I just have to take care of the easy stuff and be there for Tiana. She's still a child and she needs my love and guidance to deal with this tragedy. You would be surprised how many other ills have fallen upon this already bad situation."

"Well Ms. Menden, I want to help anyway I can. Have you been able to make arrangements? Do you need to gather some funds."

"Oh baby, that ain't what I'm speaking to. We been able to make arrangements just fine if you talking on the money side. Randall's Funeral Home has been more than kind and plus I had that insurance for Kieron that you made me purchase from the school." She chuckled.

"Remember how I chided you on how silly it was to waste money on that insurance. But after all that ranting and raving about it being unnecessary, look what done happened. I guess that's one more thing to thank you for. Who would have ever imagined that I would have need for life insurance for my grandchild? We could have just been another blip on the five o'clock news, asking for donations. But any who, I wasn't talking about that, either. I was speaking to something a little closer to the heart."

"What's that, Mrs. Menden?"

"That baby's momma, my daughter." She replied. "I been trying to find her. She needs to know that it's time to lay her oldest child to rest. She needs to say her final farewell to him here on this earth. But she ain't been around in so long and I haven't the faintest clue of where she is. I don't know who her friends are if that's what you would call them. That child has been out there in the world so long and hard that I can't even imagine what kind of life she's living. I supposed that I didn't want to know after a while, so I just haven't looked. Lord knows I tried so many times to bring her back to a clean life. Bring her to the Lord cause only he can save her. She ain't never listened to me. I swear I don't even know when I lost her. She was such a smart girl. I don't know how she got sucked into them streets. All I know now is that she ain't here right now when she really needs to be. She needs to be here for her babies."

"So you don't know how to get in contact with her at all?"

Ms. Menden sighed. "Not really. I put the word out to some of the folks she used to fool around with and my nephew, Rolo, has been doing the same. But I can't have that baby's body sittin' around forever. We got to lay him to rest. I know his soul is resting with the Lord already. We have the services scheduled for Saturday morning at eleven. And we gonna have a viewing on Friday night at seven. I pray that that child of mine shows up by then, but we are going on with the plan." She paused to shake her head and wring her hands a bit and then continued.

"I know she'll turn up sooner or later. And if it's later, I gotta be prepared to endure a great load of anger and blame from her. Never mind how I cared for her most of her life and now for the children she should be raising. She is still going to find some way to blame that baby's death on me. Lord knows I have done the best I can and given with every ounce of strength the good Lord has blessed me with."

I quickly reached for the Kleenex on the nightstand as Mrs.

Menden's shoulders began to shudder and tears seeped through under her closed eye lids. We sat that way for only a short time, for Mrs. Menden regrouped quickly and proceeded talking in a business oriented manner. She started running through a list of things that needed to be taken care of in the next 24 hours. She needed to get Kieron's clothes to the funeral home and go to the obituary mart. Before that she would have to sit down and write a brief synopsis of Kieron's short yet accomplishment filled existence. There were readings, musical selections, and singers to select. A list of relatives also needed to be done.

I asked if she needed me to take her shopping for a suit for Kieron, but she'd already chosen something from his closet. She always made sure that the kids had Sunday clothes just as she made sure they made it to church at least two Sundays per month. Much to her pleasure, they usually attended more often than she insisted.

Tiana's favorite part of church was the choir with their rich voices and joyful sounds. I could remember Kieron once sharing that in church he felt like a part of a huge family full of love. Even the adults that scolded him in the neighborhood had warm hugs for him on Sunday mornings. Overall, I believe that their main reason for attending church was to be with their grandmother during a time when she was filled with pure happiness, joy, and peace.

The sun was beginning to set and I knew it was time for me to head home. I told Ms. Menden that I would call her the next day and made her promise to call if she needed anything at all, even just an ear for listening. After hugging her I headed out to my car. Tiana was sitting on the stoop, as promised, talking to her girlfriends. I told her that her grandmother wanted her upstairs for dinner right away. Then, I hugged her and whispered that I wanted her to promise to eat and to make sure that her grandmother did the same. I proceeded to my car as she immediately dismissed her company. She called another goodbye and thank you as I was unlocking the car door. I waved and put my thumb to my ear and pinky to my mouth signaling for her to call. Once I turned on to the main road, I instantly felt totally drained. I was tired and hungry and couldn't wait to get home.

# 6

After stuffing myself with chicken chow fun, I felt ready to call it a night. I clicked off the television and put on Oleta Adams Evolution cd. Her rich inspiring voice was always calming to me. Her insightful lyrics inspired me to do things. I could listen to her in any mood and feel sustained and satisfied with the variety of her musical creations. There was an underlying theme of God and Love in an everyday living way. After twirling to "Window of Hope" a couple of times, I set about clearing the remains of my dinner and laying out my attire for the next day. I pulled out a set of satin pajamas and danced my way to the bathroom for a quick daily facial. For the second night in a row I treated myself to an extended hot shower as I continued to serenade myself.

By the time I'd finished lotioning from head to toe and slipped into bed the cd was ending and the silence left was instantly filled with a flood of thoughts running through my mind. At first they were of Kieron and his family, which was understandable. I had spent the whole day dealing with their issues. But the next rampage of thoughts caught me a little by surprise. I began thinking about my relationship with Karl again. Relationship? There was no longer a relationship. But he of course didn't know that yet. Or did he? It was time for me to call Corie and find out what had transpired during my hide away vacation. I was extremely nervous about calling her. Was I ready to hear what she would say? What did she say to Karl? I know he'd called. Did he actually talk to Corie? Was she able to keep her cool and keep her mouth shut? Did she remember what I told her to say? Shoot, I just needed to call her and find out or I would drive myself bonkers with all the questions overloading my brain. I took a few deep breaths, yanked the cordless off the base, and dialed Corie's number.

"Hey girl, guess who." "Hooker, it's about time you called! Where are you? You know you got some nerve running off all wigged out and then not calling nobody for days on end. You know that's some insensitive mess." I had to interrupt her or she was liable to blow a head gasket.

"Corie. Corie!" I shouted into the receiver. Girl, slow your roll. I'm sorry. I know I should have called, but just calm down. Okay?"

"Fine then. But you got some nerve. You know you wrong. Now, where in the hell are you?"

"I'm home, snuggled in the safety of my luscious leather sleigh bed. You know the one you drool over every time you see it." I teased.

"When did you get home? I can not believe your trifling butt."

"I got in late last night and then I had a work emergency that I've been dealing with all day. That's why I'm just getting around to calling you."

I left out the whole shabang about putting off the call due to the fear of having to deal with the Karl drama. She was my girl but she didn't need to feel all my weaknesses.

"Well, are you feeling better? And where did you finally end up?"

"I stayed with Paully. I didn't even go see my parents. I just needed to have sometime to release and gather my thoughts in peace. And there is no way that my mother would have given me the space to do that. She would have spent every waking moment trying to make it better and that would have driven me crazy."

"So you spent the whole time couped up at Paully's?"

"Not even. Girl we had a ball. We hooked up with my girl Cocoa and ate, drank, and laughed a bit. But we did talk about my situation, too. It felt good to talk it out and get some comfort. By and large, Paully is my best friend and being with him was probably the best medicine. Oh and he told me to tell you hello."

"Girl, you mean that fine piece of chocolate asked about me? Oh baby, tell me more."

I had to laugh.

"I don't believe I said he asked about you. I said that he said hello. So cool your pants. You are so crazy."

"Come on Rhap. Why can't you hook a sister up?"

I could hear her feigning a pout as she changed the subject.

"Well anyway…just forget you. Let's get to the important stuff because I know that's why you called."

My heart jumped and started ticking triple time. The time had come to hear about Karl. It was clear from her tone that she had spoken with him. What was said was what I was anxious to hear about. I was not afraid, although if I'd really thought about it long enough I could have made myself so. Other than feeling anxious I believe a part of me was a bit hopeful. Maybe I had made a horrible mistake and grossly misunderstood what I'd seen that night in Beacons Court's parking lot. I had to mentally pimp slap myself. I know that there was basically one explanation for the scene I'd witnessed. And only a fool would reason differently.

"Rhap, you know that I was rounding up a eight day work week when I went to that party, right?

"Yeah, I guess I remember something like that."

Corie was constantly putting in major hours on the job. She was head chef at a relatively new eclectic restaurant in the Highlands. In the year that she'd been with them, the restaurant had experienced great success. The ambience and uniquely flavorful dishes kept regulars regular and new comers numerous. Corie had a graphic design degree, but her passion was tantalizing taste buds. She envisioned that her artistic nature would ultimately lead her to ownership of a successful dinner club of her own.

"Okay, well that fool of yours called me at 8:00a.m. on my first day of rest. The first time the phone rang, I snatched myself out of sleep so hard that I thought I had pulled a neck muscle. Then the connection was so bad with his cell phone that I couldn't identify who it was before we were disconnected. Oh, but he called back a few minutes later and I had to hop off the toilet to catch the phone."

I was a little scared now, because Corie hates to be awakened before noon on a good day. So I knew she was surely pissed when Karl called that morning and there was no telling what she would say or how she'd say it. "He sounded all irritated asking for you and junk. Never even bothered to apologize for ringing my phone that early in the morning."

"What did you do Corie?"

"Chill girl, I was cool. I remembered what you said and believe me if you weren't my girl I would have let him have it good. But I played it cool. Besides, I wanted the asinine gigolo to sweat. He was all asking where you were and why I was I answering your phone. I told him that you had forwarded your phone to me because you had an emergency and had to go out of town to get the situation under control. Then he started asking what happened, where you had to go, and if you'd said anything about meeting him in Florida. Let me tell you that I laid it on thick then. I was like…Baby, I'm not sure what happened. She was all upset and rushing to take care of what ever it was that I couldn't bring myself to ask her any questions. I just promised to watch out for things here, told her not to worry, and for her to be safe. I told him that I expected you to call but I didn't know when."

"Then what did he say?"

"Girllll, after I put it down like that he was acting all concerned and telling me to tell you to call him ASAP when I heard from you. He even left his cell number and the hotel number."

"That's it?"

"Hell naw, he called back that night and the next day he called three times. After I got those messages I waited until I went to work and called his cell. I told him that you'd left a message that everything was doing better and then I rushed off the phone."

Corie fell into a fit of laughter. She was so pleased with herself that I had to chuckle a little myself.

"Girl, then I just avoided all his calls. But he only called a few more times after that, going by the messages I got. So what's your plan now girl? Are you going to read him the riot act?"

I had to think a moment. Let things settle in my mind a little.

"I'm not sure yet. Now that I know what happened while I was away, I can probably put together a plan on how to handle Mr. Cheat. Rest assure, it will be a good plan. I want him to know that playing me was like playing with fire. I want him to feel the burn."

Corie laughed again. I knew she was loving that. Shoot, she probably wanted him to suffer more than I did. She probably wanted to put some hurting on him herself. We talked a little more about some pay back options. Then, I carefully steered the conversation away from Karl. I filled her with the joys of my visit home, leaving out the emotional rampages and crying spells. Corie also tried to convince me again to get her hooked up with Paully. She's known me long enough to know that I do not, will not, and never have played match maker. If she ever got with Paully it wouldn't be with my help. Besides, I didn't think that she was right for my buddy anyway. Don't get me wrong. I cherish them both. But together? Definitely not! But I would never tell her that.

After I hung up with Corie, I was feeling a little solemn. So, I put on some Jonathan Butler real low, turned out the lights and let him lull me to sleep. The mission planning could wait until the morning.

I awakened from an exotic dream in a sweat. I looked around the room franticly trying to get my bearings. My eyes rested on the alarm clock across the room on my dresser. It read 3:38 a.m. I was finally aware of my surroundings as well as the layer of sweat covering my neck and brow. What was I dreaming? Why did it make me sit straight up in my bed? Why was my heart racing? I took a few deep breaths and laid back down with a sigh. I closed my eyes and tried to remember the dream I'd just left. It came back instantly and clearly along with an aching sense of need for Karl.

We were walking into the lobby of an elegant hotel sparkling of crystal and fine Italian marble. The area was busy with employees and patrons, yet their faces and voices were blurry and muffled. The only face I could see clearly was Karl's. We were walking hand in hand. Neither of us spoke a word but our eyes were communicating our happiness. We strolled past the crowed lobby as a pathway opened before us, leading us toward golden elevator doors. I could feel everyone watching us enviously. The elevator rose swiftly and we walked to our room without ever breaking eye contact. Once inside, Karl began slowly smothering me with kisses. Kisses so sensual and enveloping that I was forced to seal my eyes shut. I could feel him wisk me across the room to the bed. I felt as if I were flying. Then I could feel the warmth of his body covering mine like a down feather comforter, caressingly soft and warm. It was blissful. I felt the need to look into his eyes and whisper my love to him. So I willed my eyes to open. But as they did I was alarmed to see nothing in front of me, beside me, or around me. He was gone!

That's what had awakened me. Damn, what was that all about? I rolled myself out of bed and headed for the bathroom to wipe away the moisture and sweat brought on by that crazy dream. As I sat on my throne, crazy thoughts started rummaging through my brain. Why was I dreaming about him? Why was I dreaming about him that way? He was the villain. He was sleeping, caressing, and loving someone else. Or maybe the dream was trying to tell me something else. Maybe I was wrong. Maybe I had grossly mistaken the situation. Corie didn't say that he sounded guilty about anything. She just said that he sounded very concerned about me. You know I could be wrong. If I am wrong I could be blowing my chance at a lifetime of happiness. But it's not too late. I can make it up to him. He'll never even have to know about my misjudgment. Wait a minute. Am I crazy? I didn't make a mistake. I know what I saw. I know that what I saw summed up all the strangeness in our relationship of late. Naw, this is whacked. I am putting him in the wind.

I had made up my mind and I went back to bed. But I couldn't get back to sleep. I kept second guessing myself and running the mind video of that night over and over. Was there even a slim possibility that he could be innocent? I checked the time. It was 4:15. I jumped out of bed and grabbed some sweats out of the dresser. I was going to make a run. I needed to get some questions answered.

Before I could change my mind, I headed my car on the path to Karl's house. I hadn't a plan, just an urge to go there and hopefully find some comfort. I crept past his three bedrooms, two bath, full basement ranch home scanning for signs of life within. I'd settle for an illuminated room or the faint flicker of a television playing. I could see nothing but darkness from my position in the car. I circled the cul-de-sac, drove back down the street, over to the next street, and then back up his street. I parked two houses down from his and cut the lights. Cautiously I walked back to his house and made my way to the left side of the dwelling where

I could see that his bedroom window as dark and sealed. Even though I knew then that he wasn't there, because he religiously sleeps with a window cracked for fresh air all year through, I tip-toed back to the front to peer into the two car garage. Through the darkness I could make out his Harley parked against the back wall, the ivory and chrome glistening through. But the absence of his vehicle made my heart drop. I knew he was in town or at least I believed he was. And if so, where would he be at five o'clock in the morning.

I returned to my vehicle and headed to my next destination. The Beacon Court's parking lot was relatively full and quiet. As I entered I saw a young man exiting the first building dressed in jeans, work boots, and some type of uniformed jacket and cap. He unlocked and entered a pickup parked in front of the building, obviously on his way to begin another work day. I averted my eyes as to not make eye contact. Once past him I began to scan the other parked vehicles. I tried to remember which building I'd dropped Corie at that evening of the party. Suddenly, I remembered that the building letter was G. I continued toward building G. The night sky was beginning to lighten ever so slightly and with the parking lot lighting, vision was good.

As I passed the F building, I caught my breath as Karl's green SUV came into view. It wasn't parked where it had been the other night, but it was parked damn near where I'd been sitting when I had my heart pimp slapped. I stopped right behind it and checked the license plate. There it was in bold black lettering BIGICK. BIGICK, his macho code for his endowment. Presently in my mind the vanity plate was an extremely accurate description of who he was as oppose to what he had.

I slumped down in my seat as my eyes misted over. Suddenly, the urge to get out of there before I convinced myself to do something stupid overcame me. I quickly fled anxious to get home. Amazingly, my tears dried quickly and I made it home safely. Well, I may not have gotten the relief I was hoping for from my excursion, but at least I had relieved the doubt that had filled me a couple of hours before.

I turned off my alarm clock, undressed, slid back into bed, and closed my sleep heavy eye lids.

# 7

I was awakened by the phone ringing and I snatched it up without thinking. Thankfully, it was just Tiana instead of Karl. I instantly made myself a promise to call Karl and announce my return. I'd have to figure out what to say exactly but I could do that later. I needed to see what was up with Tiana first.

"Good morning T. What's going on? Are you okay?" I asked groggily.

"Yeah, I'm cool. I just wanted to ask a favor."

"Sure. What do you need?"

"I was wondering if you could take me to get my hair hooked up for...uh...well you know for tomorrow. I gotta go with MaDear today to the funeral home and I think we gotta go to get flowers and stuff so I'm not sure what time we'll be done. But I was kinda thinking that maybe I can find some time somewhere and maybe you can set up a walk-in for tonight or tomorrow. But I understand if you can't cuz I know it's last minute."

I interrupted her before she could work herself into a frenzy.

"Hey, hey! Tiana it's not a problem. What about your grandma? Is she getting hers done, too?"

Tiana's silence told me that she hadn't thought about that. Her reply confirmed it.

"I...umm...probably."

"Tiana, I'm sure I can work something out, but let me speak to your MaDear so I can pull it together. Don't worry. We'll get you hooked up."

Tiana put her grandmother on the line. We talked about her agenda for the day. She did need something done to her head but her schedule was kind of full. She was more concerned about looking her best for the funeral on Saturday than the wake on Friday. I told her I'd call my stylist and see what we could work out appointment wise. I asked if she needed me to drive her around but she already had a nephew or cousin doing that for her. I told her I'd come by the house later or leave a message about the hair care. Then, I updated Tiana and told her to call me when they got a break and we'd get together. I didn't want to put that request on MaDear and I knew that Tiana was watching her grandmother's back and trying to catch all the loose ends.

After talking with Tiana, I phoned Montana, my hair stylist. Montana and I have been together for the last eight years. Oh now that's my girl. She is a true blue friend and she can lay a head. I wasn't sure but I had high hopes that she would be able to help me out. I rarely ask for favors, except to get an early morning appointment on a day other than my usual second and fourth Wednesdays, every once and a while. So, I just might be able to pull this off with a little sweetness and a lot of begging.

"Good morning, Salon Absolut."

"Montana?"

"Hey Rhap. Girl what's up with you calling this early? You must need a hot date hook up."

"Ha, ha, you're so funny. Def Comedy must be ringing your phone day and night." I teased.

"Okay girl for real though, what's going on? How ya feelin'?"

"I'm good, Montana. How are you?"

"Fine as wine, baby. Fine as wine. So what's up?" she asked again.

"Not too much, but I do need a favor." I replied ever so sweetly.

"See, I know my business, girl. Come on with it."

"Now hold on, it's a favor for me but not for me. See, I was wondering if you could do a special beautifying session for a couple of friends of mine. It's a little girl and her grandmother. One of the little guys that I counsel died and his sister and grandmother want to have their heads done for the wake and funeral. Well, mostly for the funeral on Saturday. They are still doing some running around today and may not be freed up until late."

"Damn girl, I am so sorry to hear that. I mean about the kid. Too many kids are dying so young these days. It scares me to death. But look, what time are we talking because I have a few things that I must get done tonight, but you know I'm going to help you out."

"Tan, honestly, I'm not sure. I may not know a time for a few hours and even then it might not be accurate."

She seemed to ponder for a moment in silence.

"Girl, I know it sounds crazy, but I will bring them over personally." I said.

"Oh that's fine. I'm just trying to see something. I have some personal appointments that I know I can't get out of. Today is going to be tough to do. What time is the wake tomorrow?" she asked.

"I think six or seven." I responded.

"Well, what about if I do an in home appointment first thing Friday morning, say about 7:00? You said it's a mother and daughter?"

"Grandmother and granddaughter." I corrected.

"Okay, I could do them both in about two hours. I'll bring Mya and we'll knock it right out and then they'll be set for the wake and funeral."

"You wouldn't mind doing that? And what about Mya? That's a lot to ask of an assistant."

Montana laughed. "Girl, I got this."

"Well then, I will check with them and get back to you. But let's plan on doing that. I'll call you after I talk to them and give you the address. And you can call me at home tonight if you need to, okay?"

"Yeah Rhap, it's all good. I'm happy to help. Hey, how are you doing? You okay girl?"

"Listen to you playing Miss Concerned. I'm fine. The kid that got killed was a good kid. Really special. I'm going to miss him but yeah I'm okay. Look girl, let me go and get some things done. And thanks, sweetie. I'll call you as soon I can."

It felt like a double expresso day. It was one of those days that I would need twice as much of my energy reserve in order to accomplish the days' duties. But, I was ready to get started. Dressed in a black Donna Karan pants suit, pink silk knit sweater and black Kenneth Cole ankle boots, I headed out to my office. I had two afternoon standing appointments. The sessions would likely go quickly. I had Rayton, who loved to talk about his superb athletic ability, but tended to avoid discussing his cleptomaniac tendencies. He'd been caught stealing everything from candy bars to school cellos. What he planned on doing with a cello, I can't imagine. He was currently on probation and fighting to stay eligible to play football for the park. And since his Probation Officer and coach required proof of his therapy attendance, Rayton was usually very punctual. My project for him was to get a summer gig so that he could start earning money to legally purchase items he desired. Then maybe he would develop a sense of pride in being able to acquire things you want through hard work.

The other appointment was my Teen Anger Management Group. Instead of touching on loss and grief, I planned to let this be a catch up session. I would have them relay their weekly adventures. Next, I'd ask them to pinpoint a time in the last week they felt anger that was on the verge of or became incontrollable. Situations that may have made them curse, strike out, or want to cry. Then, I would have others give their views on the various situations. Finally, we would use the last few minutes as a quiet time when everyone would write in their personal journals, which all clients are required to have. I would put on some light jazz, today would probably be Terrence Blanchard, and type up my notes while the group was working. One of the rules was not to talk during journal time and surprisingly I rarely had to issue any reminders. They seem to really enjoy the time, even the ones with very poor writing skills. Every once in a while someone would ask to share a journal entry. Sharing is always voluntary because the kids know that journal entries are accessible only to themselves and their therapist, me.

Rayton's session went quickly. He was unusually quiet due to a bad cold and we ended the session early. I recommended that he start taking something for the cold before it turned into a hospital stay and sent him on his way.

I decided to call Paully. I was missing him and hadn't spoken to him since I'd been home. He wasn't at home and I opted not to call his cellular. Then I had a notion to call Trayu. I thought about how good I felt with him and wondered if he was still thinking about me. Baby boy was fine and sweet but he was kinda young. I started daydreaming about kissing him, having his arms around me, and feeling his touch. He eyes had a sparkle that sparked something inside me and his brilliant smile made my heart flutter. Maybe there was something between us. Maybe he could bring me joy like Anita Baker used to sing before her music sabbatical. Or maybe I was just looking for a replacement for Karl. If that was the case, I couldn't pull Trayu into my drama. I would have to settle this thing with Karl and put it to rest. Naw, I better wait to call Trayu. He, at least, deserved that much consideration. But I would call Karl for sure as soon as I wrapped up my next session, which was starting in about fifteen minutes. I got up from my desk to stretch, take a restroom break, and grab my second extra shot cappuccino from the Starbucks on the corner.

The Anger Management group was full of energy. It appeared that the majority of members had had rough weeks. They all had a story or two to tell and surprisingly some even took partial responsibility for their actions. We spent more than half the session talking about their emotional mishaps. Therefore, I had to cut the questioning and advice session short in order to leave time for journaling. I didn't want to leave out any part my planned agenda, so shaving a little time here and there seemed to be the best solution. One of my little men, Willie, shared that he had been trying to use prayer to help him kept his anger under control.

"I find that when I pray for help and strength it seems like I don't even hear the people that usually irritate me. It's kinda weird cuz my moms is always talking about praying for strength and I'm starting to believe that she might be right. I swear it's been workin' for a brutha'." He testified.

I chose his as our closing comment for that part of the session and directed the group to take out their journals. Lauren asked for some paper and a pen because she forgot her journal and I went to get them for her. When I returned to the group from my desk I noticed that another young lady didn't have anything out to write in.

"Rita, do you need something to write with?" I asked.

"Nope. I don't feel like writing so I ain't gonna write. This writing shit ain't nothing but crap anyway." She snarled.

I had to take a deep breath to calm myself before I replied. Lil' Sis just came out of a box on me out of nowhere.

"Hold up." I said with a low voice full of intensity. I'm not sure what is going on right now but there are a few things that we need to get straight on the quick. First one being that you need to remember why you are here and that I'm here to help you. So, if there is something you need to talk about in private, we can arrange that. Secondly, we do not use profanity in this group because there are many more effective words in the English language. The last point is extremely important for you to understand and remember and that is that I will not be disrespected by anyone for any reason. And your tone just then was very disrespectful and I am not having that. Therefore, I'm going to ask you to check your attitude and if you can't, then you need to take a moment and decide where you want to be. If it's not here, then I can respect that but if it is then you know what the rules are for this group." So if nothing else you better remember that everyone will be respected and respectful in this office.

I rested my back against my chair. I hadn't realized that I had leaned forward to present my point. I guess that I hadn't calmed myself as much as I had thought. But I guess that my point had poked someone, because one of the guys said something to Rita.

"Come on Rita, dag girl, why you trippin'. You know what's up. Here write on this." And I heard paper being ripped from a notebook.

I didn't even look up. I just made some quick notes on my tablet. The silence following our little episode reminded me to turn on the music. I walked toward my desk, turned on Terrence and slid into my desk chair. A few deep yoga breaths and I was able to push the incident to the side and type my notes. By the time the timer went off, indicating the ending of our session, I was not even thinking about Rita's attitude. I walked over to the group and instructed them to wrap it up. As everyone was leaving I noticed Rita looking at me out the corner of her eye. She was lagging behind a little and I figured that she was trying to be the last to leave. I could read uncertainty on her face and I understood. These kids had not yet mastered the art of humble apologies. In their minds, apologizing was a sign of weakness. I continually worked on helping them to understand and develop the craft, but it was slow moving. Rita was let off the hook due to the fact that another young lady had sequestered my attention. As Rita slowly walked through the door, she snuck a peek at me and I gave her a wink letting her know that all was forgiven. She gave a little smirk and left.

With my office finally empty, I took a moment to relax with a bottle of water. My midtown view always put me in the mood to chill, but I realized that I was hungry. This was an unsettling thought because I'd often met Karl for lunch on days like this and he loved to try new midtown restaurants. Suddenly, I wasn't hungry and I knew it was time to call Karl. I couldn't be letting him affect my life or my daily routines. Yeah, I was going to call and there was no better time than the present. Before I dialed his number I reminded myself to stay nonchalant, not to talk too much, and to give up no information concerning our relationship status. Now, I was ready.

"Hi. Karl? Guess who?

"Rhap?"

"Yes," I replied with a slight giggle. "Is this a bad time?"

"Hell no! How are you baby? Where have you been? I've been worried about you. I didn't know what was going on or what to think. Is everything okay?"

"Hey hold on you're drowning me in questions. Now let me see. Yes, things are better and getting better everyday. I can't really go into details right now, but rest assured that I will fill you in entirely. I'm sorry about the vanishing act. Trust me, it couldn't be avoided. Look, I can't talk long, but I wanted to touch base and check your schedule to see when we can hook up."

"Wait a minute. You mean that you can't spare some time right now to talk to your baby? Come on now, be real."

I cringed on my end of the line at the sound of his voice pleading with me and referring to himself in such terms of endearment. But I bit the inside of my cheek and mustered up a response.

"I'm sorry Karl, I know it sounds crazy but I came back to a whole new set of problems. Well, not really a problems so much as issues. One of my clients was killed and I'm helping the family out."

That seemed to bring him down a notch and opened a new door for my exit from the call.

"Oh, I'm sorry to hear about that? Who was it?"

"It's Kieron. He was shot last Saturday. It was a shock and the family is taking it very hard, especially his sister. Anyway, I don't really want to get into it right now. I need to go run some errands to help get prepared for the funeral on Saturday. I'm trying to be as helpful to his grandmother as possible because I know this has to be one of the hardest things she's had to deal with in her life."

He was slow to respond.

"Of course it must be. I understand. If I can help with anything don't hesitate to call. And don't think that I don't realize that this must be difficult for you as well. So take care of yourself too baby."

There was that "baby" mess again. This time it sent a chill down my spine.

"Don't worry, I will."

"Oh and I expect to see you as soon as possible. I mean as soon as you find a free moment, I want it. Maybe I could come by tonight and rock my baby to sleep."

"That's so sweet." I said through a grimace. "I can't tonight but don't worry, we'll get together soon and I'll make sure that we have more than a moment. I want us to have plenty of time."

I busted into a smile. I was so clever sometimes that I surprised myself. Yeah, I wanted to have plenty of time to share with him, but it was certainly not for the reasons I knew he was visualizing at the moment. When we got together, he was going to get off alright. Told off! I was instantly anxious to see his face when I busted him out. But for now I figured that I better go to the florist, that way I wouldn't feel like a liar, since I had used the Mendens as an excuse to get off the phone with Karl.

# 8

Tiana paged me while I was ordering a gardenia plant accentuated with two dozen white roses. I only purchased green plants for funerals, anniversaries, and birthdays because they symbolize life and constant growth. We all need to be reminded that through everything good or bad we are destined to expand our knowledge, wealth, and appreciation of life.

I answered the page only after identifying that the number was not Karl's. It was 5:30 and Tiana had just been dropped off at the apartment to wait for some people from the church to drop off some things. She said that MaDear had gone back over to the funeral home to take Kieron's gold hambone chain and the pocket watch that one of the church elders had given him on his thirteenth birthday. I didn't ask her if they'd been able to view his body yet. I figured she'd mention it if she wanted to talk about it. I gave her the low down on the hair appointments and she was pretty excited. It wasn't etched in stone, because I needed to talk to Mrs. Menden about it first. But Tiana was definitely up for the early morning personalized beauty session.

Tiana asked me how soon I would be coming by and I decided at once to go over as soon as I finished up at the flower shop. She probably didn't want to be home alone. So, I told her I'd see her in about twenty minutes.

On my way over to Tiana's, I called Corie and told her about my conversation with Karl. She was so proud of the way I handled the call and wanted to know how I was going to cream his behind. I cut her off and ended the conversation by letting her know that she would be the first to know when I put a plan together.

Corie's talk of creaming his behind actually took my thoughts to the opposite of its intended meaning. Did I actually want to cream Karl one last time before I ended it? He was sleeping around on me. But I'd always made him use condoms even though I was on the pill. I didn't need any surprises arising from any of our sensual encounters. And that included any diseases. Oh shit! Maybe I'd already put myself in harms way. Shoot, the medical association and the government still didn't know everything about AIDS and if they did I truly don't believe that they would actually tell us everything. Actually, having one last romp and then busting Karl out and dumping him as he tried to drift off to sleep would be very gratifying. Now that was definitely something to think about. I could get a nice suite at the JW Marriott and falsify a very romantic evening before dropping the bomb. That would kill him. The playa getting play'd! Now that would be something. I smiled to myself as I parked in front of Tiana's building. She was waving to me from one of her front windows.

I gave her a big hug as I walked into the apartment. She had the music blasting from her bedroom. That told me right away that she was uncomfortable being alone in the apartment.

"Girl, would you turn that music off? You're going to bust one of my ear drums. I know you can't hear anyone knocking at the door with that music so loud."

She threw her hands up and laughed.

"That's why I was sitting in the window. Ms. Austin, you're a trip. I know you play your cuts loud sometimes, too. So don't even front."

And I couldn't deny it, cause she and Kieron had both busted me a couple of times when they showed up early for appointments or when I was giving them a lift home.

"T, just go turn it down, girl."

"Alright, alright,... hypocrite."

"If you're going to spill it, you better be able to spell it, little girl."

"H-Y-P-O-C-R-I-T-E" she belted out as she stomped back to her bedroom.

That girl is a stone character.

She returned with a couple of Pepsis and iced glasses. We both positioned ourselves back in front of the window and started chit chatting.

Tiana started off by recapping her day.

"I think that we got most of the stuff done today except that we have to pick up the programs tomorrow at twelve. Then we have to go to a family viewing sometime tomorrow. I don't know what time, but I hope MaDear can handle it. Are you coming tomorrow night, Ms. Austin?"

"Of course I'll be there." I responded.

"I know that it's gonna be packed up in there tomorrow night and at the funeral. Kieron had choke friends. Everybody liked him. Especially the girls." She laughed then continued.

"But he didn't give none of them chickenheads too much of nothing. No time, no money. He was always full of sweet talk, though. But he said that he was going to wait until he finished high school before he got serious with any girl. Kieron didn't want to get stuck up with no kids you know. He wanted to be a good father and be able to provide right for them. So, that meant waiting until he finished school."

As she drifted off in thought I tried to change the subject.

"And I'm sure he would have been. Who's suppose to be coming by? Did your grandmother tell you what time they were coming?"

"Oh I don't know. Somebody from the church, I don't remember who she said. But somebody from school is supposed to bring my school work over too. MaDear called the school for it. I don't know how she managed to remember that but I ain't surprised. I mean, I'm not surprised. But you know Ms. Austin" she said as she looked over to me. I'm going to finish school. I'm going to graduate college, too. I'm going to do that for Kieron and MaDear. I would probably do it anyway but I know that it would really make them happy and you know that kinda motivates me even more."

"That's good to hear, Tiana. You have what it takes, that's for sure. And I want to be there to watch you receive your parchment."

"What's parchment?" she questioned.

"Your diploma. It's the type of paper it's printed on." I replied.

"Oh, that's cool. I hope that Meek finishes high school. He called last night to check up on me. He's still sad. I could tell it in his voice. He was talking about how he was gonna still look after me just like Kieron did. He was like, "You still my little sister and I'm gonna watch out for you". I know he means well, but he can't be no Kieron. Can't nobody take his place."

"Tiana, I understand that, but I don't think that he wants to take Kieron's place. It's more like he's saying that he is going to honor Kieron by looking out for you. Doing what he knows Kieron would do and want him to do. You did say that they were best friends, right?"

"Yeah, they were just like brothers."

About that time Tiana spotted a middle age woman walking up to the building that she recognized.

"Oh dang, that's Mrs. McIsaac, the Assistant Principal. Why they send her over here." She said as she put down her soda and turned in her seat to face the door. She didn't move to the door until she heard the knock.

Mrs. McIsaac was very polite in greeting and gave Tiana a little hug. Tiana invited her inside and introduce me in a gracious manner. I was so proud of her etiquette. Mrs. McIsaac took a seat on the sofa with Tiana and started going over her assignments. She told her that she would have two weeks to get the assignments in to her teachers. She asked Tiana if she knew when she would be coming back to school and Tiana told her that she would probably be back next week. I wondered if Tiana would be ready by then but I was pretty confident that she wouldn't go if she wasn't ready. My thoughts were interrupted when I heard my name. Tiana was telling Mrs. McIsaac that I would help her during our session if she needed help with her work. I didn't know how the conversation got to that point but I concurred.

There was a knock at the door and I told Tiana that I would get it. Two women and three young girls were weighted down with sodas, cakes, and a large pan of macaroni and cheese. I let them in and Tiana stood to greet them with hugs. I took the case of sodas from one woman and led the others to the kitchen which was spotless. I took the remaining items from the visitors and offered for them to go visit with Tiana.

When I returned to the living room, Mrs. McIsaac was standing with Tiana at the door. We exchanged parting pleasantries and she made her exit. I introduced myself to the other visitors and took a seat. They didn't stay long and soon Tiana and I were sitting back in the window. Tiana asked about my vacation and I gave her the happy and fun version.

"I would like to see Chicago." Tiana said as I heard the deadbolt on the door turning. MaDear was home. She came in with a guy who looked to be about my age or slightly older. He hugged Tiana and introduced himself but I can't recall his name. He made sure that MaDear didn't need him for anything else and departed.

Tiana filled MaDear in on the visitors and was directed to go get started on some of her school work. Tiana turned sad eyes towards me and told me not to leave without saying good-bye. She knew that her grandmother was stressed and probably wanted to talk adult talk.

Once alone, Mrs. Menden flopped down on the sofa with a sigh. I asked her if she wanted something to drink. She requested some water, so I made her a tall glass of ice water. As she kicked off her shoes, she commented. "I'll tell you, these are some trying times. Lord have mercy."

"You've had a busy day. Just rest a while. I can leave and you can call me later and I'll give you information about your hair appointment."

"Oh no baby, I'm fine. What did you work out?"

I told her about Montana's offer and she was just as thrilled as Tiana. I told her that I would bring them to the house and that she didn't have to do a thing. I would even stay to help her get ready after her hair was done. She gave me a big hug and sat back and closed her eyes for a moment.

"You know that I still don't have word on that daughter of mine. I just don't know what else to do. She might be locked up in jail or something. I just don't know." She said.

"You know you could call the police and have them run a check on her name and see if it comes up in the system." I suggested.

"You know what? That's a good idea. I could ask that nice officer, the one that was at the hospital with us. He called this morning to give me an update on the investigation. They don't have anything yet but the was sure nice of him because he didn't have to do that. I could give him a call."

"Why don't you go on and do that Ms. Menden? I'm going to head home and you call me if you need me to do anything for you. I will be free most of the day and then I will be at the wake. What time is it, again?"

"Seven to Eight. And the Funeral is at eleven on Saturday." She said.

"Okay then, I better be going."

Mrs. Menden called Tiana into the room and I said my good-byes and headed home.

While in route to the crib, I called Montana with an update and confirmation for the morning. My day was finally winding down and I was ready to sit back and unwind a little before turning in for the night, but I knew that I had a few calls to make first. I took a quick shower and threw on some of my old faithful Russel sweats. Then, I sat down with a cup of tea and put a call in to Corie. Although she was just getting out of the shower, she was more than happy to talk to me.

"Rhap, I have to admit that you are a much better woman than me. If he let your absence last weekend slide so easy, it proves that he has something else on the side. No man lets his one and only get away with something like that. If his woman disappears without an explanation, his mind goes in a frenzy with all types of accusations. But if he has someone else on the side, then his mind just focuses on the fact that his play is still intact and he has something to fall back on. Rhap girl, he ain't shit. I would have gone off on his behind. And you just played it off, huh? I can't believe that. What are you going to do?"

"Well, I told him that I would call him when I got a chance so we could get together. I'm thinking that I will meet him at one of our favorite restaurants. I know it needs to be a public place. I can't be alone with him, plus, I think that I will be better able to keep my composure with other people around. You know I'm not trying to embarrass myself in public."

"I know that's real." Corie said in agreement. "So, how are you going to tell him?"

"Well, first I'm going to try to get him to talk about his meeting in Savannah and see what he says and how he says it. Then, I'll let him know that he is cold busted. I want him to know how much he hurt me. I really want him to feel my pain. Finally, I will tell him that I'm finished with him. So what do you think about that Corie?"

"It sounds like a good plan. But aren't you going to ask him about the hoochie?"

I had thought about that at one point but the thought was too painful. I wasn't trying to cause myself more heartache by trying to figure out what she had that he didn't find in me. And I couldn't figure out how knowing anything about this woman would help me, mentally or emotionally. So, I pushed that thought so far back in mind that it actually gave me a shock when Corie broached that subject. But I found an answer for her.

"I thought about that, I did, but Corie I don't want to know anything about her. I don't care anything about her. She didn't break my heart, he did."

"Yeah, you're right about that, but I think I would want to hear what he had to say about her."

"Corie, what do I want to hear that for? Whatever he says is probably going to be lie. What is he going to say? That she means nothing to him, that she was just a fling? That won't do me any good. I just rather not know. I just want out of this and to get on with my life." I explained.

Corie seemingly understood my point.

"Dag girl, I guess you are right. At least I hope you're right. I don't want you wondering about her and him later on."

"I'm not, Corie. I'm not. I plan on erasing him from my life. That's the only way I can mend my heart. So, I'm not going to be worrying about him or his back up babe. I promise."

"Alright then girl. I know you know what you're doing. Well, that's enough of that. What's going on with your patient?"

"My client, Corie, not patient. I'm not a doctor." I corrected.

"Whatever. Did they have the funeral yet?"

"No, the wake is tomorrow and the funeral is Saturday. Montana is going to go over to their apartment and do their hair tomorrow morning. Isn't that sweet?"

"For real? That is sweet. Is she going to do it for free?"

"Oh, girl, I didn't even talk to her about payment. But I wouldn't expect her to do it for free and I won't have them paying either. I'll pay her. Corie, I'm so glad you brought that up."

"That's what friends are for." She laughed. "But look girl, I need to get out of here. I'll call you later."

"Okay girl, I'll holler at ya."

I needed a break after talking to Corie. She had messed me up with that talk of the other woman. I decided that a short nap would do me a bit of good, so I went to my bedroom to grab an afghan and pillow off of my bed. I always take my short naps on the sofa in order not to get too comfortable and sleep too long. That idea was shot to the cane fields when Karl rang my phone. Once again, I forgot to check the fool caller ID.

"Sup baby?" He said.

The feeling that overcame me was strange yet expected. Hearing his usual nightly greeting made me warm inside from its familiarity. Tears filled my eyes and a knot grew in my throat. I couldn't believe that this was happening again. How would I be able to get him out of my system? Well, first I had to give him his exit papers and this call would provide the perfect opportunity to get the ball rolling.

"Hey. I was just getting ready to call you. I'm dog tired and can barely keep my eyes open but I wanted to call you before I passed out. I want to hook up as soon as possible. How does Saturday sound? I have that funeral in the morning but I could meet you right after. I figure that five o'clock would be a good time. What do you think?" I rambled.

"That sounds great baby, but I was thinking that we could get together much sooner than that. Like in about twenty minutes or less depending upon how many lights I catch." He replied seductively. But I was not even going to get caught up that quickly.

"Baby, you know I can't wait to see you but I'm a zombie and that's not what state I want to be in when we get together. I want to be rejuvenated so that I can hang in there with you. So why don't I take this time to get some much, much needed rest and we will see each other on Saturday. Oh, I just had a great idea. Why don't we meet at Margaritas." I was on a roll. He loved Margaritas with its rich and subtle Cuban atomosphere. It offered more than Cuban cuisine and attracted interesting patrons from artist to fortune 500 executives. Karl couldn't get enough of this place.

"Okay baby." he pouted. "I won't pretend that I'm happy with not seeing you tonight but I know you need to rest. Maybe I can spend the night tomorrow and give you a little pampering." He suggested.

"Oh baby, that's not going to work, either. I have too much going on with the wake and funeral. And I need to be on call for Tiana and her grandmother." I added a little whine to my voice to feign disappointment and make my tiny white lie believeable.

"Damn baby, you are making this really hard."

"I'm sorry Karl. It can't be helped. But it will all be over soon. Meanwhile, I have got to get some sleep. I'll try to call you but I can't promise. But I will be at Margaritas at five o'clock on Saturday come hell or high water. Okay?"

"Okay baby, you get some sleep now and dream of me. I love you sweet thing." He cooed.

Ewww! I could just url.

"Good Night." I said and slowly hung up the phone. I was sure glad that that was over. Now, I had a little time left to prepare myself for the confrontation.

# 9

Montana, Mya, and I arrived at Tiana's at about 7:30a.m. I knew they were awake for Tiana had paged me at 6:30 that morning to verify what time we were coming. I knew that she was just calling out of nervousness, because I'd talked to both she and MaDear the night before and confirmed the time. Tiana was watching for us through the front window. Montana hit the floor running and Ms. Menden's head was under the kitchen faucet within minutes of our arrival. Mya's first duty was to retrieve the supplies from Montana's Explorer and set everything up for the ready. I helped Mya until she took Tiana to the sink. After which, I put myself to use ironing Tiana's and MaDear's clothes. In a little more than an hour, both Tiana and MaDear were getting the finishing touches on their manes. Mya was working on Tiana and Montana on MaDear. MaDear had taken a liking to Montana and they were chatting away.

"You have beautiful hair Mrs. Menden." Montana complimented.

"Thank you. I don't do nothing to it 'cept keep it clean and neat. But I can't wait to see it when you're done cause you sure keep Ms. Austin's hair looking pretty."

"Well thank you, young lady. I do my best to keep my clients happy, even friends like Rhapsody."

"I sure am glad she has good friends like you cause only a good friend would do such a nice deed as you coming here today. And I want you to know that I really appreciate this." Mrs. Menden said.

"It's my pleasure. Rhap knows she can count on me. Besides she has helped me out plenty over the years. Heck, if it hadn't been for her I don't know where my child would be now."

"Oh, she counseled your child, too?" Mrs. Menden asked.

"Yes she did. Well, actually she counseled both of us." Montana replied.

Montana was exaggerating a little. Neither she nor her daughter,

Dakota, were ever clients of mine. At one time, a few years back, Dakota was going through a rough transition from adolescence to adulthood. She was barely eighteen, searching for her niche in life, and giving Montana the blues. Dakota was staying out late, flipping off at the mouth to Montana, and talking about moving out after her high school graduation. Montana was mad, frustrated, and scared to death. Her anxiety began to effect her physical being to the extent that one of her friends suggested that she see a doctor for medication or to seek out a psychiatrist. Montana was totally against taking crazy pills, as she called them, and there is a deep rooted phobia among African Americans about seeing psychiatrists. It stems from the whole "Don't air your dirty laundry" syndrome instilled by African American elders. You are taught to keep what happens in your home inside your home. So, Montana found herself in yet another dilemma. She knew that she needed help but none of the available options were acceptable to her. Then, she had a brainstorm and decided to take a compromising risk. She called me and asked for a friendly but confidential meeting. I of course agreed and when she told me what was bothering her I knew that she had made a major sacrifice of her pride to come see me. I promised her pure confidentiality from my heart and set about trying to comfort and offer advice. Montana had touched me because I knew the level of trust that must exist in order to lay your personal, heartfelt fears on the table. I listened and advised her and also agreed to talk to Dakota.

Dakota was just another young lady searching for her niche in the world. She had always been strictly obedient and respectful to her mother. Now, she was experiencing some peer pressure. No one was telling her to be disobedient but the free lifestyle that many of the popular kids led made her hungry. She started wondering if she was missing out. She wondered whether the plans she had for her future where actually hers or her mother's. It wasn't that she felt she was heading in the wrong direction. She just wanted to feel that she had a choice, that she wasn't just being momma's girl. She wanted to feel some control. I understood her completely, yet I understood Montana's concerns as well. So, I set a meeting for the three of us to sit down and discuss both sides of the equation. Amazingly, they both readily agreed as long as I was there to mediate. As it turned out, we had to meet a few times but they were able to establish a better line of communication and understanding of each others feelings. Montana understood that she had to let Dakota make her own decisions as an adult and rely on the fact that she had given her a strong foundation. And Dakota understood that the last thing Montana wanted was for her 4.0 G.P.A daughter to end up working a minimum wage job and shacking with some no good joker who only expected her to cook, please, and supply him with rugrats. Montana was a single parent who worked endless hours to provide for her daughter and demonstrate strong values. She worked hard to build her business and to keep insurance and savings for any emergencies but she didn't want all of that hard work to go down the drain by bailing Dakota out of irresponsible jams.

The last meeting the three of us had ended tearfully with Dakota promising to always try to make wise decisions and Montana promising to love, respect, and always have an open ear for her daughter. Since then things appear to be fine between the two of them. Dakota opted not to go to Michigan State but enrolled in Therapeutic Massage school and took on a part-time gig at Krogers grocery store. She is child free but has a steady boyfriend in the Air Force.

"Now that is sweet. Sometimes I have to talk to Ms. Austin myself but I mostly appreciate what she has done for my grandbabies. She is a blessing from heaven if I do say so myself." Ms. Menden continued as Montana sprayed on a light coating of holding and sheen.

Tiana was finish and she ran off to the restroom to check the results. When she returned, she was all smiles and proceeded to thank Mya and Montana with hugs. She even threw in an extra hug for her MaDear. MaDear laughed and sent her away to get ready for the family viewing. Montana and I helped Ms. Menden get dressed while Tiana and Mya chatted in Tiana's bedroom.

I left with Montana and Mya with the promise to return by 6:00p.m. I went home and took a shower and a nap. By 5:30 I was in the car headed back to Tiana's. As soon as I arrived, MaDear pulled me into her bedroom. She explained that she needed someone to stay at the house while they were at the wake. It was likely that people would stop by to drop off food and cards. Some neighbors had offered to wait at the apartment but MaDear didn't feel comfortable with that, so she was asking me. And of course I said yes. Sure, I wanted to go to the wake, but I wanted to be there for MaDear and Tiana. So, if they needed me to stay at the apartment, that's where I would be. I could say my farewell to Kieron at the funeral.

As the hour of departure for the funeral neared, a sullen quiet slowly drifted into the apartment. I was actually kind of glad to see the limos arrive so that we could get on with bringing some closure to this tradegy. This day was not one that I looked forward to facing but it couldn't be helped.

Never have I attended a funeral so rich with youth in mourning. So many sad faces and tear soaked tissues. In thinking on how emotionally draining attending funerals of family and friends is for me today, I can't begin to imagine how I would have been affected at that age. These were mere children just as was the gentle being now laying on display at the altar of this church. I couldn't recall knowing of any deaths so young when I was growing up. I'm sure there were some; I could remember none that had touched my life. Sadness in those times were usually caused by restrictions, spankings, or not getting an item of the current fashion trend.

Here I was sitting in a church full of mourners in petite dresses, dark slacks, and white shirts. Some of the kids in attendance sported Ekco print shirts and neatly pressed jeans that represented the stylish flair I remembered from Kieron. The side choir station held seven young ladies dressed in black skirts, white blouses, and white gloves. Obviously, physically prepared for the flower girl duties, yet most of their delicate hands held tissues to wipe the tears that appeared to be rolling down precious stained glass.

I walked in before the family, against the wishes of Mrs. Menden and Tiana, in order to have the opportunity to find decent seating for myself. As I entered the church, I quickly scanned the seating availability for my options. I wanted to be close enough to Tiana but not hindering the path to a quick exit should the need arrive. On rare occasions, I have attended funerals where I am overcome with claustrophobic feelings of grief and envy. Those too very intense emotions battle for dominance within me. They smother me and I am forced to engulf as much fresh air as humanly possible as soon as possible. It always begins with the sinking feeling of having lost someone special. I would no longer be able to experience the unique attributes that made them special to me. There would be no new memorable occasions. It was all over...finite. Then, I try to steer my thoughts in a more positive direction. So, I begin thinking about how the deceased was lucky. Their suffering from illness was over. They no longer had to deal with the pain and anguish that worldly living brings, hunger, thirst, poverty, fear, pain, sadness, and disappointment. Then the panic would set in and I have to find my way outside. I could only hope that it didn't happen to me today.

I pulled off my jacket and placed it over my purse to save my seat. It was time to take one last glimpse of Kieron's earthly casing and offer a final prayer for heavenly peace unto his soul. The walk to the front of the church was short and before I knew it I was looking down on Kieron's young stone face. Disbelief was suddenly upon me as fresh as the day Tiana came to tell me of his death. I knelt and said a quick Our Father and then returned to my seat.

The family was lined up at the church entrance and the preacher stood in front of them, prepared to lead them in with prayer scripture.

There had been no music playing, but now the organist was softly tapping out "His Eye is on the Sparrow." The sound of the preacher's voice reciting scripture signaled the mourning congregation to stand. Tiana and her grandmother followed the pastor and two other ministers up the center aisle. Both were being escorted by gentlemen. I recognized one of the men as a cousin I'd met once at their home. The other I presumed was a church usher or one of the funeral attendants. About mid way up the aisle, Tiana slipped away from her escort and attached herself to her grandmother's side. I watched them continue up the aisle towards me; I couldn't help but wonder how either of them would get through this. But, they are both very resilient and that would definitely work in their favor.

Tiana caught my eye as they passed me and I reached out to touch her shoulder. The family procession was relatively large. Meek came in with his aunt. His face told the story of sleepless nights and weariness. He walked slowly allowing his aunt to drape her arm around his shoulder. After the family was seated a group of approximately eight young men slowly strutted up the aisle. They looked a bit rough around the edges, some with cornrows, thick gold chains with heavy medallions, and gold grills. Their clothes were baggy yet crisp, clean, and neat. I thought that maybe Kevin was in the group of hard, young mourners. Never seeing him, if I had to guess, he was probably the one young man wearing blue slacks, a short waist jacket, and tie. His eyes were extremely sad and slightly swollen. Tiana said that Meek told her that Kevin was really messed up, which was why he hadn't been by the house.

When everyone was seated it was clear to see that the church was packed. I wondered how many people actually felt the absence of Kieron's mother. I knew that it was definitely on Ms. Menden's and Tiana's mind. Although Tiana would never admit to it, she wanted her mom with her. She had come to realize that she didn't need her (because of MaDear), but that could not diminish that desire within to have her mother at home, drug free, functional, loving, and happy. There was no telling where she was holed up. They knew that she wasn't in jail or the hospital from the report from Officer Kelp, whom had befriended the family since the tragedy. And the word was out on the street for her to contact her mother as soon as possible. I was sure that she would turn up. Maybe even before the service was completed.

The service was short and sweet. The preacher spoke of Kieron and his family with endearing admiration. The musical selections were solos performed by an adult choir member and a junior choir member. The older woman, I recognized from the prayer session at

Tiana's place, sang His Eye is on the Sparrow. I was touched by the teenage girl who sang the old spiritual, "The Storm is Passing Over."

I spoke to Tiana outside of the church. I told Tiana that I would meet them back at the church hall for the repass. She seemed alarmed and asked if I was coming to the cemetery. I told her that I would. My emotional gauge was on full and I still had to meet with Karl later, but I knew I couldn't let Tiana down so I headed to my car to join the procession to the burial site.

The Church hall was full of people and delicious aromas by the time I arrived. I'd made a quick stop to buy some tic tacs. I slowly scanned the medium sized room and spotted MaDear at the table near a stage at the front of the room. Tiana was standing a few yards away holding two cups of punch and talking to a clean cut young man. I walked toward Mrs. Menden and tried to stifle the grumbling in my stomach. As I neared the table, she motioned to me, while giving a request to one of the helpers to get a chair and a plate for me. The attention was a little uncomfortable but I was not going to pass up the opportunity to eat. Tiana sat down a few moments later and kept an eye on her MaDear.

The food was delicious and I wanted to go for seconds but didn't want to walk into my meeting with a poofed belly. Instead, I opted to just have another cup of the delectably refreshing sweet tea. I excused myself and began to walk to the beverage table. Tiana was standing next to the beverage table at the dessert table. She was talking to the same young man that I'd seen her with earlier. This time I noticed that he had quite a handsome face. He was dressed attractively in black cuffed slacks and a crisply pressed long sleeve grey shirt. He sported a precise bald fade and had a mellow and mature air about him. It was difficult for me to determine age. Was he a friend of Tiana or a friend of Kieron's? I guess it really didn't matter. I was just curious because he seemed to be giving Tiana a lot of attention today. The other thought that came to mind was that it was the first time that I had ever seen Tiana actively involved in conversation with any boy other than Kieron. Could he be her boyfriend? Naw, she had never mentioned having a boyfriend or even wanting one for that matter. I decided to ask Tiana about him later. Meanwhile, I took my drink back to my table and listened to the ladies chatting around me.

At three o'clock, I made a gracious exit. I wanted to freshen up before my meeting with Karl. I stopped by my office, washed my face, brush my teeth, reapplied my lip stick and blush, took a spritz of my Joop, and was on my way. I took my time because I wanted to be fashionably late so that I could make a charming entrance. I didn't want to beat him to the restaurant for fear that I would find a way to talk myself out of the meeting before he arrived. If I did happen to arrive before him, my plan was to go directly back to my car and wait fifteen minutes. He had never been more than ten minutes late for anything since I'd known him. But there was no need to worry because I spotted him as soon as I walked through the door. Luckily enough he was busy reading the New York Times, looking very buppyish. I was able to regain regular breathing rhythms as I approached the table.

Karl smiled as he stood and greeted me with a kiss meant for my lips, which I conveniently averted to my cheek. He apparently missed the gesture and helped me to my seat before retaking his. He reached for my hand immediately and started professing how much he'd missed me. I gave a little sniggle and took a nervous sip of the water in front of me. "Baby you look beautiful. You sure that you're coming from a funeral?" he smiled.

"Karl, that's not cute. Yes, I just came from the repass." I snapped, which I immediately regretted. I didn't want to let myself get worked up. I needed to stay cool in order to play this thing out smoothly.

"Are you hungry?" he inquired.

"Actually, I ate at the church."

"Well, I'm starved. Starved for you and food." He said with a devilish smile. And what a gorgeous smile it was.

I lowered my head to take another couple of sips of water. He was going to make this hard for me. I could feel my stomach tightening with an urge similar to an oncoming url. I better get this thing over with.

"Rhap?" he called. I had no idea of what he had just said so I quickly apologized.

"I'm sorry Karl. I'm just a little off kilter."

"Oh my poor baby, it's okay. You do look a little tired. Don't worry I'll hook you up later with a little relaxing massage. Let's start off with an appetizer to build up your energy." He said as he motioned for the waiter.

I could not look him in the eyes for fear of losing it, so I focused on the waiter. Karl placed an order for onion rings and buffalo wings. I ordered an Amaretto Sour and he had his usual Coors Light. The waiter left to place the order. Karl took my hand again and started running his thumb back and forth over my knuckles and fingers.

"I love you. And I have been aching to hold you in my arms. I'm so glad you're back. I was missing you baby. Were you missing me?"

"Of course." Was all I could get out and luckily the waiter arrived at that moment with our drinks. As I took my first sip I decided to get down to business. It was time. I didn't know how much longer I could last. So I took my first look of the evening into his eyes.

"Karl, what does loving someone mean to you? I mean how does it make you feel and how does it move the path of your existence?"

"What?" he asked quizzically.

"You know, how has loving me affected the way you think and go about things? I know it sounds crazy, but just humor me and give me an honest answer." I could feel the seriousness in my facial expression and I knew that he saw it. He searched my eyes for a moment trying to get a handle on where I was coming from.

"Baby, since I met you it...it seems that I feel more...more at ease. I feel as if...as if my search might be over and I'm...I'm content and happy. But baby I know that you already know that, don't you?" He said.

I took a sip of my cocktail.

"You know I felt that way too, Karl. As a matter of fact it's as if you took the words straight from my heart. I felt like the happiest woman alive. My heart felt free."

He took hold of both my hands then. But I was not to be stilled. I forged on.

"That was until I happened upon a scene last Saturday night, at the Beacon Court Apartment Homes, that revealed to me that what I thought I had, was just a dream. I had been tricked and deceived. While I believed that I was living in a cocoon of love, I had actually been living in a pit of lies."

A wave of gloom covered his eyes. His expression transformed into a slab of granite. But only for a moment. He was good. He was real good, for if I hadn't been staring into his eyes I would have missed it. Fortunately, I didn't miss his slight, yet clear, admission of guilt. And somewhere deep inside I realized that I had still been holding on to a slither of hope that I was wrong. That I was the love of his life. Hey, but I snapped out of it as he opened his mouth to speak. I quickly yet gently placed my right index finger against his lips.

"Karl, I saw you. I saw you baby. Coming out of that woman's apartment half naked, when you were suppose to be sitting in a hotel room in Savannah looking forward to a romantic weekend with me. But you were not in Savannah and you were definitely not thinking about me. You don't have to say a word. I don't need an explanation. I don't want to hear anymore of your lies. I just want you to know that I know that you used my heart. I really truly loved and trusted you. I gave you my entire heart unconditionally and faithfully. And you accepted it Karl."

Tears began to form and I knew that I didn't have much longer.

"You accepted all of me and slowly trampled all over my heart. You had me convinced that you loved me. You convinced me that we had something real special. But it was all a lie. And I won't be a party to it any longer. Yes, I know that I am responsible for allowing myself to get caught up in all of your untruths and I will find a way to deal with that. But Karl I just want to tell you that you were wrong. You were dead wrong. I know that I didn't deserve it and I will no longer be a part of it.

I pulled the remaining hand from his grip and wiped away the tears that stained my cheeks. As I did so, he tried to speak again.

"Rhap, I don't know what you think you..."

I cut him off.

"Karl, don't." I shook my head. Don't. I just came to say thank you for the lesson."

I reached into my purse and pulled out the first bill I felt.

"I learned that lesson well." I continued as I place the twenty on the table and stood.

"Good-bye" I whispered and slowly turned and walked out of the restaurant.

# 10

On my drive home I felt good. I was so proud of myself. I stayed calm and cool. I never raised my voice. My words were piercing and I knew that I got to him. I had reached that place within where the innate sensitive and compassionate element dwelt. This whole thing might not be life changing for him, but I was positive that it would weigh heavily on his mind for a while. I saw it in his eyes. His adventure of sporting love had turned into something unpleasant. Yes, I had pulled it off and I felt wonderful.

I called Corie as soon as I got home and found her at work. I gave her the low down on the confrontation and included every minute detail. She was so entranced by my tale that she never interrupted me. There was even a stunned silence between us as I finished talking. When she finally spoke she was cheering me and cursing Karl. I laughed so hard at her that I gave myself the hiccups. I was full of myself.

"Girl, you would have been so proud of me. I handled that junk like a pro." I gloated.

"It sure sounds like it and I hope he felt every blow you threw."

"Oh, he felt it alright. He might even wake up sore tomorrow." I laughed.

"Ms. Rumbling Rhapsody, new welter weight champ, how do you feel after your victorious bout?" Corie said in her mock boxing official voice.

"I feel good, Ms. Corie. I feel real good. I knew I was the better fighter and I proved it in the ring tonight."

We both cracked up. When we finally caught our breaths, I told Corie that I was going to let her get back to work and I was going to fix myself a glass of wine to celebrate. I was feeling gooood.

While I was in the kitchen taking a chilled wine glass out of the freezer, the phone began ringing. I ran into the living room to grab the cordless phone that I'd left laying on the sofa. As I turned it over in my hand I saw Karl's name lit across the little display screen.

"Ha, I know he won't even try this. He couldn't possibly think that I would want to talk to him. Then again, yes he would with his cocky behind. Well, too bad Big BK, you will not be having it your way today." I said out loud to myself as I threw the phone back onto the sofa and pranced back into the kitchen. But just as I started opening a bottle of Banfi Rose' Regale, I start wondering if he'd left a message. If he did, what did he say? How did he sound? Was his voice cracking? Did he sound sad? Before I knew what was happening, that earlier good feeling was slowly replaced by the all too familiar sinking feeling in my chest. The realization that I was burned and alone was back to crush me once again. I felt low and unlovable. I couldn't understand what I had done wrong and why something so awful had to happen to me. What had I done to deserve this pain? I couldn't get Karl out of my mind. In no time, I found myself huddled on the sofa in a fetal position, crying like a baby.

Paully called at the height of my intense ballin' session. I could barely choke out a decent hello through my tears. I wouldn't had even tried if I hadn't recognized Paully's number on the caller ID. Paully was coming to the rescue once again. Who would even believe that he would have the sixth sense to call me at that precise moment. I will probably never be able to explain our surreal connection but it was of no importance at that moment. He immediately asked me what had happened after hearing my anguished greeting. I was able to choke out that I'd finally confronted Karl. He was unable to ask another question for I was sobbing uncontrollably into the receiver. Paully just waited quietly until I spoke again.

"Paully, I'm so sorry I know that's no way to greet a BFF. I'm just having a moment. It will pass. So what's poppin'?"

"Aw come on Rhap, don't play me like that. Just tell me what's going on. That's what I'm here for. Okay?" he reasoned.

"I love you, you know that?" I proclaimed.

"I know and I love you, baby girl. Now tell me what happened with old dude. He didn't hurt you did he?"

I could feel the heat in Paully's voice and it made me feel warm inside and actually brought a smile to my lips. He really did love me and I knew it.

"No Paully, he's stupid but he's not crazy. No, I played it real cool and he had no idea that I was upset with him. He thought I was going to spill my troubles to him and let him make me feel better. It was real easy to let him have it while he was sitting in front of me all sauve and smug. When I told him that I knew about the other woman he tried to come back like he didn't know what I was talking about. But Paully, he couldn't come back fast enough. The guilt in his eyes slapped me in the face as soon as he comprehended what I was saying. It was the best thing that could have happened, though. It enraged and motivated me even more to let him know that I was shutting down his game. It enabled me to stay cool and keep control of the situation. You would have been so proud of me. I was soooo cool and I felt great afterwards. But as soon as I was alone with my thoughts, I just lost it. I feel so empty, so alone."

The last few words came out in barely a whisper. I was fighting back tears and choking down the cries in my throat. Paully's continued silence was puzzling. I didn't know what he was thinking or if he was even still awake.

He finally spoke.

"Rhap, it's cool. You're going to have some days like this. You'll probably have more than you can imagine and longer than you imagine. But you'll make it through all of them. And I'll help. You can call me anytime."

"Thanks Paul, but you don't need to have me crying on the phone to you all the time. I'll get over it and be okay." I reasoned.

"Look girl, I said you can call me anytime and I mean that shit, so stop trippin'."

I knew then that I needed to change the subject and I did it quickly.

"So, how's Tanya?"

"She's real cool cuz I put her in the wind." He laughed.

"What? What happened?"

"She was trippin' too much. I ain't got time for that drama. Ain't nobody got papers on me. And you know it."

"Paully, I hope my surprise visit didn't mess things up for you. Cause I sensed that she was a little uneasy about me being there."

"Please Rhap, she was just a trip. It was time for her to go. Can't hold a brother back, you know."

I couldn't help but laugh at him. He has always been so full of himself and he's always been cute about it. That's why there are so many women walking around with hearts scarred courtesy of Paully. Don't get me wrong, he isn't a bad person and he doesn't go around using women. He treats them very well and gives much love. The problem is that Paully has not found his soul mate. He believes that each person has a soul mate or two and he is determined to wait for his. Meanwhile, he dates. He may talk junk about being the ultimate player, but Paully never dates more than one woman at a time. He shows them sensitivity, kindness, understanding, dependability, fun, and even some love. And the females eat it up like a tender T-bone steak smothered in sweet Vidalia onions. What he offers is what all women long for. Unfortunately, either Paully starts to feel like he's hindering his search for Mrs. Right or he senses that the woman he's with is looking for something lifelong, and he eases out of the relationship ever so gently. He does it with such expertise that the jilted never walk away feeling that he intentionally hurt them. Most often they feel that they are responsible for the fall of the relationship. It has always amazed me, but I love him still.

Paully changed the subject just as quickly as I had a moment earlier. I knew he was trying to steer clear of a conversation centered on how he had done it again. He always felt a certain level of guilt when he put another filly out to pasture.

"Did you have a hard time getting back in the work groove?" he asked.

"No, with all the drama, I felt like I hadn't been away. Oh wait. I haven't talked to you, so you don't know what happened when I got back. Man, one of my kids was killed while I was gone. He was shot. So, I've been working with that since I hit the red clay. We just buried him this morning.

"Dang, that's messed up."

"Yeah, he was a good boy. But I'm more worried about his little sister. He really looked out for her and tried to keep her on the right track. He encouraged her and made sure she stayed out of trouble. They came to me as a pair and I don't know how she's going to deal with coming to see me without him. I hope she continues. Man, I really don't want to lose her." I explained.

"Aw, don't worry about it. You're probably just what she needs, especially after losing someone so close to her. She most certainly will need to be around people who understand her pain."

Paully was such a comforter and what he said made total sense. Tiana would need understanding ears. I believed that I could offer them.

"Paully, you're so insightful. Have I told you lately that I love you?"

He laughed.

"Alright baby, I'm going to get going. I'll call you in a few days. You keep your head up and bump that knucklehead. He wasn't worth your time from the get go. Stay strong and remember that you can call me anytime. Okay?" he said.

"Okay. Love Ya. Bye." And I hung up the phone feeling the twinge of lonliness once again. I couldn't think of anything better to do than to just go to bed. So I washed my face, brush my teeth, slipped into some satin, put on some Shirley Horn, and cuddled under the comforter.

Sleep wouldn't come to me no matter how hard I tried. I tossed and turned for at least an hour before I thought about calling Cocoa. I dropped that notion almost as quickly as I'd picked it up. I just didn't feel like talking about Karl anymore. I had to get over him and I might as well start now. I knew that I had many more days of lonely tearful episodes awaiting me in the near future but right now I just wanted to steer clear of the raw emotions. The chance that she wouldn't ask me about Karl was slim to none. So, I picked up the Beverly Jenkins novel on my nightstand instead. That only lasted a few minutes before I realized that I surely had no interest in reading of a budding romance, especially since I was so far from one. Then I had a brainstorm to call

Trayu. A glance at the clock showed me that it wasn't too late, only ten o'clock which meant that it was only nine o'clock his time.

I surprised myself at how franticly I searched for Trayu's number until I found it in the inside pocket of the coach hobo bag I'd taken on my trip to Chicago. The phone had barely rung once when he answered.

"Hello." He said.

Did he sound much older or was it simply that I kept viewing him as so much younger than I? Could be.

"Hi, is Trayu in?"

"Yeah, this is he. Who's this?" he inquired.

"Oh hi, it's Rhap. Canyun's sister's friend." I said.

"What? I can't believe it. How you doing? I can't believe this?"

"You said that already." I laughed. "I'm fine. How are you?"

"Great now!"

"It isn't too late to call is it? I mean I didn't disturb anyone, did I?"

Now it was his turn to laugh.

"Snap! I know I live with my momma and all but I do have my own line. Besides, you called my cell phone."

"I'm sorry, I didn't mean anything by it. I was just trying to be considerate." I covered.

"Ms. Rhap, you can call me anytime, anyday, for anything. It's been a while. I know you're back in Georgia. Canyun said you left a couple of days ago." He said.

"Oh, so you've been inquiring about me have you? Well, you have me on the line now. So what is it that you want to know?"

"I already asked. What took you so long to call?" he said.

He was a cutey for sure. And he had a good sense of humor. I could really get to like him. Yeah, I could like him a lot.

"Well, I've been really busy since I got back. My days have been so full that when I get home in the evenings I can't think of anything but going to bed. I just finally talked to Paully tonight. You remember the guy I was with that night."

"Yeah, I remember him. You guys are suppose to be the three musketeers or something, right?"

"I guess you could say that. We've been friends since forever. We don't see each other as much as we should but our friendship is still strong."

"That's cool. So tell me what's up with you." He said.

"Nothing much. I just wanted to call and say hi."

I was getting a little jittery. I was beginning to think that calling him was a bad idea. Maybe I wasn't ready to be talking to a man. But it wasn't like I was trying to get with him. I just needed someone to talk to that would take my mind off of the pain in my heart.

"I'm glad you called. I've been thinking about you a lot since the last time I saw you. I really would like to get to know you better. You have a great personality. You have that special little something going on." He said.

"Look Trayu, I don't want you to get the wrong impression. I'm like…I'm not really looking for a relationship. I mean emotionally I'm not ready for a relationship. I like you too but I…I was just hoping that we could be friends. I mean that's all I'm looking for right now."

There was a pause between the both of us. I wasn't sure what he was thinking nor was I sure what I was thinking. Maybe I had jumped on the defensive too quickly. It wasn't like the man said that he wanted to marry me or even date me for that matter. He just said that he wanted to get to know me better. Yet the silence lingered until I finally broke it.

"I'm sorry Trayu. I didn't mean to come out of a bag on you. Shoot, I'm just in a bad place right now. I just ended a relationship. And I believe that I'm the only one suffering from its demise. And I guess I'm just a little edgy. But it has nothing to do with you. Understand?" I pleaded.

"Rhap, it's cool. I didn't know all that. But it's cool. I ain't going to lie, you have been on my mind and in some of my dreams, too. I was diggin' you from the first time I saw you, but ain't no pressure. I am just glad you called." He replied.

The phone beeped, signaling an incoming call. I waited for the caller ID to register. Shoot, it was Karl again. My heart started racing and I couldn't breathe. It must have been obvious that I was distracted because Tray tried calling me back to attention.

"Rhap. Rhap?"

"Yeah, I'm here." I said dazily.

"Oh, I thought you clicked over to the other line without telling me."

"No, I'm here."

"You can answer your other line. I'll wait." He said with the sweetest tone, which was good because it snapped me right out of my daze.

"Oh no, whoever it is can wait. It can't be more important than talking to you. Right?"

He laughed at me but I know that my comment made him feel good. How could it not. I then took the conversation back a few thoughts. Anything was better than thinking about butt hole trying to get me on the line to feed me more lies.

"I really enjoyed hanging out with you in Chicago and I would like the opportunity to get to know you better. I was looking forward to talking to you again. Why don't we just start over. But first tell me about this dream stuff." I teased.

"Oh no, don't even go there. I'm not revealing anymore. Maybe I'll tell you once I get to know you better. How do I know you won't take what I say and try to use it against me? A brother gotta be careful. Gotta keep my rep intact."

"Okay, okay, that's fair enough. But trust me when I say we will come back to this topic. But I'll let you slide for now. So tell me, what's been going on?"

"Nothing much. I've just been punching the clock and keeping my head above water. It's a pretty boring thang. What about you? Anything interesting happening in your life?"

Not only did I not want to talk about my heartbreak, I didn't want to talk about Kieron either. I just wanted to stay away from any emotional topics.

"No, just working like a Hebrew slave, that's all." I replied.

"All work and no fun is unhealthy, you know."

"That's what they say."

"Well Ms. Rhap, what do you like to do for fun."

"Look, I'll tell you if you stop calling me Ms. Rhap. You trying to make me feel old or what?"

"I'm sorry, just trying to be polite." He laughed. "Rhap it is, and you can call me Tray."

We talked about a little of everything and laughed a lot. He offered to be my tour guide/escort when I came to visit again and I offered to be his when he decided to make his first visit to Atlanta. He was easy to talk to and he served his purpose well that evening. We talked for nearly two hours and when I hung up I had no thoughts of Karl and no problem going to sleep.

# 11

The next week was a rollercoaster ride named agony. Karl left numerous messages and I deleted them one by one as quickly as they came. I didn't bother listening to them, that is after receiving the first two.

"Rhap, it's me Karl. Baby we need to talk. I don't really understand what happened today. You left my head reeling. I don't know what you were talking about. But I want to talk to you so that I can figure out what's going on. I know it's a mistake, baby. I know it is. It has to be. Baby, look, we can figure this thing out and it will be okay. Rhap, I love you. You know I love you. Let's not throw what we have away over nothing. Just call me baby. Please. I love you. Call me, okay?" was the first message I listened to. It had me in tears and weak hearted, but not for long. It took only until the next message started to play.

His tone in the second message had changed dramatically. Maybe he thought that he could try a more forceful tone and get results. He was wrong of course. It actually strengthened my resolve to take my licks like a woman and move on.

"Rhap, look you need to stop playing games. We aren't kids and I ain't no tinker toy. I know that you're home by now and must have listened to my message. So stop screening your calls and ignoring me. You need to stop playing around. You know that this shit ain't fair. You can't come up and accuse me of shit and not give me a chance to defend myself. I deserve to be able to defend my honor. I gave you too much for you to be treating me like this. I've been there for you and now you gonna try and shut me out for no reason. You are wrong and you know it. You are wrong for what you're doing and wrong about me. Shit! Look, Rhap, be a woman and do what you know is right. Call me and we can get together and talk. You owe me that. I'll be waiting. Bye."

He was crazier than I thought. Or maybe he just thought that I was crazy. And where did he get off thinking that he could talk to me like that. No he didn't think that he was going to use some reverse psychology and get me to feel guilty. I was not crazy and definitely not stupid. I know what I saw and I know what made sense. Besides, all his anger did was further prove his own guilt. After furiously slamming around my condo cursing him, I decided that I would not have any further dealings with him on the phone or otherwise. So when he called that night like I knew he would, I answered just before the voicemail clicked in.

"Hello."

"Rhap? It's good to see that you're finally answering the phone." He replied with just enough sarcasm to not sound mean.

"Did you get my messages? I've been going crazy trying to reach you. You weren't answering my pages either. I need..."

I cut him off unswervingly.

"Karl, I did receive your messages and there is nothing to talk about. I don't need to know any more than what I know now. Feel what you want but my vision is perfect and my eyes did not lie to me. You know that's true and any explanation that you can give will not ever be sufficient. So don't trouble yourself. Save that energy for something and someone else where it will make a difference. And please stop calling me. It's useless and truly sad. I have no desire to talk to you. This is over. Please understand that and please, please, please, just leave me alone. Goodbye Karl."

I really can't explain the mixture of feelings that enveloped me following that call, but it obviously did the trick. Karl didn't call back. I was pleased to be relieved of the emotional attempts he'd made to contact me and even more pleased that he hadn't decided to do anything more extreme, such as showing up at my job or at my place. But I would be lying if I said that I had emotionally cleared him from the plate. There were times each and everyday that I thought about him and even wished that he would call or show up. I had played out numerous reconciliation fantasies in my mind. And even a few butt-kicking ones. But I was taking things a day or moment at a time. It wasn't easy to say the least and I still cried daily. I don't mean that

I broke down on a regular basis, I just managed to keep a tell-tell puffiness around my eyes. By Tuesday I was feeling stronger. I was back to my regular work schedule and feeling comfortable. I doubled up on my days at the fitness center trying to work out some of the stress and tension. I had even joined Corie on a few of her walks around Stone Mountain Park, but only after I made her agree to no conversations about Karl or anything relationship related.

Week two was slightly better with fewer tears. I was going to see Tiana for her first session since Kieron's death. The best part was that she had called me and expressed her desire to continue her counseling. I wasn't sure if she was ready, but if she wanted to give it a shot, I was going to be there. I'd also decided to ask her to join my anger management group for our death and dying session. It was planned for that week, but I was willing to postpone it for a little longer if Tiana wanted to attend. It might actually be good for her to hear other teenagers talk about their feelings and insight on the lost of friends and family. It would also be good for the group to hear from someone who was currently grieving. But I wasn't sure that Tiana would be willing or capable to share her feelings with strangers. I was going to ask her anyway and even recommend it. She might do it if I presented it effectively.

MaDear came with Tiana, not wanting her to take the bus alone, and waiting down in the lobby until the session was over. Tiana didn't complain at all about being escorted. Maybe she needed the company. Tiana was back at school and said that she was all caught up with her work.

"Kaiewa , pronounced Ky-eva, came over and we did homework together. I did all the work that Mrs. McIsaac brought by plus more. So when I went back, I was right with the rest of the class." She boasted.

"Who is Kaiewa?" I asked.

"You met him after the funeral. You know, when you first got to the dinner."

"I don't remember that."

"Yeah, you met him. I was talking to him when you came in." she insisted.

Then it clicked that he must have been the young man she was talking to at the desert table. And she was talking to him when I arrived.

"Oh, I think I know who you are talking about. You were talking to him at the desert table, too. Right?"

"Yeah, that's him."

"I remember, but you didn't introduce him to me." I said.

"I didn't? I thought I did, but anyway that's him." She said with finality.

"So, he's in your classes?" I asked.

"In some of them but not all." She responded as I sensed that she didn't want to pursue this topic any further. I would let it slide for now, I thought, as I wrote his name with a question mark on my notepad. I was going to come back to Mr. Kaiewa.

"Well, T, how has it been being back at school?" I questioned.

"It's been okay. At first my friends were acting kind of weird but I just kept joking around with them like we always do. Now they're cool."

"That's good. But Tiana, I mean how does it feel being there without Kieron?" I queried.

She paused and looked down into her lap and started fiddling with a button on her shirt. A sensitive area had been struck. I continued.

"I know that Kieron had a lot of friends and I wondered how it's been seeing them around school without him."

She shrugged her shoulders ever so slightly but didn't look up. This time I waited for a response. Although it was a tough topic, I needed to get her talking about it even if only a little. I wasn't going to push her too far, but I needed some information in order to help her. She was quiet for another half minute or so. Then she shrugged her shoulders again.

"I don't know. I guess it was pretty hard the first day cuz it seemed like all his friends made a point to speak to me whenever they saw me. They ain't never do that before. I mean, Kieron would say something or snap his head at me when we passed each other in the hall or if I saw him in the café but Meek and Kevin were the only ones of his friends that talked to me. So it was strange having all those other boys speaking to me. The girls all said hi to me but that was kinda normal. They were always nice to me, trying to see if they could get to Kieron through me. Anyway, like I said it was kinda hard that first day. I had to go to the bathroom one time cuz I started crying. It made me late for Social Studies. But that's all, Ms Austin, I ain't cried no more at school. I mean, I haven't cried anymore at school." She answered.

It was a good response and I was pleased with her openness.

"You know, Tiana, it's okay to cry. It's probably healthy to cry because you are releasing your emotions instead of harboring them inside where they can cause the kind of stress that effects you physically. And that's something we want to avoid at all cost." I explained.

"Yeah, but Ms. Austin, I don't want to be going around crying all the time. Shoot, they might start thinking that I'm going crazy or something."

"Okay, I can understand that. But what I am saying is that I don't want you to be afraid to cry when you are feeling that overwhelming sadness. Go to your counselor or Mrs. McIsaac or to the restroom like you said before. You don't even have to do it at school, but when you get home or where ever, if you need to release…release. Do you understand what I'm trying to say?"

"Yes." She said with a smile. "I promise to cry, Ms. Austin."

I had to laugh at her coyness.

"T, girl you are a trip. Now stop teasing me."

She began a hearty laugh then. It was contagious and lasted a couple of minutes.

"Tiana, come on now. Let's get back to business. I just want you to understand that you are supposed to grieve, so don't block it. Do you think you went back to school too early?" I asked.

"No way! I couldn't stay at home another day. It's too quiet and my mind is always remembering things that make me sad. At school, I have other things to keep my mind busy. No, I am glad that I am back at school. It's not that bad, Ms. Austin, it was only the first day. Things are better now." She explained.

"Okay, that's good. I was just checking. Hey? How about something to drink?" I said as I started over to the mini frig.

"Okay, can I have a soda?" she asked.

"One soda coming up."

After a few sips I continued with the questioning.

"How's your grandmother?"

"She's getting better. I think that she's worried about me more than herself. She's always checking up on me. If I'm in my room too long, she comes in and asks me if I want her to fix me something to eat. I know that she's just trying to see if I'm crying or something, cuz she knows that I don't eat that many times a day. So now I try to spend more time in the front room watching t.v. with her. Then I don't have to worry about her invading my privacy every thirty minutes." She laughed.

"Are you spending more time in your room lately?"

"I don't think so. Maybe. Naw, I'm not in there that much. I usually go in there to read, because I like to lie on my bed when I read. I do my homework at the kitchen table like always. I like to do it there when MaDear is cooking or washing dishes. So, no, I don't spend that much time in my room."

Before I knew it, time was up and I hadn't asked Tiana about coming to my next group session.

"Tiana, we need to wrap things up but I wanted to invite you to a group discussion I have planned with some other teenagers. We meet on Thursdays and it's a pretty good group of kids. And this week we are going to discuss the loss of friends and family. I thought it would be good if you attended. You don't have to talk about Kieron if you don't want to but I think that it could be beneficial to hear how other people your age feel about losing a loved one. So what do you think?"

I could tell what Tiana was thinking from her facial expression. She didn't want to come but she didn't respond immediately.

"I don't know. Let me think about it. Can I call you tomorrow and let you know?" she asked shyly.

"Sure! Tiana, you can call me anytime about anything. I told you that and I mean it. So let's go find your MaDear." I said as I rose and placed my notepad on my desk. We walked down to the lobby and

Mrs. Menden was sitting quietly reading her bible. She asked if we'd had a good talk and Tiana assured her that we had. I said goodbye and went back to my office to type my notes. I was ready to go home but I made myself go to the gym.

I had a good workout with a forty-five minute kick aerobics class and a short upper body free weight session. Exhausted, I drove home and made a small cobb salad with extra blue cheese and avocado for dinner. Then I cleaned the kitchen and my master bath before showering for bed. I was drifting off to sleep when Tray called.

"Hi, is Rhap in?"

I was beginning to really like his voice. It was cute and sensual. I smiled to myself as I answered.

"Hi Trayu. How are you?"

"Hi yourself. I'm great and you?"

"I'm doing as well as can be expected, I suppose. Naw, naw, I'm just kidding. I'm fine. A little tired but otherwise I'm fine."

"Oh, I'm sorry. Did I wake you? Man, what time is it? I didn't even check the time. I'm sorry Rhap, I'll let you get back to sleep." He said in a slight panic that was ever so cute.

"Slow your roll." I laughed. "I wasn't sleeping and I don't have to go just yet. I was just lying here in bed resting." I replied.

"Are you sure? Because I really didn't want to disturb you. I was just feeling so good and wanted to talk to someone." He said jovially.

"Well, what has you feeling so good this evening? It must be something really good to have you all pumped up like this."

"Now that you've mentioned it, I guess it's not really all that great. I just found out today that I really only need three more classes to graduate. I thought that I had at least two more semesters, so I am totally psyced. I don't know how I miss calculated but I'm glad I did. Man, I'm ready to get started. I was going to only take two classes next semester but now I'm ready to knock this out. I can handle this for sure. Then, I can get on with some other things. I'm tired of school and I want to pursue some more of my life desires. You know what I mean. I have a couple of ventures that have been on my mind that can make me some green. And you know a brother got to keep his pocket lined to make it in the world today." He paused.

"Well, that is great news. No wonder you're excited. So what type of plans do you have for post graduation?" I questioned.

"There are a couple of things I want to do. One is to build on this detailing business I have on the side right now. I know a guy that is willing to let me use part of a lot to set up for a minimal fee. I have a good clientele already and a few dudes that I can get on payroll. Canyun helps me out on the regular and he likes the pay."

There was such excitement in his voice that I held a smile on my face during his rampage. He was really cute. But I didn't have the opportunity to tell him this because he was still running off at the mouth.

"Also, I have a professor that is trying to get me hooked up with a guy he knows that wants a state of the art website to advertise his business. That's my thing you know and I if I can get some exposure then I know I can make a killing doing it. I already know that I have the talent that it takes, so it's all about marketing myself. You need to check out my personal website. It's the Ritz for real. Did I ever give you the address?"

"No. I didn't even know that you did that kind of stuff. Shoot, I might hire you to get one started for me. Yeah, give me the site address and I'll check it out." I requested.

"See. There's a lot you don't know about me. But I believe that we can have a lot of fun learning about each other."

I sensed a little something extra in his little blurb. Trayu was definitely still flirting with me. As long as he kept it clean then I was not going to discourage him. It felt good and I needed to feel good. Feel like someone wanted me. I just needed to make sure that I didn't let it go too far. I didn't want him to get hurt and I surely wasn't trying to put my heart back out on the chopping block.

"Trayu, don't even start. I told you about that. Let's not even enter that territory." I scolded and he laughed.

"Okay, I'm just kidding around. Don't get all sensitive over nothing. I'm kidding, okay?" he laughed

It didn't take much to move on to other topics. We talked a little more about his business plans and about a possible visit. I wanted to offer my place to him but decided against it. I could easily let him stay in my guest room without any worries but I didn't want to mention it just yet. I wasn't sure that we knew each other well enough and asking him to stay will me might just confuse him about what my intentions were. It would be nice to hang out with Tray on my turf. I could share some really interesting things with him. There were so many things to turn him onto that I was sure that he hadn't experienced in Chicago. Things that I felt he would be able to appreciate. He seemed quite excited about the possibility of a little vacation as well. But I was most pleased that he hadn't asked about staying with me. After a little more than an hour, I told Trayu that I needed to get some rest. He asked if he could call the next day and I told he could call anytime.

Trayu's call, once again, tranquilized me. I slept very well that night and woke to nothing except a clear focused mind and enough energy to hit the gym for an early workout. Tiana did call and brighten my day even more by agreeing to come to the Anger Management Group. So, I spent the rest of the afternoon fine tuning the plans for the discussion group. The feeling that this could be good for Tiana intensified, so that by the time the group finally met, I was tingling all over.

Tiana arrived a little early but three of the regular group members were there. I introduced them all and realized that Tiana and Rita knew each other from school. We were off to a good start. I started with an oral outline of the session which was greeted with some sighs of boredom. Then, I asked how many of them could remember losing a friend or family member. Just about every hand reached for the ceiling. Next came the question about witnessing death or someone on their death bed. And surprisingly, almost as many hands went up. When I asked if anyone wanted to share there experience, three people volunteered, none of which was Tiana. There was a recollection of a grandparent dying after a lengthy illness, watching a friend fall out of a tree, a friend dying in a house fire started by playing with matches, an uncle getting killed in jail, and of a baby brother dying from SIDS. The group listened intently to each other speak without any interruptions or snickering. The seriousness demonstrated, somewhat, took me by surprise. The next step was to ask about the feelings that the youngsters could recall. That was when they floored me.

The first one to respond was Rita. She spoke of her grandmothers' death.

"When she finally died, I was sad but not that sad. I mean that I was sad because she died but I was not sad because my mother wasn't going to have to worry about her anymore and she used to really worry bad. She was always running around doing things for grandma and trying to make her feel better. It even got on grandma's nerves and sometimes she would tell my momma to just go sit down somewhere and leave her be. And another reason I wasn't sad was because my grandma talked to me. We used to talk all the time when she was sick in the bed. I would sorta hide out in her room to get away from my little brothers and sisters but I liked it too. She would talk about her childhood mostly. Then after a while she would talk to me about growing up and making myself proud of me. You know she told me not to worry about making her or my momma proud, just make myself proud to be me. That didn't even make sense and I told her too. I thought she was just old and talking out of her head. Then she told me that she had tried to teach me right from wrong but she couldn't do no more than that. She said I had to do the harvesting. You know, like she had planted and watered the crop but it was up to me to make something of it. That's when I knew that she was going to die when she started talking like that. But she didn't seem afraid and she said she wasn't afraid. So I wasn't afraid for her. I was a little sad, like I said, but I wasn't worried about her. If anybody was going to be an angel then she was sho' gonna be one."

I was touched by her story and more so with the expression and emotion she used to present it. She had openly displayed a new dimension to her complex personality and I was proud of her. As Rita slyly wiped her moist eyes with her palms, Evan began to share his tender experience. His voice came out in a deep throated bass untypical of a sixteen year old. A voice that I'm sure gained him much play with the young ladies along with his handsome, mocha chiseled face.

"I still consider myself a big brother even though my little brother died before I had the opportunity to teach him anything. But I did help take care of him. I used to change his pampers and give him his bottle and my mother said that I was the only one that could get a good burp out of him. And I think that he would have been a good basketball player if he'd had the chance. I used to lay him across my lap on his blanket when I was watching a game. He would just lay there and look at the television, just like he knew what was going on. He wouldn't cry or nothing. But what I really liked was giving him a bottle and rocking him to sleep. He would lay on my chest and I would talk to him about the things that I had done that day and the things we would do when he got older." He paused momentarily.

"Then one morning I woke up to my mother screaming for my father. I thought that the apartment was on fire or something so I jumped up and slipped on my gym shoes and ran toward her voice. She was in her room holding Nathan, that was his name, and my dad was trying to take him from her. She was crying and moaning and holding him so tight. My dad took the baby from her and put his ear to Nathan's mouth. Then he started do the CPR stuff and I walked closer. I knew that something was wrong for real. Nathan looked ashy and weird. He didn't look like he was just asleep. Not like I had seen him so many times before. I ran to the kitchen and called 911 and told them that my baby brother wasn't breathing. I ran back to the room but Nathan still was not breathing. My mother was still crying like crazy and I tried to hold her but she only wanted to hold Nathan. My father gave him to her and she sat on the bed and rocked him, and kissed him until the ambulance got there. My dad had tears in his eyes and when he saw me looking at him, he left the room. They tried CPR when they got there all the way to the ambulance but they couldn't save him. After that my mother was sad for a long time and I guess my dad was too. He didn't stay around much longer after that. That's why I think that he was really messed up about Nathan dying. After that, I read all about SIDS, Sudden Infant Death Syndrome, so I know that it wasn't anybody's fault. But that really don't help the pain and anger. I get mad sometimes, but I still remember how cool Nathan was." He stopped after that and there was complete silence until I spoke.

"I want to thank you guys for sharing. Now let's talk about how death makes us feel. I only want you to use one word responses. You can answer at will but let's take it at an easy pace, so that I can jot down your responses. Okay, let's begin. What emotions does death bring?" I prompted.

The responses came quickly. Mad, Angry, Sad, Sick, Mean, Worried, Sorry, Pain, Frustrated, Tired, Sleepy. They were honest responses and just about everyone shared, even Tiana. I don't remember her exact response, but the point was that she had shared. The writing session went well, so well that I had to tell them twice to wrap it up. They only stopped writing when I told them that, if they wanted, we would take some time during the next session to continue the assignment. Overall, the session was a complete success.

Tiana was waiting for me to give her a lift home, so I took my notes with me to type at home. In the car, Tiana talked about how Meek had been coming by the house regularly to spend time with her.

"I think he's trying to play big brother. It's cool but he doesn't have to come by all the time. It's kinda weird seeing him without Kieron and we really don't have that much to talk about. He asks all these questions about me and my friends and I don't feel like telling him all my personal stuff. But I don't want to make him feel bad either cuz I know he's missing Kieron, too. MaDear doesn't seem to mind having him around. She likes cooking for him and he likes her cooking." She paused. He wants to go to the movies this Saturday."

"Are you going to go." I asked.

"Yeah, I think so. He's paying and I haven't been to the movies since I don't know when. Yeah, I'ma go." She said.

"Well, it will be good to get out. And it's probably good that you two have each other to talk to. Do you guys talk about Kieron at all?"

"Sometimes but not all the time. It's kinda hard you know. We start laughing about things that he use to do and then the next thing I know I'm feeling all sad and stuff. I don't like that because then I want to cry and I don't want to cry in front of Meek."

"I can understand that. Meek is probably feeling the same way. So just take things one day at a time and don't be afraid to feel what you feel." I suggested.

After dropping Tiana off, I headed home. I was in the kitchen frying porkchops and steaming some rice and broccoli when the phone rang. I checked the caller ID and recognized Tray's number. Instantly, I felt good and answered the phone with a smile. Another long conservation pursued. I was growing fonder of him with each passing moment. I was even looking forward to the time when he would come to visit. Shoot, I might even make another weekend excursion to Chi-town to see him if he kept up with the charm.

I awoke the next morning with a slight headache which gained strength as the day progressed. By noon it was close to a migrane despite the Motrin I'd taken. I finished my two o'clock and decided to call it a day and head home for the comfort of my bed. The knock at my office door jolted me and intensified the cranial throbbing. Not having the strength to call out, I walked over and slowly opened the door. Standing in front of me was a elderly delivery man holding an opaque vase full of white and yellow daisies. His cheery greeting ran down my spine from the reverberation it brought to my head. I quickly signed his clipboard through squinted eyes and told him to have a nice day. I didn't bother to look at the attached card. I just grabbed my bag and took the flowers down to the car with me.

I slept until six that evening and when I awakened the pain in my head was just a dull throbbing. I warmed up my leftovers from the night before and made a cup of lemon zinger with a starlight mint and honey. As I sat eating at the dinette I noticed the white card sticking out of the daisies. My first thought was that they were probably from the Menden Family. Then I thought that maybe Trayu had sent them. That would truly make my day and prove further that he was a great guy. Bubbling, I opened the card and instantly had my bubble popped. They were from Karl. I couldn't believe that he would have the nerve to send anything to me, least of all my favorite flowers. He was an absolute ass. The card read, "You will forever have my heart. Love, Karl." I was hating him so much at that moment that I began crying. That of course reignited the pain in my head and I put my unfinished dinner plate in the refrigerator and went back to bed. Why couldn't he just leave me alone? Hadn't he gotten the picture? I was finished with him. I wanted him totally out of my life. I didn't want to be his friend. I didn't want to be anything to him except a memory. Hadn't he hurt me enough? Was he trying to drive me crazy? My stomach was cramping from retching sobs working their way up to escape through my mouth. Soon I was racing to the bathroom and praying to the porcelain throne. Even though my migrane was back to full force, I was afraid to take anymore medicine. Instead, I took a cold pack out of the freezer, put it on the back of my head, went back to bed, and cried myself to sleep.

# 12

Tiana's Saturday movie adventure turned out to be not what she had expected. Her Sunday night call was a welcomed distraction from my somber state brought on by thoughts of Karl. Tiana was most disturbed by the way Meek treated her that afternoon. She said that he had called everyday prior to make sure that they were definitely on for Saturday. That did seem slightly strange to her, but she reasoned that he was just trying to establish the brotherly role he spoken about earlier. When he picked her up to take Marta to the Mall Theatre she was shocked to see that he was dressed rather nicely and smelled real good. She had teased him about it but he just ignored her. He paid for the movie and offered to buy any snack that she desired. Everything seemed fine until midway through the flick when he draped his arm across the back of the seat. She was uncomfortable with the gesture and got up to go to the bathroom, which is something she never does for fear of missing a good scene. When she returned to her seat she was happy to see that he had removed his arm. She thought everything was cool because he didn't put his arm there for the rest of the movie. Then when they stopped at the arcade she was alarmed again when he stood closely behind her while she was shooting hoops. He was close enough that she could feel his breath on the back of her ear. Tiana said that his proximity made her very uncomfortable. She became so nervous that she told him that she didn't want to go to Krystals for dinner because she had a headache. He insisted on stopping to at least get some burgers to go and told her that she could nuke them and eat them later. But that wasn't the end of it. When they left Krystals, headed to her apartment, Meek put his arm around her again and kissed her on the forehead and said, "Oh my poor girl has a headache. Don't worry, it will go away once you take a little Tylenol." She said she shoved him away jokingly and told him to stop teasing her. But she was not feeling jovial. She was feeling extremely uncomfortable.

Why? Because it felt like he was trying to be her boyfriend instead of her brother. Then to top it off he called twice that night to see if she was feeling alright and had just called for the second time for the day just before she had called me.

"Tiana why do you think he's trying to be more than a brother figure to you?" I asked.

"I don't know Ms. Austin, I just got that feeling. I can't explain it. Can't you tell when somebody likes you for more than just a friend?" Tiana responded.

"Well, yes, I guess you're right. But do you think that you could be overreacting?"

"I guess I could be but I ain't taking no chances with it. I don't want him to even think that I would want him as no boyfriend." She exclaimed. He is just like a brother to me. He's not Kieron, but he's like a brother because of Kieron. I will never like him like a boyfriend! It just ain't like that!"

"Okay, okay, I hear you. But it could be that your sensitivity is at a heighten state right now. And that could mean that you are misinterpreting his motives. But you should be careful just to be on the safe side." I suggested.

"I know that's right Ms. Austin."Tiana laughed.

I took advantage of the fact that we were discussing boyfriends and asked her about, Kaiewa, the little fella she was hanging with after Kieron's funeral. She said that they weren't really going together but she did like him okay.

"He is kinda different, you know. He likes to read like I do and he likes to write too. He showed me some of his raps and I told him that they sounded like poems. He says that that what raps are really, poems. But Ms. Austin, you know that most raps don't sound like anything you would want to recite to someone you want to get with."

We both laughed. Tiana hit the nail on that one.

She continued. "Kaiewa is real nice and I like being around him cause I feel like I can talk about anything and he won't look at me like I'm crazy. I dig the way that he doesn't curse and try to be all hard. I mean he ain't no punk and he can scrap but he don't really go looking for trouble. And he's always on the honor roll and wants to go to be a lawyer. That's why I think that Kieron liked him. Ms. Austin, remember how Kieron was always talking about making something of ourselves. He was always talking about me going to college and stuff."

Her voice started softening and I knew that she was starting to feel a little mellow. So I decided to bring her back around.

"Well, Kaiewa sounds real nice. He sounds like a young man headed for a bright future. I'm glad you're hanging out with him. Does your grandmother like him too?" I asked.

"Yeah she likes him okay but I don't let him come over that much because I don't want her to start asking me about him all the time. Most of the time we meet at the library. It's so peaceful there and I can read and write and do homework and talk about stuff. Shoot, if it wasn't for Kaiewa, I probably would never have started going to the library. He loves that place and he's taken me to other libraries too. But I like the one over this way because then I don't have to take the bus no where."

I could tell that Tiana really did like this Kaiewa. She kept saying that he wasn't her boyfriend, but he sure sounded like a boyfriend to me. I was hoping that I would get the chance to meet him and see if I could pick up on what made him special.

Tiana interrupted my thoughts.

"Hey, Ms. Austin, I gotta go. MaDear is home." She announced in an alerting tone.

"Oh that's good. Let me say hello to her before you go." I requested.

"Ms. Austin, please don't tell her what we talked about. Please don't tell her." She pleaded.

"Tiana, girl calm down. Don't get excited. I told you many times that what we discuss is confidential. I don't discuss our conversations with anyone including your grandmother unless I have strong reason to suspect that the information shared could place you in harms way. Then, I have a duty to discuss it with the necessary people. But I will promise you this, I will make you aware, when or if that situation

arises. So, calm down and put your MaDear on the phone, little girl."
I said with a smile in my voice.

Mrs. Menden sounded tired but greeted me well. She said she
was doing okay although she still was not sleeping very well. There
was still no new leads on the assailants that ended Kieron's life or
the where abouts of her daughter. Unfortunately, although unspoken,
there was a probable chance that neither of those two mysteries would
be solved. There are so many unsolved cases of black on black crime
that people learn to grieve for their loss and just swallow the taste
of revenge or justice. That's the only way for them to survive and
maintain mental stability. In the second case, it is well known in the
hood that the streets and drugs can be a black hole that devours friends
and loved ones whole, never to be seen again. So, one could only
pray that Kieron's family would strive and thrive through this difficult
time.

That night I dreamt of Kieron. He was in my office sitting across
from me in the conversation nook. I could see my hand moving my
pen across the notepad but the words I wrote appeared to float a
centimeter above the paper. Kieron voice was soft and gentle. He
smiled as he talked about living in their new home. His new room had
two windows and the top of the large oaktree outside brushed against
his window when it rained. Tiana was teaching him how to use his
new computer before she left for college. When I looked up at him,
he was smiling with a sparkle in his eyes. I told him that he should
reapply and he could start the next semester. Kieron just shook his
head and smiled as he faded away. I woke in a sweat accompanied by
a dry mouth and a throbbing in my head. Strangely, as I washed down
some Tylenol caplets, I felt peaceful about Kieron. I couldn't figure
out why I had dreamt of him but I wasn't worried about it at all.

# 13

I was still jonesing for Karl. I wanted to call him so bad. I cleaned the entire condo from top to bottom, even scrubbed the bathroom tile on my knees, but I couldn't shake the need to talk to him. I decided to call Paully. He wasn't at home and I left him a lengthy message expressing my state of mind. He would get an earful when he retrieved his messages. The message was somewhat comical but not enough to ease my mind. So I tried Trayu's number. Jackpot! He answered and was happy to here from me.

"It probably sounds corny but I was just thinking about you." He said.

"Oh, you slay me, Tray. You are ever so sweet to say that, my knight in shining armour." I teased.

"Come on now, Rhap. I promise that I was just thinking about calling you because I wanted to run something by you."

"Yeah? What would that be Sir Trayu."

"I was wondering what your schedule was looking like for next weekend." He asked.

"I don't think that I have anything special going on. Why do you ask?" I responded as if I didn't know what he was hinting at.

"Well, I found out that ATA has a special going on. It's like ninety-nine dollars round trip. So I was thinking that I could make a weekend trip to Atlanta sooner than I thought. But I wanted to check with you first. I don't want to impose on you and you would be the main reason for taking the trip. So what do you think?

I was smiling by the time he finished his spill. He sounded so nervous as if he was afraid of getting his feelings hurt. But the cutest part was that he stepped up and took the chance to ask. Oh, he was wearing on my heart with his cute self.

"Woah, that was a mouthful." I laughed. "That is a great price. Yeah, it would be cool to have you come down. I told you that I would like to have you come for a visit. So you're thinking about this weekend?"

"No, I was actually thinking about next weekend. I need to get some things straightened out this week and plus I didn't want to rush in on you." He said.

"Wow, I can't believe this. You are really going to come and visit?"

"Yup, I sure am and I'm also going to hold you to being my personal tour guide."

"Tray, it will be my pleasure. I'm so excited! Have you made your reservations yet?" I asked.

"Come on now. I'm not that cocky. I wanted to wait until I had talked to you. But, I'm going to call tomorrow."

At that point my other line clicked and made my heart beat speed up. I checked the caller ID and was relieved to see Paully's number.

"Tray, can you hold on a minute? That's my other line."

"Sure. Go ahead."

I clicked over and greeted Paully with a happy dappy hello.

"What's up with that? I thought you were suppose to be over there all sad by the message you left. But you sure don't sound sad to me. Have you been hitting the sauce?" Paully teased.

"Ha, ha. You are so funny. No, I am not drinking. I was just on the other line talking to Trayu. Hold on and let me say goodbye to him."

"Yeah, you do that. You don't have no business talking to that youngblood anyway." Paully chastised.

"Whatever Paully! Just hold on."

I returned to Tray on the other line. I really didn't want to let him go yet, but I needed to talk to Paully. I hadn't talked to him since my last breakdown, besides, I was kind of missing him. Tray was just as sweet as usual. I told him that I would call him later. He in return told me to go talk to Paully and that he would call me the next day after he'd confirmed his reservations. That actually excited me and I quickly let him go.

"Paully? Are you there?" I asked returning to the other line.

"Yeah, I'm here. Are you finished with your boy toy?" Paully teased.

"Paully, you need to quit. So what's going on?"

"Nothing much. I just wanted to call and talk to my best friend and make sure she was okay."

"Yeah, I'm fine. Some days are better than others but I think I'm getting stronger everyday. Keeping myself busy helps a lot." I responded.

"Oh so is that why you were talking to youngblood?"

"Well, yes and no. I've been talking to him on the phone since I've been back. I enjoy talking to him. He's pretty cool. But I would be lying if I said that he doesn't help take my mind off some of the unpleasant things presently invading my life. We've had some pretty interesting conversations and he's really easy to talk to. And! He's not that young, so stop trippin'!"

"Rhap come on now. You know that he is too young for you. Don't fool yourself into thinking that this is going to make the pain that old dude caused go away. You need to heal first." He started rationalizing.

I stopped him as quick as I could. Paully was actually beginning to irritate me. I didn't want to let it get too far, because the last thing I needed was to argue with one of my constant supporters.

"Paully, chill! It's not like that. We are just talking. I already told him that I was not looking for a relationship. That I was in no condition to get romantically involved with anyone."

Paully snapped at me so quickly that it made me jump.

"You mean to tell me that you confided in that boy? You don't even know him, Rhap. Why you telling him all your business like that?"

His tone stunned me and it took me a few seconds before I could gather my thoughts and respond. What was all the attitude about? Why was he trippin'?

"Hey, hold your horses, big fella. I didn't tell him anything except that I was not looking for a relationship. I just told him enough to let him know that I wasn't available to him or anyone else for that matter. I haven't given him my whole life story. I reserve that privilege for you. Look, don't get mad at me. I can't take that right now. I need you, baby, don't trip on me now. Okay?" I pleaded and it worked.

"Rhap, I'm not mad at you. You know that I can't get mad at you.

I'm just saying that you need to protect your heart right now and getting involved with youngblood is not the way to do it."

"I know and I'm not trying to get seriously involved with Tray. I just like talking to him. Believe it or not, we are really developing a neat little friendship. He might even be coming to Atlanta next weekend. I told him I would be his tour guide." I shared.

"What? He's coming to visit you already and he just met you. Rhap, I don't think that you should have that boy up in your house. You don't know what he has on his mind. And you don't know what he might try to do in the middle of the night." Paully warned.

I wasn't sure but it seemed like Paully was taking this whole Trayu thing too serious. It wasn't like him. I know that he was always looking out for me but he was acting like Trayu was a recently released axe murderer. I started wondering if there was something about Trayu that I wasn't picking up on. I'm usually a pretty good judge of character but it was true that I'd recently made a very bad call when I took up with Karl. I had been fooled by him and therefore I could be fooled by Tray as well. Yet, I didn't feel alarmed by Tray and I was just going to go with that feeling. Besides, I wasn't trying to bed the boy or anything. Meanwhile, I had to calm Paully down.

"Paully, I'm not letting him stay here. He's going to get a hotel room. I'm not stupid, you know."

I left out a few facts. One, Trayu had not mentioned getting a hotel room. Two, I had actually thought about offering my hospitality. But Paully didn't need that information.

"Okay. I'm going to leave it alone. I know that you know what's best for you and you're pretty perceptive most of the time. So, let's move on to something else. As a matter of fact, I was also calling tonight to tell you that I was planning to come for a little get away. But I guess it won't be next weekend. Unless, that is, that you want me to come and supervise your little visit with youngblood."

"Paully, you know that you are always welcomed in my home. You can come next weekend, this weekend or any weekend you like. You don't have to make an appointment. Not ever. But to answer your question, no, I don't need a chaperone. Now that's enough about me.

What's going on with you? Did you and Tanya get back together?"

"Come on now. You know that I don't work like that. She was blowing my phone up for a minute and I finally had to sit her down and have a nice long talk with her. I told her that I admired her for the beautiful woman that she is and that I would always treasure the times that we had together. I told her that I wanted her to know that there was no blame to be issued to anyone for our breakup. It's just that I don't feel what I need to feel for her in order to offer her the type of relationship that she deserves. Then she started that crying mess that you women are famous for. You know I hate that mess, it just gets to me."

"Paully, please don't tell me that you got soft and gave in." I teased.

"Pleeeze! I ain't even going out like that. I soothed her by telling her that she had helped me grow so much mentally and emotionally and that I would be there for her as a friend and confidant. That was all I needed to say. I know it probably left her with some hope of nabbing me in the future but that's on her."

"You mean to tell me that she fell for that jive. Please! She needs to be gone if she's that naïve." I said with distain.

"Well she is what she is and that's a woman looking for a husband and you know that when you women get the marriage bug your vision becomes distorted. I have to admit that the pressure to get married is major for women. It's like society holds marriage as a status symbol of the worthiness of womanhood and I hate it for y'all. On the other hand, I know that I can only save one and I am going to make sure it's the right one. And Tanya is not the one. She still calls but I put the fifteen minute timer on her. I'm not even going to give her any reason to hope for more than she is going to get from me. No dinner, no movies, no drinks, and definitely no bedroom aerobics."

Paully had me cracking up. He is a fool, but some of what he said was quite accurate. Women do have it hard but we are also working hard to demolish the stereotypes and pressures that society continues to force on our worth. Paully let out a little chuckle in his attempt to stop from laughing at himself.

We spent another thirty minutes or so more on the line before I started yawning. I quickly ended that call and closed my eyes to drift off to sleep before my mind had the opportunity to wander to any distracting thoughts.

# 14

The next week flew by with the growing anticipation of Trayu's visit. We spoke on the phone daily and our weekend plans became more elaborate with each conversation. Trayu had his ticket and hotel reservations at the Marriott Marquis downtown. The central location would make it easy for us to hook up and explore the city. I have to admit that I was somewhat relieved the night he told me about his hotel reservations. We hadn't discussed lodging and I was hoping that he wouldn't ask to stay at my place. If I said no, he might be offended but if I said yes, he might think that I was offering more than a place to lay his head. I still had not convinced myself that I didn't want him to stay with me. Never the less, it was safer for him to stay at a hotel.

Paully also called a few times that week to tell me that he would be coming the week after Tray. He made it clear that he would be staying with me by instructing me to wash the dusty linen on the bed in the guestroom so that his allergies didn't act up during his visit. At the beginning of the week, Paully said that he might be coming in on the same day as Tray. That made me a little nervous considering the negative vibes he'd been sending pertaining to Tray. It would make for a slightly stressful weekend and I did not need that. But relief came the very next day when Paully called to say that he would come the following week.

Something was still bothering me about the fact that Paully seemed to dislike Trayu so much and he didn't even really know him. Maybe he was seriously sensing something wrong about Trayu that I wasn't picking up on. I kept reminding myself to be careful and perceptive during Tray's visit even as I drove to the airport to meet him in baggage claim. I parked and stopped at the bathroom before going to the baggage claim area. I had a little nervousness fluttering around in my stomach which I hoped didn't turn into gas. No need to mutilate that boy's sinus cavities on his first day in Georgia. Surprisingly, I spotted

Tray right away as he stood watching the various luggage pieces circle. Damn, he was fine! He was wearing black Levis, black leather jacket, red turtle neck sweater and black Timberlands. Tray was standing with his hands in his pockets alternating his attention between the luggage carousel and the sliding airport doors. I snuck around to come up behind him undetectable by peripheral vision.

"I just don't understand why it takes so long for the bags to get from the plane to baggage claim. As long as it takes to deplane and walk all the way to the baggage claim area, they could have the luggage lined up alphabetically waiting for us. Don't you think?" I said to Tray's back.

He turned around to respond and lost his words in his radiant smile. This boy was beautiful. He grabbed me in a warm and secure embrace and kissed me on my cheek. Goodness gracious, he smelled delectable and his lips were like eygptian cotton on my skin. What was I going to do with this stunning male specimen? I wanted to press my lips against his just to see if they would melt into them. Maybe I could melt my entire body into his. I know that I wanted to try.

"Hi Buddy. I'm glad that you didn't forget to pick me up. I was starting to worry." He said with breathe as sweet as honeysuckle.

"Well, hello to you, too. And how could I forget to pick you up when you called a zillion times to remind me of your arrival time." I teased.

He laughed and pulled me back into another wonderful embrace. I knew that I was in for a battle of will for the weekend. I reluctantly broke the embrace and turned the attention back to the task of retrieving his luggage. Tray kept his arm around my shoulder until he spotted his leather duffle bag. I offered to carry his matching leather backpack but he declined. As we walked to the car I had to slow my stride because Tray was lagging behind. I knew he was checking me out and it made me a bit uncomfortable.

"How was your flight? Did it tire you out? Cause you're walking kinda slow there, Buddy." I teased.

"No, my flight was fine. I was just following you. It's not like I know where we're going, Miss Smarty Pants."

I laughed. This was going to be a good weekend. The mood was set for fun.

In the car, Tray talked nonstop about the scenery and our weekend plans with his hand propped up on my headrest. I had a difficult time answering his questions due his proximity and aroma. I had the constant urge to rest my nose and lips against his neck to feel his natural warmth.

Our first stop was the Marriott Marquis, where he took time to unpack and hang up his clothes. From there I took him to Ramona for some Italian cuisine. Then we headed over to the Martini Bar to listen to some live jazz and sip on the best Purple Hooters this side of the Mason Dixon Line. Tray and I both puffed on cigars, which was a first for me. It was not the best experience but the time spent conversing with Tray took up any slack. I was extremely comfortable with him and I couldn't deny the physical attraction. Several women, probably closer to his age, were openly checking him out. Even the waitress seemed mesmerized by his presence. The best part, though, was that Tray never seemed to take his eyes off of me other than to give the drink order or to look at the quartet. It was as if he didn't even notice the other honies checking him out, which I know he had to. An old blind man in a dark alley couldn't miss the admiring glances of those women. Even so, I felt pretty special sitting there with him.

We closed the place down and I took Tray back to his hotel. Tray invited me back to his room for coffee and I accepted. It seemed like a good idea, since I was feeling a little tipsy. Once in the room, Tray mentioned that he was hungry, so I suggested that we walk over to Micks' and grab something to eat. Micks' was still booming with customers in the early morning but we didn't have to wait long to be seated. Tray woofed down his food and was beginning to show signs of fatigue. We walked back to the hotel and I said goodbye to him outside at my car assuring him that I was no longer tipsy. We promised to give each other a wake up call depending on who awakened first. Trayu gave me another one of his wonderful hugs and I headed home with his scent lingering around me in my car, on my clothes, and on my face. That night I slept like a baby with a full stomach of warm breast milk. The day had been perfect from my long hot morning shower to the night ending hug from Trayu. I laid in my bed picturing his face at various times during our first day together. At some point during my thought a coy smile crept across my lips and followed me into slumber. I couldn't wait to see him the next morning.

Trayu beat me to the punch and rang my phone at 8:00a.m. I teased him about waking before me and he informed me that he'd been awake for at least an hour. He asked what time we would be starting our day and a light fluttering began in my stomach. It was the tell-tell sign of attraction on my part. I was totally feeling him. I told him that I would be there in an hour and a half. Before I could hang up he had more questions for me.

"Hey Rhap? What should I wear?"

"Just dress comfortably. We won't be going to any formal affairs" I joked and continued.

"No, for real, you just need to worry about being comfortable and warm. We might get some rain today. But otherwise you can be as casual as you like. I will be. We might change for my dinner plans, but it's not mandatory in the least. Okay? Is that enough to go on?" I questioned.

I knew what Tray was trying to do. He was trying to get information out of me about what we were going to do. I had already told him that I was going to plan the weekend in totality and he would only have to ride along and enjoy. That had been a hard thing for him to except. He'd been asking all kinds of questions for the last week, trying to get some idea of what I had planned. But all he got from me was questions about the things he liked to do, which only seemed to confuse him more. I was loving his discomfort. My only comfort to him was to tell him that he could trust me. I promised not to get him arrested or anything like that.

"So you are not going to tell me anything concrete, are you, Rhap?"

"Nope! Why can't you just trust me?"

"I do! But it would be nice to know something." He pleaded.

"Tray, all you need to know is that I plan to show you a good time for the entire weekend. Okay?"

"Okay." He laughed. "I'll see you when you get here."

"Bye Traaaay." I cooed.

Tray's scent engulfed my senses as he opened the door to his room. He was ready for action looking scrumptious in blue baggy Levis, black crew neck sweater, and the black Timberlands and leather jacket from the day before.

"I hope that we are going for breakfast first." He smiled while patting his firm tummy. I couldn't help to wonder if he was sporting a six pack under that sweater.

"Of course we are. I wouldn't want you passing out on me and ruining my day." I smiled back.

I parked a block away from the restaurant because I wanted to keep the suspense going. When he saw the restaurant sign, he got so excited that I couldn't help but laugh. He had been so busy running his mouth that he didn't notice the sign until he was opening the restaurant door for me.

"Gladys and Ron's Chicken and Waffles! I can't believe this! I've always wanted to eat at one of their restaurants. Have you eaten here before? Is it good? I sure hope so, cause I'm hungrier than a bear fresh out of hibernation." He rattled on.

I laughed at his boyish excitement. I loved his happy nature.

"I think you'll be pleased. It's definitely good grub and even if you're not totally impressed, you can at least say that you've eaten here."

"Yeah, you're right."

Tray couldn't decide if he wanted chicken and waffles or if he wanted to try the salmon croquettes. So we ordered a smorgasbord of chicken, waffles, grits, salmon croquettes, scrambled eggs, hash browns, coffee and orange juice. The Winans were being pumped through the speakers strategically placed throughout the restaurant as we waited for our order. We didn't have to wait long which was good because I didn't think that Tray could take a long wait. Trayu loved the food and cleaned every plate on the table. The Martin Luther King Jr. Memorial was next followed by the Cocoa Cola Pavillion. From there we walked Underground Atlanta and drove around the Atlanta University area. Tray really seemed to enjoy cruising the college area. I asked him if he would still consider going to school in Atlanta.

"Naw, that time has passed for me. I'm happy where I am in my college career. Now my focus is on just getting what I need to secure the future that I want and I think I'm doing that. So, I'll stick to my guns and finish what I've started." He explained.

I was impressed with his answer. But I was sort of hoping that he would say that he would love to move here. That way he would be closer to me. Not saying that I wanted him closer but it would have been nice to hear it just the same.

Next we stopped for a cappuccino and took a nice leisure walk through Centennial Park. We talked about my youth in Chicago and how Paully, Cocoa, and I became friends. Tray shared more of his dreams. Where he wanted to live, travel, build, and explore. He wanted to marry by thirty-five and wanted no more than three children. His wife would work even if only part-time. He didn't want a woman who expected him to be the total financial provider. Marriage was a partnership and they both needed to contribute in order to take serious stock in their life investment. Raising the kids was to be done in unison as well. Children needed to know that both parents were their teachers, support system, and pillars. He also wanted to be financially secure by the age of forty-five, although he wouldn't retire until he turned fifty-five.

When he asked me if I wanted to get married, I hesitated a moment. Then he laughed and pulled me close to his side by putting his arm around my shoulder. His warmth seemed to radiate through his jacket.

"Come on now Rhap, it's not a difficult question." He teased.

"No, it's not. I-I-I guess that I would like to find my soul mate and get married. But I realize that there's a possibility that that may not ever happen. And I think that I could be okay with that. I mean, not getting married and still being able to live a full and happy life."

"Don't you want kids?" Tray asked.

"Yeah, I'd love to have children. But I don't want to do it out of wedlock if I can help it. I know that being married doesn't guarantee having a father to raise your children. I mean that he could run out on us just like a boyfriend or a sperm donor. But if my husband can't hang then at least I can say that I gave it an honest effort. I'd want my kids to know that much. That I tried to do the right thing. Know what I mean?"

I looked over at Tray and he caught my eyes with an almost sensual stare. I wondered what he was thinking. I figured that I hadn't spooked him because he was still holding me close to him.

"Yeah, I know exactly what you mean." He said while never losing eye contact. Then he suddenly looked away and took a sip of the cappuccino in his other hand.

"It's starting to get dark. What time is it?" he asked.

I glanced at my watch.

"It's 4:55. Wow, I didn't think that it was that late. The day has flown by. Well let's see. How do you feel? Are you tired? You want to take a little break before the next event, because you might need your energy. I asked with a smile.

"Oh is it like that? No, I don't need to rest, I have the stamina and can go the distance."

The wink he added after his little comment shut me up. I wasn't sure how to take it or respond to it. Luckily, he continued.

"I would like to see your place, if that's okay. I want to see where you relax and unwind."

"Sure. No problem. We can go to my place and rest our feet for a while. If we leave about seven o'clock we should be able to get to our next destination with time to spare."

I gave Trayu the full tour of my condo. It took longer than I expected because he stopped and studied every piece of artwork in every room. I left him on the floor checkin out my cd collection while I fixed drinks. The next hour flew by as he played DJ and we talked about various artist. Tray only wanted to play the cd's of artists he wasn't familiar with. He claimed it was a way to get to know another part of my personality. I just laid on my chocolate leather sofa with my feet propped up and a cherry RC cola at my side and watched him have his fun. I finally pulled him away to go to the ESPN Zone for dinner and games, but not before promising him that I would allow him to complete his research later.

I kept my promise and we came back to my place after our play time at the Zone. We were so hyped up from all the fun that we'd actually worked up an appetite. Tray took off his jacket and went directly back to my music station and I went into the kitchen for snacks to settle our cravings. When I returned to the living room I was surprised to see that Tray had taken off his sweater and shoes and was chilling in his white short sleeve undershirt. It fit tightly and answered one of my questions. Tray definitely had a six pack and hammer arms to go with it. He was making this platonic thing difficult. Not too difficult, though. I was still more interested in his company than his body.

When Tray put on my Lili Añel CD, he decided he wanted to listen to it in it's entirety. He joined me on the sofa by lying on the opposite end of the sofa with his feet on my lap.

"Who told you that you could put your smelly feet on me?" I snapped and he moved them to my side.

"My feet don't smell any worse than yours, so chill."

And chill we did. When Lili stopped serenading us, Tray wanted to play it again. I offered to relinquish my comfortable position to restart the CD. Ever the gracious host. I laid down on my stomach in front of the system, pressed play and turned the volume down a notch. The fatigue of a long day hit me while I lie on the floor so I figured I'd lay there for a few minutes. That floor felt good and I was sure that Lili Anel's sultry voice would soon lull me to sleep, but I couldn't move.

"Hey, why'd you turn it down? You should have turned it up a little. That lady is smooth." Tray said to me as I felt him lay down beside me.

"Sorry. You can turn it up if you want, but not too loud. It's late, you know."

"Naw, it's okay. It sounds just right down here."

That's when he touched me. Not in a bad way at all. He started stroking my hair and then upper shoulder area. Surprisingly I didn't freak out. It felt soothing and in no way threatening. Maybe it was just what I needed. I don't know how long he caressed my shoulders because I fell asleep. I awakened from an aching stiffness in my lower back and attempted to roll over and get up from that hard surface. As I turned over I awakened Tray, who had obviously been captured by the same sandman bandit that had hit me. I apologized for waking him and he kissed me. It was more like a brush of the lips. It felt like someone sweeping a feather across my lips and I closed my eyes to relish in the sensation. Tray took that personal gesture as an invitation and gave me a firmer kiss. Now that one shook me up and I broke and hopped up like a jack rabbit and skittered to the restroom. Once inside I relieved my bladder and put a cold wash cloth over my face. I had to get a hold of myself before going back out into the living room.

I walked from the bathroom straight to the kitchen leaving a few words in my wake.

"I'm going to freshen my drink, do you want me to freshen yours, too?" I asked.

Tray was now sitting on the sofa again.

"Rhap......Uh...sure, that would be good." he responded.

I could tell that he wanted to say something else but I was glad that he'd left it hanging in the wings. I wasn't sure if I even wanted to know what was on his mind. I would just get him something to drink and drive him back to his hotel. We would start over fresh tomorrow. That would give me enough time to get my hormones back under control.

Trayu looked up at me shyly when I reentered the room. He looked like a little teddy bear waiting to be cuddled. I gave him a quaint smirk to let him know that everything was okay. I realized at that moment that I was feeling better about what happened only moments before. It really wasn't that serious. So I handed Trayu his drink and sat down on the sofa a couple of feet away.

"Hey...Uh...Rhap...I'm sorry about that...uh...well, I'm sorry about what happened earlier. I didn't mean to step out of line. I wasn't thinking, I just went with my gut feelings. I shouldn't have done that and I didn't mean to be disrespectful. Not at all." He explained.

I threw my head back in laughter. " No, it's cool. Tray, you didn't disrespect me. You weren't the only one with moving lips."

"Tray, I admit that it was not what I was expecting but it happened and there's no harm."

Tray's eyes widened in shock and said, "Damn, am I that bad of a kisser?"

I let out a hearty laugh and almost choked on my drink. What a character.

"I didn't mean that; the kiss was good. I was talking about the fact that I was not expecting to be kissed by you or to be kissing you. Tray the kiss was nice. Very nice." I smiled.

"Well, if it was so nice and not out of place, then why don't we give it another whirl?"

I shook my head at him and laughed some more. He joined me in my laughter and after a few minutes I felt that all tension had been lifted. That is until he asked about the kiss again. I asked him what he thought another kiss would accomplish. The fact of the matter was that I wasn't trying to get involved and I didn't want to lead him on. I really enjoyed being with him and I didn't want to do anything to jeopardize what we were building. There was also my emotional frame of mind to consider. I was fresh out of a heartbreaking relationship and felt that that made me vulnerable to overactive emotions. And presently, it was totally unhealthy for me to act on any emotions. Finally, I told him that we should just move past it and get him back to his hotel so he could rest up for the last day of his trip. Trayu wasn't quite ready to let the situation go at my detailed explanation.

"Rhap, I hear you and I agree with you to a certain extent, but I have to be honest. I want to kiss you again. As a matter of fact I need to kiss you again, at least one more time. I can't explain why, but I will promise you that I will not pressure you to go any further." He paused. Actually, I promise not to let you go any further no matter how much you may beg."

Laughter captured me once more. But I had to admit to myself that I wanted to feel his lips against mine again. I almost felt as if I needed it, too. I couldn't explain why I felt that way either, so I didn't pressure him to explain his feelings. Instead I agreed to his request.

"Tray, you drive a hard bargain but believe it or not I feel where you're coming from. How about this, we'll have one more kiss, then I'll take you to your hotel and we'll close this chapter." I suggested.

"Okay, that sounds like a done deal, Ms. Rhap."

Then he slid closer until his thigh was flush against mine. He rested his left arm on the sofa back behind my head and began searching my eyes. I couldn't take the look so I diverted my eyes to my legs.

"Rhap, look at me. Kissing your forehead was not a part of the deal as I remember." He whispered and gently pulled my chin upward with his index finger. The look in his eyes was as gentle as a lamb and for the first time I noticed light brown flecks adding enchantment to his dark brown pupils. Instantly, a wave of heat arose in my chest. He slowly began closing the distance between our faces never taking his eyes from mine. I closed my eyes as his nose touched mine. He took a couple of seconds to run his nose up the length of mine and back down. Then, I felt his downy lips touch me once and then twice. The third touch lingered and intensified in pressure. Finally I felt his lips part and the wetness of his tongue will my lips to part. As his searched out my tongue, a shiver ran through my body. That's how the kiss began but it seemed to go on forever. It was a perpetuity I didn't resist. I was thinking that he was definitely a good kisser, when he took it to another level. I could feel Tray moving his right hand as the kiss deepened. I sensed that the accompanying fondling was about to begin. But Tray didn't go for my breast or my behind. What he did instead, pierced my heart from the tenderness. Tray gently reached up and caressed the side of my face. He ran his hand over the top of my head down and around to the bottom of my jawbone. There his hand lay holding my face in place against his. Eventually I had to break for air and as I did, our eyes met. What was I to do but fall back into him. This time he pulled my body into his and I held on to his firm frame.

We went on kissing that way for what seemed like an eternity. When we finally broke, he cradled my head between his cheek and shoulder.

"I guess we should get going. What time is it?" I whispered.

Tray glanced at his watch and lifted his head in shock.

"Rhap, it's almost 3:00 in the morning. I can't have you driving at this time."

"It's fine. I'm wide awake." I told him.

"I don't care if you are or not. I'm not going to have you driving alone in the wee hours of the morning and that's a fact. I'll just call a cab and you can pick me up in the morning."

"Tray, I'm not having you take a cab, either. I said that I would take care of you while you were here and I'm going to do just that." I recountered.

"Look, it's much safer for me to take a cab than it is for you to be driving alone in the middle of the night. So, let's be real about this and call a cab."

I knew that he was right but I still didn't feel right about it.

"What about this? Why don't you just stay in my guestroom for the night and I'll take you to your room in the morning. I don't have a lot planned for tomorrow anyway because you have an early evening flight out. How about that? You can even sleep late if you like."

"Well…"

"Come on Tray, don't make this too complicated. Just say yes so we can go to bed. You already pointed out that it's pretty late. I'll get you some pajama bottoms and a t-shirt and don't worry the bottoms are mens. You should get a good night's rest. Former guests have told me that they've had the best night's rest on that bed. So be like Mike and just do it." I said with a smile.

"Okay, okay! Stop the corniness. If you really don't think it will be an inconvenience, I'll do it. Just no more corny phrases, please!"

"Then it's settled. I'll go get your PJs." I said as I started walking toward my bedroom.

After Tray was all settled in his room I stopped by to tell him goodnight. He was coming out of the bathroom connected to the guestroom all fresh and clean from a shower.

"Do you have everything you need?" I asked.

"Yup, I'm all set."

"Well, sleep well and I'll see you in the morning. And, Tray, thanks for a great day."

Tray walked over to where I was standing in the doorway.

"No, I should be thanking you for a great day and an even better night."

He gave me one of his encompassing warm hugs. I rested my head against is chest and returned the embrace. Then he pulled his head back and bent to kiss me. This time I fell into the kiss automatically. He was too much! I pulled away when he started caressing the back of my head. That was one of my weaknesses and I couldn't let myself get carried away.

"Okay, that's enough of that mister. No more kisses for you. We had a deal, remember? Now go to bed and I'll see you in the morning." I chastised.

"Okay, okay. Goodnight and thanks again."

"You're more than welcome. Goodnight" I said.

As soon as my head met my pillow, I was asleep. There was no time to contemplate the nights events and I considered that a blessing. The next morning I awakened at 8:00. I let Tray sleep since he was on vacation. The plans for the day were scarce so it wouldn't matter if we had to make a few adjustments in time. Tray greeted me in the kitchen with a jovial "good morning. I smiled and returned the greeting, instantly sensing that there wasn't any tension lingering about the night before. It appeared that it was going to be easy to move past what happened.

We decided to have an extra light breakfast of grape juice and a bagel. Then we headed back to Tray's hotel. He showered, packed, and settled his bill at the front desk. From there we headed over to the Fox Theatre for a special matinee showing of Humphrey Bogart's "Maltese Falcon." Tray was impressed by the European decor and the starry night sky donning the Fox's ceiling. I was glad to see the he was able to appreciate another one of my favorite places. He had never seen the flick and totally enjoyed it. I think that he was won over by the suaveness of Humphrey Bogart. It was a cross gender movie, both men and woman can truly appreciate it.

After the movie, I'd planned for us to have lunch at Crème's, where Corie worked. I hadn't told her about Tray coming to visit and was anxious to see what she would think about him. Of course I knew she would initially be pissed that I hadn't forewarned her, but I just didn't want her asking me a bunch of questions. I was already nervous about his impending visit and didn't need any help worrying about what would happen. Fortunately, the visit had been a total success in my eyes. Even the unexpected happenings of the night before didn't hinder the positive flow of the weekend.

The manager, Ralph, was talking with the hostess as we entered the restaurant and greeted me with a kiss on the cheek. He's a real cool dude and always showered me with perks whenever I was in the restaurant. So I was pretty confident that this visit would be no different. Tray was in for a treat. Ralph immediately escorted us to a table near one of the front windows without considering the patrons waiting ahead of us. After giving us a set of menus, he left to inform Corie of our presence. Corie didn't come out to our table until we were sharing a raspberry flan and sipping coffees. I introduced Tray and Tray complemented her on the meal. Corie ate it up like homemade peppermint ice cream at Christmas. We chatted with each other for a few minutes before she had to get back to the kitchen. When it was time for the check, Tray offered to pay for the meal. Of course I didn't allow it because lunch was a part of my weekend plans to show him a good time. He agreed only after I promised to let him return the favor on my next visit to Chi-town.

Tray was very pleased that I had decided to escort him to the security checkpoint and waited with him. Our conversation was carefree and comfortable. It had been a great weekend and a wonderful opportunity to get to know each other better. I was admittedly confused about where we were heading with the friendship, but I was not going to let it ruin my present high. When he was next up to have his credentials checked, I said goodbye. Tray thanked me again and pulled me into another one of his amazing embraces. Then he caressed the side of my face and gently kissed me, slipping me just the tip of his tongue. Another kiss planted on my forehead and he handed his ticket and id to the agent.

I felt a little melancholy on my drive home. I really enjoyed Tray's company and couldn't wait to talk to him again. I also spent a good portion of the drive home and the rest of the night thinking about the kisses we shared. Could Tray and I make it as a couple? Was he really too young for me? Was he looking for a Sugar Momma? I had to stop thinking about what was not and just be thankful for what was. I had a wonderful new friend and he'd succeeded in cheering me up. That was enough to be thankful for. Enough indeed.

# 15

Imet Tiana waiting for the elevator up to my office. I was on my way back from the snack machine in the lobby, because my cupboards were bare. I was not only surprised to see Tiana there so early, but she'd come with a surprise guest. Standing beside her at the elevator was the young and handsome Kaiewa. What he was doing there with her at this time was a mystery I planned to solve rather quickly.

"Well, fancy meeting you here, little Miss." I greeted Tiana. She turned with a shocked expression.

"Hi Ms. Austin. What are you doing down here? Are you just getting here?" she asked.

"No, I just came down to get a little snack. I've run out of my stash, so if you think you might want something to nibble on then you should get it while you're down here."

"What? I can't believe that you don't have any junk food in your office. It must be going to snow tonight." She laughed.

"Oh I see that you're just the little comedian today. So tell me who is this handsome visitor we have here?"

Tiana's face turned a deep shade of crimson. She stuck her hands into her pockets and quickly licked her lips trying to come up with the voice to respond. Kaiewa saved her by extending his hand and introducing himself ever so politely. Tiana finished up by explaining his presence.

"This is the friend I was telling you about, you know the one that was helping catch me up with my missed assignments."

Then she turned to him and touched him lightly on his upper arm.

"Kai, this is my counselor. She's good peeps and pretty cool."

Then back to me again.

"Ms. Austin, MaDear had a migrane and so Kaiewa volunteered to ride with me down to my appointment. Otherwise, MaDear was going to call and cancel because she didn't want me to ride the bus by myself. She said it's been getting darker earlier. But I didn't want to miss my session, so I was glad that he offered to come with me. Plus I don't too much care for riding the bus at night either." She explained.

"I totally understand and I'm glad you made it. You know I look forward to seeing you. My weeks are just not the same when you miss an appointment." I said with a smirk as the elevator arrived. Tiana caught my witty comment immediately and laughed all the way up to my floor.

With Kaiewa waiting outside my office, Tiana and I got down to the business of reviewing the previous week. School was seemingly going well for her. Tiana and her grades were as strong and steady as was the norm. She was looking forward to Christmas break if only for the school closing. She was nervous of the emotional effect that the holidays would bring but that was only a small part of Tiana's concerns.

"Ms. Austin, I think that Thanksgiving is going to be hard for MaDear cause she usually has a big family dinner and invites family from all over. I mean even family that we haven't seen all year long. She's tells us over and over for days how she's thankful she has us so close to her. That she is thankful for living long enough to see her grandbabies grow up. Now I wonder what she is going to be thankful for. It can't be the loss of Kieron cause that's not nothing to be thankful for. But I am curious to see what she'll say this year. I just hope she don't lose it, you know, cause I won't know what to do." Tiana shared.

"Well Tiana, I can think of a few things for her and even for yourself to be thankful for. One being that you still have each other. Another being that you were blessed to have loved and been loved by someone as special as Kieron. You had many good years with Kieron and made many extraordinary memories. Then, there's the fact that the both of you have a brand new guardian angel working on your behalf."

"Yeah, but I much rather have him here right now. Shoot, the few years he had living wasn't hardly enough and can't nobody make me believe that they were. MaDear may feel differently but that is how I feel." She paused momentarily and rubbed a bit of wetness from her eyes.

"But I think that I'll get through Thanksgiving better than MaDear. It's Christmas that's going to be the toughest for me. Kieron and I loved Christmas even when we were with our momma. We never got much of nothing but we could always count on getting something. You see, we always exchanged gifts with each other even if it was just a bag of candy or something we made. We always gave each other a gift. That's something I been able to count on as long as I can remember and now I don't have that anymore. Yeah, I know that I have other stuff I can count on but it's not the same. I don't know what I'm going to do, cause I know it's going to be hard. I've been dreaming about it. Dreams about Kieron and me putting tinsel on the tree and lights in the windows."

The dream comment alarmed me. Tiana had never mentioned anything of dreaming about Kieron. I wondered how long she'd been dreaming about him and what the dreams had been about.

"Tiana do you dream about Kieron often?" I questioned. I knew instantaneously that I had hit a sensitive spot. Tiana started playing with her Pocahontas plaits and biting her top lip. It wasn't clear why she was nervous but I was hopeful that it would come to light momentarily. My only fear was that Tiana had been suffering through horrible nightmares all alone. I would have had a hard time dealing with the fact that I had not been sensitive and perceptive enough to pick up on her distress.

"Well, I don't dream about him every night but I do have dreams about him kinda a lot." She finally responded.

"What is kind of a lot?"

"About two or three times a week."

"What are the dreams usually about?"

"I don't know. Different things I guess. Sometimes I dream about us playing when we were little. Sometimes I dream about him hooping at the old YMCA. The one that I have the most is the one where I'm sitting in my room working on the computer and listening to The O'Jays. The room is a little cloudy like somebody turned on one of those fog machines or something. Kieron comes into the room and he's looking good. He has on nice baggy white jeans and a thick fluffy white sweatshirt. He sits down on my bed. I look back at him but I don't say anything. He smiles at me, lays down on the bed, and continues to watch me. I keep typing on the computer, but I don't know what I'm typing. I can see Kieron smiling at me in the computer monitor, you know, like a reflection. I start smiling back at him and then I save whatever it is that I'm doing and stand up to go over to him. When I turn around he's not on the bed and I see him standing by the door. I follow him out into the hallway and I realize that it's not our apartment but it feels like some place I'm used to. So we go down the hall into a huge kitchen. It has a big stove, big shiny sink, long countertops, and choke cabinets. I mean the place is sweet. There's even a dishwasher. MaDear is over at the stove and she's pulling a cake or pie or cornbread or something out of the oven. When she stands up, she sees us standing in the doorway and starts smiling and laughing but I don't hear nothing. I think I can still hear the music that was playing in my room but it's not loud or nothing. Kieron walks into the room and stands by the table and he's like smiling. I'm still standing in the doorway and I want to go over and give him a hug. But when I start walking toward him, he smiles at me and walks out the back door that's on the other side of the kitchen. Sometimes he winks at me. But he always goes out that door. I don't ever remember the door being there when we get to the kitchen. It just appears. Every time it just appears. The first time I had the dream, I woke up scared and crying but now I just wake up when he leaves out that door. I'm not scared when I wake up so I can't call it a nightmare. I think that sometimes I'm kinda glad when I have the dream. I don't know what it means but it's like I like being able to see him again. He looks all happy and stuff and I like that. That's the dream I have the most."

"How long have you been having these dreams, Tiana?" I questioned wondering why she hadn't mentioned them in previous sessions.

"I don't know. I guess they started about a week after he died. Look, it's no big deal, Ms. Austin. They don't scare me or nothing. They kinda make me a little sad because I miss him, but I'll take what I can get."

I had to admit that she hadn't been looking abnormally sad during the sessions since Kieron's death. Still there was much concern on my part of why Tiana hadn't mentioned the dreams. I needed her to be open in all aspects, especially during this time of grieving.

"Well, Tiana, I wish you had told me about these dreams when they began. I want you to know that you can talk to me about anything regardless of how mediocre it may seem at the time. Do you have any questions about the dreams? I'm not a dream analyst but I can offer my opinion."

"No, not really. Well...do you think that the dreams may stop at sometime?" she asked

"I suppose that they might. What will probably happen is that you may start to have them less often and then maybe not at all. But it could be that you will have them from time to time for a very long time. Does that scare you? Do you want them to stop?"

"Not right now. It's all I have of him. I don't know what I would do if they stop, maybe it won't bother me at all."

"Or it may be that if they do stop, it's because you don't need the dreams anymore. But Tiana, I don't want you to think that the dreams are all you have left of Kieron because that's not true. You have a heart and mind full of him that you can recall upon will, forever. Kieron will always be with you."

"Yeah, you're right. Well, it's about that time, Ms. Austin. I don't want to keep Kaiewa waiting any longer and MaDear will surely be waiting for me."

"Okay, but I wanted to ask you about your little friend. I guess you two are getting pretty tight, huh?" I questioned her with a smile.

"Aw come on Ms. Austin. I told you about him already. He's not my boyfriend, not really. I mean I like him but it's not anything serious. Besides, he's not trying to have a serious girlfriend until after high school. So, you can just quit it. Okay?" Tiana was smiling and had a little blushing going on.

"Okay, okay. That's just fine little Miss Tiana. I guess we will wrap this session up. For this week's journal assignment I want you to focus on telling me about your dreams, the ones you have at night, the ones you have for yourself, and the ones you have for anyone else."

Trayu called me on the cell on my way home. I'd talked to him everyday since he left Atlanta and it felt good. He wasn't pushing the intimate issue at all and that felt even better. The most he had ever said in that regard was to call me sweet lips once or twice. Don't get me wrong, I was thinking about it a lot but I wasn't going to bring it up either. Even though I had the notion that being with Trayu would be amazing, I was not putting my heart out there to find out. Tray was holding the role of interesting new friend and that was sufficient. That is it was enough for Tray and myself, but Corie was another story completely.

Corie started the night I put Tray on the plane heading home. She called as soon as I got in from the airport.

"Who was that exquisite specimen with you today and where have you been hiding him? Give me the details. I can not believe that you haven't mentioned him. Girl, he is drop dead gorgeous! Come on now, give it up!"

Corie was stoked albeit unnecessarily.

"Corie, calm down it's not what you think. We are not together, I mean that we are just friends. I am not dating or sleeping with him. Just friends, understand, we are just friends. So just calm down."

"Oh come on Rhap, I know that you are not gonna let him get away. What's up with that? Is he married or something? I know that he is not gay cause my gaydar is always activated and he has the stamp of approval. So what's up?"

Corie was not going to let this go so I gave in. I told her when and how Tray and I met. She was a little pissed that I'd left him out of my earlier recap of my Chi-town trip. I gave her the rundown on his weekend visit but conveniently left out any hint of the lip action that took place. Corie couldn't have handled it. Well, actually it was because I couldn't have handled Corie's reaction to it. She would have eaten it up and then threw it back up in my face over and over again. After telling her about Tray's visit I told her about Paully's upcoming visit. That totally took her mind off of Tray. She wanted to know about everything we had planned for the weekend and wanted to be included as much as her schedule allowed. Although Paully and I had not made any specific plans I promised Corie that we would keep her abreast of any happenings.

# 16

The Friday Paully was due to fly in, I was suddenly bombarded with extra things to do. Initially I had planned on cleaning the house, doing some grocery shopping, and stopping by the office to finish typing some reports and session outlines. The final chore before picking Paully up at the airport was to see Montana for my monthly touch-up. As it turned out, my well laid plan experienced alterations from the time my alarm went off that morning. First, I decided to do my grocery shopping first and locked my keys in the car in the store parking lot. I had to take a taxi to Corie's, with groceries in tow, to wake her up because as I said before she doesn't roll out of the bed until noon and therefore doesn't answer her phone before her first cup of coffee. After beating on her door for fifteen minutes, she woke up, was able to locate my spare house keys and drive me home to get my spare car keys. I get back home and realize that when I dropped off my groceries earlier I didn't think to tell Corie to put the perishables in the refrigerator while I searched for my car keys. I had a tabletop and floor smeared with Breyers vanilla bean and rainbow sherbet. I cleaned that up quickly while cursing myself for being so stupid. Then deciding that the house was clean enough, I headed to my office. I settled down to wait for the computer to boot up and then realize that I'd left my briefcase at home with the files I needed. But I figured I could do the session outlines and get over to Montana's early. Nope. Didn't happen. Fifteen minutes into my work flow, Montana called and asked if I could come right away. The HVAC was down at the shop and she'd found a guy to come out and fix it that evening. This meant the electricity would have to be cut off while he worked and of course she needed to have it fixed tonight so that her busiest day of the week would not be affected.

As luck would have it, it took twice as long to get my hair done because she was squeezing me and several others in between other clients. To top it off I ran into major traffic on my way to the airport due to a four car accident on I-285. Fortunately, listening to John Tesh while working my way through traffic was enough to calm my nerves some by the time I arrived at the airport. Paully's friendly face did the rest. We stopped at Applebees for a little dinner and cruised back to my place. Paully wanted to take a shower so that he could relax, I decided to do the same. The shower did a job on me and I ended up falling asleep somewhere between slipping into a night shirt and lotioning my legs. Paully came in and tried to wake me to watch a movie. I convinced him to just watch the movie in my room so I wouldn't have to move. I can only assume that he saw some of the movie because the next thing I remember is waking to go to the bathroom and finding myself wrapped in Paully's arms in the spoon position. I paid my water bill and slid back into bed under the comforter trying not to wake Paully. He looked so cute lying there with his mouth partially open and snoring lightly. It felt good to have my best friend so near once again. At some point during the night Paully got under the comforter and I found my way into his arms again. I woke up as Paully was getting out of bed and he gently kissed me on my forehead and told me to go back to sleep. I found myself hoping that he didn't go to the guestroom to finish out the night. It felt nice having Paully hold me. Paully has always been a source of unique comfort to me, a warm sense of safety that can't easily be described and I had to admit that I was missing that of late.

Paully did return to my bed, placed my head against his shoulder, and stroked it until I drifted back to sleep. The next day Paully treated me like a little princess. He woke me with a cup of English Breakfast tea and cooked breakfast while I showered and dressed. Paully wanted to go see Marcus, a barber who apparently gave him the best cut he'd ever had the time he came for Freaknik, although it didn't look like he needed a haircut. After the barbershop we went shoe shopping at the designer outlet. Paully bought four pair of shoes and a pair of boots and even treated me to a pair of Joan and David loafers. We stopped for a little Thai before heading back to my place. Paully unpacked his bag and then we decided to go catch a movie. The topic of Tray's visit didn't come up until after the movie as we were sitting in Kilgore's Sports Bar eating buffalo wings and onion rings.

"So you haven't given many details about your jail bait's visit last week. I figure that either the visit was a big disappointment or that you don't want me to know about what really went on that weekend. So what's up, Rhap." Paully questioned without making eye contact.

"Well, considering how our conversations about Trayu have gone I figured that it was best not to bring him up to you. Paully, I don't like it when we argue especially about something so insignificant. But I can assure you that I am not hiding anything from you. There's nothing to hide."

Paully was looking at me now and I could see the gentleness begin to sparkle in his eyes. He was taking every word from my mouth straight to his heart.

"True that. But look, I don't have anything against the dude. I'm just looking out for you, you know."

"Yeah, I know and I do appreciate it, but you have been kind of brutal with the whole Trayu thing. You know that I'm not going to put myself in harms way…not after what I've been through."

"But that doesn't stop me from worrying. Look, I will try to do better so go ahead…tell me what happened with youngblood."

I had to think about it for a moment. I wasn't sure if Paully could be unbiased when it came to Trayu. I couldn't figure out what it was that set him off about him from jump street. But he was my best friend and if I couldn't talk to him then who could I talk to. So I gave Paully a general run down on my weekend with Tray. As with Corie, I left out the kissy-kissy part. It didn't fly with Paully.

"So you guys didn't get busy, huh?" he asked.

"Come on now, you know I don't give it up to just anybody." I smiled slyly.

"But you let him spend the night at your place and I would have to say that that wasn't very wise. You don't really know him."

"True. But I felt safe and he never entered my bedroom other than the house tour. He was the perfect gentleman the entire weekend. I think that you two would get along well if you took the time to get to know him. He reminds me of you in a lot of ways."

"Is that so? Whatever, let's get back to you. Did you kiss him?"

Damn where did that come from? Paully was freaking me out. Did he have my mind bugged for surveillance purposes?

"Well, yes...he did kiss me. But it was no big deal."

"So the little gentleman kissed you. Did you kiss him back or did he peck you on the cheek or something?"

"No, it was mouth to mouth and yes I kissed him back. Look, you need to stop tripping." I laughed.

Paully was smiling but I could see that he wasn't pleased.

"Was there any groping or grinding with that innocent little kiss?" he asked.

"No Paully, there was not. That's enough about that. You have the whole shebang. Let's move on to something else." I was actually pleading because I didn't like the feel of the conversation. Fortunately, the highlights from the Falcon's game caused an uproar of the bar patron's and gave me the distraction I needed.

As we were getting up from our table to leave, the evening took a turn for the worst. I spotted Karl coming into the bar. He was alone and looking absolutely scrumptious. I can still see him strutting in wearing a pair of baggy Girbaud jeans, carmel sweater, Allen-Edmond moccasin loafers, and three-quarter length suede jacket. There was nothing I could do to avoid him other than hope beyond hope that he would not notice me. Paully picked up on my distress and asked what was wrong. I just picked up my purse and urged him to get going. Luck was not on my side because Karl spotted me an instant later. He was just sitting down at the bar, shrugging off his jacket when his eyes met mine. I looked straight at him and kept walking. But he wasn't going to let me off so easily.

"Rhap. Hey, how are you?" Karl called to me as Paully and I passed him.

I gave him a slight nod and a soft, "Hi."

Paully looked at me and then at Karl and back to me again. I started shivering ever so slightly. Paully put his arm around my shoulder and hurried out of the bar. When we were down the street from the bar, he asked if that was Karl. I nodded silently as I felt tears join the shivers wrecking my body. Paully pulled me into a tight embrace. He did not ask anymore questions or make any comments the entire ride home, which suited me fine.

Back at my place I showered and let my tears swirl down the drain. Paully was sitting on the leather chaise in the corner of my room, when I came out of the shower. He was bare chested, wearing pajama bottoms and holding two chilled glasses of white zinfandel. I sat on the bed and told him that I was cool and he could go on and go to bed. Paully instead came over and sat down beside me and placed a glass in my hand. I thanked him and took a sip. The wine tasted awful against the lingering taste of tooth paste.

"Was that the first time you've seen him since you busted him out?"

"Yup."

"Are you sure you're okay? That had to be hard, no matter what you say."

"Well, it didn't feel good but I'll get over it. Shoot, I'm already getting over him. This was just a minor set back." I explained as tears unexpectedly welled up again.

Paully pulled me into his arms and cradled my head under his chin. I didn't cry much now because like I said, I was already getting over Karl. But the next thing I knew I was kissing Paully. Wait…actually Paully started the kiss but I reciprocated. It was tender and warm but grew hotter and stronger rather quickly. Soon I was lying under Paully's weight grasping the muscles pulsating in his back. Factly, my body picked up on all the pertinent muscles of his body. I hadn't kissed Paully since we were nine years old, but the man kissing me had much more than nine years of experience. Paully rolled me on top of him and my pajama top rolled up to my ribcage. His kiss intensified as did my body temperature and breathing. Paully was holding my body tight to his with one hand place on my back and caressingly holding the back of my head with the other. He moaned. It was one of those sensual moans that comes from deep within. I felt it tickling up through his chest more than I heard it. I took a few seconds to run my tongue over his lips tasting a hint of sweet zinfandel. Then he took both hands and slowly made circles on my back before sliding them into my satin shorts. That little action was enough to wake me up. I placed my hands on Paully's chest and pushed away from the kiss.

"Paully, we can't do this. I can't do this." I said as I rolled over and off the bed. Paully came up behind me moments later.

"You're right, we can't do this and we won't do this." He whispered into my ear. "Look, I'm going to go to bed and we'll talk in the morning."

I didn't respond or turn around until I heard my bedroom door close. Then I hurried under my comforter and willed myself asleep. I did not want to think about what had just happened with Paully or about seeing Karl.

The next morning Paully was up early, how early I don't know. I was awakened at 6:15 by the robust aroma of brewing Hawaiian Kona coffee. I joined Paully in the kitchen after brushing my teeth. It was hard to tell where his head was because he wore the same tender smile I've known for years. I returned his good morning, slipped a mug out of the cabinet, and began preparing my morning java.

"I have a bagel in the toaster. Do you want one?" Paully asked.

"Sure, that would be great."

As we sat down to our bagels and guava jam, Paully started the ever dreaded conversation.

"Look Rhap, I'm sorry about last night. I didn't plan on things turning out like that."

"Hey, it's cool." I interrupted.

"No...look...I'm not saying that I didn't want it to happen. I'm just saying that I don't think that last night was the right time considering what you had just been through seeing Karl and all. Your emotions were cross-wired and I should have been more aware of that. It felt good having you in my arms and I don't regret that at all. The thing is that I love you and your well-being is my foremost concern and I want to make sure that you're okay emotionally before anything else happens...you know...between us."

I couldn't figure out what to say in response when he stopped talking. Shit, I couldn't figure out what in the world he was talking about. Was he saying that he wanted to be with me? He wanted us to be a couple? Me and Paully? Ohhh, that was way too much to comprehend. But I needed to say something and whatever it was it couldn't be offensive to Paully.

"I know. I've come a little ways but I realized last night that I have a long way to go in stabilizing my romantic emotional plane. And I also don't feel qualified to consider or discuss any romantic issues at this point." I looked up at Paully and continued. "So Paully, please, let's just forget about last night and move on. We only have one day left of your visit and I just want to enjoy having my best bud right here by my side. Okay?"

Paully looked at me sideways through squinted eyes. I was worried momentarily until I finally saw a smile creeping across his face.

"Okay Baby Girl, I think I can do that. So what do you want to do today."

We spent the rest of the day in total bliss doing what we do best, just hanging out. We went by Corie's and had an exotic brunch. The three of us hit the bowling alley for three or four games. I thought that Corie was catering to Paully a bit much at brunch, with her constantly checking to see if he needed anything or had enough or if everything tasted okay. But Corie took it to another level at the bowling lanes. Paully received a giant hug each time Corie rolled a strike or picked up a spare, where as I received a simple high five. The girl was sickening. She might as well have rammed her tongue down his throat, that way I would have been spared the torture of watching her throw herself all over him.

The only relief was that Paully did not seem to be enjoying it. He kept giving me the "HELP ME" look, which I only laughed at. After bowling we made a stop at Koffe Kafe for lattes and sandwiches. Corie suggested that we go listen to some jazz or go do a little dancing, but Paully quickly claimed fatigue and a backache from whipping us in bowling. When I dropped Corie off she made me promise to give Paully her home and cell number before he left for Chicago. I laughed so hard once back in the car at the look of relief on Paully's face.

"Come on, Paully, it was not that bad. Corie's beautiful, kind, and intelligent. She's better than a lot of the other women you've been with, including Tanya."

"You're right. Man, I used to think that I was feeling her, but dang that girl was all over me. It felt like I couldn't breathe. Can you imagine what I would be in for if I put my mandingo magic on her? Oh no, I'm not...I repeat...I'm not going out like that and I don't care how fine she is. So you need to hip your girl."

I laughed even harder.

"Should I hip her up before or after I give you her digits. Cuz I'm going to give them to you because I promised her that I would. My word is my bond brother, my word is my bond." I said between giggles.

"Fine, give them to me. I ain't gonna use them and I mean that." He pouted.

This time I had to pull over because I could not see through my laughter generated tears.

Paully and I did not dare discuss what happened the night before. It was like we both knew that the only way that we could really get past this was to treat it like an unremarkable moment in a lifelong friendship. We'd been through worse and we'd always landed on our feet. Paully did sleep in my bed that night but only because we fell asleep watching Sunset Boulevard. Monday morning I drove Paully to the airport to catch the redeye. On the way home I kept mulling over what Paully said, that morning after, in the kitchen about not being sorry about what happened only sorry about when it happened. I convinced myself that I was just reading too much into what he said and decided that it really didn't matter much.

# 17

My next teen group meeting was truly inspirational. We started the session, as I promised, by letting them finish their journalling. Then, I allowed some time for sharing and they were totally into it. The most impressive statement came from Willie.

"I think that you can feel like someone has died when they leave. I mean like abandon you." He commented.

That was enough to trigger several peer responses, so many that I lost track of who was saying what.

"No, it's not the same because the person is still living somewhere, just not with you."

"Yeah, and you never know, they might come home or you could run into them one day."

"Aw come on, if someone walked out on you and left you to make do how ever you can, then they ain't coming back."

"I know, right, and they gonna make sure that you don't see them."

"But sometimes people get confused and they have to leave to get their shit...um I mean stuff...together. And when they do they may come back and try to make things right and you got to give them a chance."

"Yeah, but that don't mean that you can't feel just like they're dead."

"Yo, it may be better just to think of them as dead. If they ain't in your life then they are dead. And ain't no reason for you to feel nothing for 'em."

Then Tiana, to my surprise, chimed in.

"Yeah, but it's not the same as losing someone by dying. Even if someone abandons you and you just think of them as dead, there is always a part of you that knows they are living somewhere. A part of you continues to hope that they can get themselves together and come home. And as long as you have the hope in you, they ain't dead and you can't really feel the pain. You know, you can't grieve."

I chose that moment to interject.

"I am impressed by the comments you guys are making. It's good to hear you sharing and listening to your peer's thoughts. It's important to remember that everyone's feelings are real and just as important as your thoughts and feelings. And when we take the time to listen to others, we never know what we can learn. For example, I can see how one would want to pretend that a person, that has abandoned them, is dead. Not that I personally agree with this chain of thought, but I agree that there are different ways of coping with loss, whether it is by abandonment or by death. And I am a believer in doing whatever it is that you need to do to deal with the pain within and continue to lead a prosperous life, as long as it's healthy. For instance, drugs, alcohol, and violence are not healthy ways of dealing with emotional trauma and stress. And I know that both children and adults have made the mistake of taking such routes, in the desperate search to relieve their pain. But it's not acceptable or appropriate nor does it work."

Shyly, Tiana asked.

"So what are we suppose to do?"

I was stumped for a moment. Tiana looked so sad all of a sudden. I would never have imagined that T would have thought about doing drugs or resorting to violent behavior in dealing with Kieron's death. But I needed to say something.

"Tiana poses a good question." I said to the group. "And I don't have a nice gift wrapped answer to that question, because everyone is different. We deal with things in different ways. We feel at different levels. We hurt at different depths. The one thing that I do know is that falling into self-destructing behaviors will only mask the pain, not heal it. There are many more positive paths that lead to healing and growing. And that's what we are looking for when we lose someone special, whether by death or abandonment."

I looked over at Tiana and she acknowledged me with a slight nod of the head and averted her gaze downward.

An extended moment of silence followed and I took that opportunity to guide the group into the journalling part of the session. They were to brainstorm acceptable ways of dealing with loss or abandonment. Once the kids were engaged, I proceeded with the ritual of completing my personal notes on the session. Tiana's comment hung on the edges of my thoughts like the last autumn leaf on an old oak tree.

After covering the basic notes and questions, I rose from my seat to prepare the little surprise I had for the group. The week before, I decided to start a new group tradition to celebrate the birthdays of the group members monthly. I wouldn't do anything extravagant, just some cupcakes for the group and leather bound journals for the birthday people.

"Okay guys, take the next two minutes to finish your last thought and put your journals away." I instructed as I set the timer on my desk.

Tiana noticed the treat first. "I smell chocolate cake." She announced.

"Well actually it's red velvet. And since Tiana has alerted everyone, we might as well get started." I responded.

Everyone's eyes were instantly trained on me with a questioning glare.

"Oh stop it with the looks!" Here's the deal. Rita and Evan have birthdays this month and I baked a little treat in celebration of that. And every month, from now on, we will celebrate the birthdays of the month. Is that okay with everyone?"

After an unanimous approval, we sang a sorry happy birthday and grubbed on some red velvet cupcakes with chocolate icing. I had to admit that I put my foot into those cupcakes.

Tiana offered to help me tidy up after our celebration and I welcomed the help. That's when she informed me that Kaiewa was waiting for her in the building's lobby. Once again, he had escorted her to her session. I told her to go down and get him and that I would drop them off when we were done. And of course, Kaiewa was gracious and cooperative. Every moment I spent in his company made me like him even more. On the drive to Tiana's, Kaiewa informed me that he had recently taken an interest in Lloyd Wright, an architect with amazing historical sites throughout the world. Kaiewa now had two passions, writing and mechanical drawing, and had hopes of traveling to France and Rome to see the astonishing structures there. I couldn't help thinking at the time that Kaiewa himself was pretty astonishing.

I didn't notice Kieron's friend Meek standing out in front of Tiana's building. But as Tiana was climbing from the front passenger seat of my car, he started walking over toward her with a smile. His smile faded quickly when he noticed Kaiewa sliding out of the back seat. He stopped about three yards from the car and stared at Tiana and Kaiewa.

"Where y'all coming from?" he questioned coarsely.

Tiana looked at Kaiewa and then back to Meek before she responded.

"I'm coming from my meeting with Ms. Austin", as she turned her head to glance at me. "And she gave me a ride home."

Tiana was looking slightly uncomfortable and that concerned me, so I put the car in park in order to wait the situation out.

"So what is he doing with you if you are coming from *your* meeting? Meek questioned.

"Meek, what's up with you and the forty questions? I don't have time for this."

Now, Tiana looked more annoyed than nervous. The three of them stood there for a moment and traded glances with each other. Finally, they seemed to notice that I was waiting and watching them and the three of them turned their attention to me. I smiled a curt and cutsy smile, gave them a little finger wiggle wave, and rested my head against the headrest. I wasn't going anywhere until Tiana was safely in the house and I wanted to make that clear. Kaiewa broke the silence first.

"Hey Tiana, let me walk you to your door and I'll get out of here." He said.

They started walking towards the building and Meek fell in step right behind them. I yelled out the window to Tiana.

"T, page me later and tell MaDear I'm going to give her a call."

Tiana turned, said okay, and gave me a wink. She knew that I was telling her that I was going to call and get the 411 on the situation. I waited until they were inside the building, moved down about seven parking spaces, and waited until I saw Kaiewa leave Tiana's building. Meek was still inside but I could leave because somehow I knew that Kaiewa would not leave Tiana until he felt that she was safe. By the time I made it home, Tiana had called left a message saying that all was cool.

# 18

Paully finally called two days after he returned home from his Atlanta trip. I'd surprised and scared myself with the feelings that had arisen inside of me during those two days. When I put him on the plane, I was somewhat relieved to not have to worry about whether or not Paully would bring up that love clumsy night. On the first day after, I was still hoping he would not call. I even left the house for a late work out at the fitness center right around the time Paully got off work. You see, I figured that if he called, he would get the answering machine and leave a message. Then, I could return his call at my emotional convenience. But by that Wednesday, I felt like a woman waiting for a call from a potential beau after their first date. Now of course I knew better. Paully and I already had a relationship. A very strong relationship. But we were by no means dating and he could call or not call anytime he wanted and he would still be my best bud. Still, I was very excited to finally hear from him.

"Dude, where have you been? I can't believe that you are just calling me. I put you on a plane two days ago. What happened? Did you get lost on the Kennedy coming from the airport?" I bum rushed him as soon as I answered the phone, but he only laughed me off.

"Oh you are sooo funny and you talk too much. But on the real, what's going on? You missing me or something?"

That comment made me hesitate but not for long.

"Of course I miss you, buddy. I love hanging out with you. You're my best friend, remember? But nothings going on here. I'm just treading quietly and keeping my head above water. What's happening in the Chi?" I asked.

And just that quickly, we were back in our comfort zone. Paully proceeded to tell me about his week and the latest update on his females. He was happy to have had the little get away and was hoping to plan another one soon. I told him about my week and that I was glad that he had come to visit. When I told him about Corie sending affectionate greetings to him, he started freaking out.

"Rhap, I don't want to hear anything about her. I'm not playing girl, you need to scoop your home girl on the fact that I'm not interested in her. Tell her I got back with Tanya or that I'm dating someone else. I don't care what you tell her as long as you can get her off of me." He pleaded and it was my turn to laugh.

"Tee Hee Hee, I am not going to start telling lies to her for you. And besides, once Corie picks up the scent, there's no talking to her. I can tell her that she doesn't have a chance with you but she's not going to believe me. She is going to have to hear it from the horse's mouth. In this case, that would be you, Mr. Ed."

Paully started hemming and hawing so bad that I had to ease his mind.

"Okay, okay." I said between giggles. "Just chill Paully, she's not going to bother you. If you don't call her, she will get the message. I know she came on kinda strong when you were here but she is not the type of woman to go chasing after some dude. You are a sweetie but you're definitely not worth going fatal attraction over."

"What do you mean? I'll have you know that I have had a few woman that I've had to threaten with restraining orders." He said in defense.

"Paully, baby, that's nothing to brag about and I hope you don't share that information with too many people. But for real, you don't have to worry about Corie. Now tell me about these fatal attractions you are talking about. Here I am thinking that Tanya was the only one but now you're telling me that you make a habit of finding desperate women."

"Come on now, Rhap, why do they have to be desperate? Some women have a hard time letting go of a sweet, romantic, sexy, and understanding man such as myself. That doesn't make them desperate. You know when you've had the best, it difficult to accept less. Baby girl you know I'm the cream of the crop but do you know what the real problem is? He asked.

"What?"

He took a deep breath and answered. "I need to stop giving them my heavy whipping cream and instead just feed them my 2% milk. Because they can't take my rich, sweet creaminess."

I fell out laughing! Paully was going of the deep end. I could almost see his head swelling through the telephone. He was funny, that's for sure. But all jokes aside, I wanted to hear more about the women he was speaking of. Paully and I usually talked about our relationships pretty openly, so I was curious of why I hadn't heard about the possibility of any restraining orders being needed. Who were these women and where were they now and what had Paully done to them to make them go crazy?

I knew first hand that Paully knew how to touch a woman and I had only had a small taste of his abilities. I didn't want to even imagine what he could do in the go ahead situation. He was probably sending women's libidos off the chart. But why hadn't he told me about them? I wanted to know.

"So Paully, who have you threatened with restraining orders? I don't remember hearing about any of this." I questioned.

"Aw girl, it doesn't matter. The only thing that matters is that I didn't have to do it for real."

"But who were they?" I questioned again.

"Nobody, Rhap." He laughed. "Why you sweatin' me? You know I don't kiss and tell."

Now I was getting pissed. Why was he avoiding the question? We are suppose to share everything so why couldn't he share this? And I told him just that.

"Rhap, we can discuss anything and I'm not trying to hide anything. It's just that, you know, we've had periods of time when we didn't talk. Like when we get wrapped up in work and other things. Then when we do talk I don't think about re-hashing all of my bad date experiences. We usually have more to talk about, you know." He responded.

By this time I realized that I was somewhat overreacting and decided to back off. Why was I so interested in his past lovers anyway? They really didn't matter and if they did, I'm sure Paully would tell me. Or at least I hoped he would. Even though I still had a little bit of nagging curiosity lingering in my thoughts, I let Paully change the subject. He wanted to know what I planned on doing for Thanksgiving. But I didn't have any definite answers for him. I told him that I might fly up for a couple of days if I could reschedule my standing appointments. This apparently didn't sit well with him for some reason.

"Do you think it's neccesary to reshedule your conferences just for a weekend trip? That doesn't make any sense. You rarely come home for Thanksgiving anyway because it's so close to Christmas. Why should this year be any different? Do you have some special plans or something? He questioned.

"No, I don't have any special plans and I didn't say for sure that I was coming. But what's the big deal anyway? I think going to spend time with my family is reason enough to adjust my schedule a little. Besides I work for myself and that's one of the perks. It would be nice to have my mother's cooking on Thanksgiving. I miss her oyster dressing, pumpkin pie and hummingbird cake. And you know I will find my way over to your house for your mom's homemade rolls. My salivation glands are working overtime just thinking about it. Is that okay with you?"

I wasn't sure what Paully was all worked up over, but I was determined to defuse it by keeping a level head and not buying into his vibe. It apparently worked because Paully response was gentle.

"I know what you mean. Mom doesn't make those rolls often but she puts her foot in them on every holiday. But I could have her make a batch of them and bring them to you on my next visit."

"That sounds good but I still think it would be good for me to come home for Thanksgiving. After the year I've had, two visits in two months to see my loved ones would do my heart a world of good. Besides, adjusting my schedule won't be much of a hassle. I realized then, that I had made up my mind to go home for Thanksgiving. Paully seemingly realized it too.

"If so, that's cool cuz that means I'll get to see you sooner than I expected." He commented before frazzling me with the next question.

"Do you plan on seeing young blood when you're here?"

"Probably." Was the simple answer I gave.

"Well, do you think that's a good idea?" Was his questioning response.

"What are you talking about? Do you think it's a bad idea and why?"

Paully went on to explain that he didn't think it was a good idea because whether I wanted to believe it or not, I was leading that boy on. Those were his exact words. Of course I told him that he was crazy and wrong on top of that. I was not leading Trayu on in any way. I had been brutally honest with him from day one and I had every intention to continue being truthful with him. Paully on the other hand suggested that I was not being totally truthful to myself. According to him, deep down inside, I knew that there wasn't anything of real substance between Trayu and myself. The most that we could have would be a short live trist that would end in Trayu being burned emotionally. This would happen because he was too young to offer me what is needed in a long term relationship and I would tire of immaturity. I would need more from him emotionally and financially than he could offer.

Now that statement alone turned sour in my ears. What would possess Paully to insinuate that I was looking for money. I am not that shallow. I am self-sufficient and have never looked for any man to take care of me. True, I was not looking to take care of any man either, but I don't need anyone to take care of me. Besides, Trayu did not seem to be looking for a Sugar Momma. He has his own ambitions and is well on his way to establishing a solid financial future for himself.

Paully continued his lecture by saying that I needed to rethink the whole Trayu thing since we had shared what we had during his visit. In his opinion, a new door had been opened between us and I owed it to myself to explore what was inside. Exploring our relationship should take priority to the little fling I was having with Trayu because I'd known Paully all my life.

I was not having a little fling with Tray at all and I wasn't toying with him either. I enjoyed talking, listening, and spending time with him and I believed he felt the same way. Regardless, I was not likely going to put myself in a position where I would be hurt or to hurt

Tray. That's the type of person I've always been and Paully should have known that. I didn't bother sharing my thoughts with Paully. It would have only given him more fuel to continue talking and irritating me. Instead, I faked an incoming call and ended our conversation.

Afterwards, I sat in silence and sipped on a glass of chardonnay and chambord. The only reason I could muster up of why Paully would say the things that he said was that he was jealous. Or maybe he was trying to sway me into thinking that Trayu was a waste of time in order to clear the way for himself. Perhaps Paully had some information about Trayu that he was not telling me about because it might hurt me. Either way, Paully did not have to be so harsh with his comments and I was offended by them, especially because the comments had come from him, my best friend.

Paully, I knew, had my best interest in mind. I also unwillingly admitted to myself that he might truly have romantic feelings for me. I, on the other hand, could not committ to feeling anything more than the well formed and founded love Paully and I have shared since childhood. True, I kissed him back when he kissed me. True, his touch had made my temperature rise. True, it felt like our bodies fit together like ying and yang. All of it was true, but that was only one night. One sorted evening. A mere thirty minutes out our decades strengthened friendship. It was one night and everyone knows that anything can happen at least once, but it doesn't have to continue or last.

Could a romantic relationship last between Pauly and I? Many believe in the strength of lovers and friends. The problem was that I was not sure that Paully and I are suppose to be anything more than friends.

Paully of all people knew what to say and or do to make me feel special, appreciated, worthwhile,…just loved. In my heart there was the deepest fear that putting our relationship on a more intimate plane could destroy what we already possessed. It could be good for awhile, but if the relationship turned sour, we may never get back the simple and true thing we have always had. At the current time, Paully's friendship meant more to me than a short term romance. And unfortunately, that was all it would probably be. We knew each other too well and the games that he plays with his women would not fly with me. I would not tolerate being treated as a sidekick, who was on call for when Paully wanted to hang out.

# 19

Mrs. Menden called early on Saturday morning, just shortly after I returned from my 8:00 a.m. water aerobics class at the fitness center. My mood was light and energetic as I prepared for my shower by searching for my Erasure The Innocence cd. When I saw her name on the caller ID, I said a quick little prayer that she wouldn't be bringin' me no bad news. Things had been relatively quiet and steady for the last few weeks and I liked it that way.

My prayers were somewhat answered, as she only wanted to ask a small favor. Well, not actually small, but not too huge. She had spoken with Ms. Kendrell, Meeks aunt, and wanted to know if I were taking new clients.

"Ms. Austin, you see, she's a bit worried about Lil' Meek. He's a sweet boy and very manageable. He really don't give her any problems and he treats her with the highest respect. But she seems to think he's not handling Kieron's death too good. You know they was best friends. They was just like brothers, yes they was. Any who, she said that Meek asked her about seeing Tiana's doctor and that made her a little scared like maybe he was loosing his mind or something. Meek told her that he was still angry and sad about Kieron and that Tiana seemed to be much better. He said it's because she has you to talk to. Ms. Austin, you know I believe that too because you done helped both my babies so much I can't explain. You know I appreciate you, right?"

"Yes ma'am, I do." I replied.

"Well I sure do. You are an angel and I know it in my heart. But here's the thing, baby. I know that she don't have much money, cuz she raisin' that teenager. And I know you got to make your money and you can't do that if you see all your clients for free. And I know I'm asking a whole lot but I gotta ask. That's what my heart is leading me to do, so I'ma do it." There was a short pause before she continued in which I could hear Mrs. Menden fill her lungs with air and slowly release it through her mouth.

"Ms. Austin, can you meet with Meek and his aunt. At least a couple of times just to see if there is anything you can help him with?"

I was able to respond relatively quickly due to the fact that Tiana had previously mentioned Meek's interest in meeting with me. Consequentially, I had already decided that seeing Meek could be beneficial. It could also help me understand the situation Tiana was involved in with him.

"I believe I can arrange to meet with them, Mrs. Menden."

"But I'm not finished, dear. I don't want to ask you to do it for free, but I know that girl don't have much money at all. So do you think you can find it in that kind heart of yours to give her a discount price or something?"

MaDear was right. I could not run my business productively by offering free services to everyone. It's not that I'm a money hungry, over achieving, looking for love in all the wrong places old spinster, but I do have to make a living by which my bills can be paid. Yet I knew that whenever the need arose I would make a way to provide for those in need.

"Look Mrs. Menden, don't worry about it." I reassured her. Just give her my number and I'll make it happen. Now Mrs. Menden, let's keep this quiet, because I don't want everyone thinking that I'm giving away my expertise. This for you because you're my special MaDear. So keep smiling and make sure my little girl is on time for her appointment this week. Okay?"

"Okay", she responded in a sweet grandmotherly voice. "Oh, and I'll have Ms. Kendrell call you and you see what you can do. Bye baby."

After hanging up with Mrs. Menden, I felt a strong desire to do some personal housekeeping. Beginning with my bedroom, I cleaned the upstairs and the bathrooms. Next, I retreated to my study and proceded with the financial review. Paid the bills, balanced the checkbook, checked and calculated stock exchanges, and readjusted my income tax account. Finally, I outlined my vacation budget for the end of the year. Two trips to Chicago and a quick weekend trip to

Buford, South Carolina for a wedding were already budgeted and paid in full. I would need to shop for a few new outfits and a wedding gift. Christmas shopping would easily be covered by my Christmas Savings account. I'd developed a system of standardized gift giving in which groups of individuals received the same type of gift. Most often adults received gift certificates to department stores, muti-media stores or hotels. There was nothing like a night away from home in a luxury hotel. The children usually received gift cetificates for toy stores, bookstores, or restaurants. This year the adults would be receiving Norstrom gift cards and the children would be shopping at Borders for books and music. The few exceptions every year are my parents, brother, and my significant others. This year my parents and brother would be cruising the West Carribean in June with me in tow.

The significant other, this year was a more complicated matter. Disturbingly, Karl was the first person to come to mind. It wasn't really surprising since up until recently he was "The One" in my eyes. Still, I was taken back that thoughts of him were still lingering in my subconcious. One would think that Trayu or Paully would be the foremost men on my mind. I had spent senuous evenings with both of them and had been in semi-daily contact. So logically one of the two should be my man of the season so to speak. But that brought about another dilemma. Which one should it be? Trayu was totally darling and a breath of fresh air in my life, but Paully was my best friend and someone that I've always been comfortable with. I love Paully and would do just about anything for him, whereas I didn't think that what I felt for Trayu was love. I wasn't in love with Tray but I didn't honestly think that I was in love with Paully either. I questioned myself as to whether or not I needed to make a decision on where to focus my romantic energy. My head started a dull throbbing and that's when I made the best decision of the day to stop thinking about the two special men in my life.

# 20

Imet with Meek and his aunt the following Tuesday morning at 8:30a.m. Posting such an early time would prevent Ms. Kendrell from missing any time from work and Meek from missing any of his academic classes. I'm usually up and moving pretty early during the week, so I didn't mind the early morning meeting at all. I easily worked in a 30 minute treadmill run, a 15 minute cool down on the Lifecylce, and a cup of Chai tea before heading to the office.

They were punctual and nervous. Meek seemed determinded to avoid eye contact with me at all cost. He either looked down at his gray Timberlands or into his aunt's soft slender face, when speaking or answering. Meek's aunt's anxiety was exhibited through the constant licking of her lips and twisting of the large cubic zirconia pinky ring on her left hand.

After we stumbled through introductions, we moved over to my desk area. Generally, my pre-consults were held in a formal manner. I always position myself behind my desk with potential clients in the leather arm chairs in front of my desk. If the people can be comfortable enough in my formal discussion format then I've found that they open up easier when we start regular sessions. Regular sessions are usually held in the conversation nook with the comfortable chairs.

As I mentioned, they both looked considerably uneasy, so much so that it started to rub off on me. I dismissed the uncomfortable feeling the best way I knew how, by asking questions of the one making me feel uneasy. The first few questions were directed to Ms. Kendrell. They were fashioned to learn, from her, the reasons she was seeking help for Meek. She quietly responded that she was concerned with his overwhelming sadness.

"Meek has always been somewhat quiet. He was really a shy boy when he was younger. When he and Kieron became friends he started opening up more but he was still kinda quiet and shy. But now it's different. Since…uhm…since we lost Kieron he's not just quiet. He seems so, so, so sad. I mean I can see the sadness in his eyes and I hear it in his voice. Sometimes I see him sitting on the front steps or in front of the t.v. and he looks like he's in another world. That's when he looks the saddest." She responded while looking at Meek the whole time. She turned her focus to me when she continued.

"I ask him what's wrong and try to get him to talk to me but he always says the same thing. Nothing's wrong and he's fine. But it's not getting better and I finally broke down.…I didn't mean to cry but I am just scared.…I don't know what's going on and he won't tell me.…And he's my child…My heart." She paused as tears threatened to water her cheeks.

"But this time he at least opened up enough to tell me he wanted to talk to Tiana's doctor…you. And here we are."

Meek never truly looked up from his hands. There were just the tiniest of glances toward his Aunt while she was talking. I could tell that she meant just as much to him as he did to her. His concern for her was glimmering in his eyes. Their bond, even though they weren't mother and son, was so strong it tugged at my heart. My heart knew then I would try to help them even if my head didn't know it yet. But first I had to find out why Meek wanted to see me. Meek practically jumped out of his seat when I directed my attention towards him by calling his name. His aunt gently placed her hand on his forearm to calm him and I proceeded to ask him why he was there to see me. Surprisingly, he responded immediately although he never looked up at me directly.

"Kieron was my best friend and its' tough dealing with the fact that he is gone. I know that I'm sad and I guess I'm suppose to be sad. But sometimes I feel like I'm worst than sad. I don't know if there's a word for that but that's how I feel and I can't fix it. I've tried and I just can't shake it. But I see how Tiana is doing better than me and I know she gotta be sadder than me because Kieron was her brother and they were tight. I saw her after it happened and she was messed up, but now she's almost back to normal. Well, I don't mean normal but I can tell she's better. And I'm not. I feel the same as I did the day he died.

So I figured you could help me the way you helped her."

Meek looked like a wounded puppy trying to get his master to understand where the pain was. Now my head had caught up with my heart. I decided that I would call his aunt later that afternoon and inform her that I would take Meek on as a client. I could have told them while they were there but that's not the way I work. When I decide to accept a client, I have to sit down, analyze, and evaluate what I see as the issues and possible routes to helping them deal with them. If I can't envision the possibility of helping them, then I'm probably not the right person to help and I refer them to one of my professional associates.

Tiana was not pleased to hear that I would be meeting with Meek, although I wasn't sure why. She did not say that she did not want me to talk to him, but her mannerisms, tone, and questions made it clear that she was not comfortable with the situation.

"I thought that you were only going to meet with Meek and Ms. Kendrell that one time? She questioned.

"I don't recall saying that that was the case. It was important for me to meet with the two of them in order to see what they needed from me and if I could possibly help them. That's standard procedure in my line of work. If you think back, you will probably remember that I met with MaDear and the two of you before I started working with you and Kieron. Then I met with MaDear to clarify what was needed and what I could provide." I responded.

"Well what are you going to do to help Meek?" Tiana asked.

"Tiana you know that I cannot answer that question. First and foremost, Meek's sessions with me are confidential as are yours. Secondly, Meek's business here is just that, Meek's business. If he decides that he wants to share with you, that's also his business. But I must caution you not to ask him about his sessions with me because that is inappropriate. Just remember to respect Meek in the same way you want to be respected. Do you think you can do that?"

"I didn't say that I was going to ask him anything, Ms. Austin. And I know you're right. I just wanted to know if he said anything about me. I want to know if he plans on talking to you about me." Tiana said with concern flowing through her voice.

"Tiana, I don't know what to tell you other than the same thing that I've always assured you of. I will hold all sessions confidential unless there is a reason for me to believe that someone could possibly be in danger, at which time I will contact the necessary people. Other than that, I can speak of nothing to outsiders. Now, let's move on to another topic. Okay?" I strongly suggested.

Although Tiana obviously had more questions, she relented to my request. The conversation didn't last much longer and I was fine with that. I wasn't real sure how this situation with Meek would work out but I had committed to eight sessions and I had every intention of honoring my pledge. I secretly hoped that Meek's concerns were about himself and the healing process and not he and Tiana. An uncomfortable potential situation involving Meek and his intentions toward Tiana would put me in a strange place professionally and personally. Tiana was like a little sister to me and I wasn't sure how I would respond to Meek wanting to be Tiana's boyfriend knowing that she had no interest in him. Besides, T was too young for boyfriends especially one that was older than she. Other than that, I felt confident that I could clear up some things fogging his mind. His pain and confusion couldn't be any worse than Tiana's.

As I left my office, I decided to stop at the mall and satisfy my sugar craving with an Orange Julius. The only mall I knew of that housed an Orange Julius hotdog restaurant was a bit off my normal path in a scarestly occupied mall in the hood. The mall itself housed only one major store, Macys, a few hip hop clothing shops for the youngsters, a small music and video store, and a hair salon and barbershop. There were also a plethora of kiosks running down the center of the mall that sold a variety of products such as incense, cologne, sunglasses, cell phones, purses, t-shirts, embroided caps, and family portraits. The largest populated locations in the mall were the food court and the video game palace. As I walked past the video game palace, I suddenly thought about Tiana and Keiron. Tiana said that she was in the video game room when Kieron was shot. Then I thought. "Maybe Meek has more information about what happened that day than what he had previously revealed. Maybe that's why he's having such a hard time dealing with Kieron's death. Maybe he knows the real reason Kieron was shot that day. Maybe he knows the boy who shot him. What in the world would I do if Meek gave me some critical information on Kieron's case? I would have to report it. There's no question about that. But what if Kieron's death was caused by Meek? No, that couldn't be it because their other friend would have said something. Unless, he was upholding the code of the hood, not to be a snitch."

I snapped out of my rambling of thoughts when the young lady behind the counter asked for my order. I had to stop putting so much thought into Meek's upcoming sessions. It was important for me to stay open and let him express what he needs to express. He most likely didn't have any vital information surrounding Kieron's death, because I believe he would have divulged that information to Madear, Tiana, or his aunt by now. I would just have to see what happened when I met with Meek.

# 21

*To my lady, who makes me feel like a prince. Accept this gift and take a little time to pamper yourself, until I see you again.*

That is how the message read on the card that accompanied the gift basket delivered that afternoon. At first, I was slightly hesitant to open the card due to the phone call that came directly before the delivery. It was Karl. I was surprised to hear his voice upon answering for a couple of reasons. One being that the caller ID did not show his name or any phone number I would have associated with him. Secondly, I had not heard from him in two or more weeks. There had been no pages, no voice messages, emails, and no late night calls. I had resolved that he had finally gotten the message and settled in with Ms. Best Friend/ Lover/ Other Woman. His absence suited me just fine and I was soon hoping that his essence would no longer register in my mind or heart. I looked forward to having to be reminded of him instead of having him popping into my thoughts. He needed to become history and that was a fact. Nevertheless, there he was on the other end of my phone line.

"Hello sweetness. Wow, it is good to hear your voice. How are you, babe?"

The silkiness in his voice made me shiver and cringe simultaneously. I just stared at the phone until he spoke again. I couldn't believe this egotistical idiot. Why wouldn't he just leave me the hell alone?

"Rhap baby, are you there?" Came his obnoxious voice again. My response was meant to be just as obnoxious and stern.

"What can I help you with, Karl? In addition, I have told you not to refer to me with any of your frivolous terms of endearment. So please be humane enough to honor my wishes."

"Okay baby...Damn... I mean Rhapsody. Damn...shit girl... come on...give me a break. I'm trying to make this thing right. I don't know how we got here but I'm trying to fix it. I want to fix it."

Came his plea but I was not having any of it.

"Look Karl, you know damn well why things are the way they are and there's no need to pretend that you don't. There is nothing to fix. It's over for us. So let's not do this anymore. I'm okay…you're okay…now let's move on. Karl, I'm wishing you well. Now for the last time, leave me alone. Good bye Karl."

I ended the call with a soft voice and gentle cradling of the phone. Strategically, I left him without the opportunity for response. His annoying and pesty attempts to recapture my attention had run its course and left me with some sort of resistance factor. I still knew him and even felt him sometimes, but the sinking feeling in my gut no longer accompanied the thoughts of him. He was passing from me, though the process was slow. Therefore, when the delivery arrived, I waited until I allowed myself to relieve my bladder and grab a Cherry RC Cola from the refrigerator, before opening the box. In the box was a gift basket with a card. With a sigh, I opened the card. I breezed over the words only saying them, not ingesting their meaning. That was until I saw Trayu's name at the bottom. Then, I went back and reread the card carefully. My smile widened with each word. Upon inspection of the basket, I was amazed to see how much Tray was coming to know me. The basket contained Frango mints, Salerno butter cookies, an assortment of herbal tea bags, lemon mint bubble bath, lotion and linen spray, a gel eye mask, and a copy of Ray Charles and Betty Carter's cd". It was a basket full of many of my favorite things. It wasn't that the boy was psychic or anything. I knew how he'd known what would please me. I'd told him. I just couldn't believe that he remembered those things. Mostly, things were just mentioned somewhere in the midst of our phone conversations. And we talked pretty often. I had become to rely on Trayu's evening call to lull me to sleep. Though I had to admit that every once in a while, I would force myself to skip a day of Tray-comfort and not make or accept calls from him. On those rare occasions I had to keep myself busy with a bunch of anything I could think of. Usually I would call and catch up with my cousins, aunts, uncles and friends or I might up and clean my blinds blade by blade. On other times, I would engage in a movie marathon at one of the local movie theatres. However, no matter what I did or how much I did of it, I still tossed and turned at bedtime struggling not to pick up the phone to hear his voice. Trayu was getting under my skin and all I could do was try to maintain my composure because I liked the way he made me feel.

I called him right away but unfortunately, I was routed to his voicemail. I left a generic thank you message and requested that he call me when he got the message. I would express my thanks with more flavor when I talked to him. Why did I want to save my enthusiasm for later? Well, basically, it was because I wanted to hear the smile develop in his voice and that little rumble/chuckle he made whenever he was complimented or embarrassed. Damn! That boy was adorable. He made me shiver and made my stomach do flips.

Around seven that night, Tray called.

"Trayu, I can't believe you. The basket is beautiful! I was so surprised and extremely pleased. I know you couldn't have known this but your gift was just in time. I was in a pretty funky mood and your gesture of kindness was exactly what I needed to lift me out of my funk. What made you think of this? When did you think of this? And how did you know how to get it to me? What if I happened not to go into the office today?" I questioned.

"Come on Rhap, you go into the office everyday. I figured if I caught you early in the workday I was safe. I see I was right?" He laughed. "I'm just glad that you liked it." I'm also glad that they delivered it before noon as promised, because if they hadn't there was going to be trouble."

It was my turn to laugh. I loved the way that Trayu could make me laugh, even when laughing was the last thing I wanted to do. That was just one of the many pleasures he brought to my life. It was a great feeling and I wanted to reciprocate to the best of my ability. *To the best of my ability*, what a joke, I had no ability in the romance department. One thing I knew for sure was that Trayu was going to make it easy for me to try. That was evident by the way he drew me back to our current conversation.

"Rhapsody, my lady, I ask thee to honor me with accepting my humble gift of gratitude. And say ye that ye will allow me to be once again in your presence before the next full moon." He said in the saddest thesbian accent.

"You are so silly, it's not even funny. But I think I can grant your wish because I plan to be there for Thanksgiving. Most likely, I will be able to fit you in during my visit. I'll probably be there for a few days, but I need to give my family some attention since I missed them the last time."

Tray seemed a little disappointed in my response, stating that he'd hoped to come back to Atlanta. I told him that it wasn't a good idea because I would be extremely busy until the New Year with my clients. The holidays are highly emotional times and I usually end up increasing my daily hours and sessions per day. There was no way I would permit out of town visitors to come to spend time with me, not even family, during this time of the year. Besides, it was a real treat for me to get away for Thanksgiving and Christmas and leave all my work behind. So, I was not going to give in to Trayu's pouting. Once he realized this, he let it go and focused on setting a time that we could hang out. He wanted to plan the day for us and needed a set date and time frame. I told him that we didn't have to do anything special, I just wanted to spend a day with him. He was agreeable but I know that he was not going to let our next date be impromptu.

We spent the next hour talking each other to sleep. Tray did most of the talking. He was so excited about his upcoming apprenticeship, which would start in April. His mind was bursting with new web designs with lots of bells and whistles.

# 22

Meek's first session alone with me was an emotional rollercoaster. My initial feeling, unfortunately, was of regret because Meek kept referring every question to the topic of Tiana.

How did I think Tiana was doing? What was Tiana like right after Kieron got killed? Did she talk about Kieron a lot? Did she ever talk about him? Was I seeing both Tiana and Kaiewa? Could I make him feel better like Tiana? Could Tiana teach him what I taught her? Could he come to a session with Tiana, you know like Kieron did?

That boy had my head reeling. I kept thinking, after every Tiana question, that I'd made a mistake. Meek was more interested in getting hooked up than healing up. So I put my reroute plan into action.

"Meek, let's back up a little and clarify the guidelines for our sessions, okay?'

He nodded his response.

"Our focus is on you and what you feel that you need. When you are here with me, I am focused on you and you only. I will discuss situations involving you and others, but I will not discuss another client with you. That's confidentiality and it applies to all my clients including you. What you discuss with me here stays here. I don't even discuss it with your aunt." I explained.

"Oh, I know she ain't gonna go for that. She's cool and all but she is nosey. She gonna want to know everything, I bet." He said curtly.

"Well, your aunt knows about the confidentiality agreement and she has agreed to it. Now, it is up to you whether you discuss our sessions with your aunt. I would encourage you to share whenever you feel the need to, but I am swarn to keep privacy intact. Unless..." I paused.

"If by chance I receive information that may put you or another in danger, I am obligated to report it to someone."

"So you would snitch on me? Oh I didn't know it was like that!

Naw man, I can't do this. I think I made a mistake!" He proclaimed.

I shrugged my shoulders and maintained my serious facial expression for a few moments before I responded. "Look Meek, that's the way this works. Listen carefully to what I'm saying because I want you to be absolutely sure that you want to be here. Okay, are you ready to listen?"

Once again Meek's eyes were focused on his lap, avoiding any eye contact with me. He cracked every knuckle on both hands before he answered with a nod of the head.

"Meek, I'm here with you because you wanted someone to talk to and I agreed to do that. When I took you on as a client I pledged to do my best to help you in any way that I can. I want to help you understand what you feel and help you to deal with things in a constructive and positive manner. In order for me to do that I have to listen to you and let you express yourself in your own way. I want you to feel safe entrusting me with your feelings and emotions. I also want you to feel free to tell me anything in anyway possible, because that will help me to help you. But I am a professional and this is my career, my business, and my passion. That is why there are certain stipulations, the main ones, of which I've already expressed. I will not and cannot discuss any other client with you nor will I discuss you with any other client. And I am binded by law and my heart to report anything that could put someone in harm's way. Now hear me when I say that I want you to share anything and I mean anything that you want. And if it happens that you share something that I have to report, Meek, ninety-five percent of the time it will be because you want some help with that situation."

I glance up at the clock on the wall next to my bathroom door and continued.

"With that being said, I think you should rethink whether or not you want my help. It looks like it's time to end our session for today. Before you leave I want to give you an assignment for this week. I always give my clients a uh...I guess you would call it a homework assignment...but it's not homework really. What I want you to do is to spend sometime thinking about what types of things you want to share with me. It could be about anything or anyone. And if you can make a list, that would be great. You won't have to show the list to me because it's actually just for you. Do you think you can do that for me?"

To my surprise, Meek answered rather quickly.

"Yeah, I can do that."

"Great, and if you decide not to come back, just give me a call. Or you can have your Aunt call. Meek I really would like you to come back but it's your call. But you will have to follow my guidelines."

I couldn't tell from Meeks expression or mannerisms whether or not he would continue with his sessions. He was very sullen and never made eye contact with me, but he didn't seem angry. He slowly put on his coat and hat and left with the softest goodbye I'd ever heard. I walked him to the elevator in silence and told him to give my greetings to his aunt as he got onto the elevator. As I walked back to my office I wondered again what Meek really wanted or needed from me.

I called Corie to see if I could catch up with her and sweet talk her into having lunch with me. I hadn't seen her in weeks and I missed her all of a sudden. We usually find time to catch a meal or do a little shopping once every other week, but as I said, it had been a while since I'd seen her. It had been difficult to talk to her as well. Neither of us were really at fault. It was just that our schedules conflicted in a major way. By the time Corie rolled out of bed to start her day, I'm well into my day. Then, as I'm closing the office for the day, Corie is knee deep in food preparations and menu changes. Even her weekends had been jammed pack with private parties and other catering gigs. Her unique and tasty flare was making her name well known as the "Pretty Party Planner." I missed her but I was happy to see that she was building her clientele and making a name for herself. It was her dream and I was her girl so that meant that I would be supportive at every turn.

Corie didn't answer her home phone, so I tried her cell. She answered on the second ring with a jovial tone.

"What's up Skeezer? Where you been, girl? I miss your ass."

"Oh please, girl you don't even have time to miss me, so don't play. I was just sitting here thinking about you because I, on the other hand, truly miss you. So what's going on? Is everything cool or what?"

Corie sighed deeply before she found the breath with which to answer me.

"Everything is cool. I'm working like a hebrew slave but I'm loving it. Look girl come on down here and I promise to find the time to sit for a while. I know I can squeeze out at least an hour. I promise Rhap. Girl, I miss your crazy ass. Now come on!"

Corie was funny as all get out sometimes. She knew how to get me to do what she wanted me to do. This time was no different as I've already mentioned. I was missing her too. "Okay, Okay. Now Corie I'll be there in about an hour, so get your stuff together before I get there. I'm not going to be sitting around all afternoon waiting on you to find a few spare moments for sweet little me.

"Just come on Rhap, I got this under control. You just make sure that you're on time, because I have less time than you do for lunch, Ms. I'm My Own Boss Lady."

We both laughed and ended the call. I decided to check my messages before leaving in order to decide whether or not I would come back to the office. I did need to plan for my next anger management group but I could do that at home. I only had three messages. There was one from my mother the night before, one from her this morning and the last message was from Tiana. I didn't know how I had missed my mother's calls. She must have called both times when I was in the shower. Tiana had apparently call on my drive in, which would explain why I'd missed the call. If I'm not on the phone when I leave the house then I usually drop it in my purse. If the phone rings, it is not likely that I will hear it over my music, especially not over this morning's Bootsy Collins RubberBand Man.

Even though my mother had called twice, her standard hour long conversation, would have to wait until after lunch. So, I called Tiana back on my way to the restaurant just to make sure everything was okay with her. As it turned out, she was fine and just wanted to know if the group session was still on for the next day. That's was very promising and I had a feeling that she would be more open this time and maybe share a bit more.

Suprisingly, I found a parking space less than a block away from Corie's restaurant. I was so excited about spending a little time with my girl that I could feel the huge grin spreading across my face. My grin turned into a full fledged smile when I stepped inside the restaurant. Corie greeted me at the door and immediately escorted me to a corner booth where she had a special table setting for our lunch date. The standard white table cloth had been replaced with a black cloth overlayed with silver rectangular runner. The base plate was a square cobalt blue plate with white etchings with a white cup and saucer resting in its center. The salad and bread plate were the same color blue and the water goblets had white accented rims. The flatware was a simple stainless steel with no designs. The final touch was the center piece, which consisted of a clear water-filled glass 8 inch bowl with floating blue and yellow hibiscus tops.

"Very impressive, Corie. Did you do all this for little old me?"

Corie smiled, obviously pleased with herself.

"Do you like? I mean for real, girl."

"Absolutely, it's beautiful. Is this your creation?"

"Yup, I was thinking about using it for some of our private parties and some of my personal catering gigs. So, I thought I'd try it out on you because if your picky ass likes it, I know it'll fly with most anyone. Now come on and have a seat. I have a special menu for lunch so don't even think about asking to see a menu. You'll eat what I say and there are no substitutions." She snapped.

"Can I at least hear what we're having in case that I'm allergic to anything."

"Sure. We're having pan seared opah with a lemon tomato basil sauce, parmesan asparagus, and garlic red potato medallions. And for dessert, we have a lemon cheesecake with a graham cracker crust and a toasted pecan top."

"It sounds delicious. Let's get it on!" I responded with genuine excitement.

I had been worried about what I would say if Corie brought up Paully. I figured that she would ask me if I had really given him her number and try to speculate on why he hadn't called. Actually, I didn't know whether or not he had called her. Paully hadn't mentioned that he had but then I hadn't spent very much time engaged in long conversations with him since our last heated discussion about Trayu. Avoiding deep conversations with Paully was the best way to evade any references to our little electrifying moment. As it turned out, I was wrong. Corie had a different agenda altogether. She never mentioned Paully at all during our hour long lunch. Instead, she honed in on the other men in my life; the ex and the next as she so cleverly referred to them.

"Girl guess who was in the restaurant a couple of days ago?" she asked without waiting for a response.

"Karl, girl! Can you believe that shit? I wanted to call you as soon as I saw his trifling behind, but we were slammed. By the end of my shift, I had reasoned that me calling to tell you about him was the last thing you wanted or needed."

I replied matter of factly, "You made the right call."

"Yeah, I thought so, but check this out. He was in here with a date."

I tried to hide the jump in my chest at the mention of Karl with someone else, mainly because I hated that it was there.

"I don't know if it was the lingerie bimbo or not and he did not introduce us either." This shock I could not suppress.

"You mean you talked to him, Corie?"

"Girl yeah, see this is what happened. I always come out into the dining area to just look around and see how people are receiving my food. So what I usually do is walk from the kitchen to the matried station and back. Along the way I stop and greet two or three tables to ask how they're enjoying their meals. See, that way the patrons feel that personal touch and they get to know my face. Return business baby, return business!"

"The point please, Corie." I exasperated.

"Oh yeah, anyway, I was doing my thing and I hear someone call my name. It's Karl and he wipes his mouth, stands, and opens his arms to me. Of course I greet him cordially and I see the woman is checking me out with a fake ass grin on her face. But here's the killer, that sorry ass ex of yours has the nerve to whisper in my ear to ask how you are and to tell you to please call him. Can you believe that? I was so through with him, but I smiled, wished them a good evening, recommended the desert special and went back to the kitchen."

Corie took a long swallow of her Fresca with cranberry juice and looked at me in the anticipation of my response. I shook my head several times as I leisurely took in another healthy mouthful of food. In order to keep Corie from asking questions I chewed slowly and gave myself time to come up with a witty reply. When I was finally ready to speak I said.

"Corie I think you handled the situation well and I am glad that you did not call me. Nevertheless, you didn't save me from him. He called me the other day. I guess it must have been the day after you saw him."

"No way, what did he say?"

"Nothing, because I didn't give him a chance to say anything. I just reminded him that we were over and told him to stop bothering me. I sincerely hope he got the message this time."

Corie expressed her approval of the way I handled the situation with Karl and we resumed devouring our food.

By the time dessert came, Corie had shifted conversation topic to Tray. She asked at least twenty questions about him and another 10 about the two of us. She was mainly concerned with what I was doing or what I planned on doing with such a fine youngman or should I say a fine younger man.

"Rhap, how old is he again. He doesn't look over 23." She quipped.

"Oh you're sooo funny. He's 26, thank you very much. He's legal and he's extremely mature. If you just talked to him and didn't know his age, you would think that he was at least 30. You know what I mean? He is intelligent, focused and he has goals and aspirations. I mean solid goals and life objectives, Corie. Now, tell me how many dudes you know right now that have real and reasonable goals and aspirations? Huh?" I asked.

Of course Corie actually started running through her list of fellas and then starting knocking the losers off her list. By the time she finished, she could only name two men. One was Manford, who was married with a child and one on the way. The other was Stephen, who I told her didn't count because he was 45 years old and I was talking about dudes between twenty-five and thirty.

"Girl, that is so sad. I can't believe that I can't think of more than two men with their shit together. I need to raise the bar and meet more decent men." She complained.

"Well, that may be true but don't count out the guys that have potential. If you can see their potential, then you just might be the woman who can help them reach their potential. You know what they say. A good woman fortifies the backbone of a good man. You could be their inspiration. So you have to remember not to kill the garden, just pull out the weeds."

Corie fell into laughter at my cliches.

"Rhap, you really be trippin'. Where do you come up with that shit? I hope you don't be telling those children that mess. Girl, I can see them looking at you with their mouth's hung open...like...What is she talking about? They're probably saying, Old girl is trippin'. She said as she continued to laugh at me.

We continued to laugh and joke around as the table was cleared and then Corie was summoned to the kitchen. The cute little waiter that had been serving us brought out a steaming vanilla latte and told me that Corie would return shortly. I flipped through my agenda while I waited for Corie and sipped my latte. Ten to fifteen minutes later, she scurried out to the table and told me that she needed to get the ball rolling for the dinner crowd. She apologized but I dismissed her apology and thanked her for a wonderful lunch. I was thrilled that she had been able to spare a little under an hour for me. We hugged, kissed and promised to get together sooner rather than later.

Back in my car, Paully entered my thoughts and I decided to give him a ring. I was greeted by his recorded voice and left a quick message telling him to call his little sis. Then I put in a call to my real little brother, figuring he'd be home from school unless he had basketball practice. He answered on the second ring and immediately filled me with joy with his excitement in hearing from me. He reported on his school progress, athletic prowess, and the newest development of a girlfriend. Her name was Kera and she had enrolled at his school only a month before. She was trying out for the volleyball team and he was going to the tryouts for moral support. They were both going to try out for the track team in the spring, though he wasn't sure if it would intefer with lacrosse. We talked for thirty minutes before I asked if Mom was around, remembering her messages from earlier.

Aslen began to snicker and I asked what was the matter.

"Oooh, you are in so much trouble, so you better be glad that she's not here." He announced.

"Trouble?" I responded. "In trouble for what? Because I didn't call her back last night? I didn't even get her messages until this afternoon. She knows I always return her calls and I didn't call last Sunday because I fell asleep on the sofa. Is she really mad at me? I questioned, feeling like I was Aslen's age.

Aslen was ravaged with laughter at this point and I still didn't know what was going on. Why would I be in trouble with my moms. Aslen soon informed me.

"I don't have all the details, Sis, all I know it that Mom talked to Mrs. Ray and she said that you were in town last month or something like that. Mom said that she couldn't believe that you were in town and didn't call us or come by. She was walking around the kitchen fussing so bad that she put coffee creamer in the creamed potatoes." He shared as he was overcome with laughter again.

I couldn't believe what I was hearing. If Mrs. Ray told my mother I had been in town, there was no doubt in my mind that she was totally pissed. Not just because I didn't call or stop by, but because I visited with the Rays. I was in for a serious ear burning and there was no way out of it. Aslen interrupted my thoughts.

"Sis, I think she is going to yell at you. What are you going to do if she does? I hope I'm here when she does, because I have never heard her yell at you. Man, she's always yelling at me, so this is going to be so much fun."

I was not in the mood for teasing from my baby brother.

"Okay Aslen, you've had your fun. Tell mom I called. She can reach me at home or on my cell phone. Can you do that for me, little bro?"

"You got it, Sis. Talk to you later and next time you're in town, don't leave us hangin'. Love Ya."

As I ended the call I pulled into my garage. My nerves had worked my stomach into knots, therefore, I had to hurriedly gather my things, rush into the house, and race to the bathroom. It was a fact that I was in for a very intense conversation with my mother before the day was over. Nevertheless, I resolved to be honest with her about what happened. She would not totally forgive me, but at least she would know the whole story. She would definitely be sympathetic of the situation that I was in at the time. I could count on that.

The dreaded call from my mom came just as I finished my shower before bed. I was in the kitchen fixing a cup of green tea and filling my water thermos for the night. The shower coupled with my three mile treadmill run had helped to knock the edge off my anxiety and I was relatively relaxed. There was a little lurch in my gut when I saw my mom's number on the caller I.D., but I answered anyway.

"Hi Mom." I answered, trying to sound somewhat jovial and cut through the tension I was expecting from her.

"Don't hi me, young lady. Your ass is grass. I can't believe that you would come to Chicago and not tell the woman who nutured, birth, and raised your behind. And don't think that you are going to sweet talk yourself out of this. I am so hurt and disappointed that I could scream. Do you know I actually cried after talking to Rays. I was so surprised that I couldn't even pretend that I knew you had been here. How could you do that, Rhapsody? How could you do that to me?"

She was on a roll and suddenly, I didn't think that I was up to the challenge of trying to make her understand. Silence was my first reaction. It didn't fly.

"Rhapsody! You better stop pouting and start talking. Now!"

I realized that I was knee deep in it and there was only one way out. The truth. So, I jumped right in with a simple, I'm sorry. I spent the next hour reenacting the entire Karl drama. I didn't leave out anything except the intimate details. All of the post breakup encounters were revealed and I even told her about Paully's visit. I, of course, did not tell her about the Paully drama because it had nothing to do with the breakup that led me to ditch the family. After all the tea had been poured, Mom came through for me. She was sympathetic and nurturing. Even though, she didn't hestitate to express her displeasure with the way I handled the matter.

"Baby, I'm really sorry that you had to go through that, because I know how much you really liked that boy. I knew when you talked about bringing him for the holidays, that you felt you had something special. My heart aches for you. What I don't understand is why you felt you couldn't talk to me about it. It's good to know that you and Paully still have that special connection and I'm happy to know that he was there for you. I know that Paully will always look out for you. He's been doing that since you two were kids. But, baby, we have always been able to talk about your relationships. Why was this time different. Have things changed that much between us?"

I could hear the sadness in her voice and it was breaking my heart. It was true that I had been able to talk to my moms about my friends, friend boys, and boyfriends when I was growing up. What she didn't know, was that I didn't talk to her about all of them nor did I tell her everything. Some things were best left unsaid and kept my mother's perception of her little girl relatively clean. Still, I never intended to hurt her feelings and I didn't want to lose the closeness we both held dear. I had to try and smooth things over.

"No, Mom. Things have not changed between us. It's just that this time, I needed something different. I don't know...I think...I don't know...I needed a different perspective...I mean... a different point of view. Mom, you always comfort me when I'm down. You remind me that there are many more brighter days than gloomy and encourage me to move on. But, I this time I needed something else. I needed someone that could give hard advice. I needed an insider and that was Paully. I'm not saying that your help is any less important,

Mom. I still need you and always will, but Paully is my inside man. I don't think that he has ever hurt anyone the way Karl hurt me but I know he understands the men of my generation better than you or I. That's why I turned to him. It wasn't planned at all, mom, things just kinda happened."

I paused before admitting the final factor.

"And, Mom, the other reason I stayed away was that I was really in a bad place emotionally. The worst I've ever been and I just didn't want you to see me like that. It was easy to put on a good face for Mr. and Mrs. Ray, but I would have never held up in front of you and dad. Do you understand?" I said as I choked back my tears.

"Of course I do, baby." Was Mom's tear-filled reply.

All in all, we had a good conversation. Mom had been quite irritated with me when she called and some of the irritation might remain. But I think she understood my actions were not intended to offend her and that is what mattered. Overall, I felt much better that I'd been able to lift the weight of deception by omission from my chest and could sleep peacefully that night. We talked a bit longer about the upcoming holidays and my pending visits. The conversation ended on a pleasant note with us professing our love for each other.

# 23

The morning following our succulent Thanksgiving dinner, I took my little brother out on our very first sister/brother shopping excursion. It was his idea because he wanted to find a nice gift for his girlfriend. According to him, if he got out on the first day of the Christmas shopping season, he was bound to catch the best bargains. He could buy all of our Christmas gifts and get something special for Kera without spending his entire $250 Christmas fund. Aslen was a serious Teen Midas.

I was teasing him about being frugal at such a young age when Tiana called on my cellphone. Her agitation was apparent in her initial greeting.

"Ms. Austin, why you not returning my calls? I paged you like ten times. Where you at?" she said.

I got a little nervous because she was in hood mode speaking in broken english. She hadn't done that in quite some time. Both she and Kieron used to speak that way all of the time, but I coached them out of the habit. I didn't have to really teach them how to speak, because they were being taught in school. All I did was encourage them to use proper English as much as possible in order to communicate their needs and desires. I told them it was essential for progress in the real world and that was enough. So, Tiana's verbal slips were alarming.

"Tiana, what's wrong?" I questioned immediately.

"Nuttin', I just wanna know why you can't call me back when I page you?"

"Okay, Tiana, if nothing's wrong then I want you to calm down and remember that you are talking to me and not one of your friends down the street." I responded.

I could hear her taking deep calming breaths.

"Tiana, you know that I am in Chicago with my family and you know that I don't take my pager on vacation. That's why I gave you my cellphone number. So now, why don't you tell me what's on your mind?"

"I'm sorry Ms. Austin, honest, I am. It's just that I really needed to talk to you yesterday and I couldn't find you. Guess I wasn't thinking straight or I probably would have called your cell." She paused.

"Yesterday was a super bad day for me."

"What happened? Is your MaDear okay?" I asked.

"Yeah, she's fine. She's better than me, that's for sure. You know I thought she was going to be mad sad for Thanksgiving, cuz it's her favorite holiday. She really gets into the whole family thing and I just knew that she was going to be sick with Kieron being gone. So I planned to stay close and try to cheer her up when she got sad. But she wasn't, Ms. A, she was happy and stuff. She was cooking, baking, and singing and junk. All she did was talk about how good it was going to be to have her family all together, especially since we had lost Kieron. I couldn't believe it but I was kinda glad that she was not breaking down and crying all day and night."

Smiling, I commented. "T, that's great! So what's the problem? Why were you upset yesterday?"

"Naw, I wasn't upset cuz MaDear was happy. That's not it. It was what happened after dinner. See, she was talking to my cousin Mavis in the living room, while they were having sweet potato pie and coffee. I was sitting at the table playing trouble with my other cousins and I wasn't really paying no attention to them. But then I heard Madear say my momma's name and so I started listening. She was telling cousin Mavis that the police officer said that he had checked all the hospitals, morgues, and the jails and that my mother wasn't listed anywhere. MaDear was talking about she was glad, cuz at least she wasn't dead or locked up. But she still wondered if she knew about her baby boy being gone."

I had to interrupt her at that point because she was confusing me. I thought it was pretty good news, myself. So I still didn't know why Tiana was upset. The only way to find out was to ask.

"Tiana, aren't you glad that your mother is not in jail or in a morgue?"

"Of course, I am, Ms. A. That's not what upset me. I don't wish anything bad on my momma, not really. The problem is that Madear hadn't told me about what the officier told her. I didn't even know that she was still talking to the police. I used to ask her if they had any leads on Kieron's murder, but she would always get so worked up and make herself sick. So I stopped asking. But there she was talking to Mavis about Momma and Kieron. I felt left out and it made me mad. MaDear should tell me about that stuff before she tells anyone else. I wonder what else she is keeping from me. It makes me so mad!" she exclaimed.

Tiana finished her explanation just as I found a parking space at the mall. I took this opportunity to send Aslen inside to begin his shopping. I told him I would meet him in the food court at Great Wraps in an hour. He was happy to oblige, probably because he could use the time to find my Christmas present. Nevertheless, I was glad that he wasn't pissed at my taking the phone call during our day out. As he dashed toward the mall entrance, I turned my attention back to Tiana.

"Okay Tiana, now explain to me again why you are so upset."

"I guess because Madear didn't talk to me about what she had found out about momma. She and Kieron and me used to talk about everything. And if we asked her a question, she would always give us some kind of answer, even if it wasn't what we wanted to hear. And if I was afraid to ask her something, I could always go ask Kieron. He would just be real real with me about almost anything. But I can't do that anymore. That means that MaDear is the only one left and if she isn't going to talk to me, I ain't got nuttin."

At that point, I realized that Tiana's frustration and concern was valid. Of course, I figured that MaDear thought that she was protecting her remaining grandchild from further pain and disappointment. She probably never thought that Tiana wanted or even actually needed to know what was going on. But obviously she did. I could understand why Tiana felt the need to be informed. She was suffering through the loss of her mother and of her brother, her best friend and confidant. Then, with her grandmother neglecting to communicate certain things to her, she was feeling the anticipation of further disconnection and loss. MaDear was not at true fault and Tiana needed to understand that.

"Look, Tiana, I hear you and I think I understand where you're coming from but I want you to listen to me. Okay?"

"Yeah, okay." She responded.

"Really listen, Tiana." I emphasized.

"Okay, Okay, I'm really listening." Tiana assured me.

"Okay, now listen. MaDear has always been there for you, right?"

"Yeah."

"She has always tried to make sure that you and Kieron were safe, right?"

Tiana sighed. "Yeah."

"You even said that you have always been able to go to MaDear when you needed to, right?"

"Come on Ms. Austin. Please just say what you want to say." She said with a little chuckle.

"Fine. No more questions. Look my point is that above all else you have to remember that MaDear loves you and will do anything for you. She has been your own living guardian angel, forever on duty and never ever complains. That has not changed. Tiana, I know that MaDear is not trying to hurt you or hide anything from you. She is trying to do what she has always done. Protect you and keep you safe from harm. She probably thinks that if she doesn't bother you with the unpleasant, then you won't feel unpleasant. That's what people who love you do, especially when the one they love is a child."

"But."

"Wait, I'm not finish. Tiana, I'm not saying that you don't have the right to feel what you feel nor am I saying that MaDear is right in choosing the method of protection that she is using. What I am saying is that you should not think that MaDear is trying to intentionally hurt you. You should remember that she loves and cares deeply about you. Then, I would suggest that you talk to her. I want you to think carefully about what you want to say and how you want to say it. You may even want to write it all out first. As a matter of fact, I am officially assigning that task to you. I want you to write down exactly what you want to say to MaDear. You got that?"

"Yeah, I got it Ms. A. Thanks."

# 24

Trayu came by my parents house around 7:00 and I was nervous as shit. Cocoa would be in Brazile for another two days or she would have been there, as she so coyly put it when I'd spoken to her.

"I would be sitting right across from your moms just waiting to see the expression on her face when that young jock walks in to pick you up for a date. She is going to think you have lost your mind, fooling around with someone half your age."

And although Trayu was not even close to being half my age, he was young enough to make my mom shake a finger at me. Still, he was coming to our house to pick me up. My preference would have been to meet him at an agreed upon location, but I didn't have that option. Tray seemed bent on picking me up and meeting my family. I tried to steer him away from the notion, but my attempts were met with obvious disappointment in his voice. He reasoned that since I had driven to meet him for coffee and dessert the night I flew in, the least he could do would be to pick me up for our date like a gentleman. Then, he added .

"Unless there's a specific reason that you don't want me to pick you up."

After that comment I couldn't bring myself to deny him. I thought that I'd made my peace with it up until thirty minutes before his anticipated arrival. I was brushing on a little masscara, a rare occurrence, when all of a sudden I felt a net of butterflies in my stomach. They should have been from excitement about seeing Tray but I knew that they were actually from fear of what my parents and Aslen would think of him.

When the doorbell rang, my first instinct was to run to the door, quickly usher Tray back to the car and get the heck out of dodge. But being who I am, I decided to let the situation unfold naturally. You know, take my punches like a woman. So, I let my mother answer the door while I waited at the top of the stairs carefully hidden away so that I had a clear view of her as she welcomed him inside. As she turned around after locking the door, I searched her face for any signs of shock or disgust. There were none and I then allowed myself to release the breath I had subconsciously been holding.

When I alighted from my childhood bedroom, my dad and Trayu were talking Bears. Dad was quizzing Trayu on his knowledge of Bear history, mainly the 1985 Bear's season. Trayu did not disappoint as he rattled off the starting offense and defense. The final pleasure came from his demonstration of the Superbowl Shuffle. Aslen fell to his knees in laughter when dad joined in the Shuffle groove. It wasn't often that we saw our dad do anything close to being considered dancing. I stood in the doorway and watched my dad and my...my... uh...friend boy and smiled heartily. My mom came and hooked her arm, gave me a wink and grin, then turned her attention back to the show. I felt another ten pound weight being lifted from my shoulders and gave my mom's arm a little squeeze.

After the entertainment, my mom asked Trayu if he wanted something to eat. He looked at me and I quickly explained to my mom that we were going out to eat. My dad added his words of persuasion by telling Trayu that we should stay there and eat, so that he could teach Trayu how to play dominos after dinner. Although dad is usually pretty persuasive, his techniques didn't work this time. Trayu graciously declined the dinner invitation and reasoned that their was a neat little stir fry restaurant he really wanted to show me. His godfather was co-ower of the restaurant and he wanted to show his support. Then he offered to come back another time to get his domino lessons from dad, because he was eager to learn. That comment appeased my dad and he assured Trayu that he would teach him well.

Unfortunately, our little date was not that inspiring. The restaurant was nice. I could tell that it was a hotspot. It was located in Hyde Park off of 53rd and Harper. Its concept was to have the freedom to customize your meal. You could choose the vegetables, protein, seasonings and sauce of your choice. Your concoction would then be stir-fried and delivered to your table. It seemed like an easy way to get a perfect meal, but as I as soon found out, I was not good at creating tasty stirfry on the fly. I gave it three tries and then as in the all american past-time, I was out. Secondly, the place was so loud that I couldn't hear Tray, unless he was talking directly into my ear. And that is not the way I like to hold my conversations. I like to be able to see a persons eyes and facial expressions when they talk to me. But the drinks were extremely tasty and they kept my mood light, which meant my frustration did not show too blaringly.

The night got better. After dinner, we drove down to Navy Pier and watched the lights on Lake Michigan and talked. We talked for hours and I was content. Tray was a great conversationalist that knew how to keep one intrigued. What pleased me the most was that we talked as much about me as him. He seemed determined to know everything about me and for me to know everything about him. We'd had so many phone conversations, one would think that there would be nothing to talk about, but that was not the case. Trayu had added to his long term plan and had acquired two more web design jobs. He talked about ideas for my web page and asked about plans I had for the future of my business. But as smooth as the conversation was, it wasn't enough to ward off my fatigue. At the first yawn, Tray decided it was time to take me home.

We talked for another twenty minutes sitting in front of my house. Then, he walked me to the door and asked for a goodnight kiss.

"Trayu, sir, I don't do those kinds of things on my parents porch. If my father saw us, he would have you hog tied. And I couldn't bear to see that happen to you." I said in my Scarlet O'Hara southern style twang.

I did want to kiss him but I knew that someone or all of them were hiding behind window blinds or curtains spying on me. I was not comfortable with my mom, dad, or brother seeing me kiss anyone, so I gave Tray an extremely warm hug and a quick smack on the cheek and entered the house.

The next morning, my mother asked about my date with a quirky grin on her face. I loved to see her that way. It was that one thing that always melted my heart and put a smile on my face. When my father died, I was devastated and I didn't know how to deal with the grief. I was daddy's little girl and proud of it, but now my daddy was gone. I cried everyday for a while and so did my mom. She was not afraid to cry in front of me or with me. We often cried ourselves to sleep at night together as we talked about what we were feeling. I don't remember when she started doing it, but eventually she started talking about how we would survive and what we would do to make it happen. I believed her and we slowly began healing.

And I remember that quirky grin showing up regularly when she wanted to cheer me up or say something silly. This time was no different from those days.

As I told her about the entire date, she listened and continued to grin. She said that he seemed like a very nice guy. He was handsome and she got good vibes from him. Then she dropped the funny bomb.

"I'm glad you found someone interesting to date here in Chicago, baby. I guess that means that we will be seeing you more often."

I just smiled and she continued.

"So, you'll be here in...what?...April or May...for the dance."

She was in pre-giggle mode with a full fledged smile.

"For what dance?" I asked quizzically.

"The senior prom of course!" she responded and burst into laughter.

I heard Aslen's chuckle drifting towards me from the hallway and I knew that he had at the very least heard enough to catch our mother's joke. Right then and there I decided that I would not bring Trayu around my family again for a while. I didn't tell him about the joke or my plan for exclusion. As a matter of fact, I didn't get the chance to see him again before I headed home but we made tentative plans for him to visit after the New Year.

# 25

"I'm not coming to group then, Ms. Austin." Was Tiana's response to hearing that Meek asked to join the Anger Management Group.

I had mentioned the group to Meek in a couple of our sessions and he finally said that he would like to give it a try. He didn't know that Tiana was a part of that group of teens and I didn't think he needed to know up front. On the other hand, I wanted Tiana to know that he would be there. My hopes were that it wouldn't matter to her one way or the other, but considering the issues that she'd had with Meek, I felt it would be safer to give her a heads up.

Meek had not been sweating Tiana too much in the past month. He was still stopping by to talk with MaDear and eat a snack or two, but he wasn't smothering Tiana with attention. On the contrary, MaDear was doing the pampering and I believe Meek truly enjoyed and appreciated it. In one session he shared that he thought MaDear liked having him around like when Kieron was alive and it seemed to make her feel better. And making her smile made him feel like he was doing some good and that Kieron would be happy to know that he was watching out for his MaDear. He was still angry about Tiana and Kaiewa's friendship and about the fact the Kevin was "running" now. He said that Kevin was asking for trouble dealing with drugs and after what happened to Kieron. Instead of running drugs, he should have been running in the opposite direction. Kevin's recent behavior and the fact that the police had still not found Kieron's murderer were the main causes of Meek's anger now. Not knowing how to control his anger made it worse, which was why I suggested the Anger Management Group.

"Tiana, I really don't want you to skip group because of Meek but I didn't want you to be surprised when he showed up. That's why I am telling you now. He doesn't even know that you are a part of the group so it's not like he decided to come because of you. Besides, you even said that he has been playing it cool lately."

"I know. It's not that, not really. I mean, the group is straight and all but I just don't really think I need it. I mean, like, I'm not really angry or mad or nothing. I still get kinda sad sometimes because I miss my brother, but I talk to you about that in our private sessions anyway. So I don't really need to come to those group sessions anymore. That's all I'm saying." Tiana explained.

"Well, if that's how you feel, it's fine with me. But Tiana, I just want you to be honest with yourself about what you need and if you truly feel that you don't need to come to the group session, I will understand. You know your girls are going to miss you, though."

Tiana laughed. "Yeah, I know but we've exchanged numbers and I see Rita at school, so we'll keep in touch."

"Okay T, I need to get back to work. I'll see you later. Peeeeace!"

That tickled her.

"Ms. A, you are so crazy. But don't use that saying again. It is not you, okay. Bye." She laughed and hung up.

Our group session started on time. It may have even started a little early due to the fact that everyone was there by ten of the hour. Meek was first to arrive and helped me set up the beverages I prepared for our little birthday treat. Before long, everyone was present, milling around and talking to each other. Meek had taken post near the beverage table looking like an outsider, but he wasn't the only new group member present that day. There was Michael, a 14 year old youngman, who had been court ordered to start anger management training. He had recently and reluctantly moved in with his dad after being released from juvenile for his involvement in fight in which a girl was stabbed. Michael admitted to being a part of the fight but maintains that he didn't have or use any weapons other than his fists. Therefore, he was resentful of having to live with his dad and for being forced to take an anger management class. When Michael arrived, he claimed a seat and waited sullenly for the rest of the group to assemble.

Once everyone was seated, we took the first ten minutes to make introductions and to share thoughts about their last assignment. The assignment was to say or do something positive for one person, other than yourself, everyday for a week. Oral sharing was optional but the ten minutes of journaling that followed was not. Even Michael and Meek were required to write about the last nice thing they could remember doing for someone else.

When the timer signaled the end of journaling, I collected the journals and put them away before starting our new discussion.

"Okay ladies and gentlemen, last week we focused on positive things we can do for others. Can anyone tell me why we were doing that?" I inquired and immediately responses started flowing.

"I don't know, I guess you're trying to turn us into good Samaritans or something."

"Because you wanted us to think about doing good stuff instead of bad stuff."

"You want us to be more positive people than negative people."

"Because maybe if we do something good for someone, then they will do something good for someone else."

"But some people just ain't going to do nothing nice for nobody no matter how nice you are to them."

"That's true but I do think that Mr. Randall, my reading teacher was nicer to me this week because I said good morning to him everyday when I came in class. It was a trip to see his face the first day I stopped and said good morning, so I kept doing it just to see what he would do. The only problem is that now I kinda feel like I have to keep on doing it or I'll look bad."

Finally, I stopped nodding and responded.

"Wow, I'm impressed with your comments and I hope that everyone got a little bit of something out of being positive and nice. And as far as thinking you will look bad if you stop being nice....maybe that's a sign that you should keep doing what you are doing. It doesn't cost you anything and hopefully you learned it doesn't hurt you either."

"Ms. Austin, it may not hurt but it does take effort and that is more than I have some days." Willie said.

"Well, just do it whenever you can. That's better than nothing." I responded before moving on.

"Last week the focus was on people you come in contact with but now I want to talk about you. As you've probably heard before, adults have lots of responsibilities and concerns. There's work, bills, children, and taxes to name a few. But there's a lot going on in your lives as well. Tell me about some of the things happening in your life that you would consider positive." I challenged but my challenge was met with silence. A little bewildered, because I hoped that these kids did not feel that life was that dismal, I presented a small prompt. "For instance, you all are provided with a free education until you graduate from High School. Isn't that a good thing?"

And with that, Meek started the debate that carried us through the rest of the session.

"Everybody is always telling us to get an education and you'll be able to get a good job and have a bright future. But I don't think they know what they're talking about. I think they just want us to believe that that's the truth, but it's not."

"For real man, they living in a dream world. That's bullshit, man."

"Evan, let's keep our language respectful, now." I warned

"Sorry Ms. A. I'm just saying that I think that grown-ups just be fillin' our heads with a bunch of nonsense. It's just another way for them to control us. An education ain't all that important."

"What makes you think that?" I asked.

"Cuz the stuff that they be teaching in school don't have nothing to do with real life. Like why do I need to know what a appopative or a preposition is or what a percentage of something is? I ain't never going to have to use that stuff outside of the classroom. So why waste time on that?"

Then Rita chimed in. "Oh yeah, and all those teachers at school are sooo gay. They be boring us to tears and get mad when you fall asleep in class. The only time you don't fall asleep is when people be tripping in class. And half the time the teachers don't even do nothing when kids be trippin'."

"Yeah, for real." Several others chimed in.

"Okay, okay guys." I said with a smile. I hear what you're saying but I disagree with what was said about education just being a distraction. I know for a fact that, especially in this day and time, an education is essential. What you guys are doing right now in middle school and high school is basically building a foundation. A foundation that will afford you the opportunity to do whatever your heart desires. Secondly, Evan, knowing prepositions and appositives might make the difference in a good resume and a great resume, which in turn will convince a company that you would be a great employee not just a good employee. And knowing the percentage of taxes being taking out of your check or how much money you will save on the next Timberland sale should surely be of interest to all of you. Yes, some of the things you learn seem useless but why don't you start asking your teachers to show you examples of how things are used in the real world. Challenge them to teach you in the same way they are challenging you to learn. Thirdly, you said that the teachers don't do anything when kids are acting out in class. So tell me what are they suppose to do?"

Lauren said, "They should make them be quiet if they really want to teach."

"Yeah but they don't listen when they tell them to be quiet and some of the kids in my classes would cuss a teacher out in a heart beat."

"I know right…some of them don't give those teachers no respect." Someone said and the whole group fell into a short bout of laughter.

"Well, can the teachers have the disruptive students removed from the classroom?" I asked.

"For sho' but by the time they can get a student written up and out of class, ain't nobody trying to start working the lesson and it's almost time for the bell to ring."

"So what do you do when someone's disrupting the class?"

"Nothing but laugh, cuz it is kinda funny."

"It's funny that they are keeping the teacher from teaching and ultimately keeping you from learning? I don't understand that, unless, you don't care about having your opportunity to learn stolen from you."

"Oh come on Ms. A, now you are trippin'. What are we supposed to do?"

"I don't know but I do know that if you guys are laughing at the disruptive kids, then you are encouraging them." I paused before continuing.

"Think about this. Think back to when you were a little kid and you learned a new dance or did something funny. Your parents would laugh and ask you to do it again and after a while you would start doing it whenever you wanted to make your mom or aunt or uncle laugh. Am I right?"

Most of the group agreed.

"Well, that's the same thing that happens with class clowns. Usually when someone acts out in class it's because they are seeking attention or they are avoiding work. Granted there may be other reasons but those are two of the most basic reasons."

"So I guess what you are saying Ms. A is that we should ignore them or tell them to stop fooling around."

"Either one would be fine if you think it will work. But I think the least you can do is not encourage them and try to remain focused on what you want from school."

"Yeah but it just ain't that easy, Ms. Austin."

"Point taken but that doesn't mean that you shouldn't try."

"I still don't see the point. I don't plan on going to nobody's college so why get a high school diploma? I'm going to work on cars and motorcycles. I want to build motors and engines for mo' power. I do that right now so I don't need college to teach me that." Evan offered.

"That's great Evan but if you are going to make real money then you are going to need some training in order to learn more about what you do and new technology. You can't get around that. But you are right, you may not need to go to college but you will most likely need a high school diploma in order to get into a training program to obtain a certificate that proves you can do the job, that is if you want to work for the big money companies. And don't mistake yourself into believing that a GED is going to do it for you. It might but it will definitely not give you the edge over a youngman or younglady with a high school diploma. So why even take the chance? Why not just do what you have to for the next 4-6 years and make the way better for yourself?"

"Okay, okay, Ms. Austin, I hear ya. I see that I'm not going to win this argument so I give up." Everyone laughed.

"It's a deal. Now let's get back to where we started so we can wrap this session up. Let's see, I believe that the topic of this discussion was to identify some positive things going on in your lives as teenagers. I don't recall hearing any responses to my question. So let's see if we can get some suggestions of things that you might at least consider good."

Lauren started by offering a response.

"We can focus on our education and join school clubs.

Then a few others shared.

"You can join a sports team."

"Or be a sports team manager if you're not good at sports."

"I used to be a member of the Boys and Girls Club when I was younger and we did a bunch of fun stuff there. That's where me and my brother had learned to swim."

"Oh yeah, and you can spend more time with your family and siblings. That's a good thing."

"Did we name enough stuff, Ms. Austin?" Lauren asked.

I didn't hear her right away because I was taking notes on what was being said and of course I was a few statements behind the oral listing. So when I jotted down the last note and looked up at the group, all eyes were on me. I knew they were waiting for their assignment for the week. It made me smile because I could remember when they would sit there with their fingers crossed hoping that I would not give them "homework". But once some of them figured out that the assignments were actually self-reflections that helped them see things a little more clearly, they challenged the others to put a little effort into doing the assignments. Soon they were looking forward to a weekly challenge and those that didn't, never complained. On a few occasions, I would have a courageous member offer a suggestion for the weekly assignment.

I gave the assignment and dismissed the group. Meek's aunt was there to pick him up and he appeared happy to see her. He even introduced her to Rita, Lauren, and Evan. I was glad that Meek had joined the group but I missed Tiana. I could only hope that she was being truthful about not needing to come to the anger management sessions anymore.

# 26

orie called full of excitement about her spot in the City Cuisine magazine. It's a food and entertainment monthly that highlighted the quiet kept secrets of elegance, fun and palet pleasing food and entertainment in the metro area. One of her early lunch customers talked her into a short impromptu interview with a few shots of Corie in the restaurant. The next thing she knew, she received an advance copy of the magazine with a glorifying review of the restaurant and her unique culinary creations.

"Wow Corie, that's great! It's about time, girl, you deserve it!" I said in congratulations.

"I know, I know. Girl, I literally screamed when I saw my picture in that magazine. And I almost fainted from excitement when I read the article. I pulled about 20 copies from the nail shop and sent them to my family. Rhap, this could be the exposure I needed to get the revenue to open my own business."

She was ecstatic and rightly so.

Since the magazine hit the stand, the restaurants already good business had become great. The owner was already talking about expanding the site and possibly opening a new location. Even better, Corie's name was circulating and her private party bookings were skyrocketing. She had more requests than she could handle, which was partially the reason for her call.

Corie needed help staffing her parties and that was where I came in. She wanted me to bartend two Christmas parties and an engagement dinner. We discussed the dates and what type of services the events required. I found myself getting a little excited.

"Okay, check this out, Corie. For each party, I'm gonna do a signature drink and name it after the party host. Like for the engagement party, I will spruce up a cosmopolitan and call it The Cranberry Cranford. And then, I will teach my helper how to make that drink so that she can make that drink the entire night. Oh yeah and we can set up a party toast with the signature drink. We can use those tiny martini glasses and give them to all of the guest for a toast to the couple." I rattled off.

Corie laughed at me.

"Rhapsody Austin, you need to calm down, girl. You've got some great ideas and I like that but remember this. I have to stay within budget in order to make a profit and you have to pay any of your assistants from your cut. I want to make sure that I give each party the Corie flair but I cannot over-staff now or I will set myself up for failure. Ultimately, that means that I am going to have to work harder now which will be smarter until things get up and running well."

And I knew she was right. I could also tell by her conversation, she was ready to take on the challenge. She'd always believed that her time would come. Still I was excited to be able to help her out and decided then and there that I was going to help her out financially whenever I could. Maybe I could be an investor in her first restaurant or catering store.

❦

"What's up baby, you can stop sitting around dreaming about me, cuz you got me on the line."

An instant smile graced my face upon hearing his voice. Lately it seemed that Trayu was the one guarantee for some daily joy. His voice was forever jovial and his conversation intriguing.

"Hiii. I see we are full of ourself again tonight. But I am glad to hear your voice. So what's going on."

"Nothing much, just feeling pretty right because I believe that I found the perfect Christmas gift for my sweetest." He announced.

"Look now, I've already told you that I don't want you to buy me anything for Christmas. I just don't feel comfortable with that. I would feel better if you used your money for gifts for your family."

I actually felt that I was going to talk him out of giving me a Christmas gift. He was a man of reason at so many different levels so he had to agree with my logic, right? Nope, he wasn't having it. He changed the subject very quickly.

"Look Girl, you can stop talking all that junk, cuz I ain't buying it. You can't tell me how to spend my money no more that I can tell you how to spend yours. So just stop it. Besides that, I didn't call to talk about that. I just want to know about your travel plans for this Christmas."

I got a little nervous about how to answer that question because I didn't know where he was going with it. My Christmases have always been spent with my family. And I mean always, there has never been one when I was not at home. One Christmas, my stepfather took my mother to Africa for her gift. They left two days before Christmas and returned a week later. Mom was going to send Aslen to Atlanta to spend the holiday with me, but I went home as planned. That Christmas was a little strange because it was just the two of us but we had a great time. Alsen didn't seem upset that our parents weren't there to watch him open his gifts. He opened them with the usual urgency and excitement. Even at the age of nine, Aslen had an amazing heart. In the midst of opening his gifts and handing gifts to me to open, he stopped and set aside two of his gifts to save until mom and dad came home. He didn't want them to open their gifts alone. I laughed at him and told him that he was a better person than me because I was going to open all of my gifts.

That said, I was hoping that Trayu was not going ask if he could come to Atlanta for Christmas. I was also hoping that he didn't plan on spending a lot of time with me because I was only going to be home for three days. And I didn't get to see Paully and Cocoa when I was at home for Thanksgiving, so we had already planned a sleepover at Paully's the night I flew in. We would exchange gifts, sip, eat, and swap stories until we passed out.

So I gave Trayu a synopses of my Christmas plans. I even told him about the sleepover. It wasn't like he could really say anything to me about spending time with my good friends. He didn't know about my Paully issues, so he didn't have any reason to ask me not to go. As a matter of fact, if he had, we would've had a little problem. It's not like he could tell me who I could spend time with; he didn't have those privileges yet. But as it turned out, I didn't have to worry about Trayu taking privileges he was not entitled to.

He just wanted to figure out if he would be able to see me while I was there. He and his family was going to Miami for Christmas and he would not return until December 28th. I told him that I was disappointed that I wouldn't be able to see him while I was there but that we should plan to get together right after the New Year. He, of course, agreed and said he would get right on the plans and run them by me, in the next couple of days.

# 27

Cocoa and I met in the airport the day before Christmas Eve. Her flight from London landed at 6:12 a.m. so she was waiting for me when I deplaned. I hadn't realized how much I'd missed her until I saw her smiling face. I guessed that she'd missed me just as much from the tight embrace and auto pilot babbling. It was as if she was trying to cram months of conversations into our first hour together. We walked and talked our way to baggage claim to pick up my bags. Cocoa was most excited about her recent decision to look for a better position in the airline's corporate office. She definitely had enough years and experience to qualify for a better position. I also knew that she'd spent some time assisting in other divisions over the past few years, so it wasn't a great surprise. Cocoa was destined to climb the ladder sooner or later. The surprise was that she was looking at a position at a different airline (British Airways). I was sure that she'd find something to suite her needs soon; that meant that she would most likely have to relocate. Having her based overseas would mean that I would see her less than I already did, which brought a twinge of sadness to me.

With baggage in tow, we headed to pick up my rental car. The conversation then turned to our plans for the night. We were to meet Paully at his apartment and then go pick up the food and liquor. Cocoa suggested that we watch a couple of old movies to add a few laughs. She had Krush Groove and Purple Rain packed in her luggage.

"I hope Paully doesn't have one of his skanks over there when we get there. I don't feel like trying to be nice to one of his one night stands. We better call him as soon as we get in the car, so he can clean house before we get there." Cocoa said.

I felt an extra palpitation in my chest cavity.

"Girl, do you think he is still doing that...one night stands?" I inquired.

I felt a little jittery and nervous though I wasn't sure why. I just hoped it didn't show.

"Please, that boy has not changed much since high school. He still changes women like he changes his underwear."

We both laughed.

"Rhap, how long do you think his longest relationship was?"

"Yeah right, I don't even know and would be to afraid to guess. But Cocoa, don't you think that he might be ready to have a real relationship now that he's in his thirties? I mean, come on, he has got to be tired of playing the field." I added.

"You would think so. I really don't see or talk to him that often but every time I do, it seems that he is with someone different. I sincerely hope that he is settling down. Shit, it's some dangerous stuff out here and it wears a great disguise. Maybe we should have a little talk with him tonight cuz he could use some sisterly advice."

Suddenly, I felt the need to tell Cocoa about what was going on with me and Paully. There was no other choice. If she started reaming Paully about settling down, he would probably tell her himself, but I didn't want her to hear it from him first. So I told her. I told her everything from the first kiss to our discussions about Trayu. She listened with an open mouth and deer in headlight eyes. When I finished, I let loose a huge sigh of relief. It was good to be able to talk to her about it.

"Oh my God!" she said.

"Rhapsody Austin, I can't believe that you kept this from me. I think you guys make a cute couple and Paully needs a woman like you. Cuz you won't stand for any of his foolishness. Girl, I think this could work, so what's the problem?"

"Come on Cocoa, we have been friends all of our lives. How are we suppose to become lovers. I am not going to be another one of his sex buddies. I will not be another notch on his belt. He says that he wants an exclusive relationship but I don't know. I don't want to chance it. I could lose my oldest best friend."

"I feel you, but if you don't try you won't know." Cocoa reasoned.

"I don't know if it's worth taking that chance. Another thing is…

well, it's the way that he has responded to me talking to Trayu. It's like he's had a thorn in his paw about me and Tray from day one. And I can't help but think that a part of what he's feeling is just jealousy. Maybe he just doesn't want to see me with Tray and is mistaking those feelings as affection for me. I don't know but what I do know is that I'm not ready to have Paully be the man in my life." I explained.

I couldn't tell what Cocoa was thinking but I didn't have to wait long to find out.

"So are you saying that you like Trayu better than Paully?"

"No, that's not what I'm saying."

"Well, I can understand your concern about your friendship with Paully but I think it's worth trying. Paully is a great guy. He's a little whorish, but you know he's a good guy and he already loves you. The odds look pretty good to me from where I stand. On the other hand, this thing with Trayu, do you think you could get serious with him? He is a bit younger, girl. He's fine but young just the same." She stated.

"Look, I am not getting serious about Tray, Cocoa. We are just getting to know each other and I do like him. But I am not trying to get into a serious relationship right now with anyone. My goodness, you sound like Paully." I sighed.

"No, no, no. I not insinuating anything, girl, I'm just collecting info."

There was silence in the car at this point.

Cocoa decided to slice the air with a knife.

"Have you slept with Trayu?" she asked.

"No!" I answered quickly.

"No, we have fooled around but I haven't let it go farther than that. Girl, but it's been hard...Let me tell you...he's got some moves for sure." I smiled and Cocoa hooted with laughter.

"Naw, but for real, Tray has been the perfect gentleman and I truly appreciate that. Annnnd he gets extra props for that, too. Annnnnd, he is not that young. He's older than your brother."

"Girl, you better stay away from my little brother. I don't want to have to fight you but you need to know that I fight friends."

We both cracked up laughing. I knew she was joking because

dating Canyun would be like dating Aslen. He was just like a little brother to me.

After we calmed down, Cocoa did call Paully to tell him we were in route to his place and to make sure that he would be ready to go when we arrived. He said the he would be ready and waiting. I had to carry all of my bags inside because Cocoa didn't want me to leave anything in the rental car over night. So while I was parking, Cocoa dialed up Paully again and ordered him to come down to carry my bags. He was waiting at the car trunk before I exited the car. I walked toward the trunk and Paully met me half way and wrapped his arms around me and kissed me on the lips. Now you have to understand that Paully has always greeted Cocoa and I with a smack on the lips but this time was different for me. I was a little nervous about being that close to him again. Paully held on a bit longer than normal and I notice because Cocoa was staring at us with a silly smirk on her face.

"Uh, you think a sister could get a tiny bit of attention over here? You haven't seen me in a while either, you know." She stated with her hands propped upon her hips. And Paully was quick to reply. Me? I hurriedly walked past him to open the trunk.

Paully carried my two bags up and Cocoa and I took care of her bags. On the way up to his apartment, Cocoa got a call.

"Oh, I've got to take this call." She announced.

I took the rolling flight bag she was carrying and continued behind Paully, while she stopped in the stairwell to talk. I wasn't sure why she didn't just take the call inside Paully's apartment and I wasn't going to ask. Paully turned and faced me in his living room, cocked his head, and gave me one of his cutest crooked smiles. He looked down at my bags and back to me. Down at my bags and back to me again.

"What?" I asked.

"Should I just go on and take your bags to my room now or would you prefer that I wait till later?" He said as he took steps to close the distance between us.

I took a step back and extended my arms.

"Boy stop playing and leave me alone. You can leave my bags right here cuz I am not sleeping in your bedroom with you." I was nervous and smiling and could feel tiny beads of sweat begin to form in the small of my back.

Paully reached out and pulled me to him just as Cocoa walked through the door. He shifted me to his side but did not let me go. And I saw the twinkle of suspicion in Cocoa's eyes as she smiled at me.

"Hey Rhap, can I use your car for about an hour? I need to go fax some information right away. It looks like I might have my first interview before the new year. It'll probably be a phone interview but it's still all good."

Before I could answer Paully recommended that Cocoa take his car and that he and I would take the rental car and go pick up the food and liquor. We would meet Cocoa back at the apartment and begin the slumber party. Cocoa thought it was a fabulous idea and Paully left the room to retrieve the spare key for Cocoa.

Paully's absence was the perfect opportunity for Cocoa to tease me.

"And what were you two doing when I walked in, eh? I thought you said that you didn't want to go there with your best friennnnnnd?"

"Girl stop it." I whispered.

"We weren't doing anything. I knew I shouldn't have told you. Now every little thing is going to be something to you. I'll never hear the end of your teasing." I said and gave her a little playful shove. She shoved me back and Paully scared the both of us with his re-entry.

"You two stop that or I'll put both of you on punishment and send you to bed without any liquor."

"Please don't, daddy. We promise to be good." Cocoa answered.

We all had a good little laugh before getting back to the business at hand.

The three of us stood in the kitchen and scribbled down a food and liquor list and agreed to meet back at the apartment in about an hour or so.

Paully was driving my rental as we ran our errands. I called my mom to let her know that I had made it in and was with my crew. She knew that I was going to spend my first night in town with my friends and was cool with it. She also said that she wouldn't tell dad or Aslen because she didn't think that they would be as understanding as she was. In essence, I think that my mom just liked to feel like we had a little secret just between us. She truly loves the special mother daughter bond that we have and I enjoy making her happy. Therefore, I let her believe that she was entrusted with this special little secret that needed to be kept from the men in the family.

Cocoa was waiting for us when we returned with the pizza, ribs, and liquor. She had showered and already changed into her flannel night clothes. I asked her to take the food and put it in the oven to keep it warm and I would go take a quick shower. After showering, I joined Paully and Cocoa in the living room.

"Okay, I am ready. Paully you can go take a shower if you want and the ladies will get the food and drinks ready."

"No thanks, I'm not all sweaty and funky like you two. I can wait until bedtime to take my shower." He responded.

Cocoa popped him upside the head and walked to the kitchen with me.

I started pulling out the food and plates while Cocoa showed me the temptation cake she picked up for dessert. Paully joined us and start fixing the drinks. He was drinking a single malt on the rocks while Cocoa and I decided on a couple of glasses of Moscato to start the night.

Everything was going fine. We watched Carwash, ate and talked for a good while. Work was going well for everyone and Paully was very encouraging towards Cocoa's career change. I was starting to get a little sleepy but I wasn't going to admit it. We were having too much fun. Then, Cocoa excused herself to go to the restroom and that's when things got complicated.

As soon as Cocoa left the room, Paully leaned over and kissed me. I don't know if it was the three glasses of wine or the uncertain attraction towards the possibility that Paully and I could make it as a couple. But whatever it was, I found myself kissing him back. In fact I took the dominating role with passionate tongue thrusts and soft mewing sounds.

"Well look at this." Came Cocoa voice slicing through the passion filled air, startling me clear to my feet.

Laughing, Paully tried to cover.

"Aw I was just playing around with Rhap, trying to show her what makes the girls so crazy. You want some, Cocoa?" he babbled.

Cocoa was not buying it of course because she already knew what the deal was.

"Cut the crap and save it for a stray, DePaul DePree. I know what is going on. You have the hots for Rhapsody and have for little while. She already told me."

Paully looked at me in confusion and I shrugged my shoulders and lowered my gaze.

"Don't worry, I love the idea. Any man would be blessed to have her as their woman. You on the other hand still show strong signs of dogitis, but I think that if anyone could bring about a change in you, it's Rhap."

"What do you mean? I'm a good man and you know it. That's why the women look for me." Paully accented his statement with a solid pound of his fist to his chest.

I couldn't take it anymore. I could feel the blood warming in my cheeks and sought out the restroom refuge before anyone noticed my blushing face. I spent a few minutes filling my lungs with air and slowly releasing it until there was nothing left. I repeated this meditative breathing ten times and felt completely relaxed. When I returned, Cocoa and Paully were sitting on the sofa leaning towards each other in conversation. Cocoa was grinning hard and Paully was looking pretty pleased himself.

"Okay, I'm back so you two can stop talking about me." I announced.

They didn't deny nor confirm that I had been the topic of their discussion but promptly changed the subject. Cocoa said that it was time to exchange gifts because she was getting sleepy. I agreed and went over to retrieve the gifts I'd purchased.

Cocoa, gave me a hand crafted expresso set from Italy and Paully an alpaca pullover sweater vest. I gave Cocoa a gift certificate to Bloomingdales and Paully received box sets of Miles Davis and Marvin

Gaye. He was thrilled and leaned over to give me a kiss which I made sure landed on my cheek. Then, Paully presented his gifts. Cocoa received a bottle of Vera Wang's perfume which took her over the edge.

"Paully I can't believe you remembered, this is my shit, baby. I love you!" she said as she through her arms around him and planted a circle of kisses on his face. He laughed, blushed and hugged her back. My heart was warm with the sight of my two best friends. Whenever I'm with them I am so happy and content and I love that. I love them.

As Cocoa continued to giggle as she opened the box to sample her gift, Paully handed me a small box about the same size as the one given to Cocoa. I opened it expecting a similar gift and was surprised to see a beautiful coiled choker with a unique oval pendant attached. My mouth formed a matching oval of awe. It was absolutely beautiful and I told Paully so.

"The necklace is Titanium and the pendant is made of steel and concrete." He explained.

"Wow, I love it. Thanks Paully. I offered with a sheepish smile.

"Girl, you better give him a big old juicy tongue kiss for that gift. That ain't no Marshall's special; you might as well say he went to Jared!" Cocoa decided to add.

I shoved her in the arm and told her to shut up. A glance at Paully let me know that he welcomed Cocoa's two cents, but it didn't matter. I was not going to give him any tongue, instead, he received a warm hug and a peck on the cheek. Cocoa was not happy and was getting ready to start up again but was interrupted by her cell phone. As she looked at the caller ID, Trayu rang my phone. Although I was a little nervous about answering it in front of Paully, I realized it was the perfect way to stop the madness building in the room. So I answered and quickly told him that we were wrapping up our evening and that I would call him before I went to bed.

Paully was clearly irritated by Trayu's call but couldn't say anything to me because Cocoa was still talking to who ever had called her. After a few minutes she excused herself and went to Paully's bedroom, where she and I would be sleeping. Fearful of being left alone with

Paully again, I excused myself to go to the bathroom. As I rose to leave, Paully took hold of my arm and asked me to stay with him. I laughed, pulled away, and told him to put on a pot of decaf and we would all have coffee and another slice of cake before bed.

Cocoa was still on the phone, so I took that opportunity to call Trayu. It was a quick conversation for he had only called to see how my day had gone and to say goodnight. I promised to call him when I got settled in at my mother's. The three of us met back in the living room and did indeed have coffee and more dessert. Then we talked until none of us could keep our eyes open where hence we retired for the night.

# 28

Although it was good to be home for Christmas, I was glad to be able to rest my head on my own pillow and bend my knees at my own throne. I took two extra days of rest before going back to work and used the time cleaning up work and personal files. It had been a good year financially. My caseload was solid and close to being full to capacity. In my estimation, I could take on one maybe two more clients and still be effective, but my preference would be to keep things the way they were. My current caseload was very manageable and left enough free time for me to make plans to expand over the next two years. I was definitely looking forward to the new year.

Tiana had been reporting deligently to her private sessions, but didn't bring Kaiewa back. When I asked about him, she would talk about him and what he and they had been doing. He was still a positive influence in her life and she still claimed that they were not dating. Our sessions always went the full time and sometimes longer if I was giving Tiana a ride home. Little by little I began sensing something was wrong. I couldn't quite put my hand on it in the beginning but after every session I felt like Tiana needed to say more. I began prepping a list of questions to ask to make sure that I touched on all the important topics such as her grieving process, family relationships, self concept, and friends. She usually had something to share no matter what I asked, even if it was a just a humorous little story which usually left us in stitches.

It was actually during one of her December sessions that I finally saw the light. Actually, it was the lack of light in Tiana's eyes. It was only for a second but I saw it just the same. We were cracking up over something she said and Tiana was laughing so hard that she was on the verge of tears. I looked up at Tiana and I saw despondency flash through her eyes. I let it pass then because it happened so quickly, but I was sure of what I saw and couldn't get it out of my mind. I had to address it. The question was how.

By our next meeting I still had not decided on how to address the concerns about Tiana's emotional state. I had spoken with MaDear and she updated me on Kieron's case, which was to say that there was nothing new to add. The assailant was on the loose and would most likely stay on that way. She vowed to continue her weekly call to the homicide department. MaDear was not going to let them forget her or her grandson. She still had not heard from her daughter, but she knew that all she could do was pray for her and hope that she would recover from her illness. Their neighborhood is what truly worried her.

"It seems like everyday there are more young men hanging out on the stoops, cars, and corners. There are even a few nasty looking gals hanging out there too. It makes me nervous to walk to and from the bus stop and I make sure that I keep an eye out for Tiana every afternoon. I wish I could get her a cell phone, but I just can't afford that right now. But Ms. Austin, that baby girl is a sweetheart; she knows that I worry about her but she never complains." That was all she had to say about Tiana.

I, of course, did not share my concerns. There was no reason to get MaDear all worked up over something that could turn out to be nothing.

When Tiana arrived for her session, she greeted me with one of her bright warming smiles and looked pretty happy to see me. We started off by talking about her girlfriend Empress getting busted kissing the new boy in their Geography class.

"I told her that she liked him but she kept denying it and denying it and denying it. She even denied it today in class and tried to act like she was mad at me. Then, not even two periods later, she gets cold busted. That's what she gets." Tiana laughed.

Tiana seemed to be in a good mood, but as soon as I started asking questions about her, her tone changed. That's when I decided to just bite the bullet and ask her what was going on.

"Tiana, lately I have been feeling like you are not as happy and content as you would want everyone believe. I really can't put my finger on it and I could be totally off base with my intuition. So right now I am going to trust that you are going to honor our commitment to honesty. Even when things are difficult to share or open up about, you have to trust me. You know that I am here to help and I don't pass judgment, but I need your honesty. With that said, I want to ask you a question. Okay?"

She acknowledged me by nodding her head and whispering a tiny yes.

I was not prepared for what came next. It's not that what she had to say stumped me. I hear that kind of stuff all the time. The zinger for me was that the signal my emotional spider senses picked up wasn't nearly as strong as it should have been. Tiana was depressed with a capital d. Her schoolwork was still top notch, but that part was easy for her. Although she didn't really need a bunch of time to study, she spent a lot of her time in her room pretending to. When in actuality, she usually sat in her room and sunk herself in sadness.

"Ms. A, I don't know why I feel this way. I mean I know that Kieron is gone and I still miss him and I expect to be sad sometimes. But I feel like this almost all of the time, when I walking home, when I'm going to the store, and when I'm just sitting at home. I don't have an appetite but I eat anyway because I don't want to worry MaDear. I hardly ever want to talk on the phone with my friends or hang out with Kaiewa either. The only time I feel okay is when I'm in class working on an assignment. Sometimes I stay in class during my lunch period, because then I don't have to deal with all those people looking at me with that, I feel so sorry for her, look. I don't need their pity. All I need is for someone to tell the police who killed my brother. That's all I want. Well, that's not true. I want to be able to feel happy again." Tiana explained.

She was hurting pretty bad and struggling with what she could do. She was still grieving and I reassured her that was okay. It took me almost two years to stop thinking about my dad when he died when I was ten, but I didn't share that with her. Instead I told her that she needed to open herself to her grief and stop trying to bury it. I also encouraged her to come back to group but she declined. Tiana was not only grieving for the loss of her brother, she hated her neighborhood. She talked about young men selling drugs to anyone who will buy and boys and girls jumping people for stupid reasons.

"Tiana, I know that it was rumored that Kieron's murder was actually a drug deal gone bad but they didn't find any drugs on him or in his system. Isn't that right?" I asked. My gut instinct was leading me to my next question.

"Tiana, do you think that Kieron's murder had anything to do with drugs?"

Tiana responded with a quick no but her downward cast eyes illustrated her uncertainty.

"Well T, my belief is that at this point it doesn't matter one way or the other whether drugs were involved in that horrific incident. The evidence indicates that it's not but that won't matter to some people. You see some people always expect the worst from certain people and it doesn't matter how hard you work to change stereotypes. So you have to stop worrying about that. Deal with what's real in your life. And right now, what's real is that you have lost your brother, your big brother, your only brother and it sucks. That's what's real."

By the time I finished my spill, Tiana was looking into my face with glassy eyes. She wasn't crying, just staring as if she was watching some suspenseful movie.

"Tiana, what I'm trying to say is that you can't let the possibilities weigh you down. You don't want to do that. You want your mind and heart to stay rooted in memory of Kieron. Remember him, love him, honor him by doing what you can to make a good life. That's what you guys always talked about." I paused.

"Isn't it, Tiana?" I asked.

Tiana nodded her head and kept nodding it until she reminded me of a life size bobblehead doll. When I assigned her weekly journal assignment, she noted it and started packing her things away silently. She was surely reflecting and all I could hope for was that she would come to a positive realization.

"All you have to do is gather all the information that you want me to include on your site and we will go from there. You can add services, pictures, and even a Blog later on. The most important thing is to get it up and running so that you start getting hits. I'll even print some business cards with your site information and you can distribute those to doctor offices, schools, recreation centers, and so forth. Rhap, you better be prepared, cuz once people see your dynamic site, you are going to be bombarded with calls. Woman you may have to get a partner and hire a receptionist." Trayu rambled on.

That's the way he had been since I answered the phone. He'd called to give me his itinerary for his visit. He would be flying in on New Year's Eve morning and leaving the second of January. He was bummed that he couldn't stay longer. It's not that he didn't try, he told me, but he just couldn't get any additional days off work. To be honest, I didn't want to take any more days off from work, either.

Talking to him that night was just like talking to a kid at Christmas. He was so excited. I couldn't help but smile and giggle at his enthusiasm and animation. He'd already finished packing his bags. I jokingly asked him if he had remembered to pack my gift and that was enough to take him over the edge.

He had been keeping my gift a secret since before Christmas although he often hinted to it being the perfect gift for me. Or would openly hope that I would love the gift he'd chosen. But that night, with that question, at that time, Trayu could hold the secret no longer.

"Okay, since Christmas is over I guess I can tell you." He paused.

"But only if you say please…Come on Lady Rhap let me hear you say please."

My face was hot and flushed. But I gave mister what he wanted.

"Oh pleeeez, Trayu, tell me what you're giving me for Christmas." I cooed.

"Damn girl, don't do me like that. I should have known better than to ask you, Ms. Smooth, a question like that, but you just wait til I see you." He threatened and continued.

"I, my lady, am giving you a Tranique Original."

"A what?" I laughed.

"I custom designed webpage courtesy of Tranform Original."

"What? I thought it was Tranique Original?" I questioned.

"Yeah, well which name do you like better? I've been trying to come up with a company name that's catchy but not ghetto. So what do you think?"

"How about Tre' Unique?" I suggested.

Trayu loved the name and kept repeating it throughout the rest of our conversation, which unfortunately had to end at 11:00 due to the fact that I had an early morning doctor's appointment.

# 29

Tiana called twice during my session with Rayton. Typically, I don't take calls during a session but I was tempted to do so this time for a couple of reasons. The first being that the call was from Tiana which was highly unusual due to the fact that she was calling during my standard session hours. Tiana, if anyone, knew my session hours. She and Kieron over the years had been scheduled into the most of the segments at one time or another. Tiana knew I was not to be disturbed during those hours, unless it was an emergency. Therefore, this must have been important. The second reason was the fact that she had called twice within the hour.

I let her go to voicemail both times and made a mental note to return her call, but at the moment Rayton was my main concern. Our last three session had been full of good reports and good spirits. He had become a part of the Big Brother/Big Sister program and had already been assigned a big brother. His big brother Colin was a full time accountant and part time trainer. Colin bought Rayton a membership at the YMCA and they had been working out together twice a week. The match appeared to be successful based on his attitude and school progress. In this session, he revealed that Colin had put him in charge of picking up their energy bars and acai drinks from the GNC store every week. Colin would give Rayton the money at the end of the week and he was responsible for purchasing the supplies they'd need for the following week. The trust that Colin had shown in him, made Rayton want to do the right thing.

"I really couldn't believe that he asked me to do it. He's so serious about his body. I mean he works out like it's a job he gets paid for. That's why everybody be wanting him to be their personal trainer but he says he doesn't have time to do that. He only trains me. Colin thinks I'm a great football player and he wants me to work on my grades so I can go to a good college. Plus he trust me with his money!"

He paused.

"The tripped out part is that I never even thought about spending that money on anything, but our energy bars, drink powder and juice. For real tho'... I can see now why my moms was always trippin' on me."

He shook his head.

"She couldn't trust me. I know she wanted to but she couldn't trust me cuz I didn't give her nothing to trust. Mannn, that trust is some powerful sh...uuh...stuff."

I gave him a little wink and nod to acknowledge his effort not to swear and I wondered.

"Rayton, why do you think that you never thought about using the money that Colin gave you for yourself? What was different for you this time?

"I don't know. I did think about that, tho'. He had asked me about why I had to come see you and I told him that it was court ordered. Then I had to tell him why the judge ordered this for me. I really didn't want to but it looked like he wasn't going to let me get away with not telling him, so I did."

"And what did he say after you told him? I asked.

"He kinda lectured me a little... well, I guess it wasn't a lecture cuz it didn't feel like a lecture and believe me...I know what a lecture sounds like. But kinda like made my mind lecture itself."

"How so?"

"I don't know Ms. Austin. He was just like saying stuff to me like... Everyone that's human has made mistakes and bad decisions. And that we take from every mistake, what we want and need, not what anybody else wants us to take or learn. If we didn't take anything at all, then we could never grow mentally, emotional or spiritually. And that growing mentally, emotionally or spiritually is just as important as growing physically. And it made sense to me cuz what would I do if I stopped growing physically? I know I wouldn't like that." He finished and laughed a little."

I told him that I liked that example. It was a good comparison. Then he continued.

"The next time we met to workout, he gave me the job to purchase our workout stuff. He never even questioned me or told me not to use the money for anything else and it never crossed my mind. Maybe I just knew that he trusted me. But I don't really know what made this time different, it just was and I feel pretty good about that."

He shared a little more about how he wanted to continue becoming a better person. Judging from our discussion, his report cards, and behavior reports, he was turning things around. He had obviously turned the corner and could see the benefits of his good decision making.

It was a good session and I sent him away with the simple goal of staying on track. We only had one more session scheduled before his next court review but I was sure that I was going to recommend release.

After Rayton left, I called Tiana back on her new Trak Phone while I fixed a cup of Passion Fruit tea and prepared to sit at my desk and type up my notes. Her phone was answered by a male voice and for an instant I thought it was Kieron and my voice got caught in my throat.

"Hello? Hello?" the voice said and I forced my voice through.

"Hello, may I speak to Tiana?" I asked hesitantly.

"Sure, is this Ms. A.? The voiced that I now knew was not Kieron's asked.

"Yes, who am I speaking to, if I may ask." I replied.

"Hi Ms. A, this is Kaiewa. Tiana's friend. She just went to the restroom and asked me to hold her phone in case you called. She should be right out; can you hold for just a minute?"

"Sure." I responded. He did kind of sound like Kieron, I thought.

When Tiana came to the phone, she informed me that she was down the street from my office in the Dunkin' Donuts. She needed to see me for a few minutes and she didn't mind waiting until I was finished with my clients.

"You're lucky baby girl, I just finished up. Come on up."

While I waited, I typed my notes so I wouldn't wonder about what was up with Tiana.

I opened the door to a very serious looking Tiana. She was all bundled up and looked like she was carrying the weight of the world on her back. She came in and went directly to the conversation nook and took a seat. I looked back to the door, expecting Kaiewa to follow her. When he didn't, I asked of him. Tiana told me that he was waiting down stairs and that he had only come to ride the bus with her there and back. Then she told me that she wouldn't be there long; that she only needed to give me something. I was confused.

"Okay T, let me run to the little girls room and I will be right with you."

I returned and took a seat across from Tiana.

"So, what's going on T?" I asked.

She didn't speak right away but when she did she was as serious as I had ever seen her.

"Ms. Austin, I've been thinking about everything you've been telling me and I feel like I am ready to take the next steps in healing from losing Kieron. And I think that there have been some things that have been keeping me from being able to do that and I have to let go of them if I am going to start feeling better."

"Sounds like you're on the right track, Tiana."

"Yeah, I think so too. But Ms. A, it's kinda complicated, you know. I need you to do something for me and I need you to keep it secret."

"T…"

"Hold on." She held up a hand to stop me. I said it was complicated and I mean it. I need you to promise to keep this secret not from just MaDear, but from me too."

Now I was really confused and it must have shown on my face. Tiana unzipped her backpack and pulled out another backpack. She seemed to be struggling to lift it and with both hands, offered it to me.

"I need you to take this." She said.

"What is it Tiana?" I questioned as I looked suspiciously at the bag.

"Just take it please, Ms. Austin, it was Kieron's. It's a safe and he used to keep it hidden in my closet in the ceiling. I always knew it was there and I'd promised never to tell MaDear that it was there and never to look inside. I kept that promise and to be honest I never wanted to know what was inside. And I still don't. I don't know why Kieron didn't want me to know what is in there but I trust that he had a good reason. You have to take it Ms. A because I want to keep my promise to Kieron but I can't keep this safe. I can't give it to MaDear. If he didn't want me to know what was in the safe then I sure don't want MaDear to know."

I took the bag and dropped it by the side of my chair. It landed with a thud.

"Ms. A, I been thinking a lot about what you've been telling me and I have been trying to find a way to do what you said. I've been trying to let myself grieve and bring closure to losing my big brother. And you're right that I have been blocking it, you know, like trying to believe that I need to have answers before I can move on. But in church on Sunday I realized that that's not really true. I figure if I'm suppose to get answers then the Lord will provide them in his own way and his own time. I should be able to move on because like MaDear always says, the Lord don't give you more than you can bear. So that's what I'm trying to do. That safe and the questions I have about what's in it are blocking me from being able to let go."

"Tiana, what do you expect me to do with it. If you don't want to know what's in it what makes you think that I do?" I questioned her.

"To tell the truth, I don't care what you do with it and I don't want to know what you do with it. See I don't think that there is anything bad in there. In my mind I think that it was just a place for Kieron to keep his nasty magazines or love letters from those girls that were constantly on his jock. You know what I'm talking about, the stuff that teenage boys like to keep secret. That's what I believe is in there and that's what I'm going to keep believing."

She paused, then stood.

"Okay. I gotta go Ms A; Kaiewa is waiting for me and I need to get home before dark. I didn't tell MaDear I was coming here."

She started walking towards the door, but stopped and turned to say thank you. I gave a hug and was surprised by the strength and intensity of her hug. She held on longer than normal and thanked me twice more before quickly exiting. I tried to walk with her but she wanted to ride the elevator down alone. I didn't push it but told her to page me and let me know she'd made it home. Then I walked back to the office and made a quick inspection of the safe in the bag. It was one of those Sentry safes that had a keyed lock. I don't know why, but it gave me the creeps. So I went to my bathroom and retrieved cleaning gloves, 409 spray, and paper towels. I returned to the office and proceeded to wipe down the safe and put it back in the bag. If anyone had asked me why I was doing it, I probably couldn't have given them an answer.

Then I walked over to my desk to finish typing up Rayton's session notes. After his I started typing up notes on Tiana's impromptu session. I started typing, stopped, deleted what I'd typed, shut down the computer and left for the day.

# 30

"Tommy, I want to make sure I am clear, okay. You can open the safe."

"Yeah, Rhap, I can open this safe. No problem."

"And you don't have to look inside, right?"

I knew that he was probably thinking that I was a crazy woman and extremely paranoid, but I couldn't take the chance. I didn't know what was in that safe and was not sure that I wanted to know. Regardless, Tiana entrusted it to me and I couldn't see any way around it. I had to find out what was in the box and figure out how to dispose of it.

"Yes, yes, yes!" he exclaimed. "I don't have to look inside and I promise not to look inside. Your little dowdry box will remain safe. But next time you might want to think about putting the combination and key in a couple of different places if you want to keep your secrets safe Miss Lady." He said with a huge toothy grin."

"Okay." I smiled back and nudged him with my shoulder. He really was a nice guy but he still had too much drama in his life for me.

Tommy got to work and I sat on the workbench a few feet away. I tried to keep an eye on him without appearing to but I was so nervous about what was inside and what I would have to do if any of the contents were illegal. The only thing I knew was that, if they were, I wouldn't tell Tiana or MaDear. I would never tarnish Kieron's memory for them.

"All done, Rhap."

"What? That was quick!"

"What can I say. I do what I do and I do it well, but you should already know that. Or did you forget?"

Tommy was always on the mack but I was so totally beyond his macking.

"Whatever, Tommy. Here." I said as I handed him a fifty dollar bill. "And I'll take my safe and be out of your way. Thanks so much for doing this."

Tommy tried to decline payment and bargain for a date instead, but I insisted on paying him and told him that I would be in touch. Yes, I knew that I was leading him to believe he had a chance at a date when he had no such thing. But it was the safest thing to do considering that I had two men fighting for my affection and keeping my mind reeling. There was no room for anymore.

I carefully placed the safe back in the backpack and lugged it out to my car. I was still very nervous, actually, even more so because now I was driving around with an open safe that had who knows what in it. As soon as I got home I made sure the house was locked up tight and took the safe up to my room. Then I went back down stairs and grabbed a package of plastic sheeting and some nylon cleaning gloves. Don't ask me why. I just wanted to be careful just in case there was a firearm or something like that. I didn't want my fingerprints on anything inside. On my way back upstairs, I had the urge to pray so that's exactly what I did. I dropped to my knees on the stair in front of me and said a prayer. I prayed that whatever I found in that safe would not put MaDear, Tiana, or myself in any danger. With that done, I headed to my bedroom. Once there, I decided that I would move everything to the guestroom and open the safe there.

My heart was beating so fast and I suddenly felt short of breath. I asked myself if I could be having a panic attack and decided that I wasn't going to claim that mess. So, I sat on the bed to take some long deep breaths and summon a peaceful serene scene. That's when I remembered that I had an appointment at the salon. I was more than happy to postpone the opening of the safe but I was still very nervous, so before I left, I carried the bag with the safe up to the attic.

"Dakota, oh my God, girl you are beautiful. What are you doing washing hair? Your momma better be paying you." I said as I hugged my little but not so little unofficial Goddaughter.

"No Ma'am, I'm just helping out so we can finish in time to go do a walk through at our new house."

I looked at Montana. "New house? What new house? That's great, do tell."

Montana gave me the look and cut her eyes at Dakota before responding.

"Girl, it's no big deal. We just needed a little more storage space."

I took the hint and instantly understood that Montana was not going to talk about her personal business in front of her clients. She would listen to theirs and share many funny stories and even offer some advice here and there. But she was careful not to put her business on the chopping block for scrutiny. I knew she would give me the 411 as soon as she could get me alone.

Dakota took me to a bowl and started my hot oil treatment. By the time I came from under the dryer there were only four ladies left in the shop. Montana put me in her chair and settled in to telling me about her new adventure as she put the finishing touches on my mane. She lucked up on a sweet deal to assume the mortgage on a practically new home in Stockbridge. So she registered her current home for Section 8 and put a for rent sign in the yard.

"Why would you want to rent your place instead of selling it?" I questioned because Montana was way too picky about her things that trusting someone to take care of a house that she owned was not something I imagined she could do. But she fooled me.

"It's an investment and I think it will be very profitable. The place is almost paid for and the current mortgage is less that six hundred a month. I will be able to clear that plus some easily. I have my oldest nephew acting as property manager, so I don't have to worry about that. He and my brother and I are the interviewing committee and we are going to be very selective. I don't want just any old body in my place, you feel me?"

It sounded like a solid plan and she seemed very excited. I was happy for her because any money she made would help her help Dakota.

"Girl that's great and I wish you all the luck. Keep me informed and if all goes well, maybe we can partner up and invest in some more property in the future. Hey, we could become real estate moguls." I laughed but it wasn't that bad of an idea.

I was the last client to leave that day although my head had been finished for a couple of hours. I spent the time catching up with Dakota and laughing with Montana. Dakota was starting at a spa as an intern and Montana was starting CPR training just in case her new 72 year old boyfriend had a medical mishap. A good time was had by all but as soon as I got on I285 I remembered what was waiting for me at home and I got anxious all over again. Regardless, I knew that I would go home and do whatever I needed to lift the weight of the mysterious safe from Tiana. That much I was sure of.

Before I went back upstairs, I fixed myself a small bravery booster which consisted of Ketel One Critron, cran-cherry cocktail and a big splash of lime juice over a mound of crushed ice. With booster in hand, I reentered the guestroom, adorned the rubber gloves and prepared for the opening of Kieron's safe. I took a gulp of my drink and reached out to pull the safe closer to me, got a little nervous, took another sip and decided to go make sure that I had locked down the house efficiently.

Of course I realized I was stalling and that there wasn't any use in doing so. I only had two options. One, I could go upstairs, open the safe and dispose of the contents in a safe in a secure manner. The other option was that I could take the safe and dump it in a watery abyss or bury it in a deep trouble free grave. And since I would have to travel too far to find a satisfactory body of water and the knowledge that it would probably take my weak upper body three days to dig a hole deep enough to secure secrecy, I was left with my current situation. So, back to the guestroom I went.

Onnnne, twoooo, three, flip! Slowly, I opened my eyes.

"Oh shit!" I screamed as my first glimpse of the contents was a pistol. I took a couple of deep calming breathes and carefully lifted it from the box so I could look at the other contents.

"What was that sound?" I thought.

Something was moving inside the gun. Then it dawned on me. I shook the gun and knew. It wasn't a real gun, just a fancy BB gun. My nervous laugh filled the room and I took another gulp of my booster.

One by one, I pulled the items out and laid them on the plastic sheeting on the floor in front of me. Some of the items saddened me but they all surprised me. There was a small manilla envelop which contained about a tablespoon of marijuana and two joints. A copy of Ralph Ellison's Invisible Man, Richard Bach's Jonathan Livingston Seagull, and a SAT prep cd were held together with a rubberband. There were also brochures for Spelman and Agnes Scott college.

Under all of these items, I found a large white mailing envelop stuffed into the bottom of the safe. It had been sealed and resealed many times with different types of tape but the final layer was of duct tape. I couldn't grasp the tape with my rubber gloves and I wasn't about to take them off. Instead, I ran to my study to grab the letter opener and carefully sliced the envelop open from the bottom. Once again, oh shit, slipped from my lips as a shower of c-notes began falling into my lap.

How much money is this? Is it real? Where did he get it from? What am I going to do with it?

The questions were rapidly firing in my head. I grabbed my drink and drained it. Then I decided that I would need was another before continuing. This time I traded my cocktail glass for a full size drinking glass and made a double booster. I figured I'd need the extra bravery.

Sitting amongst the money again, I continued to examine the items in the safe's contents. I also found a picture of Kieron, Tiana, and their mother when they were just toddlers, and a picture of Kiernon sitting on a green sofa holding Tiana. They were dressed in their Easter best and had smiles like cheshire cats. There was a small birthday card with a sweet little message added to the birthday wish inside. It read, *"Miss Mitchell, I hope you have a blessed birthday. You are an angel. Happy Birthday, Kieron."*

I had no idea who this Miss Mitchell was. I couldn't recall ever hearing her name from Kieron or Tiana. Who was she and why did Kieron have a birthday card for her? I wondered for a quick moment, but honestly I had bigger issues laying in front of me. The best thing to do for the time being was to tuck the safe matter away until after the New Year. And that's what I did. I turned my energy to preparing for Trayu visit.

# 31

Paully was not pleased with the amount of time I spent with Trayu and he honestly thought that he could call and rib me out about it. My first instinct was to go off on him and hang up in his face. Instead, I took a different road.

"I'm not going to stop seeing him Paully. I'm sorry if that upsets you. That is not my intent. And I hope that it is not your intent to upset me by suggesting, recommending or, as it appears to me, insisting that I should stop seeing him. Paully, you know that I love you with all my heart and I have for almost as long as I can remember. You know that. And I know that you love me."

"Well if you know that then why are you doing this. Why give young blood the chance over me? If you really think about it, it makes much better sense to try to take the love we have to the next level, than to try to move forward with someone new. Someone who really knows nothing about you. Damn Rhap, you don't know much about him. I just don't' understand that. What's wrong with me?!!"

I could hear the pleading in his voice and it was tugging at my heart, but I just would not cave in.

"Paully, come on, there is nothing wrong with you. You are a wonderful friend. I am sure you are even a wonderful boyfriend but I can't honestly say that that's what I want or need from you. I don't know if it could work and I'm not willing to risk losing the friendship we have in order to find out. But what is more important and what I am trying to express to you is that I really like Trayu and he makes me feel happy. I don't know where it will lead but for now it feels fine. You always say that you want me to be happy and, Paully, I am."

"So you think the two of you have a future?" he asked

"I'm not saying that, Paully, it's not that simple. To be honest, I'm not looking for a future with anyone right now. I don't talk to Tray about any type of long term commitments or arrangements. We are simply getting to know each other and enjoying the process."

My hope was to clean up Paully's thoughts. I know that all he could think about was Trayu boning me, but the situation wasn't as physical as he envisioned. We had not done the do though we had come pretty close a few times. No closer than Paully and I had come that one time. I needed Paully to see beyond that. It was bad enough that it seemed as if I were choosing Trayu over Paully, I didn't want him thinking that it was all about sex.

"Rhapsody, why don't you just bite the bullet and let me be your man. Shit, it's just the right thing to do and you know it. You know it feels right and I know it feels right so let's just go do it." Came Paully's suave relpy.

I laughed and simply stated.

"Nope."

Then to my complete and total surprise, he snapped.

"This is bull! I can't believe you Rhap! What are you thinking? What is wrong with you? Did old dude mess you up that bad that you can't think straight. Did he screw your head up so bad that you actually think that it's cool for you to be messing with that boy. Girl, your name ain't Stella, so you better wake up and smell the coffee before all you have left is bitter grinds. You're too old to be running around playing the field and you know it."

Now it was my turn and he had truly pissed me off. I could feel the temperature in my body rise. The top of my head felt like it was going to blow steam at any moment. There was a low buzzed spiraling through my ears and my throat felt tight. I knew that I was becoming angry as he continued to speak. So angry that I'd actually stopped listening to what he was blubbering about and just simmered on all that he'd already said. All that he had said over the last few months. I felt pressured and disrespected. Yeah, that's what was upsetting me... pressure and disrespect...and from Paully of all people. His post was as best friend and he should not have been putting me through this. I was boiling and the fire below was almost uncontrollable. The top had to be taken off to release the pressure before irreversible damage was done.

I noticed that my breathing was rapid, so I closed my eyes and forced myself to take a couple of deep breaths. Then, I heard his voice.

"Rhap. Rhapsody?" He called.

The sound of his voice took me over the edge. I had an overwhelming desire to go totally off on him, though I knew I shouldn't. I knew I would say something or somethings that I didn't need to say. So I hung up the phone instead.

Then I realized that I was sitting straight up. I took a long deep breath and slowly exhaled until my lungs were empty. I did it again. I could feel the tension in my shoulders easing away. Then the phone rang and I saw it was Paully calling back. Inhaling and exhaling one more time, I decided that I was capable of talking to him.

"Hello."

He wasted no time starting in.

"So I guess I hit a nerve, huh? Well, don't shoot the messenger baby girl, the truth hurts." He stated ever so smugly.

I'd had enough.

"Hold up, Paully. Let me stop you right there. Let me ask you a couple of questions. Are you seeing anyone right now."

"Nope."

"Okay, let me rephrase that. Are you fucking anyone?"

Silence.

"Right, that's what I thought. Now for the next question. Is she at least three years younger than you?"

"That's not the point, Rhap. You know it's not the same."

"Paully how could you say something so stupid. You're sitting over there trying to convince me that I am some child molester, when the age difference between Trayu and I is surely no different than you and your current play toy. The only difference is that I'm not sleeping with Tray. And to top it off, you think I'm stupid enough to fall for your reasoning. Well, Paully, I'm not. You want me to believe that we could actually take our friendship to the next level but you can't even abstain from sex while you are supposedly pursuing me. Come on, I know you don't think I'm that stupid. I love you and you're my best friend and I want it to stay that way, but this is the last I want to hear about

Tray and me or Karl and me or me and anyone. You can keep me as your best friend but not by keeping up this shit. I love you but I can't date you and I'd hope you could accept that. Since you can't, then you'll have to decide where that leaves us. So think about it Paully and when you call again, it needs to be as my best friend checking on his best friend." I said and hung up.

It was hard to talk to Paully that way and it left me shaking. I was literally shaking. The next thing I knew I was running to the bathroom puking my guts up. Why? I had no idea. After praying to the porcelain god, I washed my face with the coldest water the tap would give and looked at myself in the mirror. The face before me looked peaceful and was actually cute and the eyes spoke volumes. At that moment the eyes in the mirror spoke to me and sent me into a gut wrenching cry. I cried so hard and loud that I had difficulty catching my breath. So I made my way to the side of the tub, draped a towel over my head, put my head between my legs, searched out the deepest breaths I could find and continued to cry.

When Tray called that night, I let him go to voice mail. I wasn't in any position to talk to him.

# 32

Trayu was standing outside of Delta's baggage claim leaning against the wall and looking scrumptious. He sported a charcoal grey small brim fedora, black turtle neck under a super thick hand knitted sweater, dark blue jeans and his black Timberlands. There was a nip in the air which prompted me to grab my orange leather jacket to deposit over my brown Columbia's turtle neck, but Tray looked cool not cold. The airport traffic was creeping along so I was able to take in his adorable manifestation without embarrassment. When my tongue glided over my lips, I jerked back to consciousness and composed myself before Trayu caught sight of me.

I pulled up to the curb, got out and opened the trunk without Trayu even spotting me. I walked up to him.

"Excuse me sir are you waiting for a ride." I said in a deep voice.

"No, I got one coming mannnnnn…" He replied as he finally turned towards the voice addressing him. And before I could start laughing, he pulled me into an embrace that made me sigh with relief. I had missed him and longed to feel him close to me, yet I hadn't realized it. Or maybe, I just refused to admit that I craved him. We'd spent so many hours talking, sharing, dreaming and laughing together. Trayu had become a daily part of my existence. He held and rocked me and laughed for several moments. I could feel him inhaling my scent.

"Hey, we better get out of here before I get a ticket." I said.

"If paying a traffic ticket will allow you to stay in my arms longer, then I will be glad to pay the cost." He replied as I led him by the hand towards my vehicle. I hoisted his bag into the trunk and walked around to the driver's side and he opened the door for me. He was such a gentleman and I loved it. He sat down in the passenger seat but before securing his seat belt, he asked for a hello kiss. I gave him a couple of mushy pecks on the lips and said.

"Hello, Tray and welcome back to the ATL."

He gave me one more peck and shook his head. I asked him if he wanted to grab something to eat and he did. So, we headed south over to Ehberhert's for a little brunch. I contemplated taking him to Corie's joint but didn't really want to share him. Besides, Ehberhert's was one of my favorite brunch sites because they offered some of my favorites like, salmon croquets with yellow rice and a BLT with arugula and black beans and rice. And if I was feeling a little blue, they offered the most delectable banana and blueberry pancakes served with real maple syrup. I shared all my favorites with Tray and he decided on the banana and blueberry pancakes. I, on the other hand, went with the BLT and added a fried egg.

During brunch Tray couldn't seem to take his eyes off of me which kept me in constant blush mode. He was so handsome and he had the silkiest voice I'd ever heard. He asked how things were going at work and asked if I needed to go into the office. I told him that there was no way I was giving up any of his time to the office.

I thought briefly about the safe and its mysterious contents but pushed it out of my mind quickly. I didn't have to worry about Trayu running across the safe because I had taken it up into the attic and placed it in one of my old traveling trunks that locked with a skeleton. It was hidden under my high school cheerleading uniform, cheerleading warm ups, junior and senior prom dress, and letterman's jacket. There was no way that he would ever find it, not that he would have any reason to snoop around for it. My imagination was preparing to go wild but I promptly reeled it in.

"Earth to Rhapsody."

Trayu's voice snapped me out of the daydream that threatened to ruin my joyous mood.

"So, you want to tell me what you were thinking about or am I going to have to kiss it out of you? He teased.

"Oh please. You don't scare me cuz I got your game. If you want a kiss, you can just ask for it. You don't have to create excuses." I teased back and leaned forward to give him a peck on the lips. He blushed and I felt success. I had successfully maneuvered the focus away from my day dreaming thoughts. It was important to do so as quickly as possible because I had no intentions at all of telling Trayu anything about Tiana and the safe or any of my clients at all. At that time, I pledged to myself that I would put any thoughts pertaining to work aside until I put Trayu on a flight back to Chi-town.

After brunch we made a liquor run for a couple of bottles of champagne. I had at least four at home but Trayu insisted on buying a specific label for me to try. If I had known that he wanted to purchase two bottles of Taittinger Brut Millesime at $65 each, I would have tried harder to talk him out of it. On the way to my place I asked him if he wanted to make anymore stops since the stores would be closing earlier for the New Year. He asked about the attire for the party we were to attend and after being assured that his outfit would be sufficient, he declined making any other stops.

"I'll tell you what I would really like to do, Lady Rhapsody. I would love to go to your place, strip down to our shorts and take a nice nap in each others' arms. What do you think about that?" Trayu suggested.

I couldn't help smiling at his coyness, nor could I help the tingling in my lower extremities. He definitely had my attention and the capability of making me lose control. The plan was to fight it as long as possible by keeping my weakness for him hidden. It was my belief that if he got a whiff of it, he would pour it on and that would be the end of my self control.

"Stop messing with me." I replied as I swatted his arm.

"No, I'm serious, you're the one with your mind in the gutter. I could seriously use a nap and it would make it all the more relaxing if you'd take it with me. You can just put on your pjs. I promise not to bother you." He replied.

I was embarrassed.

"Oh…uh…okay…that's fine…I could use a nap myself."

"Cool, but I didn't hear you promise not to bother me during our nap." He smiled.

I swatted him again.

"Trayu leave me alone. I promise not to bother you either. As a matter of fact I promise not to even touch you. Better yet, I'll put a pillow between us."

"Woah, hold up. Now you're getting carried away." He laughed.

His charm was going to break me yet.

I checked the house messages to make sure there hadn't been any changes in the plans for that evening. The absence of messages told me that we'd have a little more than two hours to rest. I retrieved my burnt orange swing dress from the closet and hung it in the bathroom. It looked smooth enough, but I figured a little extra steam from my shower later wouldn't hurt. Then I stepped back into my room and pulled out my white gold diamond hoops and my Cleopatra bracelet with the mandarin garnet gemstones. As I reached for my choker, my eye caught sight of the necklace Paully gave me for Christmas. Suddenly, I felt the urge to call him. I wondered who he'd be bringing in the New Year with. His plans had been vague when I asked about them last, which made me think that he just didn't care to share. Even though, I didn't pressure him for details because I didn't want to share the details of my New Years plans.

Trayu interrupted my thoughts when he entered my bedroom. He was standing just inside the doorway in an indigo pair of nylon shorts that covered his knees and a gray wife beater. He was a vision, a delightful vision indeed. I would normally describe Trayu as slender but he was far more than slender. His broad shoulders rounded out into well defined arms of steel and a chest of iron. I could clearly see his six pack through the t-shirt and instinctively felt that sinking feeling in my stomach.

"You don't look ready to take a nap." He stated.

"I know, but just give me a minute. I was trying to getting all my things ready for tonight." I responded and fumbled around in my drawers for something to wear to bed.

Trayu awakened from our nap first and as I opened my eyes he was staring at me. I was not alarmed, surprisingly, because I identified with the look in his eyes almost immediately. It was a look of admiration. A look that says, "I'm so happy to be in this place right now with you." I know the look because it appeared on my face whenever I spent time with Tray. If I was totally honest, it probably surfaced even when I talked to him at night. When he saw that I was awake he gently kissed my temple and rolled me into his arms for a warm embrace.

"This feels right. Can you feel that?" He said as our bodies meshed.

I remained cautious and instead of replying, I planted a series of slow gentle kisses on his neck and shoulder blade. I felt our bodies beginning that slow sensual dance again and reluctantly broke the embrace informing Tray that we needed to get showered and ready to bring in the New Year. He didn't argue but gave me a look that showed me that he didn't want to leave and rolled out of bed.

I waited until I heard his shower start before disrobing and getting into my shower. I washed quickly and gave my underarms a quick swiping with the razor to make sure everything was smooth and hair-free. While I was drying off the phone rang. I figured it was Corie calling to bother me so I ran into the bedroom to catch it. It was Paully.

"Hey Rhap, what's up? Why do you sound so out of breath?"

"Oh I was just getting out of the shower and I thought you were Corie calling." I said, suddenly feeling a little nervous.

"Naw, I ain't Corie. So what's up? You two hanging out tonight?" He asked but before I could muster an answer I was interrupted by a knock at my bedroom door, followed by Trayu's voice.

"Rhapsody? Are you decent or can I come in anyway."

It didn't matter whether or not Paully had heard his voice or not; I had to respond and respond quickly or Trayu would have walked in on me in all my naked glory.

"No, give me a minute. Hold on right quick, Paully." I said all in one breath. I put the phone down, shrugged on my robe, and opened the bedroom door a crack.

"Hi there, what can I do for you, sir." I greeted Trayu.

"What you trying to hide behind that door, huh. I wanna see." He teased.

"Leave me alone." I hushed back. "What do you want?"

"I just wanted to know if you had any lotion. I forgot mine and I know you don't want me ashing up on you this evening."

"Sure, I have Shea Butter, Mango Body Butter, and some Jergens."

"Great. I'll take the shea butter please."

I left the door open, retrieved the butter from the bathroom and gave it to Trayu.

"Now go get ready and leave me alone so I don't make us late." I teased as I closed the door.

Paully started barking questions as soon as I put the phone to my ear. I guess he did hear Trayu's voice. He was not pleased to say the least.

"Who the fuck is that? You got some dude up in your place? What's going on, Rhapsody?"

"I know you are not cursing at me." Was my first reply.

"Look Rhap, I don't want to hear that crap. Answer my questions. Who is that and what's going on?" he repeated.

"You need to calm down Paully." I paused. "That's Trayu and he's here to bring in the New Year. I'm not going to even ask if that's a problem because I know it is, but it is what it is. And I'm not going to debate this issue with you now because I need to get ready for dinner. We can talk about this later." I said as I walked over to my dresser and grabbed the Mango body butter.

"I can't believe this shit. I come all the way to Georgia to bring in the New Year with you and you are hanging out with that knucklehead. This is unreal." He screamed into the phone.

I stopped lotioning my calf and stared at the wall. Did he just say that he was here in Georgia?

"What do you mean you're here? You didn't tell me you were coming to Atlanta."

"No I didn't cuz it was suppose to be a surprise. But I guess the surprise is on me. But why didn't you tell me you were going to spend the new year with him? What kind of shit is that?" I could actually feel his anger coming through the phone.

"Paully, you already know why I wouldn't tell you that Trayu was coming to visit. Come on now."

"Oh please Rhap, don't play me like that. You know that's crap. If we are going to make this thing happen, you should not be even talking to youngblood. I don't believe this shit! You spend all that time calling me a player and the truth is that you are no better than me. Are you, little Miss Rhapsody?" he yelled and hung up.

I stood there holding the phone for a minute or so before the beeping reminded me to hit the end button. Paully was extremely upset. More upset than I had ever heard. I guess he had the right to be. I probably should have told him that Tray was coming for the New Year, but I really didn't want to hear his mouth. Even though, he did not have to yell at me and hang up in my face. He was the one who just popped up. I couldn't believe he called me a player. I am not a player and I was not trying to play anyone either. I had not committed to either of them but Paully knew that I liked Trayu a lot. Trayu on the other hand did not know anything about Paully's affection for me. Maybe I needed to tell Tray about Paully?

It was too much for me to think about right now. I needed to get dressed and that's exactly what I did. I quickly dressed and applied a light coating of makeup. I don't wear full make-up often but I'm quite the make-up artist. It's one of the skills I picked up in college which allowed me the opportunity to make some play money on a regular basis. The girls would line up on the weekends for me to work my make-up magic before hitting the frat parties or the clubs. I'd applied a light coating to my toes and decided to go down to the kitchen for a glass of ice water. On my way down I thought about my conversation with Paully and by the time I tried to hold the glass under the ice maker, I realized I was shaking like a leaf.

"Wow, you look amazing!" Came the shock of Trayu's voice.

As I turned to him, his smile seemed to dissolve.

"Baby are you okay?" he asked as he closed the distance between us and took me by the shoulders.

Tears slowing poured from my eyes and Tray took me into his arms.

"Rhapsody, what's the matter baby?" He questioned as he held me in his rocking embrace.

I told him. I told him that Paully had upset me. I told him that

Paully didn't like him. I told him that Paully didn't like the two of us together because he thought he wanted to be with me. I was spilling beans left and right and Trayu just held me. Tightly at first but as every confession slipped from my mouth, his embrace weakened. He never let go of me, not even after I answered his first question during my confessions.

"How long has this been going on?"

"I don't know...practically since I met you."

"Why didn't you tell me about this before?"

"I really don't know. Initally I thought he was just mad because you beat him on the billiard table but then he started trying to convince me that he and I would be perfect as a couple. And he won't let it go. Lately it seems as if we are in constant conflict and that's not the way it's supposed to be. He's my best friend!" I cried out.

I could feel his body tensing and took this opportunity to look into his eyes. They weren't cold but they surely were not warm either.

"What Tray?" I asked as I continued to search his eyes for some clarification.

He took me by the hands and stooped down to look into my eyes.

"Hey, I don't really want to do this right now but I need to know if you think you want to be with old dude?"

He placed his left hand on my right cheek. It was like I was hypnotized. I couldn't look away from his gorgeous face. His eyes were like a truth serum.

"No, I don't think that's our path. We work great as best friends and always have. I think that should be good enough."

Trayu nodded his head and asked if there were any particular reason Paully thought that the two of us should be together. I knew that he was asking if I had given Paully any reason to believe that we could be together. I didn't want to tell him but at that instant I couldn't seem to help myself. And so I told him about the making out session that Paully and I had during his last visit. Now, I didn't feel the need to go into any details. All he needed to know was that we'd shared some kisses. When he asked if anything happened during Christmas, I confessed a few more kisses. I restated that I felt that our relationship as best friends was what was most important. I also admitted that his persistence was both mentally and emotionally draining. Finally, I shared with Trayu what I knew for certain, I felt good with him. He brought sunshine to my life and an inner warmth that was new and oh so real.

That's when he finally pulled me back into his arms. I could hear his heart racing as he rested his chin on my head. Soon I was tearing up again. I didn't want to loose him.

The limo arrived at 7:30 promptly and I asked Trayu to tell the driver that we would be right down. I trucked it back to my room to touch up my make-up. He had been so sweet which totally amazed me. I expected him to be at least moderately upset after hearing about Paully, but he wasn't. Other than asking the few more questions about what I was feeling and why I hadn't told him about this situation before, he was totally focused on comforting me. Before heading back up to my room, I'd apologized for not being forth coming because that was totally on me and that admission caused me to tear up all over again.

"Wow don't you two look lovely" Corie greeted us.

Corie was already sipping a glass of champagne when Tray and I slid into the limo. She looked stunning in her black spaghetti strapped dress with the black and silver sequenced bust bank and five inch stellettos. Her hair was pulled back into an elegant bun and large tear drop clusters negated her bare neckline. Corie's make up was flawless as usual and she was smiling as hard as a child on Christmas. I greeted her with a hug and kiss.

"Girl, you look gorgeous. You really plan on turning some heads tonight." I complimented and Trayu joined in seconding my opinion.

Corie giggled and handed me a glass of champagne. I passed it on to Tray as she handed me another.

"No love, I only want one head to turn towards me tonight." She said.

"Who might that be?" I questioned intrigued.

"Girl, I'm not suppose to say anything but I can't hold it. You two just have to promise to act surprised when you see him. Okay?" Corie was practically giddy with excitement.

I made the promise and crossed my heart to seal the pledge.

"Rhap, girl, Paully finally called after all this time. He's in town for New Year's Eve and he's coming to the restaurant to bring in the New Year with us!" she said almost bouncing in her seat.

"What?!" I yelled and looked at Trayu. Apparently, Corie did not pick up on the panic in my voice or the worry on my face.

"Yeah girl, I almost passed out when I figured out who he was. I gave him my number months ago or I should say that you gave him my number months ago." Then she turned to Trayu.

"See Trayu, I asked Rhapsody to give my number to him, because they were good friends, thinking that her good word would give me the upper hand. But I didn't think it had worked because I hadn't heard from him. But this turned out to be the magical night. He called and said he was in town and wanted to know what I was doing to bring in the New Year. I told him I was hanging out with his girl and invited him to come along." She started explaining.

Trayu held a face carved of stone while Corie spoke and even when he interrupted her. He looked at me and without hesitation asked Corie.

"And he didn't tell you that he had spoken with Rhapsody?"

Corie looked back and forth between the two of us before finally asking for clarification. I looked at Trayu for guidance and he told me that I needed to go ahead and hip my girl to what Paully was trying to pull. I did just that. First, I told Corie that Paully had not called until tonight because he had been too busy trying to convince me that the two us should be together. Then I told her that we had kissed a few times but that I didn't believe that the two of us would work out. I thought I had made my opinion very clearly known but apparently I was wrong. I wanted to keep things the way they were. I reached out and took Trayu's hand in mine and told Corie that Paully just didn't want to believe that I would choose a relationship with Trayu over him.

I had to pause because I wasn't sure that I had actually said what I thought I heard myself say. A relationship... with Trayu. I had not yet admitted to myself that I was even ready to think about a relationship with anyone. Yet here I was saying it out loud to Corie and Trayu.

Finally, I told her that Paully had called earlier and became very agitated when he found out that Trayu was here with me. Apparently, he had planned on popping into town to surprise me but he got the surprise.

Corie listened with an open mouth the entire time except for when she was gulping down her champagne.

"So that's why he didn't want me to tell you he was coming tonight. I can't believe this shit! His ass is trying to play me!" Corie screamed.

Trayu quickly switched seats to sit next to Corie and put his arm around her shoulder.

"Come on Corie, now don't get all worked up over this. You are not the only one being played." And he looked at me.

My heart clenched.

"He's just playing the hand of a loser at a hot table. He doesn't feel he's being dealt the hand he deserves and now he playing irrationally. But Rhapsody said you planned a beautiful night and I want to thank you. That being said, let's not let this night be ruined. Whatever issues we have, let's put them aside and try to enjoy the evening. You two ladies think that we can do that?"

Corie shook her head and said that there was no way she was going to be able to not let Paully have a piece of her mind. She was going to let him know that she knew what was going on and tell him that he was welcomed to stay at the party but he could not sit with us. I, of course, was cool with that but Trayu took a different point of view. He was fine with Corie speaking her mind to Paully but he said that she should let him sit with us because she had already invited him to do so. Corie disagreed because she felt that her invitation came under false pretense. Trayu's response was that she would be able to show that she was a better person than he if she held true to her word. Then he added that he would take care of both of us and not let anything or anyone mess up our evening. Besides that, he was not going to let Paully believe that he could intimidate him or make him uncomfortable. He had come to Atlanta to bring in the New Year with someone special and that's what he intended to do. Corie finally agreed and Trayu gave her a little hug and moved back to my side and gave me a tender kiss. I was still not sure about his plan but I went along with the majority and braced myself for the evening.

The restaurant was definitely decorated to bring in the New Year. Corie showed Trayu and I around and provided an inside view of what had gone into the preparation and what we could expect for the evening. We were seated at a table in the subtlely created VIP section with Kraig Mitchell, a well known violinist who played with the Atlanta Symphony Orchestra, New York Philharmonic, and the Boston Pops. His first album dropped early in November and Corie had catered his album debut function at the restaurant. He had been so impressed that he rented the restaurant for his New Year's Eve party and invited Corie. The menu was her creation but she would not be working that night. Trayu, Corie and I nibbled on the tasty appetizers and sipped san Pellegrino instead of the constant flowing champagne. Corie had already had enough in the limo to create a solid buzz and wanted to save a little room for the New Year toast. Trayu and I had planned on celebrating with the Taittinger at my place later, so we were also taking it easy on the champagne. But as soon as Paully walked into the restaurant I took the first glass of champagne that caught my eye. I saw him come through the entrance while on my way back to our table. As he talked to the maitr'd, I high tailed it back to the VIP section and immediately whispered to Corie that he had arrived. Corie practically jumped out of her seat and Trayu stood to block her exit. He told her to remember to stay calm and cool and to choose her words carefully. As she nodded her head in agreement, a young lady came to tell Corie she had a guest and she was off.

# 33

As Tiana iced the chocolate mint cake she'd baked for the New Year, she felt happier than she had for most of the year or at least as much as she could remember, because the loss of her brother had consumed her life for a long time. Christmas had turned out to be pretty nice. She and MaDear spent four days at her great aunt's house in Athens, Georgia. She and MaDear had a pre-Christmas dinner the night of her last day of school. They invited Meek, his aunt, one of her aunts and three cousins. MaDear even invited Officer Kelp. Tiana was sure he wouldn't come but he'd shocked her by stopping by for dessert. The plan for that evening was to exchange gifts of no more than two dollars and The Dollar Store made it possible for everyone to participate. The next day, they were off to the country, which she was not very excited about, but once they arrived she was glad to be there.

Thinking back on it this New Year's Eve afternoon, she felt happy and proud to have such a loving family. She had expected that everyone would treat she and MaDear strangely because of Kieron's death and her mother's addiction. Fortunately, she couldn't have been more wrong. Everyone was full of the holiday spirit and spread it willingly. Her cousins asked her how she was dealing with losing her brother which made her nervous. But she decided that it would be better to answer them honestly the first time so that they would stop asking. She admitted to having good days and bad days and to never giving up the hope of the police finding his murderer. Her cousin Debbie seemed to really understand where she was coming from and gave her advice that she felt she could really use.

"Tiana, you know it's real good that you are trying to hold on to the happy memories you have. And if you could gather a bunch of pictures and knick knacks that remind you of Kieron, I can show you how to scrapbook. We have a scrapbooking club at school and I love it girl." Debbie suggested.

Tiana kinda thought the idea was corny but had decided instantly that she would give it a try for a couple of reasons. The first reason was that it sounded just corny enough to actually be helpful. Secondly, it would give her a reason to come back and spend time with Debbie. She loved the quiet and peacefulness. It made her feel quiet and peaceful inside. It was something she'd realized she'd been searching for.

The four days in Athens were filled with laughter and kindship. They cooked, played, laughed, ate, sang, and prayed together. They didn't ignore the absence of Kieron and her mom but they didn't harp on it either. Tiana liked that, too.

Now going into a new year, Tiana felt somewhat hopeful. Her family was more supportive than she could ever have imagined. Profoundly, she realized that she had spent the majority of her life being on guard from the judgement of others. She wore a shield around almost everyone except for Kieron and her MaDear. Since she was a little girl there seemed to be a constant flow of misfortune in her life from her mother's addiction and desertion to the loss of her brother in an act of senseless street violence. And because of that she always felt that people looked upon her with sorrow and shame. But MaDear never did. MaDear always made sure she and Kieron felt like they were worthy of the world. Now she kinda felt like maybe she had been wrong about some others too. Maybe they didn't look down on her.

She spent all morning cleaning the house and doing the laundry, while MaDear cooked the traditional New Years' delicacies. This was the first time that MaDear had allowed her anywhere near the washing machine and it felt good to be trusted. She had cleaned all the rooms except for MaDear's and had the final load in the dryer. She'd baked her first cake and was feeling pretty good. She'd not known what a relief it was going to be to get rid of Kieron's safe, but it was so huge. She was sleeping like a baby and felt more energized. She and her cousin, Debbie, had been talking on the phone daily. They had a lot in common. Finally, she was going to bring in the New Year at church with MaDear and Kaiewa and then have a New Year's breakfast in the church hall. Then they would have more family and friends over for New Year's dinner, complete with chitterlings, black eyed peas, and collard greens. MaDear refused to cook the chitterlings in their apartment but she didn't trust anyone to clean them correctly, either. So she cleaned them and gave them to her cousin to cook.

At church, everyone was in a festive mood; the choir was on point and the testimonies were inspirational. MaDear even gave a testimonial of her own.

"First I want to give God the glory for He is what sustains us. I know this for certain because He has brought me through many trails and tribulations.

Yes Lord! So many, but none as difficult as this year."

She hung her head and threw her hands up in praise.

"This year I lost my only grandson to the evil that lurk in our streets. He was not perfect but he was a good boy, so loving and kind and giving and smart. He was going to be somebody and it almost tore me and his little sister here to shreds. Oh yes it did, thank you Jesus. But He was not going to let it happen and sent all of you and some many others to hold us up and keep us in prayer. Thank you Jesus, praise God. And thank all of you for being there and showing us so much love. Always remember that it doesn't matter how difficult things seem, continue to look for the blessing because it's in there. He never gives us more than we can bear. Thank y'all for letting me share my story and a blessed New Year to all."

Tiana got a little choked up but was able to hold it together because Kaiewa gave her hand a little squeeze for support. He was absolutely the sweetest. MaDear's testimony sparked a few verses of "He Never Failed Me Yet".

Everyone sang in the New Year in total jubilation.

At breakfast, while she and Kaiewa were going through the line, she noticed Meek staring at them. Kaiewa noticed him, too.

"Tiana, your friend seems a little perturbed at one of us and if I had to guess, I'd say it was me."

"Don't worry about it. Just ignore him."

She'd hoped that she sounded convincing because she was not sure that ignoring him would work. As it turned out she was right.

Tiana had fixed MaDear's plate and so Kaiewa offered to fix his and her plate. When they reached the table, both Meek and his aunt were seated at the table with MaDear. Meek was sitting across from his aunt which actually separated the last two seats at the table on that side. Kaiewa placed Tiana's plate in front of the empty seat between Meek and MaDear and took the seat on the other side of Meek.

Meek started in on Kaiewa as soon as he sat down, speaking in a hushed rumble as not to attract attention. "You not gettin' what you want this time, man."

Kaiewa just looked at Meek and went back to eating.

"Yeah that right, keep your mouth shut and listen cuz you ain't gonna get the chance to hurt her. Take a good look at me, cuz I'm the soldier charged with her care and I ain't feeling you man. Real talk."

Kaiewa didn't even look at him this time. He just shook his head.

Meek's aunt noticed something because she told Meek to cool it. He cut his eyes at Kaiewa but didn't say anything else. Meanwhile, Ms. Kendrell began telling MaDear about Meek's and Kieron's friend Kevin.

"Apparently, they had been hot wiring cars and breaking into homes in the Arbor Lands subdivision during the day. Last Friday, they tried to steal a car and the owner came out with a bat. I don't know exactly what happened but one of those boys shot that man in his shoulder. They all got in the car and sped off but crashed into a mailbox. So all those boys are being held and can't none of them make bail. Kevin is going to have to stay there too cuz his mama can't come up with that kinda money and she ain't got nothing to put up for the money either. I told her she could ask the reverend to take up a collection but she is too embarrassed to do that." She explained.

Then Kaiewa mistakenly lit Meek's fuse.

"She has no reason to be embarrassed because she's only trying to help her son. Any parent would do that. MaDear, maybe you could talk to her." Kaiewa stated.

Meek went off. He turned in his seat and shoved Kaiewa in his chest.

"Shut up, man. You don't know nothing and it ain't none of your business." He yelled at Kaiewa and drew the attention of everyone in the hall. Meek's aunt had appeared behind him in a flash and hauled him out into the hallway. MaDear's eyes misted over as she said she thought it was time to go. Once she found the deacon who'd given them a ride and got in the car, MaDear reached out for Kaiewa's hand.

"Baby, don't take what Lil' Meek said to heart. He's just sensitive cause he and Kevin and my Kieron were just like brothers. So, if Kevin goes to jail then...well...it probably will feel like losing another brother. See what I mean? So all we can do is pray for him cause he is a good boy. He really is." She told him.

Kaiewa said he believed her and he didn't plan on holding it against him.

Tiana on the other hand was not going to let it go so easily. To her it was obvious that Meek was more irritated about Kaiewa being there with her than any concern about Kevin. Of course he had to care about his boy but that was no reason to go off on Kaiewa about an innocent statement, least of all in the church hall on New Years morning. She decided right then and there that she was going to sit down and have a serious talk with Meek. It was time to tell him how she truly felt because if he continued behaving this way, she would distance herself from him permanently. In her heart, she knew that was not what she wanted to do but she was prepared to do whatever she needed to continue this new found peace she'd found. This year was going to be great, she could just feel it.

# 34

Paully walked in with his arm around Corie's waist looking relatively calm. But I knew Paully. He was far from being calm; his anger was sitting right behind his gorgeous eyes. And the smile he was wearing only slightly masked the sneer. He spoke and shook hands with everyone in the area including Trayu and then he kissed me on the cheek in greeting. I sneaked a peek at Corie which she missed because she was smiling at Paully as he made light conversation with one of the guys at the table next to ours. She was still smitten with him and I couldn't figure out why, when only minutes ago she was ready to curse him out for trying to use her. Maybe the champagne was controlling her emotions.

Trayu whispered in my ear asking if I were okay and I shrugged my shoulders in response. So, he put his arms around me and whispered that everything would be fine and he wasn't going to let anyone spoil our first New Years celebration. I turned to his beckoning gaze and felt a warm smile swelling up from my heart. I believed him.

Corie, true to character, quickly put a glass of champagne in Paully's hand, made a short personal toast and sipped with him. Paully looked over at Trayu and I with a smirk on his face. I saw his eyes follow the length of Trayu's arm in its path from his shoulder to my shoulder. This was not feeling good at all.

Corie told Paully that she was going to run and get a plate of fresh h'ordevres from the kitchen for him. So, I took this opportunity to get her alone and find out what she'd said to Paully. As soon as we were outside of the room, I grabbed her by the hand and asked what was going on.

"Rhapsody Girl, everything is cool. I told him that I knew he was having a problem with you because you wanted to be with Trayu and not him."

I didn't remember saying that to her.

"I told him that I didn't appreciate him trying to use me to get to you and that if that was what he was trying to do, he could turn around and leave right now. And girl, he was so apologetic. He said that he was pissed at you at first but he was cool now cause you will always be his best friend regardless. Then he said that the thing with you had actually been a wake up call. He realized that maybe his being here was an omen that he should call me and he was glad that he did. Isn't that sweet?"

"Yeah Corie I guess it is. Are you sure that he's cool with me and Tray being here because I don't want to be a distraction. Maybe we should have the limo take us back to my place and let you and Paully have this time together. The driver could drop us off and be back here well before midnight." I suggested.

"Hell no, girl, I want you to stay. Don't be ridiculus. Paully's cool, Trayu's cool, I'm cool and you're cool, so let's just eat, drink and be merry. Besides I want to bring in the New Year with my good friends and they don't come any better than you. Okay?"

I wasn't absolutely convinced but I was going to stay anyway. I promised myself that I would stay long enough to say Happy New Years and then I was out. Trayu and I could be back at home by 1:30.

"Okay Corie, you win. I'm gonna go back in before Trayu thinks I cut out on him." I said and headed back to the VIP area.

I heard it before I crossed the threshold. Then I saw a lady leave the VIP section with a look of panic on her face. My eyes instinctively followed her as she walked towards the restaurant entrance and reached out for the security guard on duty. I knew it was too good to be true. Paully's voice was wafting through the air as I turned back to the room. Trayu was standing and Paully was in his face calling him a milk breathed punk. The next thing I saw looked like it happened in slow motion. Paully head-butted Trayu and he flew back and down against the wall. Paully stepped toward him poised to swing, but Trayu came up on one knee and swung the other leg out, connecting with Paully's groin then his chest in what seemed like one motion. Paully hit the ground on his back holding his nuts. I stood frozen as Trayu got to his feet and walked towards me.

"Rhap, I'm out of here."

I was looking at him but he didn't look angry, not really. He looked...sad...maybe disappointed...maybe even embarrassed, but not angry.

"Wait. Let me get my purse and I'll have the limo take us home." I said as I took his hand.

Someone was helping Paully to his feet but he was pushing him away and telling him to leave him alone. We made eye contact and I shook my head.

"What are you doing, Paully? What are you doing?" was all that I could say.

He didn't respond and I didn't wait. I got my bag and Trayu and I walked out. It was cold outside. I could see the air freezing as it left my body but I was in no way cold. As I looked around for the limo, Corie came running out and grabbed me.

"What in the hell happened in there, Rhapsody." She asked.

"Go ask your new boyfriend...my best friend." And the crying started. Trayu saw the tears and pulled me close and led me to a taxi. I could hear Corie calling after Trayu and I but neither of us responded. Inside the cab, I asked Trayu if he was okay. He said he was but I could see the knot forming along his hairline.

"I'll put ice on that as soon as we get home." I told him and he just drapped his arm around me and closed the distance between us.

At home I gave Trayu the ice pack from the freezer and called Corie's home phone and left her a message telling her that I would talk to her the next day. I also let her know that we were cool and wished her happy new year. Trayu decided to take a shower so he could relax.

"That sounds like a good idea. I think I'll do the same."

I glanced at the clock and continued.

"We have a little more than an hour so let's hurry. I'll put a pizza in the oven and it should be ready by the time we're done." I suggested.

"That's cool", was all Trayu said as he walked to the guestroom. He didn't give me a snide remark or silly joke or even a little smile. He just walked into the room and shut the door. I didn't know what to think. He had every right to be upset at Paully and me. Paully was dead wrong for acting the way he had in the restaurant but I also had to admit that I could have likely prevented this by being upfront with Trayu. No matter. All I could do now was crisis management and that's exactly what I was going to do.

Trayu was slicing the pizza by the time I entered the kitchen, so I pulled out the champagne and flutes. Then I went back and grabbed the plates, napkins and a couple of bottles of water.

"Hey baby, bring the pizza into the living room so we can watch the peach drop on t.v., okay?"

"As long as you keep calling me baby I'll do whatever you want." Trayu replied.

"Whatever. Just bring the food. We only have seven minutes before the the New Year rings."

With our glasses in hand we counted down the last ten seconds of the year and shouted in the new one. We drained our flutes and embraced for the first kiss of the year which was so sweet that we immediately took the second kiss. Though I couldn't put my finger on why, there was no doubt that Trayu's kissing technique was the best I'd experienced. He held me so close that I yearned to be a part of him. His passion lit me from inside out, so much so that the tips of my fingers tingled and the arches in my feet felt as if they were sitting on lumps of hot coal.

The phone rang. It took a few seconds to shake off Trayu's effect, so enroute to check the caller ID, the home answering machine picked up. It was my moms. I snatched up the phone in glee and yelled "Happy New Year". Mom, dad, and Aslen were all at home waiting for their New Year. Aslen was super anxious because it was the one time of the year that his lips were allowed to touch alcohol.

While talking to my family, the phone clicked several times and the caller id showed Paully's number twice and Corie's once. There was no way I was going to answer a call from either of them. I planned to talk to Corie the next day but as for Paully, I had no idea when I would be calm enough to talk to him. For the night, Trayu was going to be the only one getting my attention.

Trayu laid his head on my lap and chewed on a slice of pizza while I talked. It felt so natural that I didn't pay attention to his position until he offered me a bite of his pizza. I took a bite, said thank you and gave him a peck on the lips. Dad was on the phone at the time and asked why I was thanking him. I told him that I was talking to Trayu and he asked to speak to him so he could wish him a Happy New Year. I handed the phone to Trayu and he accepted it with wide eyes. When he finished shooting the breeze with my dad he handed the phone to me with the cutest little grin on his face. Once off the phone, we kissed and sipped until the bottle of Champagne was gone. Then, Trayu started.

"Rhapsody, I don't want what happened tonight with Paully to ruin our evening but I do need to know where your head is about this whole thing." He questioned.

"Well, first I want to apologize again for not telling you about my issues with him. I just thought that I could handle it without bothering you. Secondly, it was very irritating that Paully tried to gansta his way into our New Years Eve. I think he could and should have handled that differently. Third, I'm not really sure what happened in the restaurant between you and Paully but a fight in the restaurant is absolutely ludacris. I'm pretty embarrassed about being a part of that. I'm so pissed at Paully right now because I saw him head butt you and start the physical fight and he knows how I feel about violence. I know that you had to defend yourself because he was going to hit you again. I just think that the whole fight thing was unnecessary." I shook my head.

"Well, I'm sorry that things had to get physical too but your boy left me no choice. As far as what happened when you and Corie left the room, it started off relatively calm but escalated rapidly. I think that old boy got pissed off because he couldn't get a rise out of me with snide comments. He just didn't realize who he was talking to. He obviously mistook me for some young gungho hood dweller that flies off the handle at the slightest insult."

Trayu explained.

"What was he saying to you?" I inquired.

"Aw, it was just stupid stuff like, was I looking for someone to change my diaper or buy me video games. What did I think I could do for a real woman with my premature privates? But none of that phased me so he took it a step further and said something about how he had no idea that you were so hard up and had so little self respect that you would date someone so young. That's when I stood up and told him that he could say whatever he wanted about me but I was not going to allow him to slander your character. Then he stood up and laughed and said something like I wasn't man enough to stand up to him. So I said that apparently you knew who the real man was and he didn't have to worry about you being taken care of because I had that covered. And that was that. At first I was not going to hit back but when I looked up at him, I saw that fighting fury in his eyes so I had to shut it down. But Rhapsody, I am truly sorry that you had to witness that. Honestly, I tried to avoid it."

Looking at him, I could see his sincerity and I instantly rewarded it with a kiss. The passion that came through took over and before I knew it, we had worked our way to my bedroom and the bed. I felt at home in Trayu's arms and I have to admit that it was kinda scary. His caresses made my body react with all of its womanly instincts. Trayu's body also told me that Paully's question of whether Trayu qualified as being a man was invalid. He was definitely a full grown man. The temperature in the room continued to rise so I decided to relieve him of his shirt and he allowed me to do so. My kisses then traveled to his chest as his lower body went into motion against me. I returned to his mouth and he greeted me with enthusiasm which instinctively made me arch toward him. Trayu groaned into my mouth and pressed his hips down and forward against me. I reach for his waistband and was met with surprise.

He stopped. He kissed me gently one last time and then rolled off of me. I was so shocked and embarrassed that I jumped up and ran into my bathroom.

"Rhapsody please come out here, I need to explain this" he pleaded from the other side of the door.

I knew that he thought I was in there crying but I had news for him. I looked at myself in the mirror and courageously exited the bathroom. I was going to act like what had just happened was fine and dandy. I was going to say goodnight and go straight to bed. I looked him dead in the face as I opened the door and flashed him a sweet smile so he could see that I had not been crying. He took hold of my left hand.

"Rhap baby, look here, I'm sorry for just stopping like that. I know it seemed odd and awkward but let me explain. First, I want to say that I would love to make love to you. As a matter of fact, I've been waiting since the day I met you to be able to show you how much I actually care for you. You are the most amazing woman I have ever known and I want to show you that with every inch of my being. No pun intended. But I don't want to do that tonight because too much stuff has gone down. You see, I want to know that when you give yourself to me that it's because you care enough to do so and not because you are trying to make up for putting me in an uncomfortable situation. Now that may not be the case but I have to be honest and say that the events of tonight are still weighing heavy on me and so I have to believe that they are weighing on you as well." Trayu explained.

I just continued to look down at our joined hands. In my deepest of thoughts I knew that he was partially correct. Feelings of guilt were still weighing on me and could have played a small role in my comfort level in the bedroom only minutes earlier.

"Rhapsody, look at me for a moment please." He requested and I submitted.

"Do you think it would be okay if I lay with you tonight and hold you in my arms until the sunrise of this New Year wakes us." He continued.

I responded with a shy nod and led him back to my bed. What else was I going to do. Trayu had me all caught up whether he knew it or not. He pulled back the covers and slid in. Then he pulled me down next to him and as he did so I heard a sigh of relief escape his lungs. We laid there face to face sharing tender kisses and caresses for sometime before I started drifting off to sleep. I turned my back to him and he instinctively spooned me up and began a soft snore.

A ringing telephone started my New Year's morning. Corie started apologizing as soon as I answered the phone.

"Rhap girl, I am so sorry about last night. I had no idea your boy was going to act like that. He told me everything was cool and then I come back to find chaos in my restaurant. Luckily nothing got broken and most people already had their buzz so they thought it was funny. But anyway I got Paully out of there right away and we rode around in the limo and talked. Well, I guess you could say I screamed and he tried to talk. He admitted that he'd handled things poorly. But Rhap, he thinks that you should take the blame for what happened because you didn't tell him that Trayu was coming to bring in the new year with you." She explained.

"Whatever. Corie, I had no obligation to give him that information but that's neither here nor there because his behavior was totally foul. And whether he wants to admit it or not, he's the only one to blame for that." I added.

"Well, I think that deep down he knows that." She offered.

"I hope so. So tell me where did he go last night? Did he tell you?" I asked.

Corie hesitated and then told me that he had come home with her. He was in her living room on the phone with the airline trying to get a flight out to Chicago. Her news was threatening to put a damper on my mood which was something I definitely did not need. Paully and his antics had already threatened to ruin my time with Trayu once and that was enough. So, I lied to Corie and told her that I needed to get off the phone and gather the information for the website Trayu was designing for me.

"He wants to get an early start so we can spend some time together."

"Oh that's right girl. Rhap, did you ask him about doing a site for me?"

"Yeah girl, I told you that already. Did you do what I said and pull together the stuff for him to get started?" I asked.

"Yes. I think I have most of it."

I could tell by her tone that the "most of it" she referenced was actually the stuff she would gather after she hung up the phone. Even though, I told her that I would call her back later that afternoon to tell her when she could bring her site information over. She in turn told me that she would let me know when Paully got a flight. I, of course, did not want to know but I told her okay anyway.

Trayu awakened, kissed me on the back of my neck and headed for the guest bathroom. When he met me in the kitchen, I was putting the black eyed peas in the crock pot.

He walked over and hugged me from behind.

"Where are the collard greens for wealth this year?"

He smelled of shea butter and tooth paste. Delicious.

"Don't worry, they are in the freezer and will be thawed and ready to eat for dinner."

"Aw Naw, don't tell me. You are going to have some man come to your house so that he will be the first person to cross your threshold for the year?"

"No, I am not. I'm just going to count you because you're the only male crossing my threshold for the entire day.

We sat down to a breakfast of fresh mangos, low fat vanilla yogurt, and buttered English muffins. I couldn't escape his gaze. It seemed that everytime I looked up he was looking at me.

"Why are you staring at me like that? It's making me uncomfortable."

He laughed and flashed that irresistible smile.

"I don't mean to make you feel uncomfortable but I don't know that I will be able to stop. Rhapsody, you apparently have no idea how beautiful you are. Even your inner beauty shines through your eyes." He explained and gave me a wink.

"It's the truth and so you can stop blushing and just eat your breakfast. I'll try to stop staring."

I just shook my head because I knew that I was blushing and

continued to eat. We washed dishes together while we talked about what we would do for lunch. Trayu wanted to get to work on the website right away. We sat down together and organize the information he needed to get started then he sent me away so he could work without distraction. I used the time to marinate the t-bones I planned to cook for dinner and then rifled through my closet for an outfit that would be pleasing to Trayu's eye. I wanted to ensure that his interest did not wane and that he didn't have time to think about Paully. Corie called again and wanted to talk to Trayu to make sure that she had everything that he needed. I gently tapped on the study door and asked if he would speak to her. He did and when he gave the phone back Corie told me that she was on her way over. Trayu told her that he didn't think that he would be able to work on her site while he was here but if she dropped off her information he would have her up and running for a preview by the end of the next week. Then she told me that she'd made dinner reservations at restaurant Paris for 8:00 for Trayu and I as an apology for our ruined New Year's eve dinner.

"Girl, you didn't have to do that. I was going to cook tonight and give him a taste of my good homecooking." I told her.

"Please girl, you can do that another time. You guys have got to go to Paris, that joint is the truth. Besides that, I had to pull some strings to get the reservation, so come on now." She pleaded.

"Okay Corie, I'll tell you what, you come on over and I'll cook my dinner for lunch. That means you are going to have to eat lunch with us. Okay?"

"That's a deal. I'll see you in a bit." Corie agreed.

I informed Trayu of the change in our plans. In his mind, if I cooked earlier, I would be refreshed for our evening together. So he continued working while I trotted off to the kitchen to start lunch. For a nice little flair, I decided to fire up the charcoal grill on the lanai to cook the steaks.

When Corie arrived, Trayu sat down in the living room with her to go over her information. I loved hearing him talk business. He was so intelligent and sexy and funny and cute. As he went to pack away Corie's stuff, Corie walked into the kitchen.

"Rhap, that man is a catch. I see why you are so crazy about him. And I bet that if Paully saw you two together and saw the chemistry that you have, he would not try to interfere." She said.

I just shook my head without a verbal response. I didn't even want to get into a discussion about Paully or what he would or should think. My anger towards Paully was still very strong. There was no telling how long it would be before I talked to him again. Honestly, at that moment I couldn't have cared less. Corie caught on to my silence and decided to help me with the final lunch preparations. My lunch was a success with Corie and Trayu.

After lunch, Corie left and Trayu and I chilled out on the sofa and watched Bus Stop with Marilyn Monroe. Trayu only saw about thirty minutes of the movie before he drifted off to sleep. I watched a few minutes longer and then used his nap time as an opportunity to catch up on my New Year's greeting calls. I finished my calls and then listened to my messages. There were two messages from Paully. The first one was full of attitude and accusations of how I was leading him on and leading Trayu on too. And that Trayu was going to see my true colors. And that I should tell Trayu that he better stay away from him when he gets back to town because he won't be so lucky the next time. The second message was a simple statement. "Rhapsody, I'm sorry."

I awakened Trayu with gentle kisses on his face after I showered and finished my make-up. He pulled me down on the sofa with him and held me tight for just a moment until he noticed that I was refreshed.

"You've already started getting ready! Am I late? What time is it?"

I assured him that he was fine with time. Since girls take a little longer to get ready I took advantage of his nap time.

Dinner went extremely well that evening. Trayu was as charming as ever and the conversation was easy. I found myself sharing parts of me that usually did not come easy. I shared my inner struggle with relationship failures and the emotional hardship I endured after losing my father. It came through without restraint or censor. And Trayu seemed just as relaxed. He talked about his revised career plan. He planned on showing up for his internship with a draft for a new company web design.  He'd already sent an outline of his vision to his company mentor and received rave reviews. Trayu was going to rent his car detailing business to his friend, Zenon, so that he would continue to make money while he was away.  If the business was maintained well enough, he would allow Zenon to purchase all of his equipment including his pick-up truck for a good price. A good enough price that he could start up a new one if needed, but Trayu didn't plan on having to do the car detailing anymore.

Trayu insisted on driving home with little resistance from me. We cruised down I20 hand in hand listening to Frankie Beverly and Maze.  I was feeling the purest happiness that I'd felt in who knows how long.  I think he even made me feel better than Karl ever had. Suddenly I was emotionally besieged.  My heart was a cumulus cloud, my chest the open blue sky.  My heart around him so light that I felt a hollowness in my chest.  It was such an overwhelming feeling of satisfaction, anticipation and hope that it made me want to cry.  But I couldn't cry now because I didn't want Trayu to think I was crying about Paully or Karl.  On the otherhand, I needed and wanted to do something with these feelings of emotional elevation.  It deserved to be recognized and so did Trayu.  So I asked him to pull over.  My abruptness startled him and he quickly maneuverd the car off the next exit and into the nearest parking lot.  I was aware that I'd scared him but chose not to reassure him of anything, yet.  As soon as he put her in park, I unclipped myself, ran my left hand over his hair, resting it on the natural enclave of his neck.  Searching his eyes, my lips were trembling.  I closed the distance between our beings and kissed him. I wanted to start off slow and gentle, in order to transfer my passion in layers but that level of control escaped me. The initial contact was feathery light, yes, but the intensity was crashing as my tongue sought out its' mate. Trayu pulled me closer and I absolutely felt as if I would burst into tears.

We kissed and caressed like teenagers, very mature teenagers but teenagers just the same, for several minutes. Then I pulled away to catch my breath. Trayu rested his forehead against my forehead and closed his eyes.

Moments passed and then Trayu decided we should get back on the road before Johnny Law decided to question our business in the area.

Back at home, sitting in the car, Trayu changed gears on me with a conversation so unexpected.

"Hey Rhapsody we've been dancing around this whole thing and honestly I'm afraid of where it will leave me in the end if I don't take charge."

"What? Take charge of what? What are we dancing around? Trayu you've lost me sweetheart." I countered.

Okay, he hadn't really lost me. Scared me would have been more accurate. I knew that the thing we were dancing around was the type of relationship we were building or suspending. My problem was I was afraid of what he wanted to do by taking charge. I was terrified of him saying he wanted to be my main man, my one and only, my main squeeze. Was I ready for that? No, I didn't think so, but could he understand that? Those were the thoughts running through my mind in the matter of seconds it took Trayu to present his opening statement.

"Come on Baby, you know what I'm talking about. Don't do this to me." He pleaded.

With a little bit of pleading in my own eyes, I responded.

"Look Trayu, just take your time and tell me exactly what you want. You have my undivided attention."

I knew I owed him at least that.

"Okay, here it is. I enjoy coming to see you. You're easy to be with and you…uuh…you stimulate my…uuh…mind." He said with a grin.

"Ohhhh, you had me thinking that you wanted to have a serious discussion and here you are playing around."

He pulled himself together and started again.

"No on the real, Rhap. What I'm saying is that among other things and most importantly, you stimulate my mind and that's fresh you know. I feel you and I think you feel me, but Rhap baby, something's not right. I don't know if you are fighting this or if you are just fighting me. Either way, I just need to know where you want me in your life."

I couldn't find my voice although I knew he was waiting for a response. Realizing that I wasn't going to respond, he continued.

"Look Rhap, I'm sitting here trying to tell you that I want you as my woman. We work. Our chemistry, as corny as it may sound, is strong and that's rare, you know. Now what I need to know is if you feel the same way. Is it that you want to be with Paully or see other people? Are you entertaining more than my attention?"

I still couldn't muster up a response.

"I understand that that's what people do to see who will withstand the test of time, Rhap. Understand me now, that's not my game. I've been there and done that but not with you. I know that you are what I want; there's no doubt in my mind. So you need to let me know if you want me to be your man because I don't think I can just be your buddy any longer. This shit that we have is special but if you want to throw it away you need to do it now. I don't want to go into this new year chasing a shadow."

I remained stunned into silence.

"It looks like I have shocked you into silence." He smiled.

"I'm leaving tomorrow and at that time I think we should take a little time to digest all that has happened and how we feel about each other. Rhapsody, we need to figure this thing out, okay?"

I nodded my head. Trayu exited the vehicle and I followed. Inside, we both got ready for bed and met in the living room for a night cap. We watched the late news, then retired for the evening. Trayu and I slept the same way we had the night before, spooned together with fleeting kisses until we drifted off to sleep.

# 35

I had no idea that I would receive one answer about the contents of the safe so soon and I'm sure that Meek did not know he would be the one to give it to me. But he laid it right in my lap during his next visit when I had asked Meek to think about things that he would like to do with his life that could represent the positive nature of his friendship with Kieron.

It was an attempt to get him to step out of his grief and anger and turn those feelings into something good. He started talking about finishing school and going to college and getting a good job, but the mimicry was evident.

"Come on Meek. You are just spewing back what most adults in your life have probably told you that you should want. That's not what I want to hear. I want to hear your thoughts and feelings. Let's be real, okay."

He ran his hands over his face and said.

"Yeah alright. Well, it's like this. People always want to think that we always up to no good like banging and jacking and shit...I mean stuff. But Kieron was kinda different, you know. I don't mean he was no straight laced busta like old dude Tiana's diggin'."

I ignored that comment.

"Kieron weren't no punk and yeah we did our share of uhh... stuff."

He paused.

"But he did some nice shit, too. And I wanna to do some shit like that. Excuse the language, my bad." He apologized and I nodded my acceptance.

"What kind of things would you like to do?" I asked.

And that's when Meek answered the question about who Miss Mitchell was. Apparently, Kieron befriended an elderly woman in a nearby neighborhood. He would do small jobs for her such as accompany her to the grocery store, cut her lawn, pick up her medicine, and other odd jobs. Meek seemed to think that Kieron actually enjoyed doing those things because it made the old lady happy. The couple of times he saw Kieron with Miss Mitchell, he thought that Kieron looked just as happy being with her as she did being with him.

Meek continued to share.

"I think that that old lady kinda changed Kieron. I think she gave him something else to do that wasn't about this street that we been living. Like if it wasn't for him we would still be doing that same old shit and if we'd did that we would probably both be dead by now. So I guess, when I really think about it, Kieron saved my life."

Meek paused again, but this time I saw his eyes began to get watery. He was really feeling the lost, pain, love, and appreciation and I wanted him to marinate in it. So I decided that it was a good time to wrap up the session.

"Okay Meek, it looks like our time is up for today. I think it was a good session. You touched on a few important feelings and I want you to think about those this week. Think about what you could and are willing to do in order to feel that you are working on a stronger you. We'll pick up where we left off in our next session."

After Meek left, it was time to process the information I'd just received. I fixed a cup of Yerba Matte, turned off the lights, pulled up some Bob Dylan on my computer and sat back feeling pretty lucky. I only asked Meek if he knew how to get in contact with Ms. Mitchell, so he could offer to help her out as Kieron had. He gave me the street name of where she lived but said that he would have to think about my idea. He wasn't sure if she would agree to that because she didn't really know him. Sure, she had seen him once or twice with Kieron but she still didn't know him. I understood.

I knew that I should have encouraged him to pursue his desire to offer his own version on community service, but I had an ulterior motive. I had to devise a plan to talk to this Miss Mitchell and find out how she was connected to Kieron.

Miss Mitchell greeted me with the stern caution I remembered from my grandmamma. It's the expression and a tone that questions who you are, why are you here, and what do you really want. I recognized it immediately and turned on the charm. I presented the purpose of my visit quickly. After introducing myself, I told her that I had run across a card that I believed was entended for her. Then I asked her if she knew Kieron Menden. The whole while, I held the card in my hand slightly extended toward her. She did not reach for the envelop but instead looked at me through squinted cynical eyes and asked.

"If that's for me then why didn't he bring it to me himself. I ain't seen him in months, so I wouldn't hold a torch to what you say being true." She finished with a suck of her teeth.

Hanging my head, I realized that she didn't know that Kieron had been killed. So I took on the difficult task and told her that he had passed away. I added the tiny fib that I'd found the card stuck in one of his journals used for our sessions.

That's when she took the card and invited me inside. She directed me to be seated, put on the glasses hanging around her neck, and opened the envelop. After a few minutes of head shaking, she spoke again.

"I should have known that something was wrong. There had to be something seriously wrong for that boy to just up and stop coming around or calling. He was such a good boy, you know. That child's heart had been touched by God."

Then she asked how I knew how to find her with no address on the card. I told her about Meek's help. She then spent the next thirty minutes talking about Kieron's stewardship. She met him at the drug store one day when she'd left her purse on the counter at the register.

"I had gone in to pick up my prescription and ended up with three bags of stuff. Oh it always happens that way, don't it? Well anywho, Kieron came running after me toting my purse and when he saw I had all those bags, he told me to just hold on to my purse and he would carry the bags. Now you know, I don't know what made me trust that boy, but I did. So, I let him carry my bags that day and many days after. Then he started helping with things I didn't even know I needed help with. You know what else, Miss Uhmm…"

"Austin." I reminded her.

"Yeah well you know he wouldn't take any money from me at first for a long time. But I finally told him that I couldn't let him help me out anymore without paying him. My good faith wouldn't allow me to. That's when he came up with the plan that I could pay him once a month after all my bills had been paid, including my groceries and prescriptions. I let him think he was doing something but he just fell into my little trap. I sure have been missing him and I feel so bad now because here I was thinking that he had just gotten sucked into them there streets. I just figured that he thought that there were more interesting things for a teenager to do besides hanging out with some old lady. But that poor baby done gone on to glory."

She couldn't seem to give Kieron enough accolades and that warmed my heart. Finally, I eased into the suggestion of Meek taking over some of Kieron's responsibilities. She balked it at first because she said that she didn't know him. She did say that she remembered seeing one little fella with Kieron periodically, but he looked more like a knucklehead than a steward. I reminded her that Kieron did not hang out with knuckleheads nor would he have brought anyone untrustworthy around her. He obviously respected her. Then I told her that Meek had been Kieron's best friend and that he wanted to do this as a tribute to a friend's good heart. Kieron had been a positive influence in his life and he wanted to honor him with acts of good will.

Miss Mitchell didn't totally fall for it but she did agree to meet Meek and then she would think about it. That was enough in my eyes so I told her I would set it up and give her a call. I left my card with her upon my departure.

# 36

$S$itting at my desk, I suddenly felt very tired, tired enough to go to bed right then at 4:30 p.m.. It didn't take much thought to figure out the source of my fatige. Between the best friend breaker of a night and Trayu's revealing visit, I'd had a lot on my mind. As tempting as the thought of my bed was at that moment, I couldn't leave even if I wanted to because my teen anger management group was due to arrive momentarily. Today was going to be a nice light session but I definitely could not cancel. It was right after the holiday and there was no telling what issues might pop up with the kids.

All of the kids seemed to be in a good mood. The only complaints were about having to return to school. We talked about the best and the worst part of their winter break. Most of them decribed the worst part of their vacation as not getting the gift they desired. Willie said that the worst part for him was watching his drunken uncle pick fights with his dad and other uncles. They came to blows on Christmas night and the cops came and took one of his uncles away. It would have been better if they had taken the intoxicated uncle but they weren't that lucky. But even through that drama, the family gathering was the highlight of his holiday. Family turned out to be the unanimous high point for the past two weeks.

"Now I want to point out the light that filled this room when you guys talked about your holiday. It is rarely true that nothing but good things happen in a persons' life. Life is made up of good and bad things. You see, without the unpleasant things we would have a hard time identifying and appreciating the good things. Therefore, right now is a good time to practice focusing on the good times, good things, and good people in your life. When things get rough and you want to find a way out, think positive and go to those people, places, and thoughts. Understand?" I offered.

Meek surprised me with a response.

"I understand Ms. A." he said.

"Uh, I just want to say thank you because you really helped me see that I have some good things in my life. I appreciate the friends I've made in this group. When I came to this group I was in a real bad place. I had lost my best friend to street violence and I was lost in my anger about that. But I came here and found out that I was not the only one that has felt the pain and anger that the street brings. I feel that I have grown and that I can help myself by being more positive. And funny enough, it's not as hard as I thought." He shared.

A few others chimed in their agreement and thanked me for my help and the group for their support. I'm sure that my cheeks were flushed for I was very appreciative at that moment for the wonderful group of young people sitting before me. But it was nearly time for us to finish up so I set the timer and started the journaling time.

After everyone left, Meek returned and handed me a gift wrapped in Christmas paper.

"Thank you, Meek. You didn't have to do this, you're so sweet."

"You're welcome." Is all he said with a smile and then departed.

I sat at my desk to type up the session notes and open the gift. The gift was a small lotion and bubble bath set with loofa. What a sweet little gift. It made me want to pamper myself so I called Montana to see if her nail technican was in. There's nothing like a nice manicure and pedicure to make one feel pampered. Montana was more than happy that I'd called. She was finishing up her last client for the day.

"Hey Girlfriend, I can't believe it but you have come to the rescue once again." She yelled into the phone.

"What are you talking about, silly?"

"It's your lucky day, that's what I'm talking about. Look, I can't take you today; we can schedule that for another day, but I have something better for you. Meet me at Spa Oceanic at 7:00, okay. Dakota and I were suppose to go together and get our pamper on, but she can't go because she has to work. She was really looking forward to getting a massage instead of giving one. Fortunately, you can go in her place if you can make it there by 7:00. We booked a manicure, pedicure, facial and massage. So what do you say? Can you make it? Montana explained.

"What? Are you serious? I'll be waiting in the steamroom when you get there." I laughed.

We hung up and I packed up my things as quick as lightning. I figured I had time to stop at home and take a quick shower and throw on some sweats. I wouldn't have time to lotion but then again they would probably prefer working on a lotion free body. Montana was waiting for me in the lobby when I arrived. After teasing me for not beating her there, we were escorted back to change and warm up our bodies for the massage. I love steamrooms. The moist heat makes me feel like I am releasing all stress and impurities in my body. Montana on the other hand barely tolerated the heat, but she was determined to tough out her twenty minutes. I tried to help her keep her mind off of the discomfort she was feeling.

"How's the new house coming along?" I asked her.

"Whew girl." She said with a wipe of the brow.

"It's coming along very nicely. I'm only working on the living room and our bedrooms right now. The other rooms are going to have to wait until I find some good tenants in my old place. I've interviewed a few people but to be honest I didn't like any of them. I can't believe some of the rental histories I've seen. Some of them seem to move every six months and I can't work like that. I want people in there that are going to be there a year at the very least. It's hard girl and I think it's going to be hard for a little while longer. People are going to take a few months to recuperate from their holiday spending, you know what I mean." She shared.

"Yeah, you're right but you could very well get a lot of calls. You know there some people that will spend all their money on Christmas and let the rent go by the wayside. Then come the end of the month, they will be packing it in looking for a new place to stay." I laughed.

"And you know it! I'm just going to continue to pray on it and I know a responsible couple or family will come along. It's a great starter home, you know."

All of a sudden I had an idea. I didn't want to share it with Montana right then but if it worked out, it could be win-win situation for Montana, MaDear, and Tiana. The massage was wonderfully relaxing but I spent most of the time hashing out whether or not my new idea would work. On the surface it seemed like a simple plan, have MaDear complete Montana's application and along with a stellar recommendation from me she could move into Montana's old house. Montana already knew MaDear and Tiana and she saw for herself that they kept a clean house. She would be happy to have a safe responsible family living in her house and MaDear's Section 8 money would relieve any financial uncertainty. Even better, this deal would provide a way for Tiana and MaDear to move out of the neighborhood. I knew that that's what both of them wanted but could not see a clear way to make it happen. This could be just what they'd been waiting for. It was pretty simple, right? So why was I so shaky about presenting the plan to Montana? I wasn't fooling myself, I knew that I still had a small safe packed full of money that couldn't be anything other than dirty and that was making me a nervous wreck. Then it dawned on me that the money had nothing to do with MaDear and Tiana moving. So while Montana and I were sitting side by side soaking our feet, I nonchalantly presented my plan.

"Oh my God, Rhap, that's the ticket!" She exclaimed so loudly that I inadvertently splashed some water onto the floor.

"Oh my God, I can't believe that I didn't think of them. I just love Tiana and her grandmother. My house would be perfect for them and they would be perfect for it. And I wouldn't have to worry about somebody tearing my shit up. Oh Rhap, do you think they would really want to make that move? Wait…Do they pay their bills on time? I know I won't have to worry about the rent 'cause section 8 money is true but I'm talking about the other bills. I will pay the water and sanitation bill as long as it's a hundred dollars or less, but the electric and any phone or cable will be on them."

Montana was rambling and I knew from experience that it was a good thing. She was excited and although she had questions, she knew that it was a good idea.

"I have never heard Tiana or Kieron say anything about their lights or water or anything for that matter being disconnected. I don't believe MaDear would ever let that happen." I told her.

"Great! Then let's make this happen, girl. When do you think they will be able to move? Can you call them right now?"

The rambling continued.

"Okay Montana, calm down." I laughed. "I will call MaDear tonight before I go to bed. Then, I'll call you and we can set up a time for them to go see the house. How does that sound?" I offered.

"That's good. I can give you a set of keys and you can take them whenever you're ready. There's furniture in the house but I can get that out of there without a problem."

I just shook my head at her because she was so excited that she was shaking her leg and making the nail technian's work very difficult.

That night I was true to my word and I called MaDear and told her about the house. She was so happy. I thought I heard tears in her voice as she asked if I was serious. She wanted to move right away but figured that it would be better to wait until the end of the month. That would give her enough time to check the place out, get her paperwork changed, check out the schools for Tiana, and get packed up. She'd been in that apartment for so many years that it would likely take a while to sort through her things.

"I don't want to take a lot of old stuff to my new house." She proclaimed.

She was so cute. Already she was calling Montana' place her house. That was MaDear's way to just claim what she wants. Little did she know, that house was hers even before she knew about it.

MaDear asked me not to say anything about it to Tiana until she'd had a chance to tell her. She thought that she would be excited but wasn't sure.

"You know teenagers, sweetie. You think that they are going to want chocolate ice cream because that's been their favorite since they was babies. And low and behold, they want strawberry ice cream. You never know what way they goin' come at you but I'm going to keep my fingers crossed on this one." MaDear shared.

It was going to be hard not to mention the house to Tiana during our next session if MaDear had not filled her in on the proposal but I was going to keep my word. MaDear had made a good point.

Although initially I thought Tiana would be more than happy to make this move, there was a possibility that she would bolt and run away from the idea. The more I kept thinking about it, I was coming up with reasons why the whole moving out of the neighborhood wouldn't work. Moving from your comfort zone is not ever easy. Tiana would have to change schools...not easy...She'd have to leave her friends and favorite teachers...not easy...She'd wouldn't see Kaiewa everyday... not easy even though she would probably not admit it...Tiana would have to learn a new bus route to get to me...not easy...leaving behind the space they shared with Kieron... not easy. There was a lot to consider and that made me make the conscious effort not to think about it anymore until I had to.

# 37

"I can drive down on a Friday night and we can pick up some day workers on Saturday morning and get them moved in in no time. Then we could have Saturday night and Sunday morning to spend together before I head back. Are they going to buy any new furniture? If so, I could pick that up for them while I'm there, too."

Trayu was a little more excited about this move than I thought he should be. He'd asked me about coming up to Chicago for a weekend and I told him that I didn't think I could make any weekend plans for a couple of weeks because I wanted to help MaDear and Tiana get organized and moved. In return he quickly developed a plan to get back to Hotlanta to see me. I don't know why but his eagerness was a bit unsettling to me. I had feelings for Trayu without a doubt and they were pretty strong feelings. But I was not sure what I wanted to do with those feelings.

When I left him at the airport at the start of the new year, I confessed that I was uncertain about what I could honestly offer him of myself even though I liked him a lot. And I promised to spend some real time focusing on finding some solid answers.

"Trayu, even though I feel like I should be standing on solid ground by now, I have to admit that I'm not. My heart was broken in a way that I never would have expected and it has been difficult for me. You have been good for me because you make me feel happy with your joyful and inspiring personality. You make me feel special and wanted and I can't pretend that I don't like to feel that way. I need to feel that way and I want to thank you for giving that to me. But, that being said, Trayu, I don't know if I am emotionally ready *(my body was physically ready, that I knew)* to give what it takes to build a relationship at this time. I just don't know. I do know that you make me want to. I'm glad you told me what you were feeling and I promise to do some soul searching for the answers I need. I also hope that you will stick

around while I do this but I'll understand if you feel that you cannot."
I shared.

He asked if Paully had anything to do with why I was not sure that
I could commit to building a romantic relationship with him. I took a
reflective moment before answering.

"I don't know. I think that he is connected to my thoughts on
whether or not my heart is ready but I'm just not sure to what degree.
If you are asking again if I want to be with him, then I can tell you
that I don't think so. I can also say that I probably would never have
considered it if he hadn't presented the possibility. But it's complicated
because Paully has been my best friend for so long."

Trayu looked disappointed in my response and it broke my heart
but there was nothing I could honestly and forthrightly do at that
time.

We parted with some passionate kisses and lingering hugs.
When I got back in my car to drive away I felt a hollowness in my
chest and by the time I stopped at the light at Riverdale Road I had
tears streaming down my face. I had to pull over before getting
onto the highway because I couldn't control the flow of tears or the
small cries that accompanied them. If I didn't know before, I knew
then that Trayu held a special place in my heart. I was missing him
already.

Now here I was a couple of weeks later and I was still speculating
whether I wanted to be his woman. And he was still trying to make me
see the light by being there for me whenever and however he could.
Today it was by offering to come and help MaDear and Tiana move
into their new house.

"Trayu, that sounds like a good plan but unfortunately I don't
know when they will be ready to move. So I don't think that you
should make any plans to come down." I said.

He got real quiet and I realized that I'd probably hurt his feelings.
What was I to do? Luckily enough I was saved by the bell. My caller
id showed that Meek was calling me.

"Hey Trayu, I need to catch this call. It's one of my clients." I
informed him before saying good-bye and clicking over.

Meek was calling to see if we were still on for Saturday morning. We were to go over and have him officially meet Miss. Mitchell. She'd called me a couple of days after my visit and said that she'd been thinking about Kieron and what we had discussed. She thought that it would be a good way to honor Kieron's memory by giving another young man an opportunity to practice good citizenship and service. She wasn't commiting to giving Meek a job but she did want to meet with him. Then she would decide if she'd deem him trustworthy or not.

"I think that it would be helpful to have someone come by a couple of times a week to run a few errands for me so that I don't have to use the old nasty cabs they have around here. I just don't feel safe in some of them. And I could use a little help around the house sometimes. Now, I know that boy can't hold a torch to Kieron but I owe it to him to give his little friend a chance. So I'll interview him and see what he has to offer but don't go telling him that I'm going to give him the job because I'm not saying that." Miss Mitchell informed me.

So I honored her wishes and told Meek that she was open to meeting with him but she wasn't sure if she really needed to have a new little helper around. He seemed to be okay with that although he had called me several times since that conversation to ask questions about what he should do when he met her.

"Ms. A, I just want to make sure I don't do anything wrong and make her mad. She look like she get mad easily." He said.

"Meek, you can not worry about that. I don't even want you to worry about what you are going to say to her."

"But I'm so nervous. Man, I really want to be able to do this. I think I need to do this, Ms. A, I really do."

I could hear the nervousness in his voice. It was pulling on my heart strings. "Just do this, Meek…think about why you want to do this good deed and how important it is for you. Then just be yourself. It won't be any harder than meeting me for the first time and you did a great job showing me that you were a young man trying to do the right thing. I think you will be fine. Okay?"

"Alright." He replied.

"Good, now go listen to some music or read a book so you can take your mind off of it. I'll call Saturday morning when I'm on my way."

After getting off the phone, I ran upstairs to take a shower before heading out to pick up Tiana. MaDear told her about the house and Tiana seemed both nervous and excited. MaDear told Tiana that she knew that making a move like that was scary and that she wouldn't force it on her. When Tiana told MaDear that she kinda wanted to move but that she was nervous, MaDear came up with a really good suggestion. She told Tiana that she wanted her to go take a look at the house first. Then if Tiana liked the house and thought that she would like to live there, MaDear would turn in the application and they would start packing. Today was the day that Tiana was going to take a tour of Montana's house.

Tiana was sitting on the steps when I pulled up and MaDear was standing in the foyer doorway. I got out of the car and walked up to give MaDear the envelope in which I'd stuck several pictures that Montana had given me of the house when I picked up the keys from her. It was only fair that MaDear had an idea of what the house looked like even though she'd told Tiana that the decision would be hers. I knew that MaDear would be surprised when she opened the envelope and saw the pictures so I hurried back to my car and Tiana and I were on our way.

On the way over to the house I asked Tiana if she was still nervous and she claimed not to be.

"I don't know why but I woke up this morning and the nervousness was gone. I mean it was all gone. I didn't feel anything but excitement. I can't wait to see our new house." She said.

"Oh, so it's already your new house." I laughed.

She just smiled and said. "Yup, that's what it is. I can't explain it but I just know that this house is supposed to be ours. This is it Ms. Austin, this is it.

I feel really good about it and I know that MaDear does too. She ain't telling nobody about us moving yet but she's goin' have to soon."

"Girl, what if the house looks like a shack? Is it still going to be your house." I laughed again and so did she.

"Ms. Montana is too sharp to ever live in a shack." Tiana commented.

We stopped for a smoothie and to walk over to the Marta station and pick up a bus schedule to check the routes that ran near Montana's house, Tiana's new house as she continued to claim. We went back to my car and I pulled the map from my glove compartment. While we drank our smoothies we talked about bus routes and times that would enable Tiana and MaDear to get around. It looked like they wouldn't have too hard of a time resuming their lives in a new setting. The most difficult route they would have to endure was the route to Tiana's school which was a three bus trip. She wasn't bothered by the bus route and even thought that she might decide to change schools next year to be closer to home. I silently suspected that Tiana was looking forward to changing schools anyway. If the move actually took place, maybe I would suggest that she transfer right away.

The first time, I passed right by the house and circled around the next street over. I drove slowly to see if Tiana would spot the house without me having to tell her, but she didn't. I pulled into the drive way and Tiana started with an incessive giggle.

"Oh my God, Ms. A, this is so cute! I love it already. And look at the flowers by the front door. They are so beautiful! MaDear is going to love them. She loves flowers and now she can grow them in her own yard. Ms. Austin, thanks so much. I love it!" she rambled on.

Laughingly, I responded.

"Hold your horses, little girl. You haven't even seen the inside yet."

As we walked up to the door I retrieved the keys from my purse and handed them to Tiana. She grabbed them, giggled, and ran the rest of the way to the front door. By the time I reached the threshold, she was inside. I didn't hear what I'd expected, which was screams of delight. I walked inside and didn't see Tiana, so I called her name and heading straight ahead past the living room and towards the kitchen, peering into each room along the way. Then I spotted her standing in the kitchen. Her back was to me and she seemed to be staring at the back door to the house. It looked so strange that I slowed my pace and quietly walked to her side craning my neck to see the expression on her face.

Tiana had tears streaming down her face. I immediately reached out to her.

"Tiana, what's wrong?" I said and sent her into sobs. I pulled her into my arms and told her it was okay even though I had no idea what was the matter with her. After a minute or so as her breathing started to calm, I asked.

"Tiana, what's the matter? Why are you so upset?"

She shook her head and looked at me with the most innocent eyes.

"Ms. Austin, I think I know this ....no, I know this house."

She looked at me with such intensity and sincerity that I believed her even though it didn't make sense. And she repeated.

"I know this house, this kitchen, this door." She stated as she pointed to the door leading to the back yard.

"Okay, Tiana, okay. It's okay."

I guess that she figured that I didn't believe her, so she started to explain.

"Ms. A, remember when I told you about how I had this dream that kept creeping into my sleep? You know the dream about Kieron and I being in this strange house? You remember how I said that sometimes I was glad to have the dream because Kieron looked so happy?"

"Yeah." I answered.

Tears began to re-mist her eyes.

"This is the house. I can't believe it but I know this is the house. I don't remember seeing the outside of the house but this is the kitchen for sho'. And Kieron went right through that door."

She pointed at the back door again and broke out crying once more. I pulled her under my arm and let her cry.

"It's okay babygirl. Don't worry, you don't have to move into this house. We'll find another place for you and MaDear. It's okay. I'm so sorry. I didn't mean to cause you more sadness but I'll fix it, okay."

Tiana stopped crying and looked at me.

"No, Ms. Austin, I want to move into this house. I think we are suppose to move into this house. I mean, I think Kieron found this place for us so we got to move here."

I just nodded my head as I felt tears well up inside me.

"Okay, okay, in that case I think that we should continue the tour of your new home."

After the tour, I took Tiana home. We talked about the dream she'd been having as we drove along.

"That dream would come to me every other night it seemed like. Shoot, it got so it didn't even bother me anymore. I kinda looked forward to it coming to me cause I just loved to see Kieron's face. He looked like an angel and like I said he looked sooo happy."

"That's good, Tiana."

"Yeah, I thought so too but then they just stopped. I didn't want them to but they did. Sometimes I would try to think about Kieron as I went to sleep, thinking that it would make the dream come back, but it didn't."

"Really? When did you stop having the dream?" I asked.

"I don't know... maybe a few of weeks ago... I don't really remember."

As I turned onto her street, Tiana got a little jumpy. She was tapping her hands on her knees and smiling and humming. I'd barely put the car in park and Tiana was out of the car. She ran up the stairs and bum rushed her grandmother cooking in the kitchen. MaDear was caught off guard and dropped the wooden spoon she was holding. It bounced off the linoleum and splatter red sauce on both Tiana and her grandmother. Tiana didn't seem to notice as she rambled on about the house that she and MaDear would soon move into. She described everything from the flower beds in the front of the house to the swinging bench in the back yard. Tiana told MaDear about the room that would surely be the one she would want because it had a bay window looking out into the backyard where she could pray and read her bible while looking at the flowers and tomatoes, Tiana was sure MaDear would plant. The fact that they would both have their own bathrooms caused MaDear to jump up and clap her hands. Tiana giddily rambled on for sometime about the house but never once mentioned the dream or the fact that she thought the house had been hand picked for them by her brother Kieron. I wasn't sure why she didn't nor was I very concerned. They looked so happy. I couldn't remember the last time that I remembered either of them looking authentically happy and therefore nothing else mattered. Tiana and MaDear may very well be on their way to happiness again.

# 38

Tuck and Patti were not doing their job of taking the edge off of my mind. The cd had switched over to Shirley Horn but I was still feeling uneasy. It didn't make sense to me. Tiana and MaDear were so happy to finally be moving into a house. MaDear said that she had all but given up on giving Tiana a yard of her own to play in but the time had finally come. Tiana might not want to have play dates in the yard but she could surely sit outside and write in her journal. And she was darn happy about that. So what was messing with me? I didn't think that it was Trayu, because I had been honest with him and that usually keeps me sane. So what then? I was still a little pissed off at Paully. That could be it. He hadn't called and I was not going to call him. He was going to have to get over himself and come to me if he wanted to save our friendship. That could have been it but it didn't feel like it was.

"What was it?" I kept thinking but nothing was coming not even fatigue.

I decided to take a hot bath in lemon and lavender, rub myself down with baby oil, and crawl into bed with a little Thelonius Monk on the box. When I passed the guestroom on my way into my bedroom I was drawn inside. Then I knew. I needed to pull out Kieron's safe and look at the contents again. I adorned my nylon gloves and unwrapped the safe which I had moved from the attic to the shelf in the closet. The last time I'd closed up the safe, I'd thrown the contents inside haphazardly in order to get it out of sight.

This time I took everything out of the safe slowly, sorting the contents. The items such as the pictures of Kieron, Tiana, and their mom were put in the pile with the college brochures. I put the b-b gun in a manila envelop, folded it over and wrapped in duct tape. The money, I sorted into piles by denomination. By the time I'd emptied the safe I felt a touch of relaxation flowing down my neck into my shoulders, so I ran down to the kitchen to make a cup of lemon tea with two starlight mints. When I reentered the bedroom and looked at the money I suddenly realized that there had been a lot of money in that little metal box. So I sat down to count it.

The phone rang and shook me from the daze. My hand seemed to float over, pick up and answer the phone.

"Uh hello?" I said.

"Hi there, babe. Were you sleeping?"

"Oh, hi Trayu. No, I wasn't sleeping."

"Are you sure? You sound a little groggy."

"No, I mean yes I'm sure. I'm awake." I said.

"Okay, then why are you talking so slow and low? Do you have company or something?" He questioned nervously.

That's when I realized that my head was not into any conversation at the moment, but it had nothing to do with Trayu.

"No, no, Tray, that's not it at all. I'm sorry, I'm a little preoccupied right now. I was working on some paperwork and I was in the midst of trying to come up with the right words when you called. I'm sorry baby, my mind is just focused on this stuff. Is it okay if I call you before I go to bed? It won't be very long because I just finished a cup of hot tea and I can feel the sleep coming down."

"Sure, if you feel like it but I'll understand if you're too tired."

I could hear the doubt in his voice and it gave me that sinking feeling in the chest.

"Come on Tray baby, don't do me like that. I just have to finish up this paperwork and I'll call you back. I promise. Now give me a little kiss." I cooed.

That made him laugh but he gave me a round of smooches through the phone anyway.

"Well, I guess you found a way to make a believer out of me cutie pie, cuz' I know you would not be saying that kinda shit so loud if you had company. Call me later, baby. Bye."

Trayu always did something real nice to my insides. He was so ... oh I don't know... so everything. I couldn't wait to call him back. In explaining my lack of focus when he called I had been as honest as I could. It was true that I was dealing with some paperwork although the paper was actually money. And it was also true that I was trying to come up with the right words albeit the right words to describe the awe in discovering that Kieron had 14,750 dollars in that safe. Where in the world did he get that kind of money. The majority of the money was in hundred dollar bills but there was two thousand in twenty's and three thousand fifty in fifty's. I couldn't begin to image how or why he would have that much money.

Surely, MaDear and Tiana didn't know that he had that kind of money. Maybe it was someone else's money and he was holding it for them. Maybe he had been saving all the money that Miss Mitchell paid him for his services. Not a chance that she'd paid that child fourteen thousand dollars. She was on a fixed income. Maybe he stole it from the perp that shot him. No, that couldn't be it because the boys said that the perp was looking for drugs. That only left drugs. There was weed in the safe. It was only a small amount but it was there so I knew that Kieron had been doing something drug related. Then again, such a small bag of weed was most likely for personal use. Shoot, I had no idea where he could have gotten that money but it couldn't be good. Then again, maybe it could. Suddenly I felt better. I neatly packed away the money and the bb-gun in the safe and took the rest of the stuff and stored it in the bottom drawer of the dresser.

A long hot shower replaced my intended hot bath and oatmeal lavender baby lotion replaced the lemon lavender soak. It did the trick because I was so sleepy after my shower that I was yawning when Trayu answered the phone. He was so happy that I called. And I was feeling pretty happy talking to him. I told him about the joy I felt from bringing a little happiness to Tiana and MaDear. Trayu in return told me that I deserved to feel joy from bringing myself a bit of happiness. That struck a chord within me and I knew that he was right. I had to put some time into seeking that joy, but I needed to get Tiana and Meek situated first. We talked, he sang, and I drifted off to sleep. He called to me softly until I heard him and then he told me to hang up.

Meek was very nervous about the meeting, but he looked very handsome in his starched jeans, tan long sleeve dress shirt, and freshly brushed Timberlands. The braids he had been sporting for the last couple of months were gone and replaced by a two inch curly afro.

"Wow, look at you, mister all dressed to impress." I complimented.

"Thanks. My aunt wanted me to wear a tie and some dress shoes but I told her that you told me to be myself and she know I don't wear no tie and dress shoes unless she makes me."

I couldn't help laughing.

"Why you laughing at me, Ms. Austin? Do I need to go change?" He asked anxiously.

"No, Meek, you look absolutely great. I'm just laughing because you are so candid about some things and it's never what I expect. Look, don't worry everything will be fine. And if you don't get this job be assured that another is right around the corner. So just relax." I told him and he nodded in acceptance.

My gut told me that Miss Mitchell was going to give Meek the job. She put up a good hard natured front but I sensed that she really wanted to do this. It appeared that she'd made a difference in Kieron's life but unfortunately his life had been prematurely extinguished. Meek was an opportunity for her to make a difference for another young man who wanted to be a better person. But on the chance that I was wrong, I had made a couple of calls and secured two places for volunteer services. If this situation didn't pan out with Miss Mitchell, Meek could volunteer at the nursing home in Edgewood or at the Dialysis Center at the Veteran's Hospital.

We arrived at Miss Mitchell's and I let Meek take the lead and ring the doorbell. As we'd practiced, Meek greeted Miss Mitchell, introduced himself and extended his hand. She gave him a brief handshake and turned her eyes towards me.

"You're a tad bit early, I see. It's a good thing that I was prepared to take visitors." She complained then looked back at Meek.

"Well, come on in since you're here. I guess it wouldn't make much sense for me to have you stand out here for another twenty minutes even though it would serve you right if I did."

Once inside we were seated in the living room area where a cross word book lay open on the table and the television mumbled through a commercial. Miss Mitchell went to the kitchen and returned with a pitcher of lemonade and three clear plastic tumblers. I looked over at Meek and he seemed a little more nervous than he was on the ride over. I took an exaggerated deep breath and gave him a slight nod of the head indicating that he do the same. He took the hint.

Miss Mitchell poured three glasses of lemonade and distributed them without asking whether we wanted them or not. Meek and I sipped from our glasses in unison. He quickly, yet, quietly told Miss Mitchell that the lemonade was good.

"It's just kool-aid so it's not nearly as good as my fresh squeezed but I'm glad you like it." She responded.

We took a few more sips and absent-mindedly looked at whatever program was running on the television. Another glance at Meek told me that the lemonade had washed away some of his nervousness. Then Miss Mitchell picked up the remote control and clicked the television off. She looked at me then Meek and began to speak. I was a little thrown off because although she was looking a Meek, she was definitely speaking to me.

"Well now, I suppose we should get on with this meeting. Since this is about this young man, Ms. Austin, I think it would be best for you to wait for him in your car." She explained.

I was perplexed, but I stood up and picked up my purse. Then I looked at Meek and gave him a reassuring wink.

"That sounds like a great idea. Meek I'll be out in the car when you finish."

Meek nodded his head and Miss Mitchell said.

"Oh he'll be fine. But don't run off anywhere because I can't take him home."

I assured her that I would be waiting outside and then made my exit. I wasn't really worried about the meeting/interview. The best scenario would be for Meek to get the job with her because it would help him through his grieving and give him something positive to work on. But if it didn't happen that way then he would have at least interviewed with one of the toughest interviewers around. This interview would be a good start for Meek.

While waiting in the car, I was able to check my voice mail and send a few text messages. The radio played oldies from the seventies and eighties and I sang along. I was singing loudly when Meek tapped on my passenger side window. He was smiling and I knew that he'd gotten the job.

"You landed the job, didn't you" I asked with excitement as he climbed into the car. He shook his head.

"No, not yet. She said she would let me know by Monday. Oh, and she said she would call you. But I think I did good. She seem kinda mean but she ain't no monster. She asked me a lot of questions about me and school and my aunt and about how me and Kieron became friends. I didn't like all those questions but I kept telling myself to just do me. So I answered everything she asked me and it wasn't bad. I even think that she was impressed with me, but we will see." He said.

"Well, if your smile is any indication of how things went, I'll say you're probably fine."

That night it seemed like the goods news would never stop coming. First, my little brother called and told me that he'd been selected to participate in a exchange program. Aslen would travel to Paris, France for the last quarter of the school year to study. He was so keyed up that I could have sworn that I'd heard him giggle. I couldn't believe that he or my mom didn't tell me that he was applying for such a program, but I was happy for him. Aslen said mom was hesitant at first. She'd signed the application and gathered all the papers he needed but she never really thought he'd get the slot. When he did, she ranted and raved about the fact that she couldn't send her baby to live out of the country. Then dad came to the rescue. Initially he inquired about being a chaperone for the trip.

"What? There is no way that mom is going to have both of her men living in France for two months. She would go crazy with loneliness and worry and she'd drive me crazy in the process." I said.

Aslen laughed.

"I know, right, she would be freaking out. But the chaperone thing didn't work out anyway. Then dad went into "Daddy can make it happen" mode.

He found a flat to rent and booked a seat on our flight. So, he will be in Paris with me for 17 days and then fly back home." He explained.

"No kidding? I'm sure that made mom happy."

He laughed again.

"Not at first, Rhapsody. You should've heard her. She was tripping so hard about me being so far away. She was like saying I was too young and I could get kidnapped and I wouldn't like the food. Mom found something new to complain about everyday. Finally, dad was like… "Look, you can't keep making excuses; you're either going to let him go or you're not. You're either going to crush his dream or you're not but this is a chance of a lifetime and I'll tell you now that I want him to do it."

"After that, mom continued to make excuses but she also started buying clothes and things for me to take to Paris with me. So, I'm going to Paris!" He screamed into the phone.

I was so happy for him and I told him that I would try to come and visit while he was there.

The next bit of good news came from Montana. She called to say that MaDear called and said she was ready to move in as soon as Montana gave the okay. Montana said that she told her that she could move in tomorrow if they wanted to. She'd told MaDear that she had a bedroom suite for Tiana and since she would have to get a truck to deliver the bedroom suite, she would just have the movers come and move the rest of their stuff, too. I told Montana that she was full of it. She knew that she didn't have a bedroom suite just sitting around; she was going to go out and buy one for Tiana.

"So what." she whined.

"And you're going to hire movers for them, you little stinker. I think I'm going to start calling you Little Jeanie, since you are always granting wishes."

We laughed and laughed. Then talked for a while about a little of nothing. We did make plans to get together and help MaDear and Tiana get settled into their new home. While we were talking, Miss Mitchell called.

"Hey Montana, I need to take this call. Keep in touch and we'll make this happen. I'll see you next week at the shop." I told her before clicking over.

Miss Mitchell was very direct. She got right to the point as soon as I answered.

"Ms. Austin?"

"Yes. How are you Miss Mitchell." I tried to raise my voice to that jovial octave but it had no affect on her.

"I'm fine and I hope to stay that way. Have the child come over on Monday at 4:30p.m. Kieron was usually here by 4 o'clock so it shouldn't be a problem for Jeremiah." She suggested.

I was thrown back for a moment when she referred to Meek by his formal name. I knew his name because he was my client but I also knew everyone including his teachers and pastor called him by his nickname, Meek. Hopefully, her calling him by his first name would not cause a problem.

"So are you saying that he has the job?" I asked.

"He does for now but I reserve the right to terminate services at my discretion. And you need to remind him that I don't want any funny business. He needs to behave respectfully and responsibly. I will not accept anything less." She barked.

"Okay that is great. He seems determined to do his best. I'll call him and let him know. And would it be okay for me to call you later this week to see how things are going?" I asked.

"Sure, but you better believe that if things do not go well, I'll be calling you."

"That's fine. You can call anytime. I'm just happy that you're giving him a chance and I know that it means the world to him. Thank you again, Miss Mitchell, I really appreciate it."

I got off the phone, looked at my watch, and decided that 9:45p.m. was not too late to call Meek with the good news. So I did. He immediately told his aunt and I could hear her yelling joyfully in the background.

Meek asked me if he should dress like he did for the interview.

"No, I don't think that's necessary. I would suggest that you not wear any of those blinged out and gangsta'd up t-shirts or allow your pants to sag. I do believe that it would be disrespectful to Miss Mitchell."

He agreed and said that he was going to pull out his boring t-shirts and put them aside for the days he goes to work.

After getting off the phone with Meek, I went up to my room and pulled out my clothes for church the next day. Then, I called Corie to see if she would be in service on Sunday. We didn't always make it to the same service especially not lately because I hadn't been in a few weeks. But after a week like this week and a day like this day, I couldn't resist going to the sanctuary to give thanks.

Trayu called as I was riding back home from picking up some Chinese food for dinner. I told him about all of my good news which thrilled him.

"Rhapsody, you are such a good person so it stands to reason that good things would happen to the people around you. I know that I believe that is why things are so good for me right now. Funny thing is that I was doing some school work and started thinking about something my father used to tell me when I was a kid. He used to recite this poem for me when putting me to bed and I started asking him to tell it to me when we were riding in the he car. I used to ask him so often that my moms even learn to recite it by heart. I don't know if I even knew what it meant until I was a teenager and then I developed a whole new love for the poem."

"So what is the poem?" I asked.

"It's called "If" by Kipling. I've never recited to anyone other than my mom and pops and my 5th grade teacher, Mr. Botomb. So you should feel priviledged." He informed me.

"Okay, let it be recorded that I feel priviledged to have you recite your "if poem" to me. Now get on with it will ya."

Trayu cleared his throat and began reciting the poem with such concentration and solemnity that I was entranced.

"If you can keep your head when all about you
  Are losing theirs and blaming it on you,
If you can trust yourself when all men doubt you,
  But make allowance for their doubting too;
If you can wait and not be tired by waiting,
  Or being lied about, don't deal in lies,
  Or being hated, don't give way to hating,
And yet don't look too good, nor talk too wise:
If you can dream - and not make dreams your master;
If you can think - and not make thoughts your aim;
  If you can meet with Triumph and Disaster
  And treat those two impostors just the same;
If you can bear to hear the truth you've spoken
  Twisted by knaves to make a trap for fools,
Or watch the things you gave your life to, broken,
And stoop and build 'em up with worn-out tools:
  If you can talk with crowds and keep your virtue,
' Or walk with Kings - nor lose the common touch,
  if neither foes nor loving friends can hurt you,
If all men count with you, but none too much;
  If you can fill the unforgiving minute
  With sixty seconds' worth of distance run,
Yours is the Earth and everything that's in it,
And - which is more - you'll be a Man, my son!"

There was a moment of silence when he finished speaking. I guess I was waiting to hear more because I was so rapt with the words he spoken that I didn't want them to end. The poem touched on what seemed like everything that made life meaningful. And that's almost exactly what Trayu said.

"You liked that hunh? Yeah, I can tell by your silence. Or I guess it could mean that you didn't get it but I don't think that's possible. So that means you got it and you like it and I'm glad."

I admitted to liking it and let him bask in his poetic glory.

"Yeah that poem is pretty deep. You know like I said at first I just like it because I liked my dad telling it to me, but as I got older the words made more and more sense to me. Now, it's like my life creed. I figure if I can do all that it says, I'll be a pretty good man and that's all I really want to be."

"That's deep Trayu." I told him.

"Whatever, Rhap. You need to stop teasing a Man." He laughed and continued.

"Look, Rhap, I feel that at this point in my life I can do a lot of the things that my father wanted. What he thought was important. But I know that I'm not finished. And Rhapsody you are one of the most important things that I need in order to know that I can complete my journey. I want you in my life and I believe that you are supposed to be with me. I know that I cannot make you believe it too but I will continue to do my best to help you see that it's real. The problem is that you have to let me through your emotional blockade so that I can have that opportunity…so that we can have that opportunity." He paused.

"So what do you say, Rhapsody? Can we do this? I'm not trying to pressure you but I need some kinda response. It's only fair."

He sounded like he was trying not to sound like he was pleading but he didn't quite pull it off. I couldn't hold it against him because I knew in my heart and mind that it was a fair request. He deserved to know whether he was spending his time and effort on something instead of nothing. And in fact, I had been thinking about the future of Trayu and me lately. Seeing MaDear, Tiana, and Meek moving on in their hopes for a brighter future, made me think even more seriously about my future. My thoughts were interrupted.

"Hey look Rhap, don't misunderstand me now. You know what I want. I want you and I believe that we are good together. You know that you are what I want. But if I am not what you want then you just need to let me know cuz gaming is not what I'm about. So with that said, I also want you to know that I could be your friend if that is all you have to offer. I'm not going to shit you into believing that I would be able to do that right away. I ain't that strong. My heart does bleed red you know. I'm a man but I'm not made of stone, so what's up?"

I had already made up in my mind what I was going to have to do at that point. I suppose that I'd subconsciously been thinking about this because I knew this day would come. I wasn't sure when he would get to this point or that he would do it so eloquently but I knew it was coming. So I gave it to him. I told him that I appreciated his honesty and his most sincere expressions of affections towards me. I knew that he needed answers and I was actively working on clarifying those within myself in order to offer them to him. Time was of the essence but I needed a little more of it. Then I explained that I wanted to wrap up the loose ends on Tiana's move and Meek's job. Once I felt that everything was in place for them to maintain, I would be able to apply full focus to my next move.

"So Trayu, I'm basically asking for just a little more time. I know it seems unfair to you but I promise to have some very straight, very definite, very well thought out answers for you on . . . let's say. I glanced at the date on my phone and did a quick calculation. Uhh, let's say February 14th." I suggested.

"Okay, okay. That's a bet. I can't wait." He replied.

I knew he sounded a little bit too excited about the unknown and realized that it was because of the date I gave him. Shit, I wasn't thinking but there was nothing I could do about it now without hurting his feelings more than I already had. So instead I ended our conversation and told him that I would be talking to him.

Fear started creeping its way into my chest, up through my shoulders, and tried settling in my head. It wasn't going to rest there and drive me crazy so I shook it off and out for the time being. I would deal with the what ifs at another time.

# 39

The next week went so smoothly it almost scared me. Meek started his new job and was quite pleased with it. Montana got the moving details all ironed out and MaDear and Tiana would be moved into their new home on Sunday afternoon after church. Then, Corey called and informed me that she had completed her business proposal and a business loan application. We made a lunch date so I could look over her paperwork.

I took the family photos in Kieron's safe and had them professionally framed for Tiana. Dakota and I went to Sam's Warehouse and purchased enough food to fill the cupboards for the Menden Family. Then, with a small portion of the money in the safe, I purchased two yearly passes for Marta and five hundred dollars worth of Visa gift cards for MaDear to use at her discretion. Finally, I opened a trust/college fund for Tiana with the remaining fourteen thousand. I wasn't sure how I was going to explain the money when the time came for her to receive it but I figured that I would be able to come up with something by then.

By the time I left the bank, I had to double-time it back to my office for the group session. We were back down to our original number of five because of the few releases that came at the beginning of the new year. Meek continued to come to the meetings and Tiana continued to decline rejoining the group. The weekly topic was a focus on meaningful and obtainable life resolutions.

"Now guys, I want you to think about small things you can do to assist you in being the person you ideally want to be. Don't give me any of those cliché resolutions that don't mean anything no matter whose making the resolve, such as I'm going to lose weight, I'm going to start studying three hours a night, I'm going to stop dating scrubs, or I'm going to stop going with multiple girls at the same time."

The kids laughed.

"I'm for real y'all. You're laughing but you know it's true. You hear people saying that stuff every year and then they go back to their same old ways. I don't want you to do that. I want you to make resolutions that make sense and are doable. Instead of saying you're going to study three hours a night, maybe just commit to staying after school once a week for tutoring in one subject. Or instead of saying that you are going to stop having multiple girlfriends, start dating and letting the girls know that you are not ready to have a steady girlfriend. See what I'm saying, focus on taking small steps and committing to those. Then when you accomplish those you'll experience that high of success and you'll naturally take the next step up. Got it?" I explained and most of them nodded understanding.

"Okay, let's take a five minute break and come back and jot down some ideas. Then you are going to let at least one other person look at your ideas and help you choose one to start focusing on."

"Do we have to write more than one?" someone asked.

"I would really like for you to have a minimum of two, but if you can only think of one I'll accept that. Let's just be for real about what you say you are going to do, because this is all about you. I'm not going to check up on you, it's all on you. So don't even bother making resolutions that you think will please me. Okay?"

At that, everyone broke out for the restroom and snacks and I set the timer so I wouldn't go past time. Then I grabbed a Ginseng Root and set to the task of typing up my notes. I was able to get down a brief outline before my thoughts started wandering to some of my own personal resolutions. I needed to put Tray's and my relationship in a real place. I was either going to let him go or move forward in a relationship. Unfortunately, I didn't feel that I was ready to do either one. Then there was Paully, I was faced with almost the same issues, except that I had much more history with Paully and he was my best friend. Still, I needed to put our situation in a real place and stop ignoring its' importance.

The timer went off and shook me out of my daze. I told the kids to start generating ideas if they hadn't already done so. After a few more minutes we reconvened and they shared their promises with a peer. Surprisingly, they had all done a great job in honing in on some obtainable goals, like, taking out the trash before being asked and substituting the word "nigga" with "man". Meek's resolution was to tell his aunt that he loved her at least once a week. When he shared his resolution one of the other boys in the group decided to change his resolution to doing the same to his mother. I sneaked a peek at Meek and I believe that I saw him blushing. He seemed to feel more and more comfortable and at ease in the New Year and he rarely brought up Tiana in our private sessions anymore. That was progress.

I gave the group the weekly journal assignment, which was to make a list of all the beautiful things they saw during the week. The assignment was met with some male resistance.

"Come on Ms. A., you trying to punk me out with this one." Willie said.

"What I look like talking about something being beautiful. If that's what you want me to do then all you gonna git is list of girls names. Beyonce, Ciara, Keisha Cole, Rhianna…you know what I mean." He continued.

All the kids laughed and the boys sent daps flying through the air.

"Okay, okay. Let's pull it together. Let's just say that you should right down all the beautiful or cooool things you encounter this week. Okay, if you think it's "Fi" then it's probably beautiful to you. Now, you guys get on out of here and do the assignment, alright?" I told them and ended the session.

Corie and I met at Mama Mia's for a quiet dinner and to look over her proposal. Mama Mia's is a quaint little Italian restaurant nestled in the Stone Mountain village. Seating is somewhat limited but the food is absolutely divine and the service makes you feel like you're visiting your favorite aunt. We nibbled, read and talked until the entrée was placed in front of us and then all bets were off. We attacked our food and moaned our delight in the savory cuisine. Corie's proposal looked fine to me. It was very organized and well put together. She seemed a little nervous.

"Rhap, I don't know what I'm going to do if this doesn't fly. I want this so bad I can taste it. It's all I ever wanted, girl. Have you ever wanted something so bad that it made your heart ache whenever you thought about it?" she questioned.

The food in my mouth suddenly felt foreign. I couldn't figure out what to do with it. I knew I should swallow but I couldn't seem to figure out how to do it. Corie had struck a nerve and a super sensitive one at that. Yes, I absolutely knew what she was talking about. I thought about Karl and realized that I hadn't wanted him that way. Not even when I was with him and waist deep in love. Not even after I realized that his heart did not belong to me the way I thought it had. Not now. Not ever. What about Paully? My heart ached when I thought about him but I realized at that moment that my aching was from the apparent breach in our life long friendship. Then there was Trayu. He was younger and lived in another state but I ached for him. I knew it but what I didn't know was exactly why. Trayu made me smile from the inside out, he showed genuine concern for my well being and he did not appear consumed by possessing my womb. He was in so many ways, what I had been looking for yet a sense of uncertainty lingered within me.

"Rhap, girl you are not even listening to me and I'm pouring out my heart to you." Corie shot at me across the table.

"Girl, I'm sorry. My thoughts carried me away." I apologized.

"So, why don't you just tell me what's going on then because your thoughts have been carrying you away on a regular basis for sometime now. Every time we talk, and you know that's not as often as it should be, it is guaranteed that you will drift away at some point during the conversation. So what's going on? Are you still feening over Karl? You know you can tell me." Corie offered.

It was tempting but I decided against sharing my thoughts for a couple of reasons. One reason was that I knew Corie and Paully were still communicating. I didn't want to put her in the position of keeping my business a secret but I didn't want Paully to know anything about my love life either. The other reason and probably the most important was that I needed to figure this relationship thing out myself. I had all the information that I needed. All that was left was to decide how I was going to handle things. The plan I'd fooled around with required some fine tuning but I was sure right then and there that it was the best thing to do. So I assured Corie that everything was fine.

"No, I'm good. I'm sorry about daydreaming but I'm glad you made me aware of it. I promise to try and do better. You know that I've had a lot going on since the breakup with Karl but things are on the upswing. And for the record, Karl is no longer an issue with me at all. I feel freed. So there is no need to worry about that."

We laughed at the finality of my tone, changed the subject back to her business adventure and got back to eating.

# 40

Tiana couldn't decide who to tell about her move. She still talked to and hung out with her girls at school but she didn't really talk to them on the phone as much as she used to. All they talked about was boys and parties. And if she got quiet for too long, they always thought she was sad because of losing Kieron. Then they would start speculating on what happened and why it happened and if they was ever gonna catch who did it. It never occurred to any of them that she wasn't saying anything because she didn't care about what they were talking about. One, she was not thinking about any boys except Kaiewa but he was still not her boyfriend. Two, she wouldn't go to one of those teen clubs for all the gold in the pot at the end of a rainbow cuz every week something popped off and someone got hurt. Three, they couldn't understand that she had come to a resting place with Kieron's death. The police may never find the shooter but she knew justice would be served in some other way. Tiana also knew that Kieron was safe and at peace from her dreams and the miracle of the house. He was looking out for she and MaDear and Tiana knew it in her bones.

In the end, Tiana decided to tell her closest girlfriends about her moving, on the Friday before the move. She didn't give many details but promised to keep in touch and give them her new phone number when she got it. Kaiewa was the only one who knew where she was moving. He was going to help them move in on Sunday and have dinner with them. When she turned in her textbooks to each teacher at the end of class, they all said the same things.

"What school will you be attending? Make sure you get into your gifted classes. Don't stop studying and keep up those grades. And good luck."

Then there was the one comment that really shook here. Every one of her teachers said it to her, even Mr. Fincher who never had a kind word for anyone said it.

"I'm going to miss having you in class."

Tiana never imagined that any of her teachers would actually miss her. She'd never heard teachers say that to any of the students that transferred or moved. It made her feel good inside. Maybe teachers did notice those who worked at learning. She left school that day feeling encouraged and that was a good thing to take with her.

Moving day was here and Tiana was busting at the seams with happiness. The movers showed up at 11:00 in the morning followed by Kaiewa, Ms. Austin, and Ms. Montana in that order. Her room was packed and Kaiewa was helping her dissemble her bed. When Kaiewa asked her what they were going to do with Kieron's bedroom furniture, Tiana told him that they were giving it to Goodwill.

"MaDear asked Meek if he wanted it but he said no. He did take Kieron's comic books and his cds. I didn't want those anyway and I kinda think that Kieron would have wanted Meek to have them."

Kaiewa asked if Meek had been bothering her about the move.

"No, he's been real cool lately. He said he was happy that we were moving out of these apartments and made me promise to keep in touch. He was going to help us move but when I told him that you were going to help too, he backed out. So, she said with a chuckle, I guess that he still doesn't like you, Kaiewa. But for real I think he was just going through a phase cuz now he is acting cool like old times."

The movers seemed to get the stuff into the truck in no time. MaDear wanted to take one last walk through to say goodbye to the old place. A few neighbors came out to say goodbye to MaDear and Tiana, then they were off. The moving process was even quicker for the movers because to MaDear and Tiana's amazement, there was less to move in. Both MaDear and Tiana started crying when they saw their new bedroom furniture. Tiana couldn't believe that she had a television in her bedroom. She immediately ran to her grandmother asked her if she could keep it. MaDear agreed but only if she promised to do her homework in the kitchen away from the television.

"No problem MaDear! I love doing my homework while you cook anyway, so that's easy." She screamed and ran back to her room where

Kaiewa waited for her.

MaDear screamed as well when she realized that the refrigerator, freezer and cabinets were well stocked. She wasn't sure who to hug so she hugged everyone. Then she opened one of the kitchen boxes stacked against the wall, pulled out her tea kettle and preceeded to go about the task of making tea for everyone. Montana went to the livingroom to pay the movers and tell them that they could take the stuff left in the truck to Goodwill.

Tiana came running into the kitchen to question the adults about where all the new furniture and food came from. MaDear, shooed her away and told her not to question from where blessings flow; just send up thanks for them. Then she was sent to her room to finish unpacking while the grown-ups talked.

But that didn't keep Tiana away. She reappeared moments later with the framed family photos. Tiana ran up to her MaDear and showed her the pictures. MaDear's eyes suddenly became heavy with tears as she looked at the photos.

"Where did these come from?" she asked Tiana.

"They were on my bedroom nightstand." She said and looked at me with revelation in her eyes.

"I found them stuck in Kieron's journal in my office." When I saw them, I thought they would make the perfect house warming gifts." I explained.

Tiana knew it was a lie. She also knew where they had come from, but she wasn't going to say a word.

"I'm going to go show Kaiewa. He's never seen my momma before." She proclaimed and ran back to her bedroom.

Back in Tiana's room Kaiewa was helping her unpack when she suddenly felt like she wanted to cry. She tried to hold back the salty tears that stung her eyes but her attempts were futile. And unfortunately, Kaiewa sensed the change in her mood immediately. He put his hand on her shoulder and asked her why she was crying. Tiana responded.

"I don't know. I'm not sad. I don't know. I guess I'm a little sad." She shook her head.

"But I love our new place; MaDear loves our new place. It's what she's always wanted. If she hadn't spent all her money trying to help my mama and then taking care of me and Kieron, she would have had a house a long time ago. So I know she is finally going to be happy. And I believe in my heart that Kieron is finally happy too. You might think I'm crazy, but I think that Kieron found this house for us and brought us to it." She explained.

"Maybe you're going to miss that lame schoolhouse and your friends." Kaiewa suggested.

Tiana knew that that wasn't exactly true either. She was looking forward to a new learning environment. It really couldn't be any worse than the present school. And the friends she wanted to keep in touch with, although there weren't many, she could call. Instantly, Tiana admitted to herself , the real issue. She was going to miss Kaiewa. And she told him so.

"The only person I'm going to miss is you. Who am I going to really talk to now? Nobody understands me like you do. That's what's making me sad." She said as fresh tears started flowing.

With a quick look back at the opened bedroom door, he pulled her into his chest and tried to soothe her. His warm embrace was not nearly as comforting to her as the words he spoke.

"Tiana, you're not going to miss me because I'm not going anywhere. No, you won't see me at school everyday but I'll be talking to you everyday. And if it's okay with your grandmother, I'll come and visit you. To tell the truth, I'm glad you're getting out School Hood Rock. You have to know that you're better off. This is your chance, Tiana, so don't blow it by worrying about the little things. Shoot, you've inspired me to find a way to get out of there, too. It's time for me to make a move. So don't worry, we'll be okay; I'll make sure of that." He told her as he looked into her eyes.

Tiana did feel comforted and gave him a tender smile. Then, Kaiewa began teasing her about being a worry-wart and Tiana pushed him away. Soon they were caught up in a round of laughter and shoving. The kid's play was a welcomed distraction for the adults in the kitchen. After making tea for everyone, MaDear sat Montana and I down for what had the makings of a serious conversation. She began by describing the life she dreamed of as a child in contrast to the life she actually lived. MaDear spoke of the highs, the lows, the accomplishments, the defeats, the good plans, the mistakes. But through it all, she was never without blessings. Some blessings came when she asked for them and many came when they were needed yet unexpected. This was one of those times. She never expected to be able to bring a smile back to Tiana's face after losing Kieron or to give her a house to grow up in. Yet the day had come and she wanted to thank us. MaDear was offering tearful thanks to us when bubbling laughter drifted into the kitchen. We smiled at each other. Then, MaDear yelled to them to stop goofing off and get Tiana's room in order so they could start unpacking the other boxes.

The unpacking went on well after twilight. Tiana and Kaiewa actually completed most the unpacking by themselves. They were like little robots picking up things, asking few questions and disposing of the empty boxes. Montana ordered pizza and we all sat down to eat dinner at 7:00 p.m. MaDear's pastor arrived at the house as the pizza deliveryman was leaving. She was so happy to see him that she looked like she was going to cry. He was a regal man with a quiet presence. He was dressed in grey slacks and a standard black clergy collared shirt. Warm greetings were given to everyone and then Pastor offered a prayer of thanksgiving and a blessing for the new house. As we all formed a band in the livingroom with our joined hands, the words of prayer seemed to fill the room with warmth and joyful peace. Reverend ended the prayer, looked around, took a deep breath and exhaled.

"Sister Menden, the spirit tells me that this place is truly your home. Nothing but goodness dwells here. So, keep in prayer and all will be well with you and this little one." He shared resting a hand on Tiana's head. With that everyone sat down and enjoyed the first dinner in the new place. Before the preacher left, he walked through every room in the house and blessed them. Then he walked around the outside perimeter and did the same.

Shortly after dinner, the contagious yawning infected the house. The weight of the food accompanied by the excitement of the day apparently made everyone feel sleepy and tired. Montana announced that she needed to get home and I followed suit. It was noticeable that Kaiewa really didn't want to leave but he didn't have much choice in the matter. If he didn't get a ride home now he wouldn't get home before ten o'clock and his mom would have a fit. She didn't typically bother him about his whereabouts because she trusted his judgment but she didn't trust the streets.

"Trouble has a way of finding its way into the night and if you're around, it will find you." She would say. So, everyone said their good nights and headed out for home. Tiana walked Kaiewa and I out to the car. As I closed the car door and rolled down my window, Tiana handed me an envelop with instructions not to open it until I got home. Even though I promised to do so, Tiana called me while enroute to take Kaiewa home. At first, I laughed at the thought that she was checking to make sure I was keeping the promise then, suddenly, I was afraid that something was wrong so I said a quick silent prayer before answering.

"Hey Ms. A," greeted Tiana.

"Hey yourself. What's up little one?" I inquired.

"I just wanted to thank you again for everything."

" You're more than welcome and get some sleep so you'll be refreshed for your first day in your new school."

"Well, that's exactly what I wanted to talk about. I'm looking forward to going to my new school but I'm also a little nervous. MaDear wanted to take me up there for the first day. But I don't want her to see that I'm nervous and I probably won't be able to hide it tomorrow when we get there. So I told her that you were going to pick me up and take me. Then she could stay here and put her kitchen in order. She was all for that. So, what about it, Ms. A, can you take me to school tomorrow? I mean would you please take me to school tomorrow?" asked Tiana.

There was no way that I was going to say no to her. Tiana was such a sweet young lady and tried so hard to do the right thing that I just couldn't say no. So I agreed to escort Tiana to her new school and make sure she understood her schedule. Before getting off the phone, Tiana thanked me again.

"I feel like tonight is the dusk to the dawn of our new start. It seems like after Kieron died, MaDear and I were running in place. We were going about the everyday things without really participating. I felt like I was just existing and that the things I was doing everyday really didn't mean anything. But I think things have been changing lately and now I feel like I'm in a good place. This is good and you and Ms. Montana are due for some heavy blessings for all you've done. Thank you, Ms. Austin, thank you."

I received a call from MaDear later that night as I was preparing for bed and got almost an identical speel of thanks. I didn't need thanks, not at all, because MaDear and Tiana's happiness was thanks enough. With that thought, I opened Tiana's envelop. Inside was a beautiful card but what captured my heart was the folded stationary Tiana placed inside the card. It was a poem Tiana had written.

*Sunrise greeted me unexpectedly*
*Unexpectedly processing through the night*
*Can I go on to develop a better me*
*When for every step I feel pulled away*

*Tell me how*
*Can you make it happen*
*Tell me how*
*And you'll have my buy in*
*I want to know how*

*What is expected is often not enough*
*Not enough to fertilize for growth*
*I want progress traveling through me*
*Traveling to you to everyone touching me*

*Tell me how*
*Can you make it happen*
*Tell me how*
*And you'll have my buy in*
*I want to know how*

# I WANT 2 KNOW HOW

*When you look*
*Look at me I want you to see*
*A mirror of strength and profoundly amazing destiny*
*I have only one me*
*Only one mind*
*Only one heart*
*But many hopes and many dreams*
*I want them to remain clean*

*Tell me how*
*Can you make it happen*
*Tell me how*
*And you'll have my buy in*
*I want to know how*

# 41

February 13th was a mother-daughter day. Mom picked me up from the airport. She didn't want me to rent a car when there was a spare at the house. Since I wanted this visit to be as pleasant as possible, I agreed to use the Cougar if needed. When she pulled up at the airport, I noticed that she'd had the car detailed recently. The charcoal exterior was bouncing the early morning sunbeams off and out to anything standing still and the tires resembled thickly glossed lips. Mom was smiling from ear to ear as she came around the car to grab my bag for the trunk. I grabbed her, kissed her and embraced her.

"Mommy, your hair is gorgeous. Look at you! You are cutting up with your girbeau jeans and jacket." I complimented her and she dipped into a curtsy and patted the side of her hair.

"Thank you, love. I do alright for an old lady." She smiled and walked around to slide in behind the steering wheel.

"You look wonderful, Rhapsody, that's a good sign. How do you feel, though?" she questioned.

"I'm good." I replied.

She wasn't asking about my physical well-being and I knew it. She was referring to the lengthy discussion we'd had a week ago about my romantic dilemma and what to do about it. I told mom about pretty much everything. I told her about the escapade on New Year's Eve and the way that Paully behaved afterwards. Mother already knew how much Paully meant to me as a friend and was shocked at his behavior. But she also defended his honor by rationalizing that Paully has always been my number one protector outside of she and my dad and that is probably why he'd acted so irrationally. I can't say that I bought that reasoning but I didn't dismiss it as a possibility either. I believed that I was past being angry at Paully yet I knew that Paully was still not in a safe place emotionally to talk about us. I had no plan to bridge the gap in communication for now.

As for Trayu, I told mom how well I thought Trayu handled the fiasco on New Year's Eve. I shared how he didn't hesitate to let me know that I couldn't deny my part in cultivating the tension that made the evening so volitale. Then, I told her of the many conversations with Trayu about our intentions for each other. She now knew how Trayu made me feel mentally, emotionally, and physically. She also knew how I felt about the age difference and the miles between us. Even though I knew that she and dad liked Trayu, she surely did not indicate that she thought he was my soulmate or that we could have a future together. Her advice had been simple yet enlightening.

"Rhapsody, baby, I believe you already know what you need to do. You just want me to validate that it's the right thing to do. You've been doing this since you were five and you wanted to decide whether or not you give one of your two boxes of crayons to a girl in your class who didn't have any. You said she had to borrow crayons everyday and the kids, including you, were getting tired of her breaking their crayons. I bought you a new box of crayons and your dad came home with another box that night. Then, after saying your prayers you asked me if you should give one box to that little girl. Do you remember that?" Mother asked and I confirmed my recollection. "Good, so this time is no different for you or for me because I'm going to give it to you straight, knowing that I know that you already know what to do." She paused.

"You cannot choose who you fall in love with. Sometimes you learn to love someone who comes into your life but that's not the same as falling in love with someone. So, baby, know that you have the right to love. You also need to remember that you can never justify playing with a person's heart. If you want to be with them, then commit to that. If you don't think that they are the right person then leave them alone. If you are not ready to decide or commit then walk away and let them live. Free their heart for whatever is waiting for them. Now, Rhapsody, I'm not saying that any of this is going to be easy to do but it's the just thing to do. If you plan on having happiness in your life then you better be willing to do the work and make the sacrifices and live through the pain.

Paully is going to have to do the same and do it in his own time. So you need to let him do that. He'll be back, maybe not like before, but he'll be back."

I guess she noticed the slight intake of breath.

"Aww baby, don't take it like that. When he finds his way back, it may even make your friendship stronger. It could happen but you would do well to prepare yourself if things don't turn out all rosy, Okay?"

I said okay and she continued.

"And as far a Trayu goes, Rhapsody, you know that you're not ready to make this commitment. I know it because I hear it in your voice. You need time to find your way back to being emotionally healthy enough to nurture a romantic relationship. So do what you require in order to take care of you. But baby, you can't hinder that boy from having the opportunity for happiness in a committed relationship with someone. You may want to, but don't. You wouldn't want that done to you." She paused.

I'd taken her advice to heart that night and now being in her presence seemed to strengthen my resolve. There was no need for her to lecture me again. So now we were on our way to The Orange for a light brunch. Then we headed over to Thousand Waves for some sauna time and hot stone messages. After the massages, we spent about an hour in the tranquil area reading and sipping green tea.

Mom insisted on driving out to Woodridge Mall to shop. I usually hate the drive out there because it feels like riding a country mile with ornery chickens annoying you with quick movements and irritating clucking. But this time I hardly notice the ride at all. We talked and laughed and sang all the way to the mall. Once we were there, the shopping bug bit me and I ended up leaving with two new pairs of jeans, a pair of Z-coils, a woven leather belt, and a beautiful light blue linen tunic. Mother on the other hand, left with what she came for which was a bottle of Blenheim Bouquet, which she claimed not to be able to find anywhere else. It was dark when we left the mall and rush hour traffic was in full swing, so I drove back to the city. Mom dozed throughout the interstate obstacle course run. By the time I pulled off the expressway on 79<sup>th</sup> street, she had gotten her second wind and suggested that we catch a movie. I was somewhat tired but agreed to go. In order not to wait an hour before the next movie, we ended up seeing a quirky little animated PG movie about farm animals. Mom and I laughed and remained glued to the movie until the credits ran. Then, we headed to the house to see my dad and Aslen. At home, mom warmed up some smothered porkchops and rice for dinner while I spent some quality time with the fellas.

Aslen and dad enthusiasticly filled me in on the upcoming trip abroad. I believe that dad was more excited than Aslen. They both had grand plans of what they would do and see and eat. Dad was sure that this would be a life changing experience for Aslen. He was just as sure that he was going to miss my mom something terrible while they were there, but he needed to do this for Aslen.

"Your mother was never going to let him go without one of us and I couldn't let my boy miss out on this once in a lifetime opportunity." He said and Aslen and I nodded in agreement and slapped each other a gripping high five.

Although he didn't say it, I knew that dad needed to take the trip for himself as well as Aslen. Dad has always gone far and beyond what most parents do to strengthen the bond between he and his children. When I was young, I called him my Stepped-In dad instead of my step-dad, because of the way that he stepped into the role without ever seeming to realize that I was not his biological daughter. Of course I knew it but he made it so that I never felt it and that made me love him even more.

Dad asked about Trayu and I that's when I told him that he was the main reason for my visit. This sparked Aslen to tease me about having a Valentine. I quickly shut him up by asking him about Kera. Aslen did not like discussing girls in front of either of our parents. Dad wanted me to invite Trayu over for dinner, but I explained that it would have to wait for a later time. I was only making a popcorn visit and wouldn't be able to get back to see them again before I flew home to Atlanta. Obvious disappointment silenced the conversation momentarily. Mom broke the silence by announcing that dinner was served. We had a wonderful family dinner together and then dad drove me downtown to the Drake Hotel so I could make my late check-in time.

Trayu was to meet me at the Art Museum, so I sat perched next to the lion reading the Defender and waited for him. Trayu approached me from behind and scared me with a bear hug and a Happy Valentine's Day greeting. I screamed and proceeded to playfully beat his shoulders when I realized it was him. He ceased my good-humored pounding with a fervent embrace and passionate kiss. The butterflies in my stomach began fluttering about and I was instantly happy to be there with him and only him.

"Where's your car?" I asked.

"It's in the garage. Do we need it now?" he responded.

"Would it be a problem? I think it would be better to drive to the restaurant."

"No problem. Let's go. Now, are you going to let me in on what you have planned for us on this Valentine's Day?"

I didn't want to go into details but I did tell him the basic plan for brunch, a couples massage, dinner and a night at the Drake. His approval shone threw in his bright smile and a shoulder hug and kiss on my temple. On the way to the car we talked about school and work. Trayu had also added the links to my new website that he'd promised. The website looked amazing and I had responded to quite a few blogs. If things kept going as well as they had, I would have to enlist the help of another psychologist. I maintained professional relationships with several but there were only a few that I would consider partnering with. When Trayu asked how Corie was doing, we fell upon a somber moment as both of us remembered the New Year's Eve fiasco. He then asked me how Paully and I were doing. I told him that I had not spoken with him and therefore couldn't say that we were doing anything or anyway. In addition I shared that I was not angry with him anymore but that I still didn't want anything from Paully other than our friendship. Trayu seemed to accept my response and then changed the subject.

After retrieving his car, we drove the 3 quick miles to Wishbones for some blackened catfish and grits. Trayu circled the block several times in search of a park close to the restaurant; in the end we still had to walk 4 blocks. The wind seemed to whip around the buildings to lash us with a razor attack. True to his chivalrous spirit, Trayu pulled me under his arm in an attempt to shield me from the blistering wind and share his body heat.

We didn't have to wait long to be seated and ordering was no problem. Over brunch Tray asked for time guidelines for the night. Then finally said.

"Okay Rhapsody, I won't ask anymore questions, but I do need to know if you can squeeze a break into your plans around 5:00 so I can go pick up my dad from work. My Mom's car is in the shop so she's driving his 'til Tuesday. I offered to loan him mine but he's old school and doesn't believe in driving another man's car."

I laughed at him and his dad and assured him that it wouldn't be a problem  Actually his interruption was going to help me carry out my plans.

After brunch, I took Trayu over to the hotel to drop off his bag and park the car. The day had warmed up a little bit by then. The clouds had cleared and the tops of the Sears Tower and the Prudential building were clearly visable. I changed my shoes for the walk over to the spa where we basked in a relaxating couples massage. Trayu was a little apprehensive about his very first massage but perked up when he realized we would be in the same room.

"I can't wait to hear you moaning next to me." He teased.

"Well, considering that this is your first massage, the odds are that the majority of the moaning will be coming from you." I teased back and shut him up.

I didn't bother telling him that although I'd had many massages and herbal wraps, this was my first couples massage. Even so, the 65 minute session went well. The moaning was minimal and we were separated by a screen, which made me much more comfortable.

We stopped for coffee and a bagel across the street from the spa and chatted. Trayu was hooked on massages now.

"That was the ticket. I don't think I ever felt that relaxed. At first I thought the whole process was going to be extremely sexual but it wasn't. It was definitely sensual but more relaxing than anything else. I think I even drifted off to sleep for a minute or two. Yo, I can't wait to do that again." He rattled on.

"I'm glad you enjoyed it. You know, if you go to one of the massage schools you can get one for next to nothing from one of their students." I told him and he became almost giddy, that is as giddy as any man can get.

Back at the Drake, we took turns showering and changing clothes. I went first while Trayu slipped into a short nap. He looked edible laying across the heavenly thick down comforter, sleeping peacefully. I gently kissed him on his head, cheeks and lips to awaken him for his turn in the shower. He pulled me down on top of him and kissed me into a feverish state before rolling me onto my back and leaving me panting as he walked into the bathroom.

I grabbed my notebook from my purse and went over my "to do" list for the evening. I'd tried to keep things simple yet special so that I could focus more on the two of us than the mechanics of the evening. I scribbled a quick note to let Trayu know that I was going down to the front desk in case he finished his shower before I returned. Leaving the note on the pillow, I headed down to make sure that the champagne, fruit and cheese would be delivered on time, which now meant that it would be there when Trayu returned.

I could smell his cologne as soon as I opened the door. My chest swelled and my old friends, the butterflies, took to flight. This evening had all the designs of an emotional rollercoaster. Suddenly, my thoughts were interrupted as Trayu ambushed me, clad in a black wife-beater and fitted cotton boxers. He picked me up and twirled me around and around as he kissed the crook of my neck. I giggled and melted into his arms and chest until he laid me onto the bed. He was apparently even dizzier than I because I was able to easily maneuver my way on top of him and pin him down to the mattress. Now it was his turn to laugh.

"Oh the lady has some moves of her own, I see."

I responded . "Moves? Oh, you have no idea." And planted a kiss on him which quickly entered the passion zone. His soft lips and sleek tongue accompanied by his intoxicating scent was euphoric and addictive. My insides were so heated and moist that I was sure the room should have been steaming up. I'm pretty sure that it was my hips that began the slow seductive dance but they did not dance alone. Trayu was definitely an experienced dance whether he was prone or not. My passion for him made me kiss him deeper as my hand roamed for evidence that he felt the same way. And he did! But before the confirmation was sealed, he slowly pulled away and reminded me that he had to finish dressing so he could make his run.

I was momentarily irritated that he would just stop like that. Who would turn off the burner right before the water in the pot started to boil? Apparently there was one person and he was dressing right before me. But instead of showing my frustration, I grabbed a bottle of water from the table and downed 2 / 3rds of it before offering it to Trayu.

"What time do you think you'll be back?" I asked.

"It should only take me about an hour, an hour and a half at the most. Don't worry, I'll be back before you know it. Now let me jet." He explained before he quickly kissed me and left the room. I stared at the door in his wake wondering how I was going to get through the night with my composure and dignity in tact.

A knock at the door jolted me and I quickly checked the peep hole. The champagne and pupu platter had arrived. I pulled the candles from my backpack and arranged everything on the suite dining table. Then I retrieved Trayu's presents from my luggage and placed them beside the sofa next to the wall, out of sight. With everything in place, I went to the bathroom to freshen up and continued to chill in front of the television awaiting my date's return.

Two hours later, I was still waiting. I resisted the temptation to call him so not to seem needy or desperate, but I was getting nervous. Our dinner reservations were only thirty minutes away but the restaurant was in the hotel so I wasn't worried about that. What bothered me was that the longer I waited for him the more I thought about the decision I'd made. I was 98% sure that it was the right decision but that didn't stop my mind from second guessing. So in order to clear my head I snatched up the room's ice bucket and tromped down to the ice machine. Then I drained the wine cooler of water and replenished the ice. Still, no Trayu. I checked my cell phone for messages or missed calls. There were none. So I called Cocoa and surprisingly she answered. She was on her way to JFK airport for her next round of interviews. I would be home in Atlanta long before she'd make it back to Chicago. As soon as she started her inquiry as to why I was home, Trayu walked in. I jumped and let out a little yelp because I hadn't realized he'd taken a key card with him. Quickly, I ended my call and greeted him.

"Babe, I'm sorry it took so long, but my dad got off a little late and then I had to take him to Jewel's to pick up his prescription. I would have called but can't find my phone. I think I left it here. Have you seen it?" He explained as he started looking around. Then he spotted the treats on the table and turned to me with the biggest smile.

"This is so nice. You went all out didn't you? Are we eating in tonight?"

I accepted a kiss and informed him that we had dinner reservations. He suggested I call his phone and we soon located it. It was hidden between the pillows on the bed. Trayu checked the missed calls and immediately teased me about not caring enough to even call to check on him. I just threw my hands in the air and recountered by saying he could have called to tell me he was going to be late.

"Babe, I would have called but I don't know any numbers by heart and my dad doesn't have a cell phone. But, I guess I could have found a land line and called my phone; I just wasn't thinking clearly." He offered with such a serious face that I had to reassure him that I was only ribbing him. Then, I checked my watch. There was no time to spare, we were already 10 minutes late for our reservations.

While Trayu took a leak, I grabbed the first two gifts and stuck them into my purse. I had miles of smiles on the short trip down to the restaurant.

"What are you smiling so hard about, Lady Rhapsody?"

"Is it not okay for a woman to smile when she's happy?"

"What are you so happy about?"

"What? I'm happy about being right here with you right now!" I replied with an even bigger smile. It's very possible that at that point my smile resembled the huge one Miss Ceely often gave Shug Avery in the Color Purple.

We were seated and as soon as the waiter finished his speel and left us, I slid Trayu's first gift across the table. He feigned anger at the fact that I didn't tell him we would exchange gifts at dinner, but I told him not to worry about it and just open the gift. He loved the watch I'd purchased. It was a Swatch with a slight retro Swatch look. I'd chosen a silver face with a blue band to match the color of his car. I decided to give him the second gift as our salads arrived because his reception expressions were to die for. His reaction to the Mr. Roger's Quotes did not disappoint. This time he leaned across the table and pecked me on the lips. I loved his smile, I loved the gleam in his eyes, and I loved the heat of his touch. The slightest touch from him made my blood boil and my core yearn for more. That is what I thought of while I munched on my arugula and lemongrass salad.

Chicken was the meal choice for the night. Although, I don't know what Trayu's reasonings were, mine were based on simplicity and acid avoidance. The last thing I needed was a night of playing "hold the bubble", cuz we were not pooting buddies yet.

Dessert was a decadent dish of crème brulee', which we shared. I wasn't stuffed but pretended to be and Trayu devoured the majority of the dish.

"Hey do you want to order another one to go for your midnight snack? We have a refrigerator in the room." I suggested but he declined.

My plan to pay for dinner was foiled when Trayu deceptively paid the bill on his restroom run.

Back in the room, he was eager to give me his gift but I made him wait until I took a bathroom break. I wanted to brush my teeth to rid myself of chicken breath. When I returned he'd already lit the candles on the table. A gift wrapped box, about the size of a shoe box, was sitting on the sofa. He instructed me to have a seat while he poured the champagne. I was a little set back because he seemed to have taken the lead in the evening that I'd planned but it was cute enough. Even the most self-sufficient, independent, strong, and accomplished woman admires a knightly man. So I did as he asked and waited for him to join me on the sofa. He sat next to me, handed me a flute and offered a toast.

"This is to you for coming into my life and allowing me into yours. We've had some rough times and some good times and I can foresee many good times in the future. I appreciate you putting this weekend together for us because it shows that you care. Now you know I ain't no punk but I want to say this…" He paused and a nervous cold sweat started to form. I thought he was going to say that he was in love with me. I had fallen for Trayu; I just hadn't fallen in love with him. Maybe I could someday but that time was not upon me. And if he'd professed love for me it would surely put me in an execrable position. In other words, I would be screwed.

He continued. "I ain't no punk, but Rhapsody, you have a way of making me feel that what I do and who I am has meaning. You inspire me to do and be more." Then he raised his glass and after I started breathing again, I tapped it with my own.

We sipped and kissed and then I opened my gift. I gasped at the Dooney and Bourke brown nubuck mailbag. He definitely had a knack for gifting. He'd earned another few points from me . I skipped over to the closet mirror to see how well I made my new bag look. Then I skipped back over to Trayu and planted a closed mouth kiss on his lips.

"Oh wait! I have one more gift for you!" I screamed and retrieved the wrapped MP3 player from the side of the the sofa. After shaking his head at my silliness and chastising me for doing too much, he opened the package. The device fit snugly into the palm of his large, very masculine hand.

"It's not an iPod but it has many bells and whistles. Turn it on. I've put some music on there for you." I said.

I wondered if he would know any of the songs I'd chosen. The list was a little old school.

1. Tracy Chapman- If You Wait For Me
2. Donny Hathaway- A Song for You
3. Elton John- Your Song
4. Bob Dylan- Times Are A Changing
5. Natalie cole- Miss You
6. Proclaimers- 500 Miles
7. Phyliss Hyman- Somewhere in My Lifetime
8. Isley Brothers- Harvest for the World
9. O Jays- Stairway to Heaven
10. Teddy Pendergrast-Hold Me

We attached the player to the mini computer speakers I'd packed. The first song we listened to was Hold Me with Teddy Pendergrast and Whitney Houston. Trayu vaguely remembered Teddy's sound but was thrilled at the early Whitney. "Hold up! He yelled. "That's the real Whitney. Let's start that joint again."

So we did and we did again but the last time Trayu pulled me up to dance with him. He also apparently decided to listen more closely to the lyrics because he pulled back a couple of times to look into my eyes. I didn't shy away from his gaze, for I had chosen the music on the MP3 player carefully.

Before the song ended that last time, Trayu had taken my tongue into his mouth. His oral warmth and wetness drew me nearer and fogged up my head. As he cradled the back of my head and deepened the kisses, my legs began to tremble and moisture invaded my jeans. There was no containing the moans. Trayu's breathing was weighted and although one hand was resting behind my head, he had no problem maneuvering his other arm under my legs and sweeping me up into his arms. The sudden movements jarred me momentarily but his tongue on my neck calmed any fears waiting to arise.

He carried me to the bed, gently lowered me, and climbed on top of me in what appeared to be one motion. I was blinded with passion, so I really don't know how my clothes came to rest on the floor next to the bed. I'd seen Trayu's body before but at that moment it seemed to glow. He lowered his nakedness onto mine and he felt like home.

A rhythm was started and inhibitions were forgotten. Trayu stroked, caressed and nibbled me into an explosion and then he did it again. The most amazing part was that everytime I could open my eyes, his were there to meet me.

Awakening from a passion enduced nap, I was greeted by his smiling face. He'd moved the pupu plate to the night stand and was sipping a glass of champagne. The plush hotel robe he adorned gave him that American Giglio look. I smiled at him and he kissed me on the cheek. My bladder felt like it was holding a gallon of water, but I did not want to walk to the bathroom in the buff. Trayu read my mind and handed me the other robe he'd laid across the bed. Quickly, I shrugged it on and scurried to relieve myself and freshen up a bit. When I returned, he handed me a glass of bubbly and offered the fruit and cheese. I bit into a plump red grape.

"Wow, these are so sweet, here try one." I said as I held one to his lips.

"Oh I've already tasted them and they are pretty sweet, but not near as sweet as the taste of you." He replied and took the grape into his mouth.

Immediately, my entire body flushed with embarrassment and satisfied recollection. Even though I tried, I couldn't think of one part of my body Trayu hadn't tasted and that sent a chill through me.

We both climbed up to the headboard to drink, snack, watch tv and talk. Everything was going fine when Trayu asked about taking a trip out to Jekyll Island. He was obviously visualizing a romantic weekend and that wasn't going to work. He picked up on my hesitation and asked what was wrong. There was no need to postone the inevitable any longer. I was going to have to tell him before the weekend was over so it was time to seize the moment. And so with a deep breath and another sip of the champagne, I told him of the decision I'd made.

"Trayu, I need you to know a few things. You are very special to me. What we have is rare and exciting because you get me and I admire you. You have been honest and upfront with me and I truly appreciate that. And I have done my best to be upfront and honest with you. I've spent endless hours thinking about what you've asked of me, digging deep within myself. And…although you mean a great deal to me, I'm not ready to be in a committed relationship. It's not that I want to see anyone else; I just need to focus on me for a while. It's been a tough year, I've been through a rough breakup and I lost a good friend. I feel emotionally unsettled. Healing has begun and I believe you've helped get it started. But I still have some me-work to do and I can't do it in a relationship."

At this point I began to cry. It was breaking my heart but there was no way around this. Trayu just sat there looking at me in disbelief. Then with a furrowed brow things went wayward. He stood slowly.

"I got to get out of here." He said solemnly as he pulled on a pair of Nike break-a-ways. I couldn't figure out what to say, so I didn't speak at all. I sat there teary-eyed and watched him dress, check for the room key, grab his jacket and leave. The room was so quiet in his wake. Yeah, the television was on but I swear I couldn't hear it. My brain couldn't process all the thoughts and emotions flooding in, so it left me with the feeling of being under water. I was drowning. I was absolutely drowning.

When he returned, I was asleep. I would say that I'd cried myself to sleep but in actuality I just succumbed to exhaustion with the help of the champagne. Trayu spent a little time in the bathroom and then climbed into bed. He snuggled up to me and I could smell the remnants of Maker's Mark and Black and Milds. He took a few deep breaths through his nose, taking in my scent. That was one of Trayu's quirky habits that I was going to miss. He didn't kiss me or try to do anything through the night.

I awakened with him on his back and my head resting on his chest. My mouth was so close to his nipple I could lick it without moving my head, but I didn't. Who knew how he would respond after the previous evening. Instead, I laid there and basked in the peacefulness and comfort of being there with him. I didn't know if it would ever happen again. When his arm slipped off of me, I eased out of bed, took my bag to the bathroom, showered and got dressed. Trayu was still sleeping peacefully when I finished. I guess he'd had a few Maker's where ever he went.

I went down to get some coffee and sweet rolls. Trayu was in the shower when I returned. Nervousness crept into the pit of my stomach, so I busied myself with making sure I had everything packed and ready to go. I even transferred my purse contents to my new mailbag. Trayu exited the bathroom clad in his pants and socks. He looked at me with a tilted head. I nervously said, "I brought you coffee and a danish."

He walked over to the table where I'd been standing with my purses and kissed me with his minty lips and tongue. Then said, "How about a good morning?"

"Good morning." I replied and returned his smile.

He gave me another quick kiss.

"Hey, I'll be ready in about ten minutes, okay? Breakfast is on me? Where do you want to eat?" he asked.

I hadn't planned for breakfast. My flight was at two which meant I needed to get on the train as soon as we checked out. I relayed that information to Trayu and he offered to drive me to the airport so we could grab breakfast near there. I agreed.

On the way to Midway Airport, he thanked me for the weekend. Then he apologized for leaving me the night before.

"I just had to get out of here. I needed to clear my head. I could feel myself getting angry and I didn't want to snap."

I said nothing.

"Look Rhapsody, you've been pretty much up front with me about us but I couldn't help hoping that things were going to work out for us to be together. Then after last night…the way you responded to our commencement…I just knew that we were finally on track."

Then he looked at me and said, "Tell me you didn't feel that."

"Trayu, yes, I felt the magic. It felt so right. It was amazing, I would never deny that. I could never deny that. I want to be with you, I do. But now is not our time. I've got to finish getting myself together." I paused before continuing. "Trayu, I want you in my life."

He started nodding his head. "I feel you, baby. And I want you in mine. I thought a lot about this last night and I know that I have to let you do what you need to do regardless of how I feel. Unfortunately,

Rhap, I can't be your friend right now. I just can't do it. Call it male pride or whatever you want to call it, but I ain't gonna be able to do it." He explained with angst rising up through his voice. I glanced at him quickly but said nothing and he continued.

"You need time and I'm going to respect that. And I need time, so I hope you're going to respect that. You say that you want to be with me when you get yourself straightened out and I say maybe I'll be here and maybe I won't. I'm not trying to sound harsh because I love you Rhapsody, but it is what it is. I've got to do me sometimes." And then there was quiet.

"I understand." Was all I said.

We rode the rest of the way to the airport without talking. Crazy Howard McGhee on 107.5 was the only voice in the car. At the airport Trayu asked would it be okay if he passed on breakfast. I said it was fine. I asked if he would listen to the other songs on the mp3. He said he would. Trayu retrieved my bags from the trunk. Then he pulled me to him and kissed me so passionately I felt the tears welling up behind my closed lids.

"Farewell Lady Rhapsody and be well." He said with his silly grin and bow.

I could see the mixture of emotions in his eyes and I was sorry for being the cause of his pain.

"I'll do my best, Trayu. And I love you."

With that I pulled on my backpack grabbed the suitcase handle and walked through the airport doors determined not to look back.

# Epilogue

It's been a month and I still haven't heard from Trayu or Paully. I haven't heard from Karl either, but he doesn't matter. I composed a long email to Paully but deleted it without sending it. Later, I wrote a letter and did send that one through our trusty postal service. Letter writing is a skill that seems to be forgotten but I believe we all still secretly enjoy receiving a letter in the mail. Even so, Paully hasn't written back. Corie still talks to him a couple of times a week. Apparently, he will occasionally ask of my well being but that's it. Cocoa can't believe that Paully and I are no longer friends after all these years. But to me he will always be my best friend because he's engraved in my heart. I'm not giving up the hope that we'll work our way through this.

Trayu has not called either. When I returned from the Valentine Cataclysm, I called him a few times before he finally texted me and requested an end to my calling. He was polite enough to say that I could contact him through email for webpage questions or requests only. The pain of losing Trayu is the worst, more so even than Paully. That's probably because I'm sure Paully and I will be together again, but it's very possible that I've lost Trayu for good. It's highly improbable that a man like him will stay on the market long. Knowing that still churns my insides and gives me that sinking feeling in my chest. Admittedly, I have contemplated flying into Chicago and going to his house. So far, I've been able to talk myself out of it.

Tiana and MaDear have settled in nicely. Tiana likes her school and most of her teachers. She still doesn't have many friends but that's the way she wants it for now. Kaiewa continues to call her everyday although she still claims friendship only. MaDear's yard is the prettiest on the street and she sounds happier everytime I talk to her. Keiron's murder is still a cold case as is the where abouts of Tiana's mom.

*Thanks*

First, I would like to give thanks to God Almighty for the ability, will, and courage He has blessed me with through the years. Now, I curtsy and applaud My Ladies. You know who you are. You are my readers, advisors, ears, and cheerleaders! No matter which role you played, you are so appreciated because I could never have been able to bring this dream to realization without you. Thank you, thank you, and thank you again.

CPSIA information can be obtained at www.ICGtesting.com
Printed in the USA
237745LV00001B/5/P